OH, ROSS! Lisa thought.
AFTER ALL THESE YEARS,
YOU'VE RETURNED!

Lisa ran down the hall and rushed into Ross's room, only to find it empty. She was too late.

Then the door slammed behind her, and the big, hulking one-eyed man bolted it. "No, not you!" Lisa screamed. "You touch me and I'll scratch your eye out!"

"You're beautiful. Red hair, pink skin, perfect as cream, and such a lovely body." He rushed her.

She screamed, kicking and clawing at him as he backed her into the corner. But then his arms were around her, gripping her vise-like, his hot mouth down upon the exposed portions of her breasts. Twisting both arms behind her back and turning her around, he jerked her wrists upward against her spine.

She screamed, struck him full on the jaw with her fist, frantically pulling herself away . . .

BOOKS BY BARBARA RIEFE

BARRINGER HOUSE
ROWLESTON
AULDEARN HOUSE
THIS RAVAGED HEART

FAR BEYOND DESIRE

BARBARA RIEFE

PLAYBOY PRESS
PAPERBACKS

TO ALAN
WITHOUT WHOSE PATIENCE
AND UNDERSTANDING
THIS BOOK WOULD NEVER
HAVE BEEN WRITTEN

Some hang above the tombs,
Some weep in empty rooms,
I, when the iris blooms,
    Remember.

I, when the cyclamen
Opens her buds again,
Rejoice a moment—then
    Remember.
      —MARY COLERIDGE
      On Such a Day

BOOK ONE
1866

I

Winding through the legions of black maples assembled about the house, the breeze reached the turning circle and dipped groundward, snatching necklaces of dew from the grass, tearing them and scattering watery beads. Standing in the study window, Lisa visualized a dew-drawn scythe, a twisted horseshoe, other objects. But abruptly the breeze roiled the dust in the driveway, shaping it into slender wraiths that whirled, deployed, dissolved and settled over the scattered jewels, quenching their tiny fires.

The Oriental alabaster Louis XVI clock on the drawing-room mantel under Ross's portrait announced the quarter hour. She drifted into the room, surrendering herself to the scrutiny of the painted portraits of the Dandridges. The intruding sun spread its warmth over the window-seat niche framed by antique fringe, spilled across the Brussels carpet and created a golden path pointing the way to the portrait of her late husband, Ross. The Dutch painted-leather *chinoiserie* screens, standing tall on either side of his picture, further served to isolate him from the rest of his family.

"Good morning, my darling," she said to his likeness.

She studied his picture. Then her eyes wandered slowly to her left, to Cyrus, patriarch of the Dandridge clan, founder of the largest, most successful shipbuilding dynasty in the Western hemisphere, sitting in his favorite chair scowling defiance at all who dared look upon him, one vein-knotted hand concealing the knob

13

of his stick firmly planted against the unseen floor as if he were anchoring the house against a ferocious gale.

Beside him was Gray, youthful and vigorous-looking, his salt-and-pepper mustache and sparkling eyes lending him a vaguely mischievous look. She had never met Gray; he had died in a fire at the shipyards shortly before her arrival from England. But her darling Ross had idolized this man of great humor and greater heart, as his grieving son had so often described him.

Ross. Husband, lover, heir to the Dandridge fortune. Posed above the mantel beaming his oh-so-lovable grin down at her. His eyes so alive, his tousled brown hair crowning his handsomeness.

Closing her eyes, she envisioned that fateful stormy night off Cape Hatteras: black waves sweeping over the *Monitor*'s deck, her bow nosing downward, the sea closing over her turret. Lisa could almost hear the screaming of the men trapped inside; the sound of their fists pounding the ship's metal plates, the baleful moaning of the wind, the battering rain.

The horrible, horrible war. . . .

When war was declared, the Dandridge shipyards in Providence began producing ships at a feverish rate. Ross, Tom Overstreet, the foreman, and the others put in 20 hours a day to keep pace with the demands of the Government contracts. Dandridge ship after Dandridge ship came gliding down the ways. In groups of three and four, they were fitted and manned and sent off to engage the enemy, caulking and paint scarcely dry.

Then, early in 1862, Ross had announced his decision to enlist in the Union navy. Commissioned a lieutenant, he was assigned to New York to assist that most arrogant genius John Ericsson. Working 18 hours a day, they had completed construction of the *Monitor,* christened her and sent her down the coast to confront the *Merrimac.* Ross had had no active part in that engagement, but subsequently, following General Burnside's crushing defeat at Fredericksburg, the decision was made in Washington to attempt the capture of Wilmington, North Carolina. Late in December that same year, the *Monitor*, in tow of the *Rhode Island*—a Dandridge-built ship—had departed Hampton Roads. Ross was aboard, on what he described in his last letter as "a temporary assignment."

Before the end of that week, another letter had arrived at Blackwood. She had torn open the envelope with trembling fingers:

My dear Mrs. Dandridge,

It is my unpleasant duty to inform you that your husband, Lieutenant Ross Richard Dandridge, was among those brave men whose lives were lost when the Monitor *foundered in heavy seas and sank off Cape Hatteras yesterday.*

May God in His infinite mercy ease the pain of your tragic loss and may you be sustained in your bereavement by the knowledge that your husband died a hero in the patriotic defense of his country.
                                    Yours most respectfully,
                                    John Pyne Bankhead,
                                    Capt. U.S. Navy

The letter had fluttered from her hand as she slumped into a chair, absorbing the shock with an audible groan. She recalled feeling as if two huge metal plates on either side of her had begun to close, slowly crushing the life out of her.

In the weeks that followed, she had read in the *Journal* that there had been survivors. Names were listed. There was no Dandridge among them. Hope sprung from the wreckage of despair now faded.

She studied Ross's portrait and fantasized, imagining that his lips were moving, that he was urging her to call up all the arguments against the obvious, the fragile underprops of hope. Death, after all, was far more than a letter of regret from constituted authority claiming it had occurred. Proof was wanting. The sinking, yes; the men drowning, yes; Ross among them, no. In the changeover from life to death, certain concrete rules must be observed, in proper order. You were supposed to sit by the bedside and hold his hand. You watched life ebb with the slowness and steadiness of a stone sinking to the bottom of a slough. The throat rattled, the eyes closed. The doctor examined him and solemnly corroborated his passing. The plunge into the abyss of grief followed. In due course came the preparations, the rituals and trappings for eternity. The clergyman stood at the head of the grave intoning sympathetic and reverential words; friends and loved ones assembled, heads bowed, features grim; the casket was lowered; ashes to ashes.

All of which served as confirmation, incontrovertible testimony to the certainty of it. But in Ross's case, there had been none of that.

Once more her eyes wandered to the other wall portraits, which reminded her of all that was at stake, the Dandridge heritage: the firm, Blackwood and its nearly 800 acres, $10,000,000 in real-estate holdings. An empire had been entrusted to her, one that had been founded, built upon and expanded; in time, it had attained success and power far beyond the Dandridges' collective capacities to conceive. All of it left to her keeping. At times, the weight of such an awesome responsibility fairly frightened her.

There were occasions, most often when she lay in bed at night, examining the face of the moon entangled in the naked branches of the tree nearest the window, when she was absolutely convinced that Ross had survived. Then, like a wave rolling in from the sea, logic would overwhelm the notion, drowning it like the ship. Out of the moon and the darkness would come a shower of arrows, of questions without answers. If he were alive, where was he now? Why hadn't he gotten in touch with her? Didn't common sense command that she should be the first one he would contact? Questions, questions.

Considering the situation realistically, stripped of emotional bias, how could he possibly be alive without someone's identifying him and contacting her? How many had gone to their deaths in the doomed vessel—ten, twenty, more? How many rescued? Subtract one from the other.

"Ross. Ross," she whispered and turned from his eyes.

The creature time stirred and shook itself, shedding all the years between until the memory appeared, revealed with all the clarity and immediacy of the moment. Their wedding night. Their love pledged before God, hands, hearts, lives joined: "Let no man put asunder. . . ."

Privacy. For escaping the world, the prize. Standing in the light of the night-table lamp in the small shadowy room, each disrobed the other in solemn ceremony, without a whisper, without a sound save the thunder of their hearts. Fingers finding, undoing, loosening, freeing, baring the beauty of his perfect flesh, its bronze lightened to gold by the glow of the lamp. They were naked, their arms at their sides, their bodies touching, tingling in dear, delicious torment. He lifted her, carried her to the bed and gently laid her upon the cool white sheet. Lowering his mouth, he brushed her lips. Again, again. And from within her came a great surging, her heart in upheaval setting her trembling; the urge to possess him cupped her consciousness like hands around a rose.

He kissed her. The crystal wave lifted, peaked, curled downward, crashed onto the shore, rushed forward and engulfed her with joy. *Ross, Ross, my love, my life. . . .* The play began, gently; his hands and his mouth searched, singled out and one by one subdued every source burning for his touch—until all the fires blended into one and her whole body blazed with desire for him. Still he held back, restraining. Slowly the shadows in the room dissolved, the corners vanished. Gradually the room reshaped itself into a sphere, the two of them floating in the center of it. The light grew bright, brilliant, dazzling. She surrendered. They were one, a single heart and mind, flesh and spirit. One forever, forever.

"What God hath joined together. . . ."

Ross. It had been three years since the letter—it seemed like 300 years in retrospect. Empty house, empty arms, empty heart. Love wrenched from it. Love that had been like a cool fire smoldering within, established, tended, protected, shared with a husband as devoted as one heart to another can be. A love to endure till time's final moment, only to be snatched from her as a flower at its most beautiful is torn from its roots to wither and die.

In her time of torment, when she had reached a point where she had become so firmly entrenched in grief and loneliness she was convinced that nothing or no one would ever be able to extricate her, into her life had come Jeremy.

To stir the dormant embers of the cool fire and bring her heart back to life.

Jeremy. The first man she had become attracted to since Ross. More than attracted; so fascinated as to astonish herself. His presence, the touch of his hand, his whispered words of affection had so turned her heart that she felt as if she were being split in two.

Jeremy had fallen in love with her. Shyly voicing his feelings, he had just the past week seized her impulsively and kissed her. And the cool fire had blazed upward, consuming her with desire. Releasing a flood of passions too long quiescent.

The clock struck nine. Far down the driveway at the

approach turn, a horse and rider appeared. Jeremy! On time as usual. The clatter of hooves on gravel brought one of the maids scurrying to the door, smoothing her apron and fussing over the bun at the back of her head.

Lisa stood at the foot of the stairs watching through the door-side window as Jeremy dismounted and the overgrown gnome Enos Pryne took the reins and led the horse slowly away toward the stables. The maid opened the door, curtsying. The mere sight of Jeremy made Lisa aware of her heartbeat, aroused sudden impatience with anyone else present and stimulated the need to forcibly restrain herself. No man but Ross had ever inspired those reactions in her.

"Good morning, Lisa." He surrendered his hat and surtout to the maid, who stood gaping at him admiringly.

"Jeremy. Isn't it a lovely morning?" she said. "The pussy willows and hepaticas are starting already."

"The sun is perfect," he said and followed her into the study. He walked across the room to the window, where he had left her half-finished portrait. Pulling down the cloth covering it, he stared at his work.

Tilting her head, Lisa eyed the canvas critically. "You're flattering me scandalously."

"I most certainly am not. Look closely. That's you exactly as you are, every stroke. Your skin tones; your nose deciding—though with not too much conviction—to turn up slightly at the end. You do have the most fabulous green eyes I have ever seen, so enormous, so suffused with innocence."

"Me innocent?" She laughed. "You're the one who'd better look closely."

"Today we must do something with your hair. It's been nagging at me all the way up from town. It really is awful."

"Thank you."

"I mean what I've done with it." He laughed in embarrassment. "*To* it." Selecting a brush, he began tapping the end of it aimlessly against the canvas. "It's too bright, too brassy. I'm just not doing it justice."

"Don't be so hard on yourself."

Taking up a palette, he began mixing. "I want it just right. It gets so frustrating sometimes. I wish I had a better eye."

"Your eyes are perfect."

"Painter's eye, Lisa. You've put your beauty into the hands of a fumbling amateur. Rembrandt would have no trouble with your hair."

"I like it the way it is."

"I don't. Maybe the light's too strong." He moved her chair closer to the wall. "This should soften the glare. Sit."

She did so, folding her hands in her lap. And batting her eyes impishly.

"Please. And try to relax. Don't think about yourself. Think about—apple pie."

"I loath apple pie."

"Then think about me."

"Oh, Jeremy."

He stared at her with a look betraying the temptation to stop the charade, the sitting, the small talk. He sighed. "The light's right. Head up, please, and don't slump."

Working up a color, he concentrated on her hair, tilting his head one way and then the other with every stroke, so engrossed in the effort that she hesitated to speak for fear of disturbing him.

How handsome he was, his skin bronzed and blemishless, his dancing eyes almost aquamarine. When he stared at her, his eyes absorbed her so she could scarcely tear her own eyes away. And his wildly wavy blond hair; first sight of it never failed to hasten her heartbeat ever so slightly. But even more than the sum of his physical gifts, the beauty of his beauty was that he never posed or postured. To be so outrageously attractive and oblivious of it made him so very human.

She loved this shy, gentle, beautiful man. The time his arms surrounded her—unlocking her heart, gradually freeing her from the bondage of her loneliness for the first time in three years—had seemed so natural, so sensible and necessary. And so desirable.

She gazed at him and yearned to feel his body close to her own. His mouth; she wanted to devour it with kisses. *You love him, you know you do. He knows. Don't hold back. Love him, or risk losing him.* For love was a flower floating along a stream. You reached and caught it, or let it pass and drift away out of sight.

She could not hold him off and lose him. Never. It had come too far. Her feelings were committed; her heart in the custody of his.

The voice nagged insistently. *Break the chain that binds you to the past. Look to tomorrow and all the tomorrows to come. There lies happiness. You had it once, you can have it again. Take it.*

"Your eyes. You're a million miles away." His voice erased her thoughts.

"I'm sorry. You were saying?"

"Nothing." He smiled tolerantly. "I think your hair is coming better; it's more natural."

She had seen his work months earlier and was particularly taken by a strikingly lifelike family portrait of the Slaters, his Providence cousins. At the time, she had thought him quite talented, rather like Vermeer in his gift for capturing light. He had come to Providence from Philadelphia to stay with Judd Slater and his family for an extended visit. A lawyer by profession, Jeremy had been associated with a firm in Philadelphia but had relinquished his partnership with the intention of spending two years painting full time. He explained that it was to be his first and last crack at a career as an artist. If at the end of the second year he decided that he wasn't good enough, his efforts from that day forward would be relegated to the realm of hobby. And back to law he would go.

He resumed painting. She watched him: his brow furrowed, his teeth clamped down on his lower lip, his brush whirling in the paint cup, carried to the portrait, daubing, his head cocking to one side and then the other.

"It's coming better. I'm keeping this for myself, I really am. I'm going to hang it in Carpenters Hall, right above the Liberty Bell."

"Clown!"

"I'm serious. If people can stand in line to see a bell· with a crack in it, they'll troop in from all over to see this masterpiece! Oh, Lisa, Lisa."

His palette slipped from his hand, clattering down on the taboret. Dropping his brush, he came to her, gripping her shoulders, lifting her from the chair, pulling her easily but firmly to him and kissing her. Electricity raced through her trembling body as she yielded her mouth to his, fiercely, hungrily.

"Jeremy, Jeremy."

"My darling, I love you so. I can't help myself. I fight it. I throw up a stone wall to protect you from me, but here it all comes tumbling down." Framing her lovely face with both hands, he seemed suddenly entranced by her beauty. He kissed her eyes, her cheeks. His lips found the line of her shoulder, the flesh exposed, kissing, kissing, igniting small fires.

Their embrace was broken by the faint distant sound of hammering hooves growing louder, bringing the rattle of a surrey. Sighing, she went to the window.

"It's Dr. Craven come to look in on Thursby."

"Great timing." Jeremy shook his head resignedly.

Together they greeted the doctor, a small pepper pot of a man, all nervous energy and twitching movement, his eyes crinkling at the corners, his gold spectacles catching the reflection of the sun. Dr. Alexander Craven, physician to the Dandridges and to their staff, was in his late 60s. Nearly a half century of overwork, interrupted sleep, cold meals snatched and gobbled down between crises had exacted their toll on him.

"Just a quick peek at your unsilent butler," he said, snatching off his hat. "Or should I say the lion in his den?"

"Let me have your coat," said Lisa, waving away the maid who was making a hurried late entrance.

"No need. I'll see him for only a minute." He produced a bottle containing a reddish liquid and held it up. "For the next few days, kindly see that somebody in this mausoleum gets two teaspoons of this down him twice daily. It should help get rid of the rawness in his throat. I'll be right down."

Up the stairs he flew, his coat trailing after him like the tail feathers of a crow on the wing. The door at the far end of the upstairs hallway opened and slammed shut.

Lisa examined the bottle. "I get the feeling he's afraid to try to give this to Thursby himself."

"Do you blame him?"

They laughed and Jeremy took her hand affectionately.

"The sun's getting away from us. Maybe we'd better call it a day. Would you like to go for a ride later this afternoon?" he asked.

"Can we make it tomorrow? I've a million things to catch up on."

"It's a date. Where shall we go?"

"Surprise me."

"We can go anywhere but down by the water," he said. "On the way through town, I stopped for a bite at Swinnerton's on Ernest Street. I could see the shipyards. I wanted to wave my hand and make the whole dreary scene vanish."

"I was down there last month. It was like looking at an old battlefield overrun with ghosts." Her eyes took on a faraway look. "There was one nearly finished ship sitting on its blocks like a monstrous bird. It was all sparred and rigged and completely covered with ice: a crystal ship out of a fairy tale. Staring at it through the fence, I imagined that at any moment the wind would lift it straight up into the air and send it sailing away through the sky. For all of its beauty, it was so depressing that I nearly burst into tears. The last ship ever; the end of it all."

"Which is what I've been saying. That life is behind you, darling. Why persist in clinging to it? It's become like a sack of stones tied to the stern of a skiff, slowing it, holding it back." He held her, fixing her eyes with his own. "Cut the rope, Lisa."

"How I wish I could."

"You can."

"It's not easy. I stood at the fence thinking of Cyrus and Gray and Ross and all the others—all the years, all the proud ships built and painted and polished and strung and dressed in their sails and sent to sea. How do you cut away a dynasty?"

Upstairs a door slammed. Dr. Craven came thumping back down.

"I bring bad news. The old fool will be on his feet making everyone's life miserable within two days." His eyes rolled, searching the ceiling for respite. "I've never seen such a raving hypochondriac. You'd think he was dying! He doesn't need a doctor, he needs an entire staff! Lisa, make sure somebody gets that medicine down his craw."

"I will."

"And Jeremy, let's get out of here!"

"You mean you want some company on the way down?" asked Jeremy, bemused.

"Come," Craven said, opening the door.

Claiming his hat and coat, Jeremy shrugged, shook his head, waved to her, blew a kiss and followed Craven out.

She watched them through the side window. Jeremy tied his horse to the rear of Craven's surrey and climbed up beside the doctor. Within moments, they had vanished in the trees.

Turning, she glanced through the archway into the drawing room. From where she was standing, she could see Ross above the mantel. Sighing, she started up the stairs with Thursby's medicine.

II

The road twisting down the hill widened as the house disappeared behind a screen of maples. A purple martin swooped across directly in front of them, settled on a limb and eyed their passing with evident disapproval. On either side of the road, yellow horsemint and purple-red wake-robin splashed the ground with color. The horse's hooves drummed rhythmical accompaniment to a catbird's lonely, lovely song, and the warm air was sweet with the scent of sumacs, which gathered and displaced the phalanx of black maples that surrounded the house.

Jeremy finally said, "Lisa and I met at my cousin Emily's. Emily threw a party for me and Lisa was there. We got to talking. I think we must have talked seven hours straight. It was one of those rare and beautiful arrangements nature has a way of conjuring up, bringing together strangers who spark each other like magic. You've known her for a long time, haven't you?"

"Sixteen years. I brought her daughter into this world."

"She never talks about Deirdre."

"It's too painful for her. Particularly on top of what happened shortly after she and Ross got here from England."

"That she told me about, being separated from him. She didn't go into detail."

"As far as I know, she's never discussed what actually happened with anyone except Ross. The whole grisly business was engineered by Lavinia Cartwright, who had been engaged to marry Ross's father, Gray."

"What was Lavinia after?"

"What she almost had but lost when Gray died before

26

they married: Blackwood, the Dandridge fortune, all the comfort and status that wealth and eminence can bring to anyone. Plus Ross."

The trees were thinning now, the neatly rowed, drab little homes on the edge of the city coming into view. And the sun, no longer partly obscured by the trees, flooded down, silvering the horse's coal-black mane and scattering diamonds across the blue water of the bay stretching beyond the city.

"Whatever happened to Lavinia?"

"She was caught and put in jail; however, she escaped and hasn't been heard from since. It's been fifteen years now."

"She could be dead."

"Possibly. A natural death or murdered."

"You're not serious."

"When it comes to Lavinia, you have to be serious. She made a lot of enemies in her time." He paused, reining the horse to a stop. The bay was closer now—a great flood of sapphire encrusted with sun jewels. A steamship smudged the horizon and the terns and gulls circled and swooped, white-patching the sky.

"According to my cousin Emily, the baby was kidnaped," said Jeremy, his tone questioning.

Craven nodded. "Early in the summer of 1854, Blackwood burned to the ground. Everyone managed to get out; but in the confusion, Lisa, who was carrying Deirdre, was struck from behind and knocked unconscious. When they found Lisa and revived her, there was no sign of the child. People seemed to think at the time that the fire was only a diversion to cover the kidnaping. Ross spent a fortune searching—hired dozens of private detectives— but there was no trace. No ransom note, no demands for money, nothing."

Craven slapped the horse's rump with the reins and the surrey lurched ahead, Jeremy's horse trotting behind it. They got onto the city road, passing buggies and the

Woonsocket coach leaving town bulging with passengers and a pyramid of luggage.

"Have you asked her to marry you?" inquired the doctor.

Jeremy mock winced. "You don't bother circling to get at the subject, do you, doctor?"

"Never. Have you?"

"Not formally, but we have an understanding."

" 'We have an understanding.' What a sterile way to describe two people so in love with each other that they can't see straight."

"Now you're prying."

"I was indeed." The horse picked up the pace, as if sensing the end of the run was nearing. "Emily tells me you're a widower."

"Four years. My wife died of pneumonia."

"Then you're no stranger to loneliness. I take it you really love Lisa."

"Yes. But without the trappings. That is, free and clear. No Blackwood, no Dandridge Shipbuilding. I want her to break clean with all of it, leave Providence."

"She should. It would be the healthiest thing for her. Especially getting out of that memory-ridden house. It reeks of tragedy."

"She keeps insisting that she can't bring herself to make the break."

"And you insist she must."

"For her own sake, not mine. For her peace of mind. It's the only thing that stands between us."

"Stick to your guns."

"I mean to."

They had arrived at the fork of Douglas and Branch. Jeremy asked to be let off, untied his horse and mounted up.

"You'll make a splendid couple, Jeremy. You're right for each other. You're what she needs. Get her to say yes."

"Failing all else, I'll twist her arm. Good day, doctor."

"Good day, counselor."

III

With the departure of Jeremy and Dr. Craven, Lisa had gone to Thursby's room and given him his medicine. They chatted briefly. She noted that he was fighting to stay awake and left him to nap. Repairing to her own room, she lay down atop the great wide walnut tester bed canopied in flower-patterned toile. *A bed much too wide for one to sleep alone in night after night, especially when the sleeper recalls that it had been infinitely more comfortable being shared,* she mused.

She knew instinctively that during those brief beautiful moments before Dr. Craven had arrived, Jeremy was on the verge of proposing. Then Craven had come clattering up the drive, giving her a reprieve from decision.

Jeremy. . . . He couldn't understand.

For some reason, he seemed to think that getting Ross out of her heart was a simple act of will. It was no such thing. Losing him had filled her with pain that rooted itself as securely as an oak roots itself to earth. Even the earlier cruel loss of their child had not brought such deep-seated and enduring sadness. The agony of that deprivation had been shared, easing it somewhat. Recovering from the loss had brought them closer, strengthening the bonds of their devotion to each other.

And there was one other certainty; she could never love Jeremy the way she had loved Ross. This rising to mind, she turned and stared out the window at the chickadees patroling the naked limbs of the tree closest to the house. And immediately reconsidered.

How could she think such a thing? Such an arbitrary assumption was outrageously unfair. And this vacillating

29

between accepting Ross's death and doubting it was just as bad—and foolish. For Jeremy's sake, for her own, she must put Ross out of her mind completely. Other women who had lost their husbands had been able to do so. She would.

Unexpectedly, Alexander Craven appeared early the next morning, informing her that he'd decided during the night that the best course for Thursby would be for him to quit his bed.

Thursby, the master's master of the house, commanding general of the staff—a man who could spot a pin in a deep-pile carpet 40 feet away; a man to whom a mote of dust was anathema, a thumbprint on a spoon handle a cardinal sin and a misplaced place card at a dinner party the iniquitous act of the Devil himself—sat rigidly against his pillow. He glanced icily at Craven as he and Lisa entered the room. Lisa stood next to the Pennsylvania highboy. Cued by their intrusion, Thursby slipped down under the covers, his eyes gazing at the ceiling, suggesting he was rehearsing his deathbed scene.

"I feel much worse today, doctor," he croaked hoarsely, touching his throat with a gaunt finger. "My throat is on fire."

"You've been in bed six days," said Craven in a bored tone. "What do you say to six more? Perhaps a week?"

An expression of abject suffering seized the patient's angular features. "If it will help me spring back, restore my strength," he said feebly. "I don't become ill often, as you know, Mrs. Dandridge. But when it strikes, everything seems to disintegrate. My arms and legs and the back of my neck ache furiously. It's absolute agony to swallow; even breathing is painful. My eyes are sore as boils, my stomach, my vitals. I have no appetite."

"You have our sympathy," said Craven. "Under the circumstances, I won't burden you with the bad news."

"What are you talking about?"

"Disaster. It's slowly striking, taking possession of

the house like plague spreading," lied Craven. "Nobody seems to be bothering about the dusting. The windows badly need washing, the silver polishing, the kitchen. . . ."

"Alex," began Lisa.

"You mean to stand there and tell me that those lazy slouches—" burst Thursby, not even able to finish his sentence. Whipping aside the covers, revealing legs sufficiently bony to rival a stork's, he slapped his bare feet against the floor.

Craven gasped. "You're not getting up!"

"Don't try to stop me!"

"As your doctor, I forbid it!"

"Out of my way! Pardon me, Madam."

Lisa and Craven withdrew, giving the patient privacy in which to dress.

"You, doctor, are a scoundrel!" Giggling, she took him by the arm and walked him down the corridor and around the corner. Moments later they glanced back around to see Thursby come storming out of his room, knotting his robe cord about him, his slippers slapping against the runner as he rushed headlong down the stairs.

"Stanton, Carlson, Reilly, Chase. Everybody into the foyer. Line up!" he called.

Lisa and Craven made their way to the library—the painted room, as she thought of it. In it were the Piedmontese secretary, blue with silver molding, gilt trim and cartouches; the English Regency lacquered-and-gilded cabinet with lovely *faux*-burl panels and Siena-marble top; the neoclassic armchairs, resplendent with painted armorial cartouches; and the ceiling-high shelves crammed with volumes, their continuation interrupted only by the doors and the single window looking out upon the rose garden.

"I've never seen anyone so close to death's door make such a remarkable recovery," said Craven dryly. "We've witnessed a miracle of modern medical science."

"He may overdo it and collapse completely, of course," she murmured.

Sliding his spectacles halfway down the bridge of his nose, he began inspecting the books at eye level occupying the stack at right angles to the doors.

"What trash you Dandridges collect. Ah, Christopher Marlowe, a pearl amongst the nettles. *Tamburlaine the Great*. May I borrow this?"

"Take it."

He riffled the pages. "I'll probably forget to return it. Did you know that Marlowe died at the age of twenty-nine? He got into a quarrel with a friend over their dinner bill. Marlowe pulled a knife, but in the struggle, the other fellow turned it into him and killed him. Twenty-nine. Time to write four plays and some poetry. Such a meager output for such an enormous talent." He searched her eyes. "Precious commodity, time. People do waste it so. Have you fallen in love with Jeremy Slater?"

"Yes."

"Do you intend to accept when he asks you to marry him?"

"I wish you hadn't asked me that."

"Is that the answer you're going to give him?"

"Do you want to play clever or try to help me? I need an objective opinion. I'm so close to the thing that it's practically making my head spin. I want to say yes, but I want to hold off."

"Why hold off?"

"Well, for one thing, he's so different from Ross. I've never known two men so completely opposite."

Craven nodded. "Ross was very open, uncomplicated."

"Exactly. Jeremy's so unlike that. I get the feeling he's painting my portrait just to be near me, to legitimatize his presence while he's courting me. He hides his feelings up to a certain point, then it all comes rushing out. He never gets angry, never says anything cross or even mildly provocative. Sometimes he's so bashful I half expect him to avoid my eyes, blush and screw his toe into the rug."

"You think that because you loved Ross the way he was you'll never be able to adjust to someone so unlike him?"

"Maybe it just takes getting used to."

"Why compare them? Take Jeremy for what he is. He'll love you. He'll put you up on just as high a pedestal as Ross did."

"I'm not an urn, Alex. I don't need a pedestal." She sighed. "Ross and I were so happy—in spite of what Lavinia put us through, in spite of all our problems. I could never be that happy again."

"Nonsense. Of course you could. Bury the past, girl. When he asks you to marry him, say yes. You're still young, still beautiful. You have a great capacity for happiness, and the world owes you a bowlful."

Impulsively she kissed Craven on the forehead, causing him to blink in surprise.

"I love you, doctor."

"Then you'll do as your doctor orders."

"We shall see. Is there anything you can prescribe for chronic indecision?"

He returned the kiss. "An affirmative answer. A sure cure. That will be two dollars, please."

That afternoon started out continuing the glorious brightness and beauty of the morning. In a rented gig, Lisa and Jeremy drove out in the direction of Monton, into the countryside that was coming alive with spring. Early primrose and trailing arbutus exuded spicy fragrance and paraded their colors around the roots of the budding beeches and birches that crowded the woodland ways between the farms. Above their heads, trafficking the warm, windless air, were bickering jays and robins, sparrows, and an occasional mourning dove sent its melancholy call through the afternoon. Then, less than two miles from the outskirts of the city, the sun speedily vanished, dark clouds rolled in from the sea, the birds flew for cover and the storm broke.

Jeremy raced the mare for the nearest shelter, a

dilapidated barn filled with the damp and unpleasant odors of the rotted hay and old manure. Gaping holes in the roof funneled the deluge down upon them, forcing them to huddle in a corner in close company with the mare.

"This isn't exactly the way I planned it," said Jeremy ruefully. The horse snorted and stomped one hoof. "I wasn't talking to you."

Lisa laughed. Jeremy stopped her with a kiss.

"Lisa, Lisa." Pausing, he dropped to one knee, clasping her hands. "Will you marry me?"

"Oh, Jeremy, dearest darling Jeremy. Get up, you've got your knee sopping!"

He put the other down beside it. "Will you?"

"I'd love to. . . ."

"But?"

"I didn't say but."

"You were about to. Lisa, marry me. Give it up, all of it, every stick of furniture, every foot of land. Leave Providence, come away to anywhere. Please, shed it all; the business, the house, the lands."

"Darling, they're worth millions. If I sold them, what would I do with all that money?"

"Buy hats, give it to charity, toss it into the sea, burn it! Who needs it!"

She pulled him to his feet, slipped her arms around his neck and kissed him lingeringly. "You ask for an answer. My answer is yes. I will marry you, Mr. Jeremy Slater."

From his vest pocket, he produced a small velvet box. Snapping it open, he revealed a large oval-shaped diamond surrounded by six smaller stones. She gasped, her eyes dancing. He slipped it onto her finger.

"Oh, Jeremy."

"Like it?"

"I adore it. It's beautiful!" She hesitated.

"What?"

"All I ask is that you give me time to decide about Blackwood and the rest of it."

"How much time?"

"Ten days, two weeks."

"Ten days is a long time."

"I know, please be patient." She released his hand and turned away. The rain continued to splatter down, turning several areas in the barn into quagmires, splashing against the seat of a rusty hay tedder and the unprotected rump of the horse.

Jeremy took her by the shoulders, pulling her back close to his chest.

"Darling, it's not an ultimatum," he said quietly. "I wouldn't do that to you, I haven't the right. It's for you to decide." He turned her to face him. "All I can say is if I had never come into your life, if another fellow fell in love with you and proposed and you accepted, don't you think he'd want the same thing for you? And make no mistake, Lisa, it is for you."

"I know."

"Ten days."

She nodded and they kissed, fiercely, passionately, the rain continuing to batter the ruined roof, pouring through the holes, attacking the horse and tedder.

In her heart, the sun blazed.

IV

A few days later Lisa and Jeremy had lunch in town and afterward strolled through Roger Williams Park, reveling in the loveliness of the day, the balmy weather, the gradual greening of the city. They shared a bench with a corpulent middle-aged couple engrossed in a newspaper shared between them. Engrossed in each other, Jeremy and Lisa ignored the two and passers-by, losing themselves in mutual affection in the manner of two teenagers struck with the blissful contagion of first love.

The announcement of the wedding had gone out. Congratulations flowed in. Emily Slater was arranging a bridal shower for Lisa. The wheels were in motion, the altar and commitment loomed.

The heavy-set couple exchanged newspaper sections and a pigeon, red-eyed and scraggy-looking, strutted pompously up to Jeremy's foot, eyed him, caught sight of a female close by, inflated his feathers and set out in pursuit of her.

"Everybody wants to get married," observed Lisa.

"I'm for it." Jeremy leaned toward her, kissing her cheek. The woman seated beside Lisa rattled her newspaper and cleared her throat. Lisa and Jeremy got up and resumed strolling.

"Where shall we go for a honeymoon?" she asked. "Everything's been happening so fast that a honeymoon completely slipped my mind."

"I've thought about it. What would you say to London? I've never been there. You haven't been back in years. We can sail from New York on Monday. It's three weeks to Southampton—closer to two, actually—then on to London and wherever you like in England, to the Continent. . . ."

"Oh, Jeremy, could we?"

"Of course. I'll book passage on the *Olympia*."

At the mention of the ship's name, her smile faded. "*Olympia?*"

"Yes, she's a clipper. I can't wait to see the two of us standing on the deck, the bow skimming through the water, the wind roaring overhead."

"I came to America on the *Olympia*."

"Really?"

"It belongs to Baldwin & Baldwin, at least it did back then. Cyrus and Gray built it for them."

"Darling, if you think you'd feel uncomfortable, put it out of mind. There have to be a dozen ships crossing. The *Agamemnon,* the *Niagara*. I hear the *Great Eastern*'s due to leave sometime before the end of April."

"I'm being childish, but please, not the *Olympia*."

"Whatever you say, my darling."

Tom Overstreet, the Dandridge shipyard foreman, and his wife gave a dinner party for the engaged couple the following evening. It proved a triumphal success, attended and acclaimed by the Slaters, the Hallorans, Senator and Mrs. Evan Brockway and other longtime friends of the Dandridges who, over the years, had become Lisa's friends. Shortly before the end of the war, Tom Overstreet had retired from squinting at blueprints and chewing the ends off pipestems while wrestling with the problems of putting clipper ships to sea and keeping them afloat against the formidable opposition of wind and weather. Mrs. Overstreet had borrowed Thursby from Blackwood to supervise dinner. Recovered from his illness, Thursby had selected the menu, dictated preparation of everything down to the choice of polish for the napkin rings and ordered the servants about like an overzealous drill master.

The affair concluded shortly after midnight and Jeremy drove Lisa back to Blackwood, the carriage keeping pace with a great black cloud scowling down at them and scudding westward. It slid across the face of the moon, cloaking the woods in blackness as they came within sight of the house. Thursby had requested permission to stay the night at the Overstreets—probably, suggested Jeremy, to lecture the help on their errors of the evening.

With the exception of the front-door lamps, the house was in darkness upstairs and down.

"Tired?" he asked, stopping the carriage at the door.

"A little."

He kissed her lovingly. The cloud obscuring the moon passed over it and the pale light flooded down upon them.

"Jeremy."

Her heart raced as he took her in his arms. The cool fire burst into flame and she drew in her breath, steeling herself against the onslaught of the overpowering urge to yield her body to his. She imagined his flesh warm against her own, his limbs encompassing her. It had been so interminably long. Every night lying alone had been like ritual torture, deprived as she was, denied.

Suddenly the need to feel him, possess him, to know once again the sweet splendor of lying in embrace, the delicious tingling sensation sweeping over every inch of her body, the gentle beginning, the act, the ascent to the heights, to mutual climax, the all-pervading explosion so beautiful she could faint with joy consumed her.

V

Standing naked before her mirror, Lisa ran her hands slowly down over her ample breasts, the tips of her fingers coming together at the concavity of her stomach, down over her hips to her thighs. Her body was still attractive, she decided, still firm and well-formed where it should be. She loosened her hair, letting the abundant red waves cascade down over one of her shoulders. Thrusting her fingers into it, she began freeing the tangles. Then she stopped short at the sound of a single knock at the door.

Drawing back the antique spread of crocheted cotton and getting into the freshly made bed, she fluffed the pillows and then leaned back against them, their coolness sending a tremor down her spine. Then she pulled the sheet up to her chin to cover her nakedness.

"It's unlocked."

She blew out the candle on the bedside stand and the room filled with moonlight, a wide swath of it finding its way between the opened portiers and drenching the floor. He came in, then closed and locked the door behind him.

"My perfume." She pointed at a delicate-looking crystal bottle on the vanity.

Sitting on the edge of the bed, he was preparing to hand it to her, then held it from her. "Let me." Drawing the covers down, exposing her body, he daubed behind her ears, her throat, moving dexterously over her flesh, selecting the sensitive areas. "You are beautiful, my darling."

Setting the bottle on the stand, he kissed her and she began unbuttoning his shirt. Within moments, he was undressed entirely and lying beside her, their bodies touching at shoulder, at hip and thigh. He lay on his chest, she on her back, pulling one of the pillows out from under her head and sliding down beneath the covers. His hand found her breasts and began caressing them gently, his palms gliding over her nipples. His closeness, his warmth, the gradual hardening of his member. He moved slightly and she felt it against her thigh, tremor after tremor coursing through her. Now his chest was full against her breasts, his weight upon her, his mouth finding hers, grinding it, kindling the embers of her passion so long held in subjugation. Her heart came pounding to life. Her hands buried in his hair and she worked his mouth furiously against hers, devouring it. Their tongues probed, clashed, dueled uncontrollably.

Now he mounted her, joining their bodies. She moaned in ecstasy, clutching him in the vise of her limbs. Like a gigantic bud thrust heavenward, bursting into bloom, every nerve, every fiber, every atom of her being drove to the exquisite culmination of climax.

"My darling, my darling," she whispered huskily. "Ross, Ross."

His body stiffened, then slowly he drew himself upward out of her hold and out of the bed, crossing to the window. His shoulders rigid, he stood looking out upon the night.

"Jeremy, my God. What have I. . . . Forgive me, please, please!" She was out of the bed and standing behind him, her arms about his shoulders, her cheek pressed against his back. "It slipped out. It was stupid of me. I wasn't thinking, I swear." He said nothing. She tried to turn him around to bring their bodies together to feel his warmth, to clutch and hold him tightly. But he resisted. "Please, my darling, I didn't mean it, I didn't."

"I know you didn't."

From the pain in his voice, he might have been speaking with a needle thrust into his heart. But then to her relief he seemed to shake it off, taking her in his arms, kissing her forehead, stroking her hair.

"Forget it, you didn't say it."

"I. . . ."

"Forget it, Lisa. I will. I have." He paused, staring down at her, smiling wanly, framing her face with his hands. "It's late, I must go."

"Not yet. Not like this."

"It's all right."

"Let's make love again, please."

"If you want."

"Not if I want. Not that!"

"My darling, my wife, we will make love again."

And picking her up, he carried her back to the bed.

VI

Jeremy left for Philadelphia the next day, for three days, to clear up some legal ends having to do with his giving up his law partnership and monies due him in consequence. Enos Pryne drove the two of them to the railroad station in the cabriolet. The 9:25 for New York came puffing in on schedule, startling every horse within a city mile. While Enos waited, reins in hand, she walked Jeremy to the platform. They kissed good-bye and she waved to him as he mounted the steps. The trainman at the end car swung his flag, the engine whistled, the stack poured forth a plume of dirty white smoke as the driving wheels spun and gripped and the train slowly labored on its way. She walked with the moving train, waving as he found a window seat. He smiled down and her heart melted as she saw the kiss in his eyes.

Three days without him would be like three weeks, she knew. Her dreadful slip of the night before was still fresh in her mind, but it was a relief to see that once its effect upon him had spent i self, he had forgotten it.

The train curved away in the distance, carrying its clamor and smoke toward Westerly. Those who had come down to see people off or to welcome passengers in from Boston and the north began drifting toward the carriage lot. Enos sat waiting patiently. He had been in the service of the Dandridge family long before Ross was born. Now, she guessed, he was close to 80, palsied, forgetful at times and as lazy as a dog in the sun, according to Thursby. He was annoyingly opinionated and as nosy as a landlady "with a keyhole eye," as her father used to say. But Cyrus had insisted he be kept on as stableman. In his

42

cottage 50 yards from the house, he kept to himself, caring for the horses, carving small wooden ones and fishing rainbow trout out of the pond behind the stables. He took excellent care of the horses and vehicles. No mother ever lavished more devotion over her children than did Enos Pryne over his horses.

"You and him getting married?" This delivered in the flattest tone imaginable, as if he were announcing the fact that one of the horses was due for new shoes.

"Yes, Enos."

"That's good, I guess. My best to you."

"Thank you."

"I ain't the marrying kind myself. I'm seventy-nine and four months and never come close," he announced proudly, snapping the reins in punctuation, stepping up the mare's gait. "What about the house? You plan to sell it?"

It was a question on the minds of everybody on the staff lately, all of whom would have to be let go should Blackwood be sold. *Perhaps not, perhaps the new owner would keep everyone,* she thought. *It's all so involved, so cumbersome.*

"I honestly don't know at this point whether or not I'm going to sell," she answered quietly.

Enos screwed up his homely features and grunted. *Ill-disguised disapproval,* she thought.

It was past ten by the time they got back to the house. Enos drove up to the door, helped her out and continued on to the stables. But not before taking note of the carriage parked on the far side of the circle.

"That be lawyer Muybridge's Stanhope," he said. "I'd know it anyplace by them curtains. What do you suppose a lawyer wants with a doctor's rig anyways?"

"Maybe you'd better ask him."

"I think I will."

Both Muybridges were waiting for her in the library, according to Thursby.

"It's that time of the year, madam."

"Have they been here long?"

"Just arrived a few minutes before you."

"Show them to the living room. We'll have coffee."

"Very well, madam."

The phrase "that time of the year" referred to the fact that one or the other, or both, Muybridges came to the house early in the spring and early in the fall to bring Lisa up to date on her holdings. They would swamp her with legal advice, caution her against this, that and the other thing of a legal nature and push paper after paper under her eyes to be signed, which she would do until her first and second fingers ached.

The elder Muybridge had been Cyrus's legal counsel since the early 1830s. His only son had joined the firm in 1855. The two were look-alikes a generation apart. Junior Muybridge was tall, athletic-looking—a squash and football player of some renown during his days at Brown—a bright, though overly talkative, young man, with a wife who, conveniently, rarely opened her mouth. He was a man who prided himself on following in his father's footsteps with cautious precision, taking care never to enlarge the imprint, but to fit it cleanly. His father had also been an athlete, but the years and the sedentary demands of his profession had softened the hardened muscles, relaxed the spring in his step and added inches to his waistline and companion chin to the one given him by nature. Endless hours poring over documents had brought on astigmatism as well, and he had taken to wearing a pair of offset guard eyeglasses that gave him the look of a surprised Pekingese.

Muybridge Senior offered his hand. "Congratulations, Lisa."

"Congratulations," echoed Junior, "we hope you'll be very happy."

"Thank you both."

Senior thrust his thumbs into his lower vest pockets and began pacing slowly. "We've some rather interesting information."

Junior tapped the briefcase on his lap. "Your investments are sound as a dollar. There's nothing we'd advise you to consider changing, but——"

"A gentleman by the name of Anderson from New York called at the office yesterday. He and his people have come up with what appears to be a most interesting proposal," concluded Senior.

Thursby arrived with the coffee and Lisa poured and served. Thursby nodded and withdrew.

"What is this proposal?" asked Lisa.

Senior slowed his pacing to keep from sloshing his coffee into the saucer. "He represents a syndicate that's interested in buying the yards. The works, lock, stock and barrel."

"I see."

"I don't mean to sound cold or unfeeling, but we must all us face the fact that Dandridge Shipbuilding has seen its best days."

She stared into her coffee to conceal an amused look. "You're being very generous, Mr. Muybridge. Let's be honest. Dandridge Shipbuilding is no more."

"Nevertheless, the land—some eleven point three acres—the buildings, equipment, that nearly completed ship on the blocks, the whole of it could be worth a great deal of money. Is. As the situation stands at present, the estate is paying taxes on unused property."

"What are these people offering?"

"Close to eight hundred thousand in cash and negotiable bonds for the yards alone," said Junior. He tapped his briefcase again. "We have all the particulars."

"What do you mean by 'the yards alone'? What else do they want?"

Senior's free hand swept away from his cup. "The lot. This house, the acreage, your holdings in Westerly, all over the state."

"Slow down, please." Setting her coffee down, Lisa rose from the divan and confronted him, her arms folded.

"I suddenly feel as if the rug has been pulled out from under me."

"I don't blame you. It is rather awesome and sudden. Believe me, Lisa, we didn't come up here to bowl you over," Senior said sympathetically.

"You don't need the money," said Junior. "You don't need the taxes on the yards, but they're minuscule when set side by side with the income from all of your real estate. Frankly we were amazed at the coincidence of Anderson approaching us at this time, when you're planning to remarry. We considered the possibility that you might be leaving Providence. Mr. Slater does come from Philadelphia, does he not?"

"Yes."

She weighed their words. It seemed almost fate. On the day Jeremy was due to return, he would be expecting her decision. Now here was this ostensibly very handsome offer lining up with his suggestion and with the sentiments shared by Alex Craven and obviously both Muybridges.

"Will you be leaving?" asked Senior.

"I believe so. Yes, yes."

The words coming out surprised her, as if some power within over which she had no control had prompted their utterance.

Senior went on: "The offer is contingent upon complete purchase—the whole kit and caboodle."

"I understand," said Lisa.

Senior and Junior exchanged glances. "Then your decision is to accept?"

"Yes, everything to be included. Get started working out the details at once."

Senior rose. "You're making a wise decision, Lisa. We'll inform Anderson and get back to you in a few days." He opened his briefcase "So much for that. Now there's the usual run-of-the-mill business." He smiled. "It should take only a few hours."

It took until three o'clock.

Then both the Muybridges put on their coats and hats, echoed their congratulations, shook hands and went away in their curtained Stanhope.

An hour later it happened.

Enos arrived with the day's mail, handing it to Thursby at the front door. He loaded it on a salver and conveyed it to Lisa, who was sitting at the desk in the study going over the wedding lists. Most of the letters were responses to the invitation: the majority of them were acceptances.

There was also a letter in a dark-gray envelope postmarked Williamsburg, Virginia. She stared at it, puzzled.

The return address was the Eastern Virginia Asylum.

She opened the envelope and out fell a small rectangular piece of pasteboard.

It was a photograph showing the face and upper body of a man. A circle had been penciled around his head. There was no mistaking the dark curly hair, the brown-almost-black eyes, the handsome face—tight-lipped, unsmiling.

It was a picture of Ross.

VII

Jeremy walked by the as yet uncompleted St. Patrick's Cathedral and crossed the cobblestones of Fifth Avenue, dodging carriages and wagons. He headed west down 50th Street and turned into a six-story brick building. Entering the elevator, he instructed the operator to take him to the top floor and minutes later stepped out in front of an office door announcing Empire-Loomis Theatrical Productions. Two names were lettered in the lower-left corner of the opaque glass: N. LOOMIS, T. VOSSBACHER.

Jeremy knocked and went in. The room was filled with the acrid stench of cigar smoke and an outer office looked as if it had been ransacked. File drawers were pulled open, a wire wastebasket overflowed with discarded papers and a flat-topped desk was piled with newspapers. A large album lay open, a jar of paste and a number of clippings were scattered about the blank pages waiting to be mounted. Miniature posters of theatrical productions adorned the walls interspersed with photographs of Jenny Lind, Laura Keene, William Burton and others. The door to the inner office stood open and it was from here that the cloud of smoke was issuing. A bull-built man in his middle 50s sat behind the desk, legs up, feet perched comfortably beside his cigar box, a half-smoked cigar plugged into the corner of his mouth. He wore an ash-smudged vest, his shirt-sleeves were rolled up and his watch chain sagged across his ample stomach. Out came his cigar, allowing a broad smile to take possession of his face.

"For God's sake, will you look what the wind blew in!"

A second man, ten years younger than the first, standing at the window looking down upon the traffic below, turned slowly. He too was tugging at a cigar, blue smoke curling up from the corner of his mouth. Jeremy waved away the haze with his hat.

"How about opening a window?"

Ned Loomis pulled his feet down and, hauling his bulk out of his chair with obvious effort, proffered a hand. "Jerry boy, how are you? What a pleasant surprise. Teddy and I were just talking about you, isn't that so, Teddy?"

"Yeah." The tone was surly, and the look on Teddy Vossbacher's face was one of displeasure threatening to deteriorate into downright disgust.

Loomis eyed Jeremy. "We haven't heard from you in ages. What's up?"

Jeremy reached into his inside coat pocket and brought out a newspaper clipping along with an unsealed white envelope. He laid both on the desk.

Loomis's eyes widened as he read the clipping. "Look at this, Teddy. The boy's getting married!"

Vossbacher came away from the window, reading over the other's shoulder, his lips forming each word. Taking out the wedding invitation, Loomis read aloud: " 'Mrs. Ross Richard Dandridge and Mr. Jeremiah Roger Slater request the pleasure of your company at their wedding, Saturday, the fourteenth of April, one thousand eight hundred and sixty-six, at Providence, Rhode Island.' April the fourteenth! My, my, my, congratulations!" Again he pumped Jeremy's hand. "I hate to say it, but we were beginning to wonder, not hearing from you and all."

Sitting, Jeremy raised his feet to the desk. "What's to worry about? You knew where I was, what I was doing."

"We know only what you tell us," said Teddy in an unfriendly tone.

"How much does it look like?" asked Loomis. "Four million? Five?"

Jeremy began laughing uproariously. Muttering, Vossbacher hurried to the outer door, slamming it.

"Try ten," said Jeremy, when he returned. "Minimum."

Loomis emitted a low whistle, flicked the ashes from his cigar onto the floor and leaned back. "My, my, you are onto something, aren't you."

Jeremy described Lisa as beautiful, lonely, passionately in love with him: "And she trusts me completely."

"She sounds as stupid as they come," commented Vossbacher, pleased with his sudden flair for sarcasm.

"Myra should be half as bright."

"You shut up about Myra," snapped Vossbacher. Jeremy smirked. "Wise bastard."

"All right, all right," cautioned Loomis, "take it easy, Teddy."

Vossbacher glared. "I don't like him talking about my wife. I don't even like to hear him say her name."

"Teddy, shut up," said Loomis.

"What makes you so sure she's going to dump her money into your lap to play with?" asked Vossbacher, ignoring Loomis. "She could have other ideas. You can't tell me money that big don't have big-shot lawyers holding onto all the strings."

"You didn't hear me, Teddy," said Jeremy evenly. "I said she trusts me completely. She's even going to turn all her assets into cash, as you suggested, Ned. I asked her to and she will. She's playing right into our hands."

Loomis puffed on his cigar, fashioned a smoke ring and eyed its ascent to the ceiling. "Teddy's got a point there, though. How can you be so sure she'll hand over control of her money to you?"

"Come on, Ned. You're talking to the lady's devoted husband-to-be. Say, mind if I open a window?"

Loomis gestured. "Open the window for him, Teddy."

Vossbacher complied, but not without muttering.

The cacophony of traffic below filtered upward, dominated by the rumble of a horse-drawn trolley.

Loomis studied Jeremy. "You're doing a grand job, Jerry boy. We're coming to the end of the rainbow."

"We ain't seen nothing yet," said Vossbacher. "Everything's still going out and nothing's coming in."

"Teddy, if you want to make money, you've got to invest money," Jeremy said. "Which reminds me, I'm going to need a little bit more to tide me over till the ship comes in."

Loomis's face clouded and his eyes went to his cigar, examining its length. Silence hung like the smoke in the air. Then Loomis cleared his throat and spoke, his tone deadly serious, his eyes directed at his well-manicured fingernails. "We've already advanced you eleven thousand," he said. "That's a pretty big pile."

"Eleven thousand two hundred fifty," said Vossbacher.

"Ned, her engagement ring set me back more than two thousand." Planting his knuckles on the edge of the desk, Jeremy leaned over and peered into the fat man's face. "I need three thousand more. It's the last I'll ask for." He straightened up. "If you think about it, it's a drop in the bucket. With the best collateral in the world." He tapped the wedding invitation lying on the desk.

"You really think you're going to get three thousand dollars more out of us!" began Vossbacher, reddening angrily.

Loomis stood up. The sudden turn in the conversation had drained away his joviality. He scowled, whistled nervously and drummed the desk with his fat fingers.

"I don't believe you two, I really don't," said Jeremy. "I ask you for a paltry three thousand——"

"Fourteen thousand two hundred and fifty dollars ain't paltry!" snapped Vossbacher.

Jeremy tossed up his hands. "Incredible!"

"Not so, Jerry boy." Loomis waved his cigar. "These two pieces of paper you bring us are great as far as they go. But all they really tell us is that something good might happen."

"I tell you we're getting married!"

"I tell you congratulations, best wishes. When it happens. When everything is tied up in a neat little package with a blue ribbon around it. In the meantime, I've got to look at the whole picture realistically. And when I do, there's not a lot worth seeing, not yet. I worry about you, Jerry boy. About a hundred years ago, you stumbled your way through that law school down in Philadelphia, graduating by the skin of your teeth. Never even setting up practice, not really. Instead you got married, you started living off your wife—until she got fed up and walked out on you."

"You mean till she threw him out," said Vossbacher. "Hell, he never woulda got in with that bunch of Shylocks down there, that Wheeler & Wheeler outfit, if she hadn't paid his way!"

"That doesn't happen to be any of your goddamned business, Teddy," said Jeremy.

"Whether it is or not, he's got the facts straight," Loomis said, frowning. "So where are we? She gets rid of you, you're left without a dime, you don't dare go to your old man's relatives up in Providence and ask them for help, because all the while, thanks to your wife, you've got them believing you're a big successful Philadelphia lawyer."

"Playing the playboy painter on the side, sucking around anything in skirts." Vossbacher snickered.

"Is it my fault women find me attractive? Especially married women?"

"You son of a bitch!" Vossbacher started for him, but Loomis leaped to his feet and held him back with one arm.

"Jerry boy, one of these days I'm not going to stop him," he said tiredly. "And you just might wind up with a broken head."

"Somebody's head'll get broken, but it won't be mine."

Vossbacher leveled a finger at him. "If you so much as come within one city block of Myra and I find out, I'll kill you. So help me God!"

Loomis took out his Waterbury watch, listened to it and showed it to his partner. "It's getting on to four, Teddy. You're going to be late getting up to Yonkers."

"I ain't going, not while he's in town!"

"Teddy, we're still trying to run a business around here. You get your hat and coat, get out of here and get on that train. You talk to Brideweiser and get him to sign his contract or else. Understand? And come straight back here."

Vossbacher glared at Jeremy and stalked out, slamming the outer door. Loomis sat down slowly, stumping out his cigar and shaking his head.

"Jerry boy, you've got ten thousand women to play with. Why fool around with his wife? Is it just to get his goat?"

"I don't chase her; she comes after me. Look, I didn't come all the way down here to talk about Myra Vossbacher. I came to fill you in on what's been happening."

"And to squeeze us for another three thousand."

"I don't like that word, Ned. I've got to have that money and that's all there is to it. I'm not about to ask my bride to pay for her own honeymoon, no matter how much she's got."

"Jerry boy, what do you do with it all, make bonfires on chilly nights? You're living rent free up there with your relatives. How in God's name do you manage to spend eleven thousand dollars in a few short months?"

"I live. Graciously. In the manner of a man about to marry a wealthy widow."

"You know what Teddy thinks?"

"I wasn't aware he could."

"He claims you're a bad poker player."

"He's loony."

"Is he?" Loomis started to say something but hesitated, swinging his chair around toward the window. Then he went to the safe and squatted in front of it, twisting the combination dial, pulling open the door. Taking out a manila envelope, he counted out three thousand dollars in 50s and 100s, squaring off the stack on the corner of the desk.

"Where are you going on your honeymoon?"

"Boston."

"Very good. We've got a production opening there next week. E. P. Christy's Minstrels and the Bryant Brothers. I'll see that a couple tickets are left at the box office for you any night you please. Now, about the money." Loomis opened his desk drawer, brought out a small loose-leaf notebook and thumbed through it. "Teddy's right. It's eleven-two-fifty plus this."

"As if you didn't know."

"April the fourteenth. You should be back home when? End of the month?"

"Thereabouts."

"Giving you reasonable time to persuade her that a self-respecting husband should have a hand in his wife's business dealings, let's put a deadline of the end of August on it."

"What are you talking about, deadline?"

Loomis closed his notebook and restored it to the drawer.

"We have to consider the possibility that she may not permit your fingers in the pie. Or ask for any advice from you." Jeremy tried to interrupt, but Loomis continued. "I know, she trusts you completely. The thing is, we have this sum of money invested in you. If, for whatever reason, you're unable to get the capital we're going to need for the business ventures I have in mind, then just like that the game is over. And we're going to want a lump-sum payment of fourteen thousand two hundred plus interest from you. By the end of August."

"You've got nothing to worry about. Within a couple of months we're all going to be rolling in money."

"Let's hope so. Oh, one last thing: For the sake of your health, don't get any foolish ideas about running out on us once you're married. You can go to Mongolia, but sooner or later we'll catch up with you. And we'll take a lot more than money out of your hide."

"You're an ungrateful cuss, Ned. Here I let you and that simpleton Vossbacher in on the ground floor of the deal of a lifetime and you worry about a few measly dollars. A tiny fraction of what we stand to make."

"Jerry boy, that's the difference between us. I'm a businessman—dollars and cents, sound investments, minimum risks. You, my friend, are the riskiest venture I've ever gotten into. Has it occurred to you that you could walk out of this office and drop dead the second you hit the street? Think of the pile we'd lose!" He patted Jeremy's shoulder. "Your problem is you're an artist. When it comes to business, you think like a child. You don't think at all, really. You've got this all planned and it's all going to run as smooth as clockwork. Well, that we'll have to see, won't we?"

"Good-bye, Ned. I'll be in touch when we get back from our honeymoon."

"You mean Teddy and I aren't invited to the wedding?" Loomis half-laughed deep in his throat, building it into a loud guffaw. The laugh of a man who rarely makes jokes and who when he does so is unable to contain his self-admiration. Jeremy had gotten up to leave but paused at the door. He tapped his inside pocket holding the money.

"Thanks for the vote of confidence."

"Are you going back up to Providence tonight?"

"Probably. Oh, by the way, is Myra working in town?"

Loomis frowned. "Never you mind. You stay away from her. If he catches you, he'll put a bullet in your head and hers, too. I've put too much money into this thing to see it go up in smoke because you can't keep your hands off Myra Vossbacher! *Stay away from her!*"

"If you insist."

"I insist!" His tone softened. "Use your head. You want somebody to play with when you come to New York, I'll fix you up with six beauties. Take your pick."

"I'll find my own, thanks. Good-bye, Ned."

Descending in the elevator, his hand wandered to the money buried in his breast pocket again. It had been a little bit harder getting it out of Loomis than he'd figured on, but of course there was no possible way Loomis could turn him down—not at this stage. All that drivel about never having asked Judd Slater for a cent, accusing him of gambling, all smoke, that's what that was. . . . And where are you going on your honeymoon? He'd no doubt have Vossbacher or somebody out spying on him from now on, to protect his $14,000. Maybe he shouldn't have lied about Boston.

What's the difference, he thought. *Once we get on that ship it could be we'll never come back.*

Out on the sidewalk, he sucked in the sweet cool air and tipped his hat as two well-proportioned young ladies wrapped in mink jackets sauntered past led by their poodles. One blushed and whispered something to the other and both tittered.

The late-afternoon sun slipping into the Hudson flung its gold up the busy street as he paused to watch the traffic and mull over his situation. He could not possibly lose. Teddy Vossbacher was the only thorn, and he couldn't be bothered worrying about him. He'd had plenty of experience handling jealous husbands. Loomis was right, though: Playing with Myra wasn't overly bright, with so much at stake. If only she weren't so cooperative and so capable with the door locked and the lamp turned low.

He headed west, stopping at the corner of Sixth Avenue to buy a *New-York Times* from a newsboy squatting on a crate, his papers balanced across his knees. Jeremy handed him a dime. Getting his paper, he scanned the front page:

"THE CHOLERA
DEPRIVED OF ITS HORRORS BY PURIFYING
AND ENRICHING THE BLOOD.
NOW IS THE TIME TO USE A PREVENTATIVE.
THERE IS NONE EQUAL TO

HEMBOLD'S

HIGHLY CONCENTRATED FLUID
EXTRACT SARSAPARILLA."

"Got some change from that dime for me, son?"

The boy's friendly smile dissolved in disappointment. Fishing out a nickel and a penny, he handed them to Jeremy.

"Thank you, sir."

Jeremy handed him back the penny. "Good boy."

Turning the paper over, he opened it to the next-to-the-last page and began reading aloud, imitating a barker:

" 'Niblo's Garden: Miss Maggie Mitchell—*Margot, the Poultry Dealer.* And Paul in *The Pet of the Petticoats.* The Olympic, the New Bowery. Ah, here we are: the Winter Garden. New comedy farce in two acts titled *Woodcock's Little Game,* after which the burlesque extravaganza titled *Cinderella E La Comare.* Miss Myra Cummings as Cinderella, the Baron's youngest daughter.' "

He walked the four blocks to the Winter Garden Theater, hurrying down the side alley to the stage door, inside, past the door guard busy arguing heatedly with a well-dressed couple, the woman reeking of gin.

"Hey, you," called the guard. "Where do you think you're going?"

"To see a friend. She's expecting me."

"Wait." The man started up from his stool, but the couple was blocking his way, the woman beginning to yell at him. Jeremy ignored them, striding down the narrow, gloomy hallway separating the dressing rooms.

"Myra, hey, Myra."

A door at the far end opened and a tall blonde woman, her face lathered with cold cream, leaned out. She burst into a smile.

"Jerry darling!"

The dressing room smelled of stale cologne and roses; at least 30 were forced into a vase large enough to hold half that number. Clothing was flung about; it hung from lamp fixtures, a battered dressing screen and was piled on a tufted Turkish couch. The vanity-table mirror was fringed with tintypes and newspaper clippings and the dismal green walls were plastered with posters. A dozen framed photographs, all men, were also in evidence. The vanity itself was strewn with bottles and jars, powder boxes, an atomizer, hair brushes, combs, manicure tools and a wig stand—all designed to transform a pretty woman into a ravishing beauty when bathed in the glow of the footlights.

Myra was wearing a flannelette wrapper partially unbuttoned at the top to reveal most of both breasts. Her hair was a disaster: loose curls springing upward, outward and hanging down like coiled shavings from a carpenter's plane. Locking the door, she grabbed a towel, wiped the cream from her face, then grabbed him and kissed him, holding his mouth to hers fully a minute until he was barely able to catch his breath and had to break from her.

"You devil! You go away months at a time. No letter, not a line, nothing! Now suddenly up you pop. Oh, Jerry, Jerry."

They didn't talk long. They never did. There was nothing to talk about with Myra Cummings Vossbacher. To his recollection, there never had been. Each knew what the other wanted and that was all either cared about. Slipping behind the screen with a shrill giggle, she divested herself of her wrapper and chemise and stockings and emerged naked, reaching for him.

"Jerry, Jerry, Jerry."

She clawed at his clothing, stripping it from his body, all but ripping it in her haste to see and feel his flesh. She clung to him as he sidled to the door to lock and bolt it, fairly dragging him back to the couch, smothering his face and neck and shoulders with kisses. Pulling him down on top of her, squealing at the contact of flesh on flesh, the smoldering embers of her lust bursting into flame, she imprisoned him in her arms, crushing her lush breasts against the unyielding hardness of his chest. Then she ran her hands up the muscled plain of his back, reveling in the feel of it, the soul-stirring sensation of strength beneath her fingertips. Upward her hands traveled, finding and gripping the back of his head, bringing his mouth down hard upon her own, devouring it.

Slowly she began to writhe, twisting her hips and thighs upward, feeling his member rapidly erecting against the softness of her stomach.

"Jerry, Jerry, Jerry."

Her insatiable desire to possess him, her ravenous hunger, set her trembling; her mouth opened, her tongue thrusting, driving against his. Her body continued to undulate, silently screaming, every inch, every nerve, every fiber, to engulf and own him. Slowly spreading her thighs, she drew her hands down from his head to his shoulders, summoning her strength, pushing his body downward, releasing his mouth momentarily, easing his throbbing member down, down, down into position, a hollow gasp of overpowering lust escaping her throat.

"Jerry, Jerry."

VIII

Lisa's first reactions to Ross's picture had been those of shock and disbelief—but for the briefest possible moment only. She had quickly scanned the letter enclosed and joy mingled with an enormous wave of relief engulfed her.

He was alive! Alive!

She cried out—a scream of exultation—jumping to her feet, swinging about, dancing circles, possessed completely by sheer happiness, reveling and rejoicing in release from the pain of loneliness, the specter of nagging doubt with which she had lived for so long.

Thursby had come running, his eyes filled with alarm. She had blurted out an explanation. He had clapped his hands, shouted triumphantly, abandoned his composure completely, grabbing her hands and dancing round and round with her.

Now, the next morning, she was on her way to Ross. She stood at the glass at the end of the last car of the train looking down upon the twin bands of steel lengthening behind her, separating her from Providence and her distant destination speedily, but not nearly fast enough.

She took the picture and the letter out of her bag and studied Ross's face again for what by now, she mused, must be the 50th time since she opened the envelope. Never had she seen such a faraway look in his eyes, usually so bright and animated. And his mouth was drawn so tightly, as if the photographer had forbidden him to smile. She reread the letter:

To whom it may concern,

On Monday, four patients arrived, transfers from the Maryland Hospital for the Insane in Baltimore. The man whose picture I have enclosed is on file as a John Doe. He had been admitted to Maryland suffering complete loss of memory.

Since his arrival here, I have questioned him at great length. He has no recollection whatsoever of his life prior to his being admitted to Maryland. We have no information on where he was hospitalized before that or even if he was hospitalized.

I examined his clothing, the uniform of a Union naval officer, missing his cap and one shoe. By chance, I discovered a hole in the bottom of the breast pocket of his jacket. I found a wad of paper that had fallen through into the lining. It was only after carefully unfolding it with a tenotomy knife and tweezers that I found it was actually a letter. It had been thoroughly water-soaked and the writing was illegible, but at the top, the stationer's imprint showed the words Blackwood and Providence.

I am writing in the hope that you may be a relative, a friend or acquaintance who can give us information regarding his identity. If such is possible, I would appreciate your getting in touch with me as soon as possible.

I am most respectfully yours,

> *Dr. Howard T. Middleton*
> *Asst. Chief of Staff*
> *Virginia Eastern Asylum*
> *Williamsburg, Virginia*

She had sent a telegram within the hour and had caught the first train out of Providence the next morning, leaving Thursby with a vague explanation for others that she'd been called away to Virginia on "something to do with business" and would be back in two or three days at the most. She had also advised him to keep where she was going to himself.

Her first thought, after her heart had regained its normal beat, was of Jeremy. Examining her engagement ring, she had sighed and removed it. Poor dear Jeremy. How would she ever be able to break the news?

"Beg your pardon, ma'am." It was the conductor, an angular-looking older man as ramrod straight and as proud-looking as a general in his dark-blue uniform. "We'll be getting into New York in ten minutes. Will you be changing trains and going on?"

"Yes. I'm going all the way to Richmond. I understand there's no line to Williamsburg, is that right?"

"There's connecting public transportation or, if you want to, you can hire a private carriage."

"How far is Williamsburg from Richmond?"

"About three hours' ride—from the center of town, that is. You take the Richmond Road straight through. But it's a long way from here to there. You'll have to change here in New York and in Philadelphia, too. You won't get to Washington till after dark."

"I know. I plan to stay overnight there. You've been most helpful. Thank you."

"You're welcome."

He followed her back to her seat and explained how she was to change trains upon arriving as they crossed the Harlem River bridge and the train jangled and jounced slowly into the heart of the city.

Ross alive! Even the chilling thought that he'd been in a hospital for the insane for all these years failed to dampen her joy. She wanted to stand up and scream out to all the other passengers. He's alive! Alive! My husband, Ross, my darling!

Turning to the window, she saw her reflection through the veil of tears. She had never been so overwhelmed, so filled to bursting with happiness!

Through all of life's unexpected torments, the certainty

of uncertainties, the unimaginable, the inconceivable, one constant ran like a thread through the chain of one's days from cradle to coffin. No matter how abysmal the night, how magnificent the day, time always moved forward, the minutes dropping into the past in steady cadence. Now, suddenly, the clock had stopped dead and both hands were spinning backward, whirling faster than the train wheels, cutting into memory, pushing life back more than three years.

"Lisa, darling, some important people from the Navy Department came to the yards this morning. They want me to help untangle some problems. They have to speed up production. There's this Swedish fellow Ericsson who's contracted to build an ironclad and the Government has to have it as fast as it can get it."

"But what in the world do you know about ironclads?"

"We've turned out all kinds of ships since the clipper days."

"Not ironclads."

"Ships are ships, darling. In some ways, they're all identical. It's this Ericsson's plans. The Navy people claim he only partly draws them and that he often makes his drawings to overcome problems the same day they're to be worked from."

"The man sounds demented."

"It is a trifle scary."

"When would you have to start?"

"Right away. Rowland's already started on the hull at Green Point, Long Island. They're building the turret at the Novelty Works in New York; the machinery and mechanism for the turret at Delameter's in New York."

"It doesn't even sound like a ship."

"It certainly doesn't look like one, from the way they've described it to me. But the Government wants it before the end of February 1862."

"At least you'll be in New York. That's a long way from the shooting."

"And I'll get home as often as I can, I promise."

"How will this Ericsson like your looking over his shoulder?"

"From what they tell me, he'll hate it. But he's got a contract to fulfill and he knows he needs help. We'll get along. I'll try not to step on his toes."

"You'll still be a civilian. I mean, there's no need for you to enlist, is there?"

"Lisa, I must. I can't stay out of it any longer. It's beginning to chew up my conscience. I can't continue to sit up here in safe harbor in Providence making money hand over fist while others are being sent out to risk their lives. In Dandridge ships!"

"But you're helping to win the war!"

"I suppose so, but I don't feel like I am."

"That's the silliest thing I've ever heard!"

"I don't feel personally involved. I'm not going to be in any fighting. There's no danger; you said so yourself. But, darling, if we're going to continue to profit from this holocaust, the least I can do is behave like a patriot."

"You men. You're insufferable! Whenever the bugle sounds, you all get that same glazed look, the same champing at the bit for action! Is that supposed to be manhood on display? Do you have some great inner need to show how courageous you are? Or how rash and stupid? War, war, war! Men run away into the thick of it, and their women stand watching, shaking their heads, wondering what's so fascinating, so captivating about people shooting at one another."

She had to confess that he looked stunning in his blue uniform with gold surrounding his cap, strapped to his shoulders and circling his sleeves. His buckle and buttons were bright as mirrors in the sun, his gold-and-ivory-hilted sword stood jauntily in its scabbard.

He had come home when he was able to break away. The *Monitor* had been turned over to the Navy on the 19th of February, nine days ahead of schedule. The cheesebox on a raft had rumbled away to the jeers and ridicule of practically everyone who saw it, but had met and defeated the *Merrimac*, outmaneuvering it easily and all but blowing it out of the water. Ross's next letter was brimming over with exuberance. In response, she couldn't resist reminding him that whichever ship had won, the battle itself all but rendered wooden ships with canvas sails obsolete.

Ross had taken a well-earned leave. Then they had put him to work at the Navy Yard in Brooklyn, New York, solving other problems on other ironclads. In December the following year, he had been ordered to board the *Monitor* to examine her for mistakes in her original construction. She had been practically thrown together and too hastily pressed into service, according to Ross's last letter. He would be on board at least a week.

But the next letter had come from Captain John Pyne Bankhead, not Ross. And under the seal of the Navy Department in fewer than 100 words, he had stated that Ross Dandridge had died.

Now it appeared that Bankhead had made a mistake, one that had shattered her heart, leaving her desolate, wrapped in a cloud of gloom that resisted dispelling by anything or anyone. Until Jeremy. Poor dear Jeremy, his heart inextricably linked with hers forever—or so the two of them had believed. Love returned to her, kindled by a tall, handsome, shy man who was Ross's complete opposite, wholly lacking his fire, his flair for expressing his feelings, but able to reveal them in so many subtle ways. Poor Jeremy. The thought of hurting him upset her. And hurt he would be. Crushed.

She could not be so indurate as to write to him and explain. That would never do. No, when she and Ross got back, she would go and see Jeremy. Go for a walk or ride and tell him. God willing, he would hear her out, hide his shock behind admirable pretense, take her hands in his and wish her and Ross the best. Then tell her that he hoped that all three could be good friends, see each other often—a customary comment uttered by the loser, but something rarely realized.

She stayed overnight in Washington as planned, dining at Culver's near the railway station, and early the following morning boarded the train for Richmond. It was raining hard. She scarcely noticed. Within hours now, she would be in his arms.

IX

Stand upon the edge of the cone of Mount Vesuvius, thrusting nearly 4000 feet into the cobalt sky, the dormant crater at your back, the bottomless pit of Dante. Not so much as a wisp of vapor rises. No subterranean roaring and rumbling; no slackening or drying up of spring water nearby; no closeness or unnatural stillness of the air. The only sound at this height is the wind, as soft and warm as a blanket, although stronger than that teasing the bay below. Looking down, you see it flecking the water white here and there, like long slender feathers popping to the surface.

Close your eyes and imagine yourself propelled backward in time. It is the noon hour of August 24, 79 A.D. On the northern side of Vesuvius, a semicircular cliff creeps around your back encircling the crater and descending in long slopes toward the plains below. Monte Somma. The same wall continues around the southern half. Below lies the bay, an immense sapphire carelessly dropped by the gods. Up from the water's edge, situated on a hill between two streams, stands Herculaneum. It is presumed to be the port where Hercules stopped with his fleet on his return voyage from Iberia, hence its name. Farther south, near the river Sarnus, nearly two miles from the bay and almost at the foot of Vesuvius, lies Pompeii, also reputedly founded by Hercules. In 63 A.D., both cities were victim to intermittent earthquakes, and today, 16 years later, the inhabitants are still repairing and restoring ruined edifices.

The wind dies, the stillness becomes awesome, as if the earth has suddenly stopped spinning. An ominous muffled *rumbling is heard far below in the bowels of the crater. Vapor rises from the volcano's throat, preceding great clouds of steam. The rumbling grows louder, the mountain shakes, loose stones tumble downward, boulders are dislodged, careering down the slopes. Like a blister breaking, the seal of the crater floor splits. Blocks of stone are hurled upward and a great surging of fiery rock is released, flinging itself up the interior walls into the steaming air. Within moments, the volcano is erupting in all its fury, vomiting pumice and ashes. Down they rain, building in quantity, burying the vineyards clinging to the slopes. Reaching the base of the mountain, the deadly mixture fans outward over the coastal plain. In Pompeii, in Herculaneum, the tide of death rises against doors and windows, burying the helpless people who are huddled in courtyards and cellars. Poisonous gases asphyxiate those who attempt to flee and trap others in their homes and shops. Rapidly the mass of rock and ash creeps above the eaves of the buildings; then above the rooftops, smothering the city under 20 feet of lava in a single enormous burial vault.*

The rumbling ceases. The eruption is ended. Vesuvius stands encircled by a cloud of black dust, drained of its wrath, as silent as the twin tombs of Pompeii and Herculaneum that it has created.

Lavinia drew her eyes down from the summit of the dormant volcano, erasing the tragedy from her imagination as easily as closing a book. Arising from the plank seat of the little fishing boat, she steadied herself and turned to stand and wait as they headed into Marina Grande. To the left ahead, the fishing nets strung up to dry stretched across the beach, webbing the whiteness of the smooth-walled buildings huddled together beyond like square cakes freshly iced on a baker's shelf.

"Giorgio."

"*Signora?*"

"This boat stinks of fish."

"But how can that be?"

"*Signore* Aldoni has told you time and again that you are not to use it for fishing."

"I do not, *signora*." The old man seated at the tiller began pulling nervously at the peak of his cloth cap, his eyes dropping to search the boat bottom. "I swear."

Lavinia took hold of the brim of her straw hat against the onshore breeze and pointed her parasol as if to impale him.

"*You* are a liar!"

"Sometimes, perhaps, the mullet leap over the gunwale; I don't see them; they rot in the sun. They——"

"If you'd rather fish than run us back and forth to the mainland, if you think you are underpaid——"

"No, no. *Signore* Aldoni is very generous!"

"Too generous. If I smell fish in this boat once more, you can go and fish to your heart's content. Is that clear?"

"*Si, capisco, signora.*"

Giorgio steered the little boat between the rocks up to the stone quay, releasing the tiller, scrambling forward and fastening the forward line to the rusty metal ring. Making fast the stern, he helped his passenger out of the boat, collecting her packages and handing them up to Adolfo, a slender, sad-eyed boy who had come running at sight of their arrival. Gulls carved the sky and floated virtually motionless overhead, shrieking at one another; fishing boats came and went, their colorful sails flapping in the breeze; and bathers lay on the sand subjecting their tanned bodies to the brutal white eye of the sun. Hauling down his sail, Giorgio removed his cap, baring his naked scalp to the sun's fury, and bowed from the waist as his passenger made her way to the waiting donkey cart followed by Adolfo, his arms piled with her purchases.

"Remember, no more fishing!" she snapped without looking back.

"*Si, capisco, Signore Aldoni.*"

* * *

The slow uncomfortable ride up the winding mountain path took them past the church of San Costanza, patron saint of the isle of Capri, on the left, its 12th Century Byzantine dome gleaming in the sun, the bell hanging silent in its campanile, a brown cloud of small birds weaving about it, sewing it up with invisible threads. Now the path hewn in the rock by the trudgings of centuries rose sharply, but the donkey, its collar adorned with pheasant feathers, its harness resplendent with charms against the evil eye, continued pulling the *carrozza* effortlessly, steadily leaving the Marina Grande and the sea beyond lower and lower beneath them.

They had ascended almost midway between the town of Capri, with its vaulted houses interlaced with labyrinthine streets, lying in the saddle between Lo Capo on the east and Monte Solaro on the west, and the town of Anacapri, which was half the size of Capri and situated nearly 500 feet higher, a sprawling mass of snow-white houses with quasi-oriental roofs.

At length, the isle became visible in its entirety: a massive chunk of green-stained rock dotted with white, rising in places almost vertically from the sea—springing from it. Lavinia stared down at the view as the *carrozza* lurched forward, the donkey's hind hooves sending loose rock clattering down the path while the boy talked to the creature in a soothing tone, occasionally touching its lean flanks with a stick to remind it that should it falter, quick punishment was waiting. Lavinia held her parasol firmly, warding off the sun, shielding her face. She was approaching her 57th birthday, a fact she needed little verbal reminder of, with so many mirrors in the villa. She looked at least ten years younger, even closer to 40 on days following nights when she slept without the aid of Dr. Inglese's yellow pills. No woman she knew devoted more time and care to her complexion and figure. Fastidiously and regularly applied coloring disguised the increasing number of gray hairs appearing among the black. Lines were creamed and massaged before they were permitted to develop into wrinkles, and with rituallike consistency, she immersed herself in a bubble bath generously laced with milk every morning at 11 on the dot.

Like the enormous jewel box of some mythical giant-ess, Villa Aldoni rose before them: rectangular-shaped, Roman orange in color, accented in glistening white marble and surrounded by flat-topped Italian umbrella pines, tall conifers and luxuriant gardens. To the left, a stairway led through sylvan growth to a placid pool where a muscular statue of Triton, fist upraised defiantly, rose from the water. To the right, beyond a statue of Hermes draped with ivy, a company of olive trees lined up in parade-perfect order, basking in the sun, filling their fruit with its warmth.

The slope leveled gradually. The *carrozza* circled the olive grove, making its way down a gravel path between pink oleanders and through the formal garden to a cluster of violently purple bougainvillaea clinging to a trellis. Here the driver stopped, assisted Lavinia down and began collecting her packages.

"Thank you, Adolfo." She smiled. "Your cart may be uncomfortable, but at least it doesn't smell of fish."

He did not understand. His English was very limited. Her Italian little used. She did not enjoy speaking it, and so she preferred the company of those on the isle and in Naples who could speak to her in her own language. She led him through the entrance between two enormous oil urns and indicated a chair into which he piled her packages.

She had kept the smallest of her purchases in her pocket. Her heels clicked across the terra-cotta floor and a maid, bent with age, shuffled out of nowhere to take her parasol, hat and gloves.

"Vinnie, is that you?" A young girl's voice came from upstairs toward the front of the house.

"Be right up, dear," called Lavinia. Under a magnificent chandelier by Gouthière and up the stairs inset with marble fragments from the ruins at Ostia Antica she strode, reaching the second floor. Through the open door she could see the girl sitting in a peacock chair by her window, her left foot raised on an ottoman, the ankle tightly bandaged. Seeing Lavinia, she braced herself to rise.

"Sit still."

"I can walk."

"It still looks badly swollen. Give it time. Where are your crutches?"

She glanced about the room. It was bright and cheerful, the almond blossoms in a figured bowl on the windowsill, the cozy-looking antique bed with the porcelain doll resting between the pillows, the walls hung with the works of local painters and a 12-foot palm tree springing from an ivory pot circled in high relief in the corner farthest from her, showering its glistening leaves downward like green skyrockets falling. Near the palm both crutches leaned against the wall.

"You haven't touched them all day, have you, child?"

"I don't need them. Look!"

Before Lavinia could move to stop her, the girl was on her feet walking easily up and down the room. Lavinia searched her face for signs of discomfort. There were none.

"You're rushing it."

The girl sat, putting her leg back on the ottoman. "I'm okay, and tomorrow I'll be perfect."

"Hopefully you won't go back to scrambling over the rocks like a ten-year-old tomboy. You're getting too old for that sort of thing."

"So why do you keep calling me child?"

Lavinia smiled radiantly. "I love the young woman coming into my life, but it's sad losing the child." Lavinia kissed her on the forehead. "So what did you do to keep busy today, besides study? You did study?"

"Of course."

The girl began to detail her day, emphasizing the more boring aspects. Lavinia paid little attention to what she was saying, engrossed as she was in studying her, her beautiful red hair, her eyes as green as the bay on a broiling-hot summer day, her skin so pink, so fresh and young-looking. And yet she had grown over the winter, her figure developing, the awkward little girl vanishing into memory. The resemblance had always been obvious, but now she was beginning to look the image of her mother, Lisa. Lavinia sighed inwardly. Stretching her mind, she could almost remember when she was her age. A 16-year-old was no longer a child in this part of the world.

The girl pouted. "Why didn't you take me shopping with you?"

"Deirdre, what would you have me do, carry you on my back? Be patient. I'll be going over Saturday and you can come if you can get around town without your crutches, with no pain, and if Dr. Inglese gives you his permission."

"Great, wonderful."

"I bought you something."

"What?"

"Here." Lavinia brought out a small box wrapped in blue-and-white paper and tied with a ribbon. It contained earrings: tiny pearls set in silver shells.

"They're beautiful! Oh, Vinnie, I adore them!" Throwing her arms around Lavinia's neck, she kissed her loudly on the cheek. "You always bring me such lovely things. You spoil me so!"

"As if I could come back from Naples empty-handed with the house invalid waiting."

She held Deirdre's hand mirror while the girl put the earrings on and examined them from every angle, commenting delightedly.

A cadaverous-looking maid fully six feet tall in flat shoes appeared at the door.

"What is it, Philomena?" asked Lavinia.

"Word has come from Massalubrense, *Signora,* the *signore* will be here by dinnertime."

"Excellent."

"Cook is preparing quail."

"Ugh," said Deirdre, crinkling her nose in distaste. Philomena withdrew, closing the door with practiced discretion.

"I thought you liked quail."

"Not since Enrico told me that they catch the poor things with nets. It seems so cruel. Why can't they raise them like chickens?"

"It's a cruel world, with more that's ruthless and brutal than netting birds. You lead a very sheltered life, Deirdre, in this villa, on this isle."

"You make me sound like a nun!"

"Don't be disrespectful."

"I go to Naples. I've been to Rome and Paris." She took off the earrings, toying with them in the palm of her hand. "Someday I'll see the whole world. I want so much to go to America."

Lavinia managed a grin and a lighthearted tone to cover the concern that swept over her whenever Deirdre mentioned America.

"There's nothing there you won't find better of in Europe, believe me."

"There's Providence. I want to see the ruins of Blackwood, even though they're probably overgrown now. It's almost fourteen years. I want to see where daddy and mother are buried. I want to talk to their old friends. Get to know what they were really like. Mother was beautiful, wasn't she? You've always said——"

"Very beautiful. And your father was handsome."

"To burn to death must be horrible."

"You mustn't think about it, Deirdre. It's a sadness that's part of the past." She took her hands. "We must both keep it back there where it belongs."

"I can't help being curious."

"Of course not. And someday when you're a grown woman, there'll be nothing to keep you from going back. If you really want to."

"I don't even have pictures of them, or of Great

Grandfather Cyrus. Nobody in the family. There isn't anybody, except you."

"Do you like your earrings?"

"I love them. They're beautiful."

"Will you do something for me?"

"Anything."

"Practice a few minutes with your crutches, so you can get downstairs to dinner."

"I can get up and down without them. I already have."

"Are you sure?"

"Honestly!"

"Enrico would be delighted to see you coming into the dining room without them."

"I'll make a grand entrance." Pausing, she shook her head, her lovely hair seemingly catching fire in the light of the dying sun. "He's been gone only five days, but it seems like ages, doesn't it?"

"Mmmmm."

"With all his money, why does he have to work so hard? Why does he go away so often?"

Lavinia looked amused. "To make money. They say in the village that his wife spends money scandalously—practically tosses it into the sea." She stared down at the olive trees stationed below in line after line like soldiers on dress parade. "Enrico's a businessman, Deirdre. All businessmen work like coolies and all of them travel."

"He should let Bisetti and Dominic Serio do his traveling for him. I've thought about it. It's really very simple: They bring him the wine, he sniffs it, tastes it and tells them to forget it or to order a roomful!"

"Ha. You tell my darling that and see what he says."

"But he's hardly ever around anymore. You must get awfully lonely."

"I do, but——"

"I know: Business is business."

Again Lavinia kissed her on the forehead. "I'm exhausted. I'm going to lie down for a bit. Then I'll be changing for dinner. Give me an hour, then come and visit with me."

"Okay."

The master bedroom was well removed from Deirdre's room, toward the back of the house: a corner room looking down upon the olive trees and the serene symmetry of the gardens in the rear. Beyond the trees in the distance, grim-looking Monte Solaro rose nearly 2000 feet, the highest point on the isle.

Lavinia was infatuated with her bedroom. She had decorated it herself, every inch, from the Venetian ceiling to the 18th Century painted-and-lacquered Venetian furniture. The silk chaise upholstery and bed hangings produced by Scalamandré were suitable for an empress, a thought that rarely escaped her as she lay in bed resting on disagreeably hot summer afternoons.

Lying in bed now, studying the sculptured molding bordering "the most beautiful ceiling in all of Campania," according to Enrico, she considered how her life had changed and all that had happened to her since Lisa Dandridge's return. She had escaped from jail, fled the country with money borrowed from a friend, returned a year later to live in Boston, where she had bided her time collecting the clay of inspiration and carefully shaping it into the first phase of the perfect plan for vengeance against Lisa and Ross—and Cyrus: abducting the baby Deirdre. And a baby she had been—barely 14 months old on that fateful night of the burning of Blackwood. And to her delight, once Deirdre was hers, she found that she was more than just a child to feed, to hold close, to play with. She became her lucky charm. Suddenly the world seemed to open up and pour out good fortune. Everything Lavinia touched turned to gold, capped by her introduction to Enrico, his falling in love with her, his proposal of marriage, her acceptance, their return to Capri.

Now, for the first time since the sun had reappeared in her life, a dark cloud showed itself on the horizon: Deirdre, whom she adored, whom she couldn't have loved more had she been her own, was becoming a woman. The changes were coming almost daily. And the day was not far off when she would confront them and announce that she was going away for good. To work, to marry, to leave the nest.

Reflecting on this inevitability made Lavinia disconsolate. They had been mother and daughter since the finalization of legal adoption papers some years earlier. Now time was stealing Deirdrè from her. Before she was 18, she would be off to college, hopefully in Rome—although lately she had taken to insisting that she'd be better off completing her education abroad, preferably in the United States.

Why was she so set on college? Lavinia mused. Girls had no need for college. Formal education dulled the edge of intuitive wisdom. And yet Deirdre's not going would likely only hasten her marriage. Next she would be pregnant and mother would become grandmother.

What, thought Lavinia sadly, had she ever done to warrant such a discouragingly bleak future?

X

Lavinia was seated at her vanity fussing with her lashes when a gentle knock came at the door and it opened.

"Darling." Enrico pounded into the room, arms outstretched, a woolly bear of a man with a crown of white hair and a once-handsome face now sagging with age. His happy eyes were surrounded with masses of wrinkles and he breathed heavily, as if the stairs had been too much for a heart surrounded by so much weight.

"Enrico!"

They kissed and he held her close, rubbing his hands down her back possessively. "Miss me, darling?"

"Did I miss you? What a foolish question! They said eight and here you are an hour early. What a delightful surprise!" He released her, his cheery smile vanishing. "Dearest," she said, "is something wrong?"

"No, nothing. It's just that we have a visitor: Mama."

Lavinia sat down heavily on her vanity bench. "Oh God, no. For tonight, you mean," she said hopefully.

"For a week, maybe two. But maybe less."

"Two weeks!" It came out a near scream and he hastily closed the door.

"They're redoing her house—painters, plasterers all over the place. She insists she has rats, so they're cleaning up from cellar to attic, besides. She complains she can't sleep with the noise in the morning and the smells at night. Rosa suggested she go to Rome to visit her sister, but Mama said no." He shrugged, his hands helpless in front of him. "What could I do but ask her to stay with us? Please, for my sake try to get along."

78

"*Me* try?"

"Lavinia."

"I bend over backward to be hospitable to her. I ignore her insults. I wait on her hand and foot. She makes me a servant in my own house! The woman's impossible!"

"She's my mother."

"She hates me."

"Let's not get into that now."

A knock and the door opened. It was Deirdre.

"Enrico!"

"Dee-dee, my darling!" He crushed her to him lovingly and—thought Lavinia, looking on—somewhat gratefully for her timely interruption.

The three of them went downstairs to greet Enrico's mother, Enrico raving all out of proportion over Deirdre's "amazing" recovery from her injury. His mother stood at the bottom of the stairs, a small bundle of a woman who jerked about nervously like a wren sensing danger. She wore a new black dress and shiny black shoes and around her neck hung a three-inch silver crucifix. She took one look at Lavinia and scowled, another at Deirdre and beamed and a third at her son, which Lavinia decided was unabashed pity. While she chatted with Deirdre in Italian, Enrico drew his wife aside and whispered to her.

"Tell Philomena to put her in the guest room overlooking Triton. She loves the pool and his muscles."

"She can stay in the pool for all I care!"

"Please, darling, try."

"If I try any harder, I'll burst!"

"Sssssh."

In the four-way conversation that took place subsequently in the drawing room overheard by Trojans battling Greeks in high relief on all four walls, *Signora* Aldoni took little notice of Lavinia. On occasion, she uttered monosyllabic responses to inquiries regarding her health, the work going on at her home in Massalubrense and a generous compliment on her "stunning" new dress.

The woman is infuriating, reflected Lavinia. Not for the reasons she herself had given Enrico—nothing so bearable. It was the way she fastened her beady little eyes on Lavinia and peered into her soul, turning it over and over, examining it as a jeweler examines a stone under his loupe. One statement only shouted out of those eyes, chilling Lavinia to the bone.

You are cheating on my son!

Never a word: not a hint to Enrico that she knew. Only those icy eyes boring into her. They said it clearly.

Dinner conversation was dominated by Enrico's persistent teasing of his Dee-dee for her poor Italian. It was intended good-naturedly, but the old woman took exception to it, citing Deirdre's mastery of the language as *eccellente*. This led, inevitably, to a serious discussion of why everybody at the table didn't speak everybody else's language with flawless fluency. The fact that Mama Aldoni spoke perfectly atrocious English seemed not to matter at all. She carried on loudly and rapidly, knife in one hand, fork in the other. Waving them over the bones of her quail, she rattled on so rapidly that Lavinia failed to understand half of what she said. And said as much. Seconds later she regretted it, telling herself she ought to have known better. It provided all the opening *Signora* Aldoni needed.

"I am Italian! I speak Italian!" she shrilled, pounding the table with the hilt of her knife, rattling her plate. The serving girl rescued it, bearing it off to the kitchen. "Do you know why I speak Italian, Lavinia? I'll tell you why: Because I am in Italy. You are in Italy. Why don't you speak Italian?"

"My Italian, I'm afraid, is rather mediocre, Mother Aldoni."

"I think it's perfect," commented Enrico.

"You keep out of this, Rico. I am asking you again, Lavinia: Why don't you ever speak Italian? If I were to come to your country and stay for so many years, I would learn your language."

"She knows our language, Mama," interrupted Enrico.

"She does, Grandma Aldoni," said Deirdre.

"She prefers English," said Enrico. "She has a right——"

"You be quiet like a good boy! You too, Dee-dee. I'm talking to *her!*"

The sound of the garden door opening terminated the inquisition abruptly. Everyone's attention was drawn to Philomena as she accepted a white envelope from the young *carrozza* driver, placed it on a salver and marched it into the dining room.

"Excuse me, *signora*," she said to Lavinia, "it seems to be urgent. It is for you."

Lavinia exchanged glances with her husband, shrugging. Then she excused herself pointedly to her mother-in-law, tore open the envelope and read:

> *My darling,*
> *I must see you tonight. It is absolutely imperative that you loan me another 200 lira. I love you desperately. My body hungers for you. Tonight! Tonight!*
>
> *F.*

"Anything wrong?" asked Enrico.

With a presence of mind upon which she would later congratulate herself, Lavinia covered a yawn, begged everyone's pardon and shook her head.

"I wonder, I really wonder." She murmured.

"About what?" asked Enrico. All three sat as if frozen to their chairs, staring at her.

"Jane Chambers."

"The Englishwoman?"

"She's been planning to meet me for lunch on Thursday in Naples at Da Vinci's on Via Carlo Poerio. This makes the third time she's postponed. I'm beginning to think she doesn't even want to see me again, let alone lunch with me."

"Her banker tells me she has the brain of a bird."

"What was her excuse this time?" asked Deirdre.

"Doctor's appointment. Can't possibly be broken." She paused, looking from one to the next. "Deirdre, you and you, Enrico, and mother, of course, we'll all have lunch together on Thursday at Da Vinci's. They have the most delightful *mozzarella in carrozza*."

Enrico shook his head. "Count me out, I'm afraid."

"You're not going away again!" Lavinia crumpled the note, clenching it tightly in her fist under the table. "Say you're not."

"I must."

"Where this time?"

"Geneva."

"How long?"

"Three, maybe four days. They claim they're having difficulty with a shipment of Torre Giulia."

What difficulty?"

"They insist some of it is bad. Aldoni wine bad, can you imagine?"

"You, the president of the company, have to go up in person?"

Lavinia's affected indignation was beginning to rise. Inwardly she couldn't have been more delighted at the news.

"I can patch up things up in an hour. But this is the opportunity I've been waiting for to meet their top people face to face." He rubbed his hands together. "Watch me talk them into ordering our Moscato della Murge, maybe even our Zagarese. I can open up a whole new market for us!"

She was more than delighted: She was overjoyed. Not that Fernando's note hadn't upset her terribly. It wasn't the money. She had plenty to keep him in decent clothes and all the other niceties that distinguish a gentleman from a *contadino*. What had shaken her was his demand that they meet that very night. And sending the note to the door! The fool, the handsome, virile, hard-muscled, delicious fool! Perhaps *he* could afford to take chances;

she could not! What if she'd been out at the time? What if Enrico had come home earlier, intercepted it and, thinking it something that required an immediate answer, had torn it open and read it!

She'd strangle Fernando the next time she saw him! And she'd have to send dear, faithful Philomena down with an answer within the half hour. She'd tell him she couldn't possibly leave the house with Enrico there. Still, as soon as he left for Geneva, she'd rush to Fernando, to his arms, to his bed.

She pictured the bed in the room, the shades drawn against the heat of the day; Fernando's lean, brown body lying against her, the weight of him pressing her down, her legs locking his, the glorious beginning, the squeal of delight escaping her lips.

Abruptly she was aware of eyes on her. Glancing up from her plate, she saw Mama Aldoni staring stilettos.

XI

The rain struck the window and threaded its way down to the sill in patternless profusion. Staring at it, Lisa sat in silence, overcome in rapid succession by confusion, disbelief and stubborn refusal to believe Dr. Middleton's words.

Her driver had located the Eastern Virginia Asylum at the corner of Henry and France Streets in Williamsburg. Under the steady downpour that had accompanied her all the way from Washington, he had let her out at the front door. Moments later she had been ushered into the gloomy and stark-looking admissions office. There the orderly who had answered the bell left her with Dr. Middleton.

He was much younger than she had pictured him, a fussing, nervous man of medium build with a thinning thatch of brown hair and eyes that shot about the room like those of a small boy advised it was filled with hidden Easter eggs. It became obvious at once, however, that the doctor's uncontrollable eyes were not searching for anything, merely avoiding hers. They had exchanged introductions and he had offered her a chair, but he himself continued to stand. The door to the inner office was open and an orderly in a rumpled cotton jacket and trousers sat at a desk thumbing through a sheaf of papers, humming tunelessly to himself. Middleton closed the door, eliminating the distraction.

"Where is he?"

"I'm afraid I have disturbing news."

"Has something happened to him? Why isn't he here? Is he hurt? Ill? Doctor, look at me, say something!"

"He's gone."

"Where?"

"Late last night he and another patient escaped."

"Oh, my God!" The rain lines on the glass parted and joined and slid toward the sill. A fleeting picture of a mammoth cloud showering the world flashed across her mind as the doctor explained. She did not hear a word.

"I sent you a telegram—to Providence. Of course, I knew you'd already left, but I thought perhaps someone there might know where you'd be staying overnight on the way down and——"

"How did this happen?"

"It seems that one of the wire-screen locks was broken open. They bent the screen."

"Where could he have gone?"

"Who can say? The local police were informed immediately and they in turn alerted the Norfolk police. They're combing the entire bay area. They'll find them."

"They won't hurt him?"

"There's no reason to. He's not violent."

"Who is this man he's with?"

"May I get you some coffee?"

"No. What's his name?"

"Harlan Kimbrough. At least that's the name on his file here. He's originally from Norfolk. He's known to have friends there. People he could go to to hide him, maybe get him aboard a boat."

"With Ross."

"Mrs. Dandridge——"

"I want to know more about this Kimbrough. Is my husband in any danger from him?"

"No, we don't believe that he is."

"Why was he in here? What was the matter with him?"

"Mrs. Dandridge——"

"Say it, Doctor!" She slapped the flat of her hand against the table loudly.

"If you'll calm down, I'll tell you what I know."

"In heaven's name, why are you making me pull every word out of you?"

"We, that is Dr. Parmenter, the chief here, and I, believe Kimbrough is perfectly sane. But it appears he's wanted in Alexandria for beating a man to death."

"Good God!" She shot to her feet, pounding her fists against the table and holding them planted firmly. "You're saying my husband is out there somewhere with somebody who can kill him as easily——"

"I don't think Kimbrough will harm him."

"You don't think, but you don't know, do you, Doctor?"

"Please sit down."

"He could be lying dead in an alley this very minute!"

"Please."

She sat slowly. The feeling of numbness had passed, replaced by confusion, disbelief and anger.

"Dr. Parmenter and I think that Kimbrough deliberately faked insanity in order to be admitted here. He was in a hospital in Newport News for some sort of minor stomach disorder. He went berserk and tore the place apart. They threw him into our laps. When your husband got here from Baltimore, Kimbrough latched onto him, became his friend and protector."

"Some protector. Good God!"

"Believe me, he won't hurt him!" It was the first time Middleton had raised his voice, and the effect upon her was instantaneous. She became mollified, lowering her own voice.

"He could turn on him in a second."

"Why should he? He's perfectly sane. I'd stake my life on it."

"He's a killer."

"He killed in anger. There's no psychopathic history."

"Why did he gravitate to Ross? Why did you let him?"

"We can't prevent that sort of thing. We have eighty-nine patients here and only three doctors. We can't hold their hands. They make friends; they make enemies. Kimbrough took a liking to your husband. He respected him; you might even say he held him in awe. In spite of losing his memory, Mr. Dandridge is clearly a man of breeding and education—everything Kimbrough is not. Such relationships are not unusual in places like this."

"About Ross, who's responsible for putting a sane man into an asylum? Loss of memory isn't lunacy!"

"Whoever he was taken to when he was saved made that decision."

"Why not an ordinary hospital?"

"I suppose because it's a mental condition. Not something you can bandage, or put a crutch under, operate on, or give pills for."

"It's outrageous and you know it! Another thing: How is it his ship sank, he survived and yet not a single soul could identify him?"

"Who would be able to?"

"The other survivors, Doctor, obviously. There were forty-six. You mean to sit there and tell me not one could have come forward?"

"It must have been a hectic time, everybody scattered all over. Either that or nobody knew, nobody asked. So he was officially designated dead."

"While he was unofficially alive. Some clerk in the Navy Department gets word to Captain Bankhead and with a flourish of his pen, the good captain does away with my husband. A pen-and-paper execution!"

"Unfortunately these things happen."

"Not easily, I'm sure. It must have taken at least twenty people down the line to keep the lie alive, not excluding you."

Middleton glared resentment. "May I remind you that it was I who found that letter."

Suddenly she felt exhausted, completely sapped of the nervous energy that had sustained her. "I apologize," she said quietly. "I can't blame you. I'm very grateful; I'd be a fool not to be. What infuriates me is the ease with which Uncle Sam dismisses a human life. A few words, a decision, a letter and close the file. It makes one wonder how many John Does are wandering about institutions like this when a little common sense, a little effort on somebody's part might reunite them with their families."

"I understand. I don't disagree."

"They're alive; they're walking around. Nobody christened them John Does." She paused. "I suppose with a war on and so much to do, it's naïve to expect anyone to take the time to follow up individual cases."

"The people responsible are continually shifted about, files are lost or misplaced, mistakes made. And there's so little cooperation. Men like your husband are shuffled from one hospital to another. It would take the luck of the gods to be able to pick up the thread and follow it all the way."

"Let's be candid, doctor: Nobody bothers, nobody cares." Her voice softened. "Except you. And I do appreciate that, even though it's come to this."

"At least he's alive."

"Will he still be alive when he's found—if he's found?"

"Mrs. Dandridge, as ridiculous as it may sound, he's probably better off with Kimbrough, or whatever his name is, than wandering around alone."

"Ridiculous, yes. How bad is Ross's amnesia?"

"It's total. We've only had him—let me see—yesterday was the eighth day. But in that time, I've spent a good ten hours with him. His life before he was admitted to Baltimore is a complete blank."

"Is there anything that can make him remember?"

"I had a case at Sheppard's in Baltimore. A young fellow no more than eighteen. He couldn't remember his own name. He had suffered some kind of blow on the head. We checked and finally found somebody who recognized him. We traced the name and got his parents' address. A farm way out in the hinterlands. I went out to see them, but nobody was home. They were out looking for him. Our paths finally crossed. I brought the two of them to the asylum and sat them down in an unoccupied room. I brought in the patient. They fell all over him. I remember, I had tears in my eyes. But not a blink out of him. He didn't recognize either one. They couldn't believe it, they were crushed. There was nothing I could do but send them away. But the very next morning, he woke up and his first words were 'Where're Dad and Mom?' "

"Shock."

"Right. There was the overnight delay, but it finally got through to his brain. He was released in their custody, and I saw him a week later and then six months after that. He was completely cured."

"So Ross can be."

"Possibly."

"Not even probably? What are the odds, Doctor?"

"With amnesia, there's no such thing as odds. Doctors have cured two patients, one after the other, then not cured another for years. It's not the doctor, it's the individual brain. It closes a door, shutting off a corridor. In some cases, that door can be shocked open; in some, it opens of its own accord, in its own time. In others——"

She rose from her chair. "I'm going out and look for him."

"But the police will find him."

"If they don't, if this week drags into next and there's still no clue, you know as well as I do that the police will lose interest. Or some other case will come along to divert their attention. But I won't lose interest. And I won't be diverted." Reaching into her bag, she took out Ross's picture. "Can you give me a picture of Kimbrough like this one?"

Middleton hesistated. "I gave the only two we had to the Williamsburg police. But you won't need a picture to find him any more than they will. You could pick him out of the biggest crowd you've ever seen. He's a good six foot five and completely bald, with a scar on his head—a cross, heavily welted." He drew it with his finger on his own head. "Not just tall, but a big man, well over two-twenty, two-twenty-five. A heavy drinker and a ferocious temper."

"That's nice to know."

"And they'll be together. They were inseparable here."

"I'll find them. You said Norfolk."

"Yes, Kimbrough will want to get out of the country."

"Which means I'll have to move fast."

"Mrs. Dandridge, I wouldn't if I were you. The police will be covering the docks along the Ocean View with a net. There's no way either of them can board a ship without being seen. Every vessel coming and going has to be officially cleared. You'll just be wasting your time. Besides, those docks are no place for a respectable woman."

She offered her hand. "I do appreciate your help, Doctor. And your taking a personal interest. I won't waste any more of your time."

"I'm sorry this happened." Regret crept into his eyes. "Your husband and I were really beginning to get to know each other."

"If you hear anything at all, please get in touch with the local telegraph office. I'm going straight there."

"It's on the Richmond Road across the street from the college. You passed it coming in. You're welcome to my carriage."

"Thank you."

"And good luck, Mrs. Dandridge."

She left Dr. Middleton and his asylum with the howl of a patient assailing her ears, the awful keening of a poor tormented soul ringing down the empty corridor. *How ironically appropriate*, she thought.

The rain had let up, leaving the rolling-green countryside glistening. Spring was far more advanced here than in and around Providence: dogwood, daffodils, daisies and dozens of other flowers already in full bloom, grouped about like marchers assembled for a colorful parade, preparing to lead the land into summer. From a nearby thicket came the sweet-sweet-sweet what-cheer what-cheer what-cheer of a cardinal.

Ross was alive and she would find him before anything or anyone could harm him if it took days—if it took years. God forbid it ever would, but if it took the rest of her life, she would feel his arms about her again. Bring him home to Blackwood and make him whole again.

And nothing on earth, in heaven or hell would stop her!

XII

The police captain at the station in Norfolk to whom the desk sergeant introduced her was past 60 and obviously had become part of the furniture in his untidy, stuffy office long ago. But neither age nor isolation seemed to discourage him from displaying his authority like a garishly colored sash. He held his fat chins high, staring down his nose at her and all but yawning in her face as she explained her presence.

She could see at once that he did not like her. It had not even been a year since the end of the war and the resentment of loser toward winner was all too evident on his round, ruddy face. His comments and his answers to her questions struck her as stock, the majority of them uttered before she finished the sentence.

"We're looking, that's our job. Just be patient."

"I'm prepared to offer a reward of $5000 to the man who finds my husband alive," she announced.

This raised one eyebrow, but if it impressed him beyond that, his voice failed to betray it.

"Policemen ain't supposed to ac-cept ree-wards. Not in this town they ain't."

"Five thousand."

"The mayor'd be mighty upset."

"I'll make it my business to speak with him. I telegraphed my banker from Williamsburg this morning. I stipulated the money be made available from the Citizen's Bank here in Norfolk. I've taken room at the Monticello Hotel."

"Five thousand dollahs won't find yo' husband no

quicker than the good Lord intends him to be found, if at all."

"But you say you're practically certain they're hiding out somewhere down at the docks?"

His jaw sagged slightly and he stared, as if appalled at her ignorance.

"Theah's places down theah no officer in his right mind would stick his nose into—not fo' all the money in the world. Not without ten men to back him up."

"How many men do you have down there looking?"

"Two."

"Two! But I understand there's at least fifteen miles of waterfront!"

"It's all we can spare. It's e-nough. A few questions in the right places."

She shot to her feet, suddenly irate. "It's not enough! Not nearly. A few questions in the right places won't find them. The whole area has to be blanketed with men!"

"Didn't you just hear me say that's all we can spare? This ain't Providence, you know. We'ah just a little bitty town tryin' to get back on our feet."

"Captain——"

"You-all just listen. Eleven years ago, we got hit by the yellow fever like to wipe us off'n the map. When the war broke out, we had to abandon the city. In sixty-one, the Federals burned the Navy yard. We didn't get the city back till May o' sixty-two. And you oughta' have seen the condition it was in! There wasn't a house fit to keep pigs in! Now, four years later, we still got no money, damned little trade, less than half the businesses in town open and more rascally carpetbaggers and loose niggas wanderin' round than you can shake a stick at! This year so far we've had twenty-three murders, nineteen of 'em down by the watah. Now you-all come marchin' in here high and mighty with your big ree-ward, demandin' we find yo' husband. We'ah supposed to drop everythin' and scattah all over lookin'. Well, we ain't about to! We get us a couple escaped lunatics down from Baltimore or over from Williamsburg ev'ry othah month like clockwork. Most of 'em just jump on a ship and get out. Good riddance to bad rubbish!"

"What about Kimbrough? The man's a murderer. Doesn't he interest you?"

"Regan."

"I beg your pardon?"

"That's his real name." He pulled open a drawer and fished through a number of small cards. "Wiley Thomas Regan." Shutting the drawer with the side of his knee, he swung about, facing her. "Now if theah's nothin' else, ah suggest you-all go back to your hotel and wait. If ah heah anythin', ah'll send word."

"I'm not leaving until you answer some more questions."

"What now?"

"No ship can clear the harbor without authorization, isn't that so?" He nodded. "The harbor master or whoever's in charge, doesn't he have a list of passengers and crew?"

"Customs has, but that ain't gonna hep none. Iffn' those two row out in a dory after dark and lay to east o' Cape Henry, they can get aboard any ship without the harbor master or anybody else seein' them."

"They could have gotten out last night."

"Ah would if ah was Regan. He gets caught, he gets hisself hanged."

She weighed the possibilities, her teeth assailing her her lower lip nervously. "No, last night's too soon. They had to come all the way from Williamsburg—on foot, probably—steal a boat and get across Hampton Roads. Which means they couldn't possibly have gotten here before daylight. Even with the rain, they'd be foolish to show their faces."

"So right now theah hidin'."

"Waiting to get out tonight."

"Like ah said, good riddance to bad rubbish."

He was disgusting. Without another word, she got up and left. Presently she was heading for her hotel in her rented rig, but the sight of a small gunshop wedged in between two larger buildings caused her to rein up sharply.

She bought a four-barrel pepperbox pistol and half a box of shells, then hurried off. From the position of the sun out over Hampton Roads, she estimated that she had fewer than four hours of daylight left.

Trotting the horse to the docks, she silently cursed the captain. And yet, however reluctantly, she could sympathize with his position. Announcing the reward, flaunting it, had been stupid. And questioning his judgment had only made his natural ruddiness two shades deeper. Perhaps he was right, perhaps two men were enough to check with Customs, with the harbor authority, with masters of outward-bound ships. But sitting in the hotel waiting for word was out of the question.

She would do what the police evidently had no intention of doing. She patted the loaded pistol in her bag in her lap. Hopefully, she wouldn't be needing its protection; putting bullets into dockside citizens of Norfolk or visitors from abroad would hardly improve her chances of finding Ross. Her steely determination, so much in evidence upon leaving the Eastern Virginia Asylum, came back to her. Nothing on earth, in heaven or hell, would get by her, save, perhaps, a nameless, unidentifiable ship smoking its way out of the harbor under cover of darkness, bound for God knows where!

There is a striking similarity to all waterfront areas in all ports of the world: All ports display their ships hawsered snugly in their slips, the gulls and terns above, the filthy, fetid water below. The worn pilings of Norfolk's waterfront supported 15 miles of dockside, the wooden, stone, sand and mud thoroughfares running parallel to the prows. The cargoes were piled high and awaiting lading—bales of cotton, hogsheads of tobacco, barrels of peanuts, timber and a dozen other products.

And facing the ships sat an endless row of little wooden buildings interspersed with clusters of warehouses.

Similar, too, were the men roaming about: able seamen, smartly dressed shipowners, prosperous-looking tradesmen, soot-smudged stokers, black-jacketed ships' officers and the human jetsam of the sea—unclean, unshaved, foulmouthed, leering, drunk and drugged, maimed and sinister-looking. Men with strange accents, men speaking unintelligible tongues, men with no links and few loyalties, who looked over their shoulder at life with fear and regret. Liars, thieves, scoundrels, thugs and worse.

Tying her horse and rig at a ship chandler's, Lisa gave the most trustworthy-looking boy in sight a dollar to watch them. Then she set out on foot, clutching her bag with her precious pepperbox in one hand and Ross's picture in the other.

She stopped everyone she met and showed it. "Have you seen this man? Have you seen anyone who looks like him? I will be here until sundown. If you find him, bring him to the chandler's and I'll pay you well."

The same speech over and over until her mouth became dry as sun-bleached sand. The eyes studied his likeness, the brows furrowed, the heads shook. "Sorry, sorry, don't know him. Never seen him."

She was well into the second hour and beginning to lose hope when she noticed a little man with a homely, knot-muscled face, a sparse-toothed grin, carrying a small black-and-white puppy, following her. In front of a large warehouse—*Higgins & Bothwell, Shippers to the World* —she stopped and whirled to face him.

"Who are you? What do you want? I already showed you the picture."

"I know, missus." He touched the peak of his cap and bowed his head.

"You told me you didn't know him."

He nodded. "I don't. But if he be here, they's a better

way to find him than what you're about." She stared at him suspiciously. "There is."

"Who are you?"

"The name's Joshua Lilly, the *Bombay Queen*." He stopped petting his little dog on his arm and pointed at a twin-sailed, double-stacked, paddle-wheeler badly in need of paint just beyond them.

He seemed sincere. She relaxed and smiled and began petting the dog. "He's cute."

"His name's Brandy. We're shipmates all the way from Hong Kong. I was fixin' to say down the way there is The Pelican. All the lads stop in there one time or 'nother. It's a barn of a place inside. Instead o' you goin' from lad to lad, why not go into the Pel? We'll ask for attention, and you can announce you're lookin' for him and there's a reward."

She thought a moment. If she said anything about $5000, she'd probably be seized, locked up and held for ransom.

"A hundred dollars. And I don't have it on me. It would be paid first thing in the morning at the Citizen's Bank."

"Just you follow me, missus."

The Pelican was a "barn of a place," but it looked and sounded and smelled like no barn she had ever been inside in England or America. A thick curtain of tobacco smoke hung like a pall from the ceiling over a clutter of round-backed chairs, stools, benches and bare tables. The music of a musette came drifting out of a far corner and a lusty chorus boomed a chantey. Grog, ale and beer flowed like rivulets gathering at a falls, and those present still upright, who were not quite as intoxicated as those spread snoring on the tables and stretched out on the floor, were doing their best to catch up to the condition rapidly. The racket over the feeble strains of the music was ear-splitting and the stink—a mélange of cellar mold, tobacco, green cabbage soup, camphor and body odor—was enough to send one hand to her mouth to keep down her midday meal. Joshua made way for her to the center of the room, helped her up onto a table and bellowed for silence. She spoke. The men crowded about the table and took turns studying the picture, but they only looked, reflected, shook their heads and walked away. Disheartened, she was preparing to leave when a tall ginger-bearded man came shouldering through the crowd up to her. He took hold of her arm.

"I know where he is, Red. Come along."

"You haven't even looked at the picture."

"Hey, Bob——" began Joshua. He got no further. The tall man swung his free fist backward and, like a gate slamming shut, caught him full in the face, sending him sprawling. The next thing Lisa knew, she was being hurried out a rear door and down a narrow alley.

"Let go of me!"

"Just shut your face." His free hand darted out like a snake striking, snatching her bag from her.

"Give me that! How dare you!"

"Will you lookee here. A toy popgun." Tearing the bag out of his hand, she wriggled free, glaring at him, her heart pounding, her throat tightening with fear. She turned to run back the way they had come, but he brought up the pepperbox, aiming it squarely at her. "Is this thing loaded? You try running for it or screaming, we'll find out, won't we?"

"Pig!"

"Is that any way to talk to a good samaritan who's trying to help you?" He gestured her ahead of him with the pistol. "Turn left at the end, through the fence gate and up the stairs. Go on."

"I'll fix you for this," she snapped.

" 'Course you will."

"There are laws against kidnaping."

"Hurry it up."

He was three steps behind her, their heels clicking against the brick walkway. Halfway to the end of the alley, he fired the gun, the shot echoing loudly within the narrow confines, the bullet slamming against the side of the building on their left. It frightened her so that she screamed.

"You bastard!"

"She's a beauty, ain't she?"

"Where are you taking me?"

"You'll know soon enough."

They entered what appeared to be a deserted warehouse and started up a flight of wooden steps at the back. By the time they reached the third floor, the effort and her mounting fear had her gasping for breath. Pushing by her, he flung open a small door.

Slivers of sunlight slipped through the rotting wallboards, illuminating the musty interior. The place was empty but for a heap of torn and dirty sailcloth that filled one corner. Beside it stood a narrow door painted blue and marked PRIVATE.

"Through there."

She hesitated until she felt the muzzle of the pepperbox against her back. Her mind whirled. Middleton had warned her not to go near the docks. Why hadn't she listened? Why hadn't she asked the captain for an armed man to go along with her? Why hadn't she taken the trouble to hire two bodyguards? Why the grand rush into certain peril?

They reached the door and he knocked a complicated signal.

"It's Bob, sir." Silence. Then a chair scraped the floor, footsteps and bolts thrown. The door eased open two inches. A single eye peered out of a rosy glow at her.

"She's looking for her husband, sir. She's offering a reward."

"Is she?"

The door opened all the way and a short, powerfully built man in a striped shirt and heavy woolen trousers stood leering at her with one eye, the other awry in its socket, staring blindly.

"Good job, Bob. Come in, lovely lady."

Again she hesitated, again the pistol muzzle against her back. She entered. Bob handed the pepperbox to the other man and strode away singing. The one-eyed man bolted the door behind her.

The room was small, almost tiny and overfurnished: a desk, chair, file cabinets, bookcase and, on the right, a door leading into an adjacent room. She leaned against the door warily, and he set his hands against it, his arms stiff, locking her in place.

"And who might you be?"

Ducking, she slipped under his arm and backed quickly against the desk.

"Unlock that door! I told him and I'm telling you, this is kidnaping. You can go to jail. I'll see to it!"

He was paying no attention, his good eye wide and staring at her breasts, the tip of his tongue moving from one side of his mouth to the other. Up came his hands to fondle her breasts, but she sidestepped out of his way and moved around the desk.

"You touch me and I'll scratch your eye out!"

"You're beautiful."

"Open that door!"

"Red hair, pink skin, perfect as cream, and such a lovely body. You're getting me all excited. You don't do such a thing, you know, walk around the docks like you were on a Sunday stroll, talking money, reward. You could get gang-raped and your throat slit as easy as turning around."

She screamed, kicking and clawing at him as he backed her into the corner. But then his arms were around her, gripping her like a vise, his hot mouth down upon the exposed portions of her breasts. Twisting both arms behind her back and turning her around, he jerked her wrists upward against her spine. The pain shooting down from her shoulders was excruciating. She screamed, tears welling in her eyes. He half-carried her into the other room, flinging her onto the bed, slapping her brutally.

He was no man, but a jungle beast, his babbling, meaningless talk trailing off into a series of obscene guttural sounds issuing from his throat. His hot breath poured over her face and neck and her mounting dread caused her to cry out in abject terror. He had been gripping her wrists, holding her down, but her cry brought a snarl, his face twisted maniacally. He struck her full on the jaw with his fist. The pain shooting to the top of her head was like a cleaver dividing it. The room whirled, faded into a formless gray mass, and a black curtain smothered her senses.

The dull throbbing in her jaw awakened her, her eyelids flickering, the room gradually coming into perspective. She was lying on the bed naked, spread-eagled, her wrists and ankles tied to the four corners, a gag over her mouth, the knot pushing hard against her teeth.

The door opened and he stood there at the foot of the bed, stripped, his one eye fired with lust at the sight of her, his mouth working lecherously. Slamming the door, he came at her.

XIII

Of all the unspeakable horrors that traffic the imagination, the insidious depravity that man and monster are capable of inflicting in nightmares and hideous fantasies, none she had ever imagined could approach the abuse to which he subjected her from the moment he joined his body with hers. He delighted in hurting her, in poking, pinching, twisting and squeezing her most intimate parts. He did not say a word, uttering only a sequence of disgusting sounds. Every muffled squeal of pain elicited a chuckle; every groan, a satisfied leer; every unendurable agony that caused her to scream soundlessly into the gag brought a roar of laughter.

Her body gradually became a single solid mass of suffering, mercifully numbing as he continued his depredations upon her. She prayed for unconsciousness to return, for death and release.

And the more intolerable her anguish, the more he enjoyed it. After what seemed a lifetime, he finally tired of torturing her, arose from the bed and put on his clothes. She was only dimly aware of his presence when he spoke; his voice seemed to come from miles away and she could barely understand what he was saying.

"You're beautiful. I'll be back in a little bit, and we'll start all over again. There's a whip I want to borrow. You'll love it. And I've got some business to attend to." He leaned over the bed, his eye an inch from her own. "Business you'd be interested in, lovely lady. You'll fetch a nice price. And you'll love where they take you. China's beautiful this time o' year. By the time you get there, the lilies'll be in bloom."

She heard the outer door close and lock. Gritting her teeth, ignoring the blanket of pain spreading over her body, Lisa raised her head and looked about. Then she tested all four bindings in turn. Her wrists and ankles were tied so tightly that they ached furiously; however, she discovered that the ties were only looped over the knobs of the bedposts. Fighting off the pain, she began throwing her body from side to side, twisting every which way, struggling to pull loose any one of the ropes. It was useless. She noted, nevertheless, that her struggling had increased her freedom of movement so that she could almost turn on one side now. Her heart quickened as hope seized it! Pulling both ankles and her left arm as tightly as she was able, she inched her body toward the right headpost. The rope had become visibly looser, but she was still unable to slip the loop up over the knob. She resumed her writhing, all but wrenching her hands and feet from their sockets. Again she tried for the right headpost. Again she failed.

Her heart beat wildly; she had to unbind herself, recover her clothes and flee this awful place! Again she writhed, thrashing about, straining at the three ropes in an effort to yield sufficient play to the wrist rope to lift the loop free. The rope was hard and stiff; if she could only lift it, it would clear the knob. Struggling, straining, disregarding the agony in her wrist and ankles, she fought the weakness rapidly stealing over her as her strength ebbed. She tugged and thrust. The loop inched upward, higher, higher to the top of the knob and over!

In seconds, she had freed herself. Grabbing her clothing and shoes, she raced for the door. Then she stopped short, freezing. Steps, muffled, faint, but coming closer, louder. Dropping her things behind the door, she looked about desperately for the pepperbox, but he had evidently taken it with him. Rushing to the desk, she jerked open the top drawer. No gun, no knife, no—a letter opener! Snatching it up, she ran back and stood flat against the wall, trembling in fear as a key fumbled in the lock, the door opened and he came in. He turned to close the door, and his eye widened at the sight of her. But she was already in motion. Holding the letter opener high, both hands gripping the handle, she stabbed at him wildly. The opener jabbed into his good eye. He roared and fell backward, his arms flailing the air, blood spurting from the eye, crimsoning her naked breasts.

XIV

Dazed and in shock, she had dressed quickly and run out, leaving him sprawled on the floor roaring in pain, his hand cupping his blinded eye, the blood-stained opener lying nearby.

How she found her way to the ship chandler's she would never know—staggering, half-running past arms stretched out to delay her, coming within sight of the shop. She saw at once that her horse and carriage were gone. In her time in hell, the sun had gone down, and darkness had crept over the city, shrouding the harbor. Stars and a quarter moon riding high on the back of a cloud softened the blackness and silvered the water across Hampton Roads.

"Missus." It was Joshua at her elbow tugging at his cap, his homely face masked with worry. "I been waiting and waiting for you. Bob Talbot knocked me cold, the dirty rat. When I woke up the two of you was gone." He paused and smiled. "But I been checking around and I've got news about your husband."

She gasped and grabbed him by the shoulders with both hands. "Where is he?"

He pointed up the harbor toward the bend. A huge freighter, a slender plume of black smoke trailing above its wake, was turning, heading toward Cape Henry and the open sea.

"He's on that ship, the *Crown Pearl*, bound for Singapore. Him and a big bald-headed lad with a scar here." He drew a cross with the tip of his finger on his cap.

BOOK TWO
IN PURSUIT OF THE PAST

XV

"Singapore!" Fred Muybridge Senior's eyebrow shot up his forehead, all but dislodging his glasses. "Surely you're not——"

"No, no, no. Though if he were heading for the moon, I'd follow him," said Lisa quietly. "His ship will be making a two-day stopover at Pernambuco, Brazil. I intend to be there when he comes down the gangplank. Along with everything else, I want you to alert the *Crown Pearl's* owners that I'm on my way there and fill them in on what this is all about."

"I wish to heaven *I* knew what it was all about. It's all bits and pieces."

"Precisely why we're having this meeting. Fred, bear with me, please." She caught herself. "Oh, before I forget. As soon as you get back, cancel the sale to Anderson. Explain what's happened."

"Of course."

Her thoughts flew back to the night of horror, the previous night, and the dreadful sinking feeling in her breast at the sight of the freighter slipping around the bend in the distance. The only thing that kept her from losing heart completely was Joshua Lilly's disclosure that the *Crown Pearl* was: "One of the slowest ships in trade, with a maximum speed of less than eight knots."

Any Dandridge clipper, so she'd been told at least 10,000 times, was capable of attaining 20 knots. So the game was far from over: She could book passage on the first clipper following the same route. Which she'd promptly done.

"I can be waiting for him in Pernambuco!"

Senior scratched one cheek thoughtfully and began picking nits.

"But what if you don't arrive in time?"

"Twenty knots against eight, better than twice the *Crown Pearl*'s speed. It's well over four thousand miles to Pernambuco, a three-week trip. I can beat him there easily, even with his thirty-hour lead!"

"Thirty hours?"

"My ship leaves at three this afternoon—the *Olympia II*, believe it or not—carrying corn and tobacco." She nodded agreement with the awareness in his eyes. "I see you remember. Sixteen years ago, I came over from England on the *Olympia I*."

"Ironic."

She glanced at her watch. "It's almost noon now. Three hours and I'm on way."

"I confess I've lost all track of time," he said in bewilderment. "I got your telegram, raced around town doing what you needed done, literally ran for the train and suddenly here I am in a hotel in Baltimore, of all the godforsaken places!" He cast a disapproving glance about the room, taking in the dusty portieres, the dirty windows, the cheap, run-down furniture. She watched him in amusement.

"I was in a big hurry; I couldn't afford to be choosy about accommodations. I'm not even sleeping here overnight. It's just a place for us to meet and get everything straight. I'm sorry I've had to put you to so much trouble on such short notice."

"I'd be hurt if you didn't, considering the cause."

"You say you got in touch with Jeremy."

"Yes, he's supposed to be here at one o'clock. I'm sure he's as curious as I was as to what you're up to."

She sighed audibly and, going to the window, stared

down at the street below filled with fruit and vegetable vendors and shoppers, each individual cart collecting its cluster of patrons like honey attracting ants. "I'm going to loathe and despise this one o'clock meeting," she said solemnly. "To hurt someone you care for so deeply, someone you've pledged your love to."

"He'll understand. He's not a child."

"I *hope* he'll understand."

"I still have so many questions whirling around in my head, Lisa. Why Baltimore? Why aren't you catching a ship out of Norfolk?"

"There are next to no clippers down there, coming or going. I'd have to wait a month. I'd miss him in Pernambuco entirely. Then, too, this makes it easier for you and Jeremy, doesn't it? You don't have to come so far."

"Far enough." He squirmed uncomfortably in his chair, then got up. "Why I'm sitting, after all the sitting I've done getting down here——"

"Let's go over things one more time."

"Very well. I'm to tell Thursby the whole story, only swear him to secrecy."

"For now."

"All the household help is to be kept on at full salary regardless of how long you're away. I'm to cancel the deal with Anderson and his syndicate. I'm to explain the entire matter to Emily Slater, also swearing her to secrecy."

"Just in case, after Jeremy and I talk, he decides to leave Providence without telling her why. She has to know; she's helping with all the wedding preparations." Lisa looked grim. "I seem to have stirred up a huge mess."

"For the best reason in the world!"

She brightened. "It certainly is. Thank God he's alive and all right."

"How can you be absolutely certain he's on that ship? Just because your little friend with the dog said so?"

"Because he described Kimbrough, I mean Regan. To a T. I'd planned it that way."

"I don't follow you."

"When I was showing the picture of Ross around the docks, I took great pains never to mention Regan—no name, no description, nothing. Joshua Lilly volunteered his description. He had to have seen them."

"Clever girl. You can be very grateful to that little man."

"Grateful's not the word. There's five hundred dollars waiting for him in an account in his name at the Citizen's Bank in Norfolk. That's something else you can check. I want to be sure he gets it."

"Speaking of banks: You have your letter of credit?" She nodded. "Where nobody will find it."

"Least of all another of those princely gentlemen like the one you ran into in Norfolk. That's what has me on tenterhooks, a lone woman running about the docks." He shook his head and frowned. "How are you feeling now?"

"Awful."

"You should be in a hospital. At least see a doctor."

"There's no time. I pretend I don't feel anything and the soreness just isn't there. It actually works when you have as much on your mind and as much to do as I. A good night's sleep and knowing I'll be seeing Ross before much longer are all the tonics I need."

"You've a lot of courage."

"Nonsense. I'm a thoroughgoing coward. I simply have to find my husband and bring him home, and there's no easy way. Any wife with a husband like Ross would do the same."

"It could be done for you."

"No, it couldn't. I'd go out of my mind wondering what was happening, waiting for word."

"I hope, for your sake, that it turns out to be as simple as you make it sound."

"I'll bring him back, I promise!"

The bell in the church steeple directly across the way

tolled the quarter hour. They talked further, ordered lunch brought up from the hotel kitchen and Muybridge left after wishing her luck and Godspeed.

As the church clock sounded one, she opened the door to greet Jeremy.

XVI

He took hold of her to kiss her and, for a fleeting
moment, she considered turning her cheek to his lips.
But no, that was no way to start things off. Kissing her
warmly, he came in.

"To say this is a surprise is the understatement of all
time." He beamed. "Mr. Muybridge says 'Get on a
train for Baltimore,' simple as that. You, my darling,
owe me an explanation. I mean, I go to Philadelphia, I
go back to Providence, you're not there, Thursby tells
me you've gone running off to Virginia, 'Something to
do with business', I sit cooling my heels and the next
thing I know——"

She touched his mouth with her fingertips. "Jeremy,
sit down. I have something terribly important to tell
you."

His smile vanished, then returned, but without
warmth—more a nervous expectant grin. He sat looking
up at her inquiringly, his hat on his lap. "Has something
happened?"

"I've found Ross; he's alive."

His cheeks paled, his mouth opened slightly, as if he
were about to say "My God." But, as quickly as her
words took effect, he changed his mind, relaxing with
an awesome effort of will, leaning back, clapping his
hands together once and shaking them in a gesture of
victory. "That's marvelous! Fabulous!"

A wave of relief passed over her. He would take it
well after all. She explained, hurrying her words, until
his hand came up, stopping her in midsentence.

"Let me get this straight. He's on a ship heading for Singapore?"

"Yes, my ship is leaving in less than two hours."

"Terrific! I'll go with you!"

"Jeremy, you can't. I couldn't ask you to."

"You're not. I'm volunteering."

"It's very generous of you."

"You'll need protection. You can't pick up and go scurrying halfway around the world, a woman alone. And Singapore, of all places. That's no place for an armed *man!*"

She explained that she was only going as far as Pernambuco and would be reaching there well ahead of the *Crown Pearl.*

"It's still dangerous. And I'm still going with you!"

"No you're not. There's no danger. I'll be on board the *Olympia II,* a ship Ross supervised the building of, strangely enough. I'll be traveling first class. The owners' representatives are expecting me. Jeremy, Jeremy, I hate myself for doing this to you. It's too cruel."

"You win, you lose." He tossed up his hands in a carefree gesture, then he sobered. "I'll get over it."

Reaching into her bag, she took out the engagement ring and handed it to him. "It's still beautiful, Jeremy. I'm so sorry it has to be this way."

"I'm happy for you, Lisa. I feel as if an anvil dropped on me, but if this was meant to be, and it obviously is, I couldn't wish you more happiness. And success in finding him."

"You're an extraordinary human being, Mr. Slater. A very special man."

"Don't be silly. What would you have me do, jump out of a window?" He laughed. "I do intend to get roaring drunk, possibly get into a fight—and I may end up taking a trip to darkest Africa to get you out of my system."

"Oh, Jeremy." Tears filled her eyes and she put her

hands against his cheeks. He closed them together and kissed her fingertips gently.

"Please, Lisa, this is no time for tears. You should be up on a table dancing, singing, cheering your lungs out." He fixed her with a profoundly earnest look. "God bless the two of you. May you be happy together for a thousand years."

"Thank you."

"I mean it with all my heart."

"I know you do. I'm terribly sorry I had to drag you all the way down here."

"Don't let that bother you. I love train rides."

"I'm sure. It's just that there was no other way. I couldn't go and leave you a note. I wouldn't know what to say, what words to use. I had to tell you to your face. It seemed the only decent thing."

"I'm glad you did it this way. I appreciate it." He got up, turning his hat in his hands nervously and smiling. Patting her cheek affectionately, he started for the door.

"Please don't go yet. There's so much I still have to tell you. I've said it over and over again in my mind."

"There's nothing more to say, darling. Look at it this way, we've had weeks and weeks."

"Wonderful times, Jeremy."

"Happy times. We liked each other; we fell in love."

"Yes, we did."

"We can be thankful we met in the first place." He waved one hand melodramatically. " 'Tis better to have loved and lost.' Isn't that so?"

"Can we shake hands?"

"Oh, God, no! A peck on the cheek, maybe, a wave." He threw her a kiss. "Even that, but please, no handshakes."

"Will I ever see you again?"

"Who knows? I suppose I am the sort who turns up like a bad coin."

"Penny."

"Whatever it is. Good-bye, Lisa, and good luck. I hope with all my heart that you find him, he recovers and the two of you are happier than you've ever been before."

He walked out, closed the door and hurried down the hallway, down the stairs to the lobby. The smell of cigar smoke wafting over a potted palm coming from an overstuffed chair overstuffed with an elderly man wearing a derby reminded him of Ned Loomis's office. And Ned Loomis.

This was "Marvelous! Fabulous!," all right! Like being shot by a cannon. Good God, she might as well have pulled out a knife and slit my throat! he thought.

He stopped and leaned against a pillar near the revolving door. He was in some fine mess now. Once it hit the newspapers, Loomis would set Vossbacher on his tail and the two of them would wind up in an alley together with old Teddy grinning down a foot-long pistol, preparing to blow his brains out!

Still, Loomis was smarter than that. How do you get more than $14,000 out of a corpse?

He went outside, drank in two great lungfuls of fresh air, cleared his head, slowed down his spinning brain and took stock. Ross Dandridge. If she never found him, or better yet, if she found him dead, she could still eventually end up Mrs. Jeremiah Roger Slater after all. She would, that he'd see to. So the nuptials were delayed. So what? They'd be a long time married— $10,000,000 long!

Leaving her hotel so soon hadn't been overly smart, though. Better he'd stayed and argued with her, convinced her that he had to go along to protect her. That way he'd be out of Loomis's reach and on the spot when she and Ross were reunited. And could get rid of him before they started back.

On second thought, it made considerably better sense to let her go off alone. Once she'd fetched Ross back to Providence, he could dispose of him in an hour; a freak accident, something stupendously clever. She'd gotten over his death once, she could get over it again. Mrs. Lisa Allworth Slater. It had a nice ring to it. Mr. and Mrs. Jeremy Roger Slater announce the birth of Jeremy Junior.

Maybe things weren't as black as they looked. He'd have to kill Ross, though. There was no way around that. He couldn't possibly compete with him. Get rid of him permanently this time, long before Loomis's August deadline. Her trip down to Brazil and back to Rhode Island would take her the better part of a month. Plenty of time to devise a perfect plan for eliminating one superfluous husband.

"Jeremy, old fellow, you are positively brilliant. Who else would have swallowed such news so manfully, without so much as losing your smile. The great good loser. You made it easy for her; for that, she'll always be grateful."

A young couple coming the other way down the sidewalk stared at him.

"That man's talking to himself," said the woman.

Her companion half laughed. "He must have money in the bank."

Jeremy didn't hear. He was too busy planning his next move, so engrossed that he failed to see the beautiful blonde passing him on the heels of the couple. And staring at him. Had he noticed her, he most certainly would have turned his head to follow her with his eyes.

And he would have seen Teddy Vossbacher emerging from the hotel ten strides behind him, a beatific smile surrounding the cigar in his mouth. As if he'd just heard something both interesting and immensely gratifying.

XVII

Her fingers stole through his thick curly hair, guiding his head downward, joining his mouth to her own. Their tongues met, gyrating furiously, and her heart thundered in her breast as the heat of his naked flesh against her body flooded through her. The little room seemed to shrink, the glare of the sun sneaking through the apertures on either side of the drawn oilcloth shades becoming progressively fiercer. She moaned as they continued to gorge each other's mouths. Then his deserted hers, moving to her breasts. She squealed and began thrashing about the bed wildly, writhing, her pale supple body glistening with tiny beads of perspiration.

"Now, now, now, now!"

"Not yet, *mio caro*, soon." His husky voice seethed with lust for her. She could tell he had to have her!

"Now!" Her arms encircling his neck closed tightly, bringing his mouth back upon hers. She could feel his muscular legs slipping between her own, his pulsing member touching the insides of her burning thighs. "Now!"

They began thrusting, twisting, grinding, driving as one. Encompassing his manhood, she gasped in mingled astonishment and joy at the strength and awesome power of it. Stripped of awareness of her surroundings, she abandoned herself to him totally, rising swiftly into a cloud of ecstasy, through and beyond, driving to the heights of all-consuming climax.

Locked in the firmament, the sun bathed the moving earth, the tides ebbed and flowed and time stretched its unseeable thread closer to eternity. She lay on the bed, the sheet drawn over her nakedness, her perspiration saturating it. He had gotten up and pulled on his trousers, his bare feet slapping the floor as he went to the window to raise the shade. She followed him with her eyes, reveling in the tawniness of his lithe, young body, his catlike movements. The shade flew up, the brilliant white light hammering against her eyes, eliciting pain and snapping her lids shut.

"Close that, Fernando!"

"We need more air in here. *Tutto èstagnante.*"

"Speak English." She turned over, frowning at him.

"How do you say?"

"Stagnant."

"*Èstagnante,* stagnant." He shrugged. "They are the same."

"You promised me you'd speak Italian only when you whisper words of love." She shaded her eyes with one hand. "Damn, open the window if you must, but close that goddamned shade!"

He obeyed, then went to the dresser and got out a clean cotton shirt. When he put it on, however, she saw that the pocket was torn and hanging down absurdly.

"Take that off and put on one that isn't ripped!"

"It's only the pocket." Gripping it, he ripped it off. "There."

"Why can't you wear one of those lovely new ones I bought you at Giopello's in Naples?"

"I save them for night."

"Liar! You love looking like a tramp. I buy you beautiful clothes and all I ever see you in are rags."

"Comfortable rags."

Raising her arms, she gestured, pulling him toward her with her fingers. "Come, let's make love."

"Are you crazy? What do you think I am, a bull? Besides, I have to go out."

"Where?"

"Business."

"What business?"

"My business, *mio caro*. It's all right for me to have my own business, isn't it?"

"Don't be impudent." Taking a wad of money from the dresser, he thumbed through it hurriedly, then pocketed it.

"What do you do with all the money I give you?"

"Put it in the bank. I'm saving up to buy a new boat."

"You're a liar. Come, beautiful liar, come and hold me, kiss me."

He hesitated but then went to the bed and pulled the sheet down slowly. He ran both hands teasingly up her body, fondling her breasts briefly, touching her mouth with his fingertips, bending over to kiss her. But she was too eager for him, too intent on stealing his mouth. Stiffening, he pulled back his head, straightening his body.

"Bastard!"

"That's me."

"Wait for me. I'm going with you. What time is it?"

"Close your eyes." Running up the shade, he glanced out at the clock in the steeple of San Paolo. "A quarter to five."

She jumped up, hurling the sheet to the floor. "Good God, Giorgio's waiting for me."

"The old man with your boat? So what?"

"I must get back to the villa, that's so what! My mother-in-law!"

"You should see your face, Lavinia. You look petrified. I don't believe it."

"The old bitch drives me out of my mind. You can't imagine! If I'm not home by sundown, she writes it down in her little book so she won't forget to tell Enrico."

"What does she think you are, my sweet, a twelve-year-old? A virgin?" He laughed heartily.

"It's not funny, Fernando. You're stupid, sending

that note to the house the other night. She watched me reading it at the dinner table. She knew who it was from, what it was about."

"You showed it to her?"

"Don't be an ass, for God's sake! She didn't have to see it. She knows what's going on; she senses it—intuition. Oh, how I wish she'd die! I wish to hell!"

"Wish to heaven, *bello*, you may get better results."

"It's no joke. If she ever catches us, if she ever gets proof that she can take to Enrico, she'll break her legs getting to him! She can't stand the sight of me, of her son's money in my sinful hands. God, how I despise her!"

"Does she ever come here to Sorrento?"

"Who knows where she goes? She floats about like a wraith." He stared blankly. "Wraith, *fantasima, apparizione!*"

He lit a cigarette, using it to light one for her and proffered it to her. "When does your husband go away again?"

"He won't be back for another two days." A provocative leer pulled up the corners of her mouth. "We can see each other tomorrow and the next day—in the morning, though. I have to be back when he gets home sometime in the afternoon."

"How considerate. You enjoy playing the dangerous game, don't you?"

"That's a stupid thing to say!"

"You should see your eyes when you talk about his comings and goings, and how you're going to do this and that. They catch fire."

"We're unusually observant today, aren't we, my darling." She paused and studied him archly. "Where did you say you were going?"

He patted his pocket bulging with the roll of lira. "To the bank."

"The bank closes at four."

He scowled. "I told you before, *mio caro*, I don't

appreciate your nose poked into my affairs. If you can't give a trusted friend a few lira without smothering him with curiosity——"

She interrupted, laughing mirthlessly. "A few lira? I must have given you at least ten thousand these last three months."

He took the money from his pocket, holding it out to her. "Take it."

"Oh, Fernando, stop teasing. You and your Latin temper. Stop looking so gloomy and put upon. I'm sorry." She took the money and, throwing her arm around him, jammed it back into his pocket. Then bringing the other arm around, she embraced him, kissing him passionately, working her naked body against him, rekindling the fire in her loins. Easing her gently away, he smiled, kissed her cheek and, plopping his straw hat on his head, hurried out the door.

The beautiful bastard, she thought, closing the door after him and returning to the bed. *Too beautiful and too young for me to hang onto very much longer— even with money.*

Wrapping the sheet about her, she went to the window and raised the shade. Grimacing against the brilliance of the lowering sun and shielding her eyes, she watched Fernando hurry down the stone steps. He swung his arms, moving easily, barely touching the steps with his toes. And tipped his hat to an old couple dragging themselves by. Her hand went to her face, and turning about, she looked at herself in the cork-framed glass hanging over the dresser. She was twice his age, maybe more, although he swore he was 28. He looked barely 21. And she? Preparing to turn the corner into late middle age. Or was it early old? Why in the name of mercy did old age come so fast, at such breakneck speed! One day the lines were faint, barely distinguishable, the skin firm, the eyes clear and bright, the hair alive, healthy-looking. The next day. . . . Better she die in agony than ever reach Mama Aldoni's years and resemble her, an upright corpse. Her hands crept to her naked breasts, caressing them where Fernando's warm, wet mouth had been. He loved her breasts. Ross had loved them. He and Ross were much alike physically, had identical builds. Fernando's hair was darker, perhaps, but it had the same curl. A Latin Ross was what he was.

Dressing, she thought about Ross and Lisa, rolling back the years as easily as a wave slides down a beach. If Ross had survived the war, he would be 38 now, perhaps showing a gray hair or two, but still slender and rugged-looking, well-muscled and as hard as Fernando, despite the difference in their ages. And Lisa, three—no, two years younger. She'd take care of herself; she wouldn't have changed much. Side by side, Deirdre and she would look more like sisters than mother and daughter.

"Good God! What am I doing standing here daydreaming!"

She dressed, collected her bag and parasol and got out, leaving the room in a shambles.

She half ran down the long winding sun-baked steps into Via Passo, past San Paolo and the Plaza Di Vittoria thronged with people and sea birds down to Ninfeo. Giorgio waited in his little boat. He tipped his cap in greeting, bowing from the waist, smiling.

With Mama Aldoni firmly entrenched at the villa, Lavinia didn't trust Giorgio. Associating one with the other was logical. Old people, even those separated by the chasms of class, had a predilection for spreading gossip among their peers. Small wonder, with so little to take up their time, so little they could do. She wouldn't be surprised in the least if Giorgio ran to the old bitch and told her he'd taken the *signora* to Sorrento today and watched her climb the hill to a house halfway to the *cattedrale*.

How stupid of her! In her haste to leap into bed with Fernando, she had forgotten the customary purchase, something for the house, for Deirdre, for herself—anything to make it appear that she'd been out shopping again.

The boat smelled of dead mullet, having been free of the odor on the trip over. She quelled the urge to upbraid Giorgio.

"Giorgio, I'm so sorry I'm late."

"Is almost sundown."

"Will you forgive me?" she asked coquettishly. His face broke into a broad toothless smile and he blushed. "You do forgive me." She patted his hand affectionately and with his help moved toward the stern and sat down.

"Here we go!" she exclaimed brightly, holding her hat and parasol against the breeze.

XVIII

She fell on her love's bosom, hugg'd it fast,
And with Leander's name she breathed her last.

Deirdre closed the book over the ends of her fingers
to keep her place. Hero and Leander: Surely no two
lovers ever loved as they. To reason that life without
him would be no life at all, to join him in death, the
river closing over her head.

Drawing the brim of her hat lower to shut out the
glare of the early afternoon sun, she let her eyes drift
to the pool. She marveled at the beauty of the cloudless
azure sky reflected across its surface, and the tall conifers, thrusting straight down, lending the water the illu-
sion of depth. And in the center of the pool, rising,
lording it over his placid realm, the naked Triton on
his horse, his powerful chest and biceps, his right arm
raised, the elbow bent. How handsome he looked, in
spite of his eyes blindly staring. She imagined him
alive, his eyes black, piercing, fixing her in their gleam,
his beautiful sunlit chest rising and falling with every
breath. Her glance lowered to his genitals, but at once,
he became stone again, motionless and unfeeling. And
the stains and weatherworn cracks girdling his wrists
and his horse's neck visibly marred the handsomeness of
the two of them.

She turned her attention back to Marlowe, to *Hero
and Leander*, to finish reading the argument of the sixth
sestiad. But the sound of the *carrozza* coming up the hill
prompted her to close the book. Over the brow of
the hill into view came donkey and cart with a lone

126

passenger. Jumping up from the bench, she ran toward them waving and shouting.

"Enrico! Enrico!"

The boy stopped the beast and Enrico got down from his seat, briefcase in one hand, suitcase in the other. He gestured to the driver and the *carrozza* went on out of sight around the end of the house. He stood smiling, waving and, she noted, swaying slightly, as if the breeze slipping up the hill were affecting his balance. But coming up to him, throwing her arms around his neck and kissing him loudly, she knew it was no breeze but anisette. He reeked of it and his eyes showed a slightly glassy look.

"Dee-dee! Dee-dee!"

Dropping his case and bag, he seized her arm and steered her off into the pines out of the sun.

"You can't imagine what's happened!"

"What? Tell me."

"The Swiss, my darling, they want to practically buy us out! Everything we bottle. And they are drowning in money! I tell you these four days have been the golden days of my life!"

"Better even than you expected!"

"Fantastic! I shall be the wealthiest man in all Campania!" He stopped short. "Where is your mother? I must tell her."

"She's taking her nap." His smile faded. "She had to go to Sorrento this morning to see about something. I don't know——"

"The new furniture for the drawing room, probably. I asked her to check on the delivery."

He paused, staring at Deirdre. The sunlight filtering through the trees fell across her generous breasts like a golden sash, defining their contours, their sculptured beauty. She was babbling on, effusive in her congratulations and compliments on her father's good fortune. He half-listened, his eyes on her breasts gently rising and falling, the cotton bodice over them accentuating their ripe fullness.

"Dee-dee." His hands shot out snatching hold of her arms, his bear head snapping down, his mouth going to her cleavage, nuzzling it, then kissing her breasts voraciously. One hand slid down her body, caressing her, pulling her close to him so that she could feel his organ stiffening. She cried out, struggling to pull free, but he held her fast, his hot mouth fairly burning her breasts, his voice husky, rasping.

"Bellisimo, bellisimo."

Wrenching free, she ran from him, stopping a few steps away, whirling about, staring fearfully.

"Enrico." It was a voice full of astonishment and pain. Her eyes glistened with tears. "Please stop, please!" She continued to back away. "Please."

The word repeated tightened her throat, choking her, so that only a whisper came forth. He did not hear. Her awe, her fear, her helplessness stoked his lust as he pressed forward. Having touched her, having felt her flesh beneath his eager fingers, tasting the fire with his lips, he had to possess her!

The animal in him was aroused. His eyes were reduced to slits, his tongue gliding back and forth over his lips lasciviously. His breath hissed from his throat. Backing away, continuing to whisper pleadingly, she came up against a tree, throwing one arm up to push aside a branch. Slipping by the tree backward, her heel catching a root that all but tripped her, she repeated his name, begging him, hands clasped imploringly, to stop.

"Enrico, please."

He was not a man but a savage beast stalking its prey, consumed with lust, trembling in anticipation, his great shoulders rolled upward, hunched forward, his body bent slightly. Hurrying his step, he came to her.

"Daddy, Daddy, dearest Daddy. I—love—you." Lifting her face to the sun, she began sobbing uncontrollably.

Her words, the sound of her crying ripped through the curtain of his concentration; the effect was like a whip cracked in his face. The look of lust vanished and he straightened, dropping his hands to his sides and staring about in confusion. One hand wandered to his forehead, scratching it. And in place of the beast was a man bewildered, a man who appeared to have lost something. It was as if a chunk of time had dropped out of both their lives, so quickly did the change come over him.

"What am I doing, dear God in heaven!" he whispered hoarsely. Crossing himself, he clasped his hands and shook his head. "This can't be—no. It didn't happen. It couldn't."

Pity welled up inside her as she stood rooted watching him. In seconds, he was so filled with shame and embarrassment that he could not look at her. He turned his eyes to one side, then the other, closing them absurdly as they passed her. And he worked the air with his hands as if trying to pull words of apology out of himself.

"I—I—oh, dear God!" Again he began casting about, jerking his body one way, then the other, searching for a door to open and flee through before he shriveled up in disgrace and humiliation before her eyes. Then both hands flew to his cheeks, pressing them, fattening his lips ludicrously.

"A priest. I must see a priest! I must confess! I have sinned! I have sinned! God forgive me! Holy Mother, hear me, forgive me, forgive me, forgive me, forgive me."

Turning about, he staggered away toward the house. She watched him fight the branches to the road, then veer away from the house and run down the hill.

"Enrico! Enrico!" Her voice choked with grief, she could only whisper his name.

As if in a trance, she walked slowly back to the road, looking down it. He had vanished. Turning, she stumbled over his briefcase. She picked it up, holding it close to her, crying aloud, her tears splashing down upon the polished leather.

Picking up his suitcase also, she ran with them past the front of the house, the pool and Triton to the marble bench. Her book lay there closed. Dropping the bag and briefcase, she sat down and buried her face in her hands.

The shame. He might just as well have stripped her naked and gone all the way for the damage he'd done. She'd never again be able to sit across from him at the dinner table, let alone sit on his lap and muss his hair and giggle and laugh with him. It was terrible, awful! Lavinia would notice; she had an eye for the nervousness, the telltale discomfort of others. "What's the matter with you, Deirdre, the way you look at your father? Enrico, you're blushing!"

She would never tell her; she couldn't do that to him. To either of them. He was so good, too good, fine, decent.

Rising from the bench, she walked toward the garden nervously picking at her cuff, less upset now, but more apprehensive. A tree swallow followed her, hopping from limb to limb alongside, cocking his head and studying her.

Was Enrico so good? Or had he lusted for her ever since her body had begun to develop, the fire smoldering within until it blazed forth? The way he'd stared at her breasts, his face contorted so viciously, so frightening-looking, and his hands reaching.

He had kept it bottled up inside him, then suddenly lost all control, only catching himself on the brink. The guilt, like a great wind, rushed in to overwhelm him.

The sensible thing for the two of them would be to wipe it out of mind. Sift it from memory and carry on as before. If only they could. If only she could pretend it had never happened.

But that would require a capacity for self-delusion beyond her powers.

There was only one course open; she would have to pack up and run away. She would leave a note explaining to Lavinia that she was fed up with Capri, with Italy, and wanted to go to America. No, that wouldn't do at all. Lavinia would follow her, find her and bring her back. Enrico would have every *poliziotto* within 100 miles on her trail. No, she'd just go. No note—nothing. When she got to Naples, she'd buy a boat ticket for America.

The swallow tired of watching her and, twisting its brown-and-white body about, flew off toward the house, rising over the roof and disappearing.

She'd ask Giorgio to take her to Naples first thing in the morning, very early, before anyone else in the house was up, even the servants. She'd tell him she was going to visit a friend. She'd go immediately to the docks and look into boats sailing for America. And get a reservation, or whatever they required. On second thought, she wouldn't tell a soul she was leaving the isle. She'd pay a stranger to sail her over.

At that, if Lavinia discovered that she was roaming about Naples alone, she'd fly into a purple rage. The lectures she'd given her on the plight of teenaged girls in "that Sodom of a place," as she invariably described the city.

Deirdre began picking at the privet hedge, flicking the little round green leaves off the tip of her finger and glancing back the way she had come. In front of the marble bench lay Enrico's briefcase and suitcase. And Christopher Marlowe lay closed on the bench itself, his beautiful love tale the furthest thing from her mind.

Lavinia slid her hands down Fernando's back, reveling in the warmth of his flesh. For all his weight, his body felt surprisingly light atop her own, more a part of it than upon it. Not a man and a woman, but a multi-limbed creature spawned of desire, each half melting into the other, gloriously entangled.

"Prostituta!"

Lavinia's eyelids flickered, her mind jettisoning the image.

"Prostituta! Marmaglia!"

She woke with a start, her eyes snapping open. To the sight of Mama Aldoni inches away, glaring at her, spitting more words out, her normally yellow skin florid with rage.

"Sudicio maiale!"

Lavinia bolted upright. "Filthy pig? You dare call me——"

"Silence, you garbage, *rifuito!*"

"Get out of my room! How dare you burst in here!"

The old woman backed away, but not in fear. Only, it appeared to Lavinia, to display her animosity and hatred in full view.

"Fernando Crosetti, your lover. I know all about him, you bitch! Don't begin to deny it. I refuse to listen to your filthy lies. I have proof! Proof!"

Her skinny arm shot upward, a slip of yellow paper clenched in her fist.

"You're insane!"

Christ, how could she have found out? How? Giorgio, of course. Who else would betray her? Obscene animal, disgusting little peasant stinking up his grubby boat! She'd strangle him!

The old woman was running on now, flinging words out like darts of fire, spouting Fernando's address, describing the house, the way to get there, the time she'd arrived that morning, the time she'd left. A tremor passed through Lavinia's upper body. Enrico was due back anytime now! And the moment he showed himself at the door the old bitch would run to him! Her moment of triumph arrived at last; she would crucify her! And

Enrico would also. His blood would boil. She'd be lucky if he didn't beat her to death on the spot! And once he cooled down, he'd throw her out of the house, off the isle!

No, that he would not do, not with his beloved Dee-dee an innocent bystander. He would never make her suffer. Lavinia's mind hurtled forward, outstripping the moment, the hour. A score of possible punishments paraded through her mind vying for dominance.

It was all over, of that she was convinced, Deirdre or no Deirdre. She had no idea how far he'd go beyond breaking with her, however. He seldom lost his temper, but when he did, he was like a grizzly run amok—ranting, raving, pounding tables, kicking chairs, flinging about everything at hand. Worst of all was that his honor had been abased, his manhood disgraced. And he himself made a laughingstock. The family Aldoni, "for 700 years one of the region's foremost and most highly respected clans," would now be the target of public abuse and humiliation. He wouldn't be able to show his face!

"The moment Rico walks in the door he will hear of your perfidy, you fornicator! He will throw you out bag and baggage! Miserable bitch, you will get what you deserve, all you deserve!"

She lunged at Lavinia with surprising swiftness and agility, drawing back her hand to slap her face, but Lavinia caught her wrist and pushed her away.

"Get out of my room, you hysterical old witch! Out!"

"*Your* room? You poor fool. Your room, your clothes, your jewels, you've thrown them all away, stupid bitch! *Prostituta! Marmaglia!*"

"Out!"

She shoved her out the door, slamming and locking it, leaning against it, fighting to regain her composure. What could she do to forestall the inevitable? What? She'd love to knock the old bitch over the head with a brass candlestick, carry her through the garden out into the woods, throw her into the first ravine she found and pile it full of stones!

No. Giorgio. He was the key. She must bribe him to change his story, say that he had lied about the whole thing. Pretend that he'd been angry with the *signora* for continually accusing him of fishing, that he had lost his temper and invented a pack of lies about her to get revenge. Crossing quickly to her vanity, she pulled open a drawer, snatching up all the lira she could find. She counted it hurriedly: 6000, 7000, 7200, 7300— a total of 7400 lira. A fortune for the grubby old fool. Enough to buy himself a new boat and enough wine to live like a king for years!

Rolling the bills up tightly, she unlocked her door and ran down the corridor, around the corner and up the stairs to the third floor to Philomena's room.

Thank heaven for Philomena, the one person she could trust, the only one whose loyalty couldn't be bought with bribes or threats. She'd give her the money, rush her out of the house and down to Marina Grande to Giorgio. Enrico would be coming over in the public boat, that she could be sure of, since he himself had told her he had no idea of his exact time of arrival that afternoon.

If anyone could talk Giorgio into changing his story, it would be Philomena. He worshiped the skinny thing, turning six shades of pink when she so much as smiled at him and practically groveling at her feet when she spoke. The only way to make the thing work would be to give him 1000 right off with instructions. He must confess his "lies" and his reason for them, accept his dismissal and get the rest of the money later in the day. She knew he'd take it. She felt it in her bones and her bones never misled her. He had to be destitute, as was every other peasant on the isle. Not one of them could afford to put principle above his belly. Or a new boat in which to go out and fish the bay dry of red mullet!

She knocked on the door. "Philomena, it's me, let me in—hurry!"

"A moment please, *signora*."

"Damn!" Seizing the knob, Lavinia pushed the door wide. Philomena was seated at her mirror. Dressed only in her underclothing, she was half-turned away from the glass toward Lavinia and in the midst of removing a silver chain from around her painfully slender neck. Dangling from the chain was a familiar-looking silver crucifix, three inches long. The instant her eyes fell on it, Lavinia recalled that she had failed to see it earlier in its customary setting: around Mama Aldoni's neck back in the bedroom!

Caught in the act of removing it, Philomena flushed and began stammering an explanation. Lavinia slammed the door behind her.

"You bitch! You filthy traitor!"

"*Signora*, I do not have to listen to your insults."

"Deceitful pig!"

Furious, suddenly fully capable of wringing her neck, Lavinia rushed at her, hands outstretched. But like a shot, Philomena was up from her bench and twisting away, backing against the wall.

"You touch me and you'll only make things worse for yourself than they are already!"

Lavinia gulped a breath, hesitated and got control of herself. She stood before Philomena, searing her with her eyes, her fists clenched, the lira protruding from the fingers of her right hand.

"Pack your things, Philomena. You are dismissed! I want you out of this house in one hour."

Philomena laughed, a lilting, musical sound, barren of any semblance of worry. Her homely face relaxed in a broad, beaming smile.

"You are crazy! *You* are the one who'll be out of this house in one hour!"

Lavinia glared, her face pure odium; fear and loathing rose in her like a fountain, flooding her mind.

Turning away, she moved to the window, looking down on the pavement.

"You contemptible bitch! Letting her bribe you with a bit of silver. You and Judas, two of a kind."

"You and Jezebel the whore."

Lavinia whirled on her. "One more word and I'll cut your tongue out!" Her voice softened. "You know what your problem is, Philomena? A very simple one. Repulsive-looking old maids like you have been jealous of beautiful women since time began."

"Get out of my room!"

"You dare——"

"Yes, I dare! I know which side my bread is buttered on."

"That's all that trash like you needs to betray a trust."

"What trust?"

"I trusted you like a sister!"

"You used me, that's all you did. I was your messenger, your go-between, covering up for you, lying for you to the *signor*. To her. No more, you hear? I have my self-respect. I have to live with my conscience. I can no longer deceive the people who pay me my wages, who treat me——"

"Shut your mouth. You make me sick!"

Striding to her, Lavinia seized the crucifix and jerked it, snapping the chain.

Philomena gasped. "You bitch!"

Slapping her hard, the sound ringing about the walls of the little room, Lavinia then flung the crucifix out the window, stalked out and slammed the door so hard behind her that the walls shook and plaster dust came floating down from the corridor ceiling.

Back in her own room, she stood at the window turning over plan after plan, rejecting each one the instant her brain offered it. There was simply no way out. It was too late. Had she a day, 24 hours, she might be able to cook up something with Giorgio, get him to lie for her. But she was only fooling herself. He'd wilt like a dying flower when confronted by the old bitch, Enrico and Philomena. And the way Giorgio felt about Philomena.

Her heart sank as she caught sight of a familiar figure trudging up the road. Enrico—without hat or case or bag. He looked exhausted, as if he'd walked all the way from Marina Grande. His jacket was folded over one arm and his white shirt was wringing wet with perspiration, his necktie askew, his trousers brown with dust. Panic seized her, squeezing her heart like a sponge in a fist as he neared the front door and his mother hurried out to meet him. She began talking, in tones too low for Lavinia to hear.

But she did not need to hear the shriveled little bitch in order to understand what was being said. The whole business began to be played out below her in pantomime. Mama gesticulated melodramatically, pouring her story out like water gushing from a culvert. His first reaction was astonishment, unmistakable and total. Quickly it gave way to consternation, then anger, then wrath! Again and again he attempted to interrupt, but she refused to permit it, rambling on, relieving herself of her "burden of proof." Proof, proof, proof; it was what she'd been after ever since Enrico had brought the pale and haughty non-Italian heathen home to Villa Aldoni. Proof to confirm her vicious suspicions of adultery. Proof, proof, proof. Now, thanks to that traitorous hellhag Philomena, the old woman had all she required.

Lavinia was tempted to throw open the window and shout down to them. But to what purpose? What could she possibly say? The die cast had come up a crushing loss. It was defeat, as clear and obvious as the sky above, the sea below. In three minutes, it was all over. Together mother and son disappeared from view, coming into the house. Unlocking her door, Lavinia went to her vanity and sat down slowly, her back to the mirror, her eyes glued on the door. Presently she heard him coming, and when he reached the top of the stairs and started down the corridor, the sounds multiplied. The old bitch was coming with him. Of course. She'd have to be in on the kill!

The gentle knock, the door opening, his face ashen, taut with strain, looking in.

"May I come in, Mrs. Aldoni?"

His mother hovered behind him, her insufferable mouth jabbering encouragement, leering at Lavinia over first one shoulder, then the other. "Go in! Go in!"

He entered the room slowly, Lavinia noted, too slowly for one burning with fury.

"Tell her, Rico. Then beat her, thrash her within an inch of her life!"

The old woman suddenly became hysterical, waving her fists wildly, her eyes glazed with detestation. She began cursing her in Italian.

"Silencio!" roared Enrico, throwing out his arm, preventing her from coming forward. "Get out! Leave us alone!"

"I stay! I want to see the filthy bitch crawl! Shame! Shame on this house! Jezebel. Adulteress!"

She continued screaming insults and imprecations as he pushed her out, locking the door.

"May I speak first," asked Lavinia quietly, "or am I not to speak at all?"

He shrugged, turning from her, but not before she caught the sudden rush of sadness invading his eyes behind the thick lenses. Removing his glasses, he shoved them down into the sweat-dampened breast pocket of his shirt and tossed his jacket onto the bed.

"I'm listening."

"I want to tell you something you will not believe. Something I cannot hope to make you believe, but I have to say it. God knows and I know——"

"Yes, yes, you love me," he said tiredly, rolling the verb off his tongue as if it were something distasteful he had bitten into and was in haste to reject.

"I do, Henry." It was a name he loved, a name she

called him only in periods of intimacy, in bed, in darkness, in each other's arms. But to use it now proved a tactical error. This she realized at once when he lifted his eyes and stared at her with a look that suggested the sound of the name from her lips under these circumstances was the last straw. "Enrico, I beg you———" she blurted.

"If you have something to get off your chest, say it!"

"Yes. I have sinned, I know. I have sought the company of another man behind your back. Why? Why should I do such a terrible thing?"

"Why indeed?" He sounded older than his mother and as weary as she had ever seen him.

"Because I have no husband. My husband is away; our entire married life he seems to be away. He comes to visit his wife and family—yes, family; she is your daughter as well as mine—between business trips. Thirty days in the month and he is here, what? Seven? Eight? But of course business is a particularly demanding mistress. And I am expected to understand and accept that, and sit home knitting, gardening, reading, killing the hours of my life patiently awaiting my lord's return."

"You can get off that tack now, before you go any further," he said tightly. "You cannot shift the blame for this so easily."

"I had no intention of shifting the blame. If I were to do so, I would put it on my own shoulders."

"You are priceless, Lavinia, absolutely unique."

"Look at me, Enrico. Please. Am I so old, so wrinkled, my looks so gone to seed that I cannot keep the husband I adore close to me for more than a few days at a time? Is Deirdre such a handful, so spoiled and troublesome that you prefer to stay as far away from her for as long as you can until she's grown up and gone off on her own?"

"Leave her out of this."

"How can I, my darling?"

"Don't say that! Don't use that word!"

"Ever again, is that it? Forgive me, it's a habit. As for Deirdre, no, I can't leave her out of it, any more than you can leave your mother and sister out of your life. She loves you, she adores you, Enrico."

"Damn you, don't talk about her! Not now!"

"When I go, naturally I'll have to take her with me. A daughter's place is with her mother."

"Some mother you are."

"Is that what you want? I mean, don't you feel something for her? Need I remind you that she's at a very impressionable age. An age when she can be hurt painfully, by disappointment, rejection."

"Lavinia, I warn you."

"She worships you. As if you didn't know. We both do."

"I'm sure *you* do. You love this Fernando what's-his-name—*Tuo innamorato?*"

"He is not my lover!"

He grunted. "What do you call him?"

"He is my husband."

"Lavinia!"

"He is you, Enrico. In his arms, I close my eyes and he is the husband I love who is off to Geneva, or Paris, or Rome, or Genoa."

He shook his head. "What an imagination, what an artful liar you are! Incredible!"

"If I am lying, may God strike me dead!"

He laughed grimly. "So suddenly I am 26, 27, whatever he is, young, strong, without a white hair on my head, oversexed, ready to romp at the drop of a lira. Yes, my business takes me away more than I'd like it to. Yes, you get lonely. Yes, temptation is always there. Yes, you're only human. Yes, you love me; you wouldn't hurt me for the world. Yes, yes, yes to all of it, but——"

"There's no excuse for carrying my fantasies into reality? Something, of course, you've never done. You are so pure."

"I took a marriage vow; you took the same vow. I have never, I swear by the Holy Virgin, *never* taken another woman to bed!"

"Not even in imagination? Not even patted a shapely thigh or a breast, stolen a kiss or two? Some sweet, voluptuous young thing who closes her eyes to your age and sees only the chance to please you for a handful of your lovely money?"

"You have to turn it onto me, don't you! To scour your conscience!"

"You haven't answered my question."

"I am not the guilty party in this mess! I haven't committed adultery!"

"But I have. Why attempt to deny the obvious? Explanations do not appear in order. So that is that. Deirdre and I will leave in the morning."

"You are an unholy witch!"

"But before we leave, I want you to know that guilty as I am, what I did has nothing to do with our relationship. I fell in love with you, I married you and I love you today at this moment more than I have ever loved you before. I cannot beg your forgiveness, I have no right to it. Will our getting out tomorrow morning be soon enough?" She rose from the vanity bench.

"Sit down."

She obeyed. "If you prefer, we can leave tonight, under cover of darkness. Perhaps that's better. If your mother can sew up Philomena's mouth, word of my sinful lapse need never get out. There'd be no disgrace, no scandal. The name of Aldoni would not be dragged——"

"Be still!" He filled his eyes with her, her face, her body. Getting up slowly, he came toward her. "You play this game unfairly, woman. You know how I feel about Dee-dee. Take her away and you take my heart out of my body." He turned, as if to keep her from seeing the sadness and embarrassment in his face give way to compassion. "I love her. I love you, God help me. I won't deny part of the blame for this is mine. I suppose in a way what happened I let happen, encouraged it."

She could feel the beat of her heart quickening in her breast. The tip of her tongue found her lips and began moistening them. *Talk, keep talking, say it, say it!* the voice inside her shouted.

"Still, what you have done is monstrous. Surely the worst disgrace of all. You and he must be punished."

"Do with me what you will."

"Don't talk, please! You've said far too much already." His shoulders slumped, bringing his whole body down and into itself. Putting his glasses back on, he faced her, his eyes enlarged by the lenses looking like those of a dead man. "If you ever see this man again, if you ever so much as nod to him in the street and I hear of it, I shall kill you. You have done more than disgrace and humiliate me." He touched his temple with his index finger. "You have emasculated me in here."

"No! Don't say that!" Tears filled her eyes, coursing down her cheeks. "I beg you, darling." She reached for him, but he backed away.

"No."

"It's useless," she said in a defeated tone. "I must leave. We both must. You and I can't possibly pick up where we left off, where I. . . ." She faltered, searching his eyes for pity, for understanding and acceptance. "Your mother would never permit it. And she's right."

"Leave her out of it." He nodded at the door. "It's between us. She and Dee-dee have no part in it. Come here." She obeyed, her eyes lowered, tears continuing to fall. Taking out his handkerchief, he dried her face. "You look absurd. You never cry, never so much as a single tear. Why now?"

"I'm so ashamed, my darling. I feel so awful, so dirty inside. What must you think of me? I got so lonely; I hungered so for you. Lying in bed alone at night sometimes I think my heart will break. If only I were different; if only I were the mousy type, the dried-up little proper middle-aged housewife. Bridge and tea and gossip and church—all the trappings of dutiful wifehood. But God didn't make me that way. I'm alive. I feel alive. I have needs, urges, fires, my feelings get out of hand." Her arms slipped about his neck and she pressed her body slowly, sensuously against him, her breasts hard against his chest. A long moment for effect, for realization and reaction. He locked her to him too tightly, so tightly it hurt. Then he began smothering her with kisses.

Breaking with her and sweeping her up, he carried her to the bed without a sound, save that of his breath coming louder and louder from his throat as his lust swelled and intensified.

XIX

There would be no need to tell Enrico that she, Deirdre, would not betray him to Lavinia. He knew his Dee-dee, knew he could trust her to keep his guilt secret.

Deirdre sat by her window looking out upon the olive trees, feeling wistful and despairingly lonely. And so sad that her heart felt like a stone. Why did such a thing have to happen? Why did there have to be an animal inside that surfaced and overruled the respectable, the civilized in people? Why attack her? She had done nothing to entice him.

She couldn't run away; she hadn't the heart to. If he had gone all the way, if Lavinia had found out, there'd be no choice but to leave and go to America. Now, with time to consider her situation somewhat less emotionally, it made no sense at all to go rushing off like a frightened chicken.

She was thirsty. She would go down the hall to the bathroom for a glass of water. No, better downstairs to the kitchen for a lemon squeeze with ice in it.

She was starting out the door when she heard loud voices. Enrico was arguing with his mother in an obscure dialect Mama Aldoni favored, one that Deirdre had never studied and did not understand. The two of them were in the old lady's room. She closed her door, and as if they both had heard the sound, the shouting stopped. Moments later Mama Aldoni came stomping down the corridor, Enrico following. Deirdre could hear her pass her door and, reopening it a crack, she watched mother, then son, pound down the stairs.

Mama left him standing at the garden door, slamming his fist against the jamb in frustration. And swearing in English. Presently the donkey boy was starting down the hill with her seated in the *carrozza*, waving her hands wildly, bawling out the world.

Dinner that evening was a theatrical fiasco.

Enrico appeared neither embarrassed nor disturbed by Deirdre's presence. Rather he seemed morose, staring glumly into his soup, his mind absent. Lavinia too was strangely silent, Deirdre thought, smiling now and then when their eyes met, encouraging her to finish her salad—"It's delicious, dear"—but making no effort at table conversation.

Deirdre examined their behavior. He couldn't have confessed to her, there was no need for that. He'd already poured his soul out to a priest, why tell Lavinia? Why hurt her unnecessarily? Nevertheless, she couldn't understand either of them. She had expected him to be subdued, self-effacing, even awkward in his efforts to conceal his embarrassment. But not angry. He had no right to that. And Lavinia, as quiet as the statues in the garden. So unlike her!

Deirdre continued perplexed through soup and salad into the main course, venison with small boiled potatoes and spinach. Halfway through his meat, Enrico suddenly swore, threw down his knife and fork and napkin, got up without excusing himself and left the table.

Lavinia made a laudable if vain attempt at pretending nothing had happened, continuing to pick at her spinach and daub her mouth with the corner of her napkin. Enrico meanwhile had gone upstairs. They could hear him overhead, the floor creaking, a door opening and closing. Only then did Lavinia comment.

"Forgive your father, dear, he's upset. He had bad luck in Geneva," she said.

"Did he really?"

"They're not interested."

"Oh." Deirdre let the matter drop, concentrating on

the smallest potato on her plate, halving it, quartering it, eating it.

Shortly Enrico came back down and went out the front door.

"Where's he off to this time of night, I wonder?" inquired Deirdre. Lavinia's expression was that of "search me." "He didn't even finish his venison. He loves venison," Deirdre added.

"Business always affects his appetite. You know that. When things go well, he gorges himself. When the buyers don't buy he can't stand the sight of food."

After dinner, they retired to the drawing room and a game of Russian backgammon. In that style of play, the game was begun with all the stones off the board. Deirdre doubled her stakes repeatedly, bearing off most of Lavinia's stones in a few minutes. She had never beaten Lavinia quite so definitively before. Obviously Lavinia did not have her mind on play. Time and again she had to be reminded that it was her turn. The first game resulted in a gammon for Deirdre; Lavinia unable to bear off a single stone. The second game started off following the same pattern.

"You really don't want to play, do you?" asked Deirdre.

"Of course I want to play."

"You're not paying the slightest attention. You're worried about him, aren't you?"

"Enrico? Certainly not. He probably forgot something at the Naples office and has to go over and get it. After all, tomorrow's Sunday."

The darkness covering the windows was pricked with stars and a half-moon pushed its straight edge through the clouds. The woods beyond the garden had come alive with the dry-throated grut, grut, grut of chorus frogs, and farther up the slopes in the direction of Monte Solaro, a hawk shrilled loudly, proclaiming its proprietorship of the isle.

Deirdre sensed that Lavinia was, for whatever reason,

in no better mood for conversation than she had been
at the table. Courteous, even pleasant in response to
questions, perhaps, but unwilling to initiate any conversation. The grandfather clock standing just outside
the door, its case gaily cluttered with floral marquetry,
struck the quarter hour before nine. Another full hour,
distinguished by Lavinia's listless efforts to provide
worthy opposition, came and departed before Enrico
returned, bursting in through the garden door. Noticing
the two of them in the drawing room, he called Lavinia
with a wave.

"Excuse your mother, Dee-dee, we have something
we must discuss."

"Of course," said Deirdre. And off they went upstairs.
Deirdre could scarcely suppress a gasp. She had never
seen him looking so. Standing in the dimly lit foyer, he
resembled a ghost, his face as white as chalk! His eyes
burned anger, or fear, or something equally potent and
possessive.

What has happened? she wondered. *What is going
on? Why did Lavinia lie so blatantly about the success
of his trip to Switzerland?*

XX

The shock of his admission sent a tremor through Lavinia's shoulders. They were in their bedroom, she seated on her vanity bench, Enrico standing with his back to the window, his face a sullen mask.

"How could you do such a thing?" she asked in pretend bewilderment.

"A question of honor, Lavinia. This is Italy, not America. In this country, a man's honor is all. Without my honor, I am naked."

"But to shoot him in cold blood! To take a life."

"It had to be. There was no other way. I only told you because you will hear about it anyway, sooner or later. I suggest you do your best to forget it. Forget him. Pretend he never existed."

"I gave you my solemn word I'd forget him. Was it necessary to murder him?" Her tone was close to hysteria.

"What is necessary is to satisfy my honor!"

"But the risk. What if somebody saw you? Everybody in the building must have heard the shot!"

Ignoring her, he took the pistol out of his inside pocket and hefted it covetously. "British. Light as a feather. Isn't it handsome-looking?"

"Put it away. I can't stand the sight of firearms!" She sniffed. "It smells of firing."

Emptying out the unused cartridges, he wrapped the gun in a piece of chamois and stuck it far back in the top drawer of the dresser.

"There's nothing to worry about. Nobody saw me enter or leave. And even if someone had, nothing would be done. In this country, a man as prominent as I has every right to put his wife's lover where he belongs." He tapped the dresser top over the spot where the gun lay. "Vengeance is the prerogative of my people."

"Nevertheless, you shouldn't have. If it comes out, if you're suspected, we'll be in every newspaper from Sicily to the Swiss border. You were the one who wanted to keep it quiet!"

"I do, but my honor was at stake."

"Of course," she said airily. She tightened her face so that the muscles under her temples became as hard as steel. How she hated this old man! If she could get between him and the dresser, she'd grab his pistol and shoot him! To wantonly kill such a beautiful animal, so young, so virile! The jealous bastard! The imbecilic hothead!

"What do we do now, Enrico?"

"Not a thing. Nobody's coming after me. I'm sure your playmate had enemies. Doesn't everybody?" He laughed coldly. "Gentlemen of his stripe have little trouble making enemies."

"So now somebody else can expect to suffer, possibly hang, for your night's work."

If this bothered him in the least, he made no sign. His thoughts had moved back to his ego and the assuaging of it.

"It makes me sound positively barbaric, I know, but I can't help admitting I feel as if a great weight has been lifted from my shoulders," he said.

"What about the weight on mine?"

"What are you talking about?"

"Your mother, she's determined to make me suffer."

"Nonsense, she'll get over it. At the moment she's a good deal more incensed with me than you. She left here swearing she'd never set foot in this house again. She wouldn't even let me go with her down to the boat."

Good, thought Lavinia, *excellent*. "I'm so sorry, Enrico. I've made a terrible mess of things, haven't I?"

"I suppose you want to get rid of Philomena, pay her and send her packing. The problem with that is she'll start babbling and never stop."

Lavinia thought fast. She'd love to get rid of Philomena. Push her off the highest mountain into the sea, the emaciated bitch! But that particular contretemps called for something cleverer than a bald plea for her dismissal. No, Philomena would be her mistress's piece of work. To be dealt with in good time, in a manner replete with the succulent taste of revenge.

"No, Enrico. I can't blame Philomena for what she did. The fault is all mine. She was tempted, but I inspired it. I'll talk to her in the morning. If she's agreeable, perhaps we can let bygones be bygones."

"As you wish. Handle it your own way. Keep it just between you two."

"I shall."

"Let's go to bed. I'm exhausted."

She shrugged. Later in bed, after she had finished submitting to his crude fumbling, after he had asserted his conjugal rights, she lay on her back with his right arm flung across her stomach, staring up at the molding. How she envied the sculptured cherubim and seraphim their freedom. And while Enrico snored loudly into her right shoulder, she imagined Fernando's smiling face materializing, hovering in midair between an angel of love and an angel of light.

Poor dear, she thought. *How surprised he must have been answering his door, opening it to a gun pointed at his heart. Such a pity. He was a grand lover, and the number of unattached worthwhile ones seems to be shrinking.* Still, with all she had to offer, she anticipated little difficulty in selecting his replacement.

Perhaps this time a blond for a change, maybe even a foreigner.

XXI

A dollar a week and no smoking, no female visitors after sundown and no cooking in the room, the landlady had cautioned. Jeremy had been hard put to keep from laughing her out the door, the fat, pudding-faced idiot! The room proved little larger than a closet, with space enough for a spring bed, a rocking chair, of all things, a washstand and what appeared to be an upright piano crate pressed into service as an armoire. And the five-floor walk-up was four more than he would have liked. Still, he had little reason to complain. A dollar a week wouldn't strap him and it would be for only a month at most, providing Lisa was correct in estimating her traveling time to and from Pernambuco. He sat on the edge of the bed puffing a cigarette and going over his plans for the tenth time since returning to New York from Baltimore. Shortly after leaving her hotel he'd decided that his failure to press his wish to accompany her had been a monumental blunder. Now he'd simply have to make the best of the four-week wait. At that, with $3000 in his pocket, he could move easily through the city in the company of Mrs. Vossbacher and whomever else beautiful, desirable and willing he chanced to encounter.

He'd have to stay out of Ned Loomis's way, though. He was presently sitting 46 blocks north of his "banker," sufficient distance to reduce the odds of a chance meeting in the street. The story of Ross Dandridge being found alive would probably leak to the newspapers. The *Times* would certainly print it. Any little crumb of news having to do with the recent hostilities seemed to find its way into the columns of George Jones's eight-page daily contribution to the edification of New Yorkers. It might prove a bit touchy trying to explain to old Ned why Mr. Slater's prospective bride had dropped everything, including Mr. Slater, to run off to Brazil after her husband. Where, Ned would be certain to ask, did that leave his precious $14,250 investment?

To be sure, nothing was to be gained groaning over the state of things. What he had to do was remain active and keep out of Loomis's way. And Teddy's. He would contact Myra, give her his address and instruct her to come uptown to see him instead of him frequenting the Winter Garden.

He consulted the calendar card in his wallet. On the first of May, a Tuesday, he would catch the train for Providence. The Dandridges would either be there or be expected shortly. Then and only then could he think seriously about getting rid of Ross.

Washing his face and hands, he changed his shirt, spit-polished his three-dollar tan box-calf bluchers recently purchased in Baltimore, straightened his tie, ran a comb through his hair and prepared to depart for the Winter Garden. Reaching the lower hallway and glancing out a side window, one of two flanking the front door, he stopped with his hand on the knob. Across the street leaning against the wall of a building, standing two steps back in an alley, was a familiar figure. Teddy Vossbacher.

Jeremy's immediate reaction was surprise, but quick second thought advised him that he had little reason for that. He distinctly recalled telling himself upon leaving Loomis's office a few days earlier that Ned would no doubt put somebody on his trail. And fetch-and-carry Teddy would be the most likely candidate. Still, sight of him watching this house told Jeremy more than he had any pressing desire to know. He'd told Loomis he'd be leaving town. He'd made no mention of coming back.

He had no reason to. Neither Ned nor Teddy had any reason to expect him back. So Teddy wouldn't have been waiting for him at the train station; he must have followed him back to Providence, then all the way down to Baltimore and back. Of course! That had to be it! Whether he'd followed him closely enough to be aware of his, Jeremy's, brief meeting with Lisa was questionable, however.

One thing was certain, heading for the Winter Garden now would be begging trouble. If Teddy was carrying a gun, he'd never let him out of the side alley of the theater alive, and probably put a bullet or two into his devoted wife while he was at it.

Turning from the window, Jeremy knocked on the landlady's door. She came shuffling to open it, her worn slippers clapping against her soles, her apron filthy with grease. She fussed with her bun affectedly and flashed him a gold-and-ivory smile.

"Yes, Mr. Fitch, can I help you?"

"I was wondering——"

Her smile vanished and she interrupted. "Is anything the matter with your room?"

"Not at all. It's just what I need. Perfect. I was just wondering, do you have a piece of note paper and a pencil I might borrow?"

"Sure, come in."

The parlor reeked of corned beef and cabbage. Everything, from the battered upright piano to the cheap, garish curtains to the furniture—most of which looked as if it had been recovered from a dump—was blanketed with dust. It resembled a house that had been shut up for ten years, then suddenly occupied and yet to be tidied.

She brought him pen and ink and two pieces of cheap yellow note paper.

"Would you possibly have an extra envelope?" he asked, sitting at a table, dipping the pen and scribbling hurriedly. She left the room to fetch an envelope. By the time she returned, he was done writing and, blowing the ink dry, folded the note and inserted it in the envelope.

"I certainly appreciate this, Mrs. Harrigan." He smiled. "My, but don't you look nice today." The instant it was out he hated himself for saying it, but he couldn't resist it. Her reaction to this unbelievable statement was to believe it. With a grin, a blush and a sudden impulse to preen—her hair, her collar, her apron. Thanking her again, he left, hurrying down the front steps and heading up the street east toward Broadway, without the slightest indication that he knew Teddy was on the other side of the street following well behind him.

It was an unusually lovely spring day: The sidewalk maples and elms showed bursting buds, the air was clear, the sun brighter than he'd ever seen it in New York. There was a freshness about the city that generally visited only following a heavy downpour. Walking briskly, he crossed 72nd Street and shortly found himself coming onto Columbus Circle. A crowd of pigeons and people had taken over the bench area at the south end of Central Park. An organ grinder was busy winding out *O Solo Mio*, while his undernourished-looking monkey foraged the group for coins, holding his tin cup high overhead with both paws. Stepping into the doorway of a men's clothing store, Jeremy pretended interest in the suits on display. Searching the way he had come in the glass, he spotted Teddy stopping to buy a newspaper, unfolding it, losing his face in it.

Poor old Teddy, Jeremy thought, chuckling. *A messenger boy turned detective. A jealous husband saddled with a beautiful, somewhat less than moral, wife. What a life his must be!*

At the corner of 57th and Broadway, a few blocks up from the Winter Garden, Jeremy walked up to a shoeshine boy and stood with one foot on his box in front of a large carriage shop.

He got his bluchers shined. Then, taking care to conceal the action with his back to Teddy, he slipped the boy the envelope, a quarter and instructions.

"Give it to the man at the stage door at the Winter Garden Theater. Make sure he puts it into the mail holder. Got that?"

"The Winter Garden. Yes, sir. It's just down the street."

"Don't point! Pay attention. I'm going to walk away now, but don't you head for there until I get out of sight. Wait a good ten minutes, then deliver it. Don't run, just walk. Understand?"

From the look on his face, he did not understand, but the quarter shining in his hand was enough to stifle his curiosity. He promised to do exactly as instructed and Jeremy left him, walking east on 57th Street, leaving the Winter Garden and Myra Vossbacher somewhere off his right shoulder a safe number of blocks away.

How clever, he thought. Inspired! If he could only see the look on Teddy's face.

XXII

Myra reached over her head and, gripping the brass uprights, pulled herself farther up on her pillow, her breasts easing out from under the sheet, exposing themselves entirely. Jeremy lay on his stomach, his handsome features wreathed in amusement, shaking his head in disbelief.

"He kills me, he really does."

"Is that a prophecy?"

"I mean it. How'd you ever get hooked up with him? More important, why do you stay hooked up?"

"Don't be stupid, darling. I'd give my eyeteeth to divorce him. He refuses to let me go. He swears he'll kill me before he'll give me up. He's the most jealous bastard in the Western world, honest to God!"

"Covetous is what he is. I'd sure as hell be covetous, too, if I were married to you, the way you run around."

"I wouldn't if you were my husband."

"Not much. I'll give you some friendly advice, sweetheart. Your Teddy is a dangerous man. He's not kidding when he tells you he'll kill you. And me."

"And six other fellows."

"Bitch!"

She laughed, throwing her head back and shaking the bed beneath them. He pushed her playfully aside and she pushed back, all but sending him off the edge of the bed. They fooled with each other, pushing and pinching, finally ending up in embrace, Jeremy finding her mouth, luxuriating in its warmth and tenderness. Then she broke away, pulling her head back and eying him questioningly.

"You're not living here in this dump, are you?"

"No. I've got a dump uptown."

"Where uptown?"

"Ask Teddy, he's been sticking to me like glue ever since Loomis put him on my trail."

"You'd better be careful with Ned Loomis." She pursed her lips, staring at him gravely and nodding her head. And running her fingers through his blond waves.

"There's no reason to worry about Ned. He gave me a deadline to produce. If that day comes and I can't, then I'll start worrying."

"What deadline? Produce what? What have those two got you tied up in?"

"A business deal."

"What?"

"None of your business. Do you want to make love again? Or no?"

"Of course, silly!" Grabbing his face, she kissed him all over. But this time it was he who pulled free.

"Don't you want to hear how I gave your loving husband the slip?" Without waiting for response, he proceeded to fill her in on the events of the morning. She laughed and laughed, then the anxious look crept back into her eyes.

"I'd still worry about Ned Loomis if I were you, lover."

"I can't be bothered."

Why should he be? Obviously Teddy had run to Loomis and told him that their business partner was back in town and had taken a room on West 96th Street. So what would Ned do? What would he do if he were Ned? Drop up and say hello, possibly. Probably. If and when he did, he'd have to be given a cock-and-bull story as the reason for the delay. Maybe tell him Lisa had gone off, say to England to bring her parents over for the wedding.

"They're very old, Ned. Petrified of traveling alone.

Never been on a ship, you know. So we've pushed the date up to late May. No problem, old man."

Loomis would buy it, he'd have to. At least he wouldn't have to dun old Ned for more money. That would be welcome news to him.

Myra flung her arms limply across his back, tightening her grip on his shoulder and pulling him over again. "Make love to me, Jerry." She picked her watch up off the nearby bedstand. "Twenty minutes, darling. I have to be back at the theater at six sharp. There's a photographer coming, a Mr. Brady."

"If he's good-looking, I'll bet he'll take more than your picture."

She wrinkled her nose witchlike and pulled him down upon her. The fire came fast this time, coursing through his body and filling hers, setting her moaning in anticipation. He made love with his hands and with his mouth, invading the small realms of sensuous delight, teasing her unsparingly. Her moaning grew louder, each sigh sustaining longer than the one previous as the pace of their play accelerated. And very shortly both abandoned the preliminaries altogether in favor of mutual possession.

This was, he assured himself, *this has to be Myra Cummings Vossbacher's greatest role.*

XXIII

Two days later, having gone out for breakfast at the diner on the corner, Jeremy returned to the house to find Ned Loomis sitting on the front steps waiting for him. A folded newspaper was thrust into his jacket pocket, a fat black cigar jammed into his face, his derby off, eyes closed, face raised to the warm April sun.

"Good morning, Ned," said Jeremy amiably.

"Well, well, well, look who's here!"

"I know, a sight for sore eyes, unexpected pleasure, the whole gamut. Come on up."

"With pleasure."

Loomis was puffing like an elephant seal by the time he reached the fifth-floor landing, sweating profusely and fanning himself with his hat.

"Some climb, eh?" remarked Jeremy. "Keeps me in shape."

"I didn't see your name on the mailbox downstairs, Jerry boy."

"It's Fitch. C for Charley Fitch. A name I'm very fond of, Ned. Been using it for years with the ladies."

"Charley Fitch, I must remember that."

Jeremy unlocked the door and ushered Loomis in, indicating the rocking chair.

"This is a coincidence," Jeremy said. "I was just about to run down and pop in on you."

"Sure you were." Loomis eyed him steadily through the haze, the smoke filling the air between them.

"The wedding's been postponed."

"Is that a fact?"

"No big problem. Just for a while."

"What might that be more specifically? Days—weeks?"

"Sometime in May." He began telling him about Lisa's parents, but Loomis cut him off with a wave of his cigar.

"Jerry boy, keep the funny stories for your lady-friends, okay? What I'm interested in is exactly what you're up to. A little bird tells me your wedding's off, dead, down the hole. You, my boy, have loved and come in second."

"That's not true. I'm telling you it's only been postponed."

"That's not what Teddy says. He was standing outside a certain door in a hotel in Baltimore a few days back, his ear glued to the wood. He heard her tell you she's going looking for her husband. Now tell me something, what would the lady want with two husbands?"

"Ned."

"Let's put that aside for a bit. We'll get back to it. Something else has come up, something maybe you haven't heard."

Pulling the newspaper out of his pocket, he unfolded it, laid it on the bed, front page up, and indicated a headline:

BROADWAY ACTRESS KILLED
IN DRESSING ROOM

Myra Cummings Vossbacher, starring in *Cinderella* at the Winter Garden Theater, is dead.

Her husband, Theodore Vossbacher, is charged with first-degree murder.

"Jesus Christ!" whispered Jeremy.

"My very words, Jerry boy."

"He actually did it!"

"So say the cops. Caught him with the revolver smoking in his hand."

Loomis began reading the article aloud, but Jeremy's mind was busy considering another matter, one that appeared invitingly advantageous to him. Teddy was as good as dead. There'd be a trial, of course, the customary routine. It would be guilty, appeal, final judgment, sentencing, a few more weeks—to give the doomed man time to reflect upon the error of his action —and the hood and rope.

Which left this overweight moneylender sitting in his rocking chair attacking the ceiling with great clouds of evil-smelling smoke holding all the strings. Mr. Ned Loomis—the only obstacle in the road ahead. Getting rid of Ross Dandridge would hardly be a problem. There were dozens of possible fatal accidents. It was merely a matter of selection and timing. As far as that went, there was a reasonably good chance Lisa wouldn't even bring him back with her. If the chap Ross was reputedly running with ran true to form, Mr. Dandridge could be out of the picture before she even arrived in Brazil.

Standing over Loomis, he stared down at him babbling on, his eyes captured by the article. Slowly Jeremy eased his way around back of the chair. Shoving both hands forward, he grabbed hold of Loomis's throat. There was a quick sharp gurgling sound and Loomis's cigar fell from his mouth, hit the floor and rolled across it. The sound changed to a steady muted choking, coming from deep down. Tighter and tighter still Jeremy squeezed, tighter, tighter, his fingertips burrowing into the fat flesh, crushing the windpipe, jerking once, twice. Squeezing so tightly that pain shot through his thumbs and fingers. Tighter, tighter. He counted to 30, slowly, deliberately. One last squeeze and jerk and release. He pulled away his hands, Loomis's head fell forward and over he pitched onto the floor with a sound like a heavy sack dropped from the height of the ceiling. Kneeling, Jeremy put his ear to the man's heart. There was no beat. Pulling down one eyelid revealed the white staring blindly, grotesquely. He sucked in his breath and fought off the nausea rising in his stomach. Moving to the window, he opened it wide and looked down. Below was a small yard surrounded by a high wooden fence. Two rust-clad refuse cans stood in one corner, a forlorn-looking rose trellis thrust into the ground at an angle opposite them. He looked around at eye level. Anything landing below could well have been thrown or fallen out of any one of the 40 windows in the buildings surrounding. Still, throwing him down would be unnecessarily risky, particularly in broad daylight.

And there was the chance that Loomis had had a word with the landlady before he himself had come back from breakfast. But that he would have mentioned, and surely wouldn't he have asked why her newest tenant's name wasn't on any of the mailboxes?

He stared at Loomis's body lying belly down, one knee drawn up, the face to one side, the eye staring, the mouth open and twisted ludicrously. Getting him out of the house without being seen would be impossible. Even if he were able to, what then?

Perhaps he wouldn't have to. *He* was the one who ought to be getting out! Leaving Loomis where he lay, Jeremy began packing his things. Moments later, he went out, locking the door, going down the stairs, stopping to take a deep breath at the first landing. He stopped for a second time at Mrs. Harrigan's door. He knocked.

The door opened a crack, then all the way.

"Mr. Fitch?"

"Mrs. Harrigan, I've got to leave town for a few days on business. Philadelphia."

"Philadelphia? My sister lives in Philadelphia. Edna, she's married to a Danish fella'. They have two children, two girls."

"That's nice. Hold my room for me. I'll be back." He handed her a dollar.

"When?"

"Three or four days, no more."

"Very well, sir. Have a nice trip."

"Thank you."

He tipped his hat and was gone, a smile on his face and his chest rapidly filling with the warmth of confidence. If the pigsty she lived in were any indicator of her interest in housekeeping, she wouldn't go near his room for as long as he stayed away. And that could be a full week, since he was now paid up until a week from tomorrow, a Friday.

It would be all the time he needed to find a town and squirrel away until the Dandridges got back.

XXIV

The *Olympia II* drove forward toward the 30th parallel and Bermuda off her starboard bow. The weather was ideal, inspired in its perfection: The wind was hard at work billowing canvas to the tautness of sheet iron, the two blues of sky and sea joined their edges at the horizon, and overhead a brilliant white sun bathed the world.

Lisa had retreated to her cabin shortly after 11 to read a book lent to her by the first mate. With the book came the information that the ship's rate of progress toward distant Pernambuco was holding at near record-breaking speed. The book lent her was Causling's *History of Sail* and in it were three entire chapters devoted to the Dandridge contribution. As she expected, Cyrus was cited as the primary contributor, but both Gray and Ross were mentioned as well as the *Olympia* and *Olympia II*. The author exhibited a dramatic flair, particularly in his descriptions, was refreshingly thorough and consistently generous in his praise.

Lying on her bed fully clothed, she placed the open book facedown on the spread beside her and untethered her thoughts, letting them drift back in time to 16 years earlier and this very cabin in the other *Olympia*. The two ships were virtually identical, but the other had been their lovers' lair on their honeymoon voyage. *Paradise afloat,* she mused.

She closed her eyes and Ross was beside her, lying on his stomach, his leg against hers, his gentle hand gliding over her fevered flesh. Her heart hammered as his fingers found her breast, cupping and caressing; his warm mouth descended, kissing lightly, describing its roundness touch after touch.

They lay upon the spread, his tawny body now juxtaposed against hers full length. White as alabaster was her skin in contrast to his, ignited with a faint pinkish glow. His hands found both her breasts and his kiss traveled from one to the other and back. Fire leaped to life in her loins and she moaned softly, bringing his head up from her breasts, his dark eyes staring, a smile relaxing his face.

And he kissed her, gently, ever gently, always, every movement, every touch gentled with affection. Her body quivered slightly as his lips met hers and the urge to devour him, to encompass his entire body with her own skimmed across the reach of her mind. She wanted him inside her, in her breasts, in her heart, captured and kept, radiating his love, sending it outward to the furthest extremities of her limbs, her mind, and her consciousness.

"I could eat you alive," she whispered huskily.

"I could let you, want you to. And be a living part of you forever," he said quietly. "What could be more wonderful? I love you, my darling. I adore you. You are the prism of my life. Everything I see, everything I hear and feel comes through you, is beautified through you."

"Love me, my darling."

Slowly, gently their bodies entwined, locking in sublime embrace, loins to loins, fire to fire, the maelstrom of passion sweeping forward, bursting the causeway of their volition, flooding the plains of their desire. And silently the cabin exploded, flaring into a blossom of blazing gold, consuming them in ecstasy.

Sighing, opening her eyes, Lisa glanced about, her attention drawn to the large unlit copper lamp swinging lazily overhead in awkward rhythm with the groaning of the ship. The cabin had a low ceiling and was small but, like its counterpart in its sister vessel, was strikingly well-furnished. The walls were paneled in rosewood richly ornamented with imitation inlaid gold. The ceiling surrounding the lamp was ivory, white-framed with handsomely wrought molding with gilded beads. An overstuffed chair with stout mahogany legs to match the sideboard and the bedstead occupied a corner alongside a lowboy, which was attached, as was the sideboard, to the wall to prevent movement in the event of heavy seas.

Stretching her limbs and closing her eyes, she dispatched her imagination to the earlier setting, to Ross, the two of them lying on this very bed making passionate love. The beginning, eagerly accepting his mouth with her own, their naked flesh tingling, touching, sealing in embrace, his desire to possess her so manifest. Now his gentle, loving hands exploring her body; his mouth finding her breast. A surge of fire raced through her thrusting its heat to every extremity. Another long, passionate kiss, soul seizing, beautiful beyond description. Then the fire drawing itself back, as a magnet draws filings, collecting itself in one enormous ember, filling her heart, setting it pounding furiously, like the bell of a steeple locked in her breast. His fire and her own merged, their bodies joining in the act and the beginning of the glorious celebration of the senses.

She smiled inwardly as she remembered how he had tried to define the height to which together they had risen. To the heavens beyond the stars, back of the stars. To infinity and beyond, to a place where time and space and all experience other than love's were outdistanced. Beyond all worlds, all eternity, beyond imagination. Into the universe of the heart.

"Ross, Ross, I love you. I adore you. I hunger for you. I am coming, my darling. Soon, very soon."

Then suddenly, unexpected, she could no longer tolerate sight of the cabin and its all-too-familiar furnishings without his presence. Getting up, she wrapped her shoulders in her shawl and went out on deck. Heavy of heart almost to the point of tears, she leaned against the rail and let the wind whip her hair playfully, loosening it with her fingers and turning her face to the breeze. It was so clean, so refreshing, so comfortably cool until it stripped a lacy tangle of spume from the sea, flinging it down the line of the ship. A few of the loosed beads struck her, chilling her face like icy darts. She turned from the rail, looked up, shading her sight from the glare of the sun, watched the skysails, fore and main, race across the heavens like clouds scudding to keep pace with the ship and marveled at the masts that connected deck and sky.

"Morning again, ma'am."

It was the first mate, a short, blocky man with a gracious smile stretching across his well-weathered face. The cleft in his chin was so deep that she fancied he could hold a pea in it, had such a thought ever occurred to him. And the furrows of his cheeks and forehead were just as deep. Yet he couldn't be very old; his eyes, the manner in which he moved, his quickness of mind and body supported her judgment that he was not yet 40.

"Mr. Guilfoyle. Isn't this the loveliest day you've ever seen?"

"The loveliest wind," he replied. "Just about perfect. Steady enough for good speed without bullying the sails." He glanced skyward, then back to her eyes. "It doesn't seem to be impressing your fellow passengers, though. You're the only one out."

"Perhaps they're poor sailors."

"Miss Osborne, the schoolmarm, hasn't been out of her cabin these three days except for meals."

"She may not be feeling well."

"It's hard to tell. She's not exactly naturally rosy-cheeked."

Lisa laughed, recalling Miss Osborne seated at the captain's table at breakast. A woman past 60, decidedly prim and disturbingly proper. She didn't like this, she didn't like that, she didn't like just about anything her senses put her in contact with. The food was somewhat poorer than she was used to, she had confided to Lisa, which Lisa took to mean inedible. The woman's cabin was stifling during the day and freezing at night. The lighting was inadequate for reading, and dozens of other things, each less significant than the previous one, were a disappointment. Still, Lisa could sympathize with her. To be a poor sailor and be stuck on a ship for almost two weeks, with no relief from the rolling, from the wind, from the weather's capricious tyranny, and with the inescapable fear of drowning holding court in the kingdom of the mind, must be far from enjoyable. But commiserating with her was becoming a conscious effort, inasmuch as all Miss Osborne did was complain. She was on her way to a teaching position in Pernambuco. Portuguese was her second language; biology her first love; travel by sea, her major hate.

There were two other passengers: a Congregational minister on his way to visit his son, a missionary in Sertania, some 170 miles inland from Pernambuco, and a dealer in "international exchange," a pompous, middle-aged gentleman from Baltimore. The minister, the Reverend Thomas Nesmith, was a sick man. Sitting opposite him at the captain's table, Lisa guessed that his liver was failing him, letting down the rest of his body, draining him of his resistance and his will to continue. His skin was a pale dry-mustard color, his lips thin and bloodless, his eyes rheumy. It appeared to be an effort for him to eat, and when anything came to mind worth voicing, it came from his mouth in halting tones. Nevertheless, he tried his utmost to be gracious and friendly to everyone, his smile ready, his eyes jewels of kindness when he spoke from his heart. *A sensitive and con-*

siderate soul, Lisa decided. *One accustomed to pleasing others, even if the effort strained his own capacities.*

The other man, Clyde Buckshaw, was a vigorous, insufferably garrulous glad-hander, a born peddler and proud of it to the point of haughtiness. Meal after meal he sought to dominate the conversation, but his fund of funny stories was fast running out and his ability at meaningful conversation, subjects requiring a suggestion of knowledge and intelligence in discussion, seemed woefully lacking. All paint and no structure was the way Cyrus Dandridge would have described Mr. Buckshaw.

Four decidedly different types, the passengers of the Olympia II, thought Lisa, as Mr. Guilfoyle rambled on about each of them—excepting his listener.

Lisa liked Mr. Guilfoyle. He was pleasant and charming, a perfect gentleman, and he was proving her most enthusiastic morale booster. Every opinion he offered, every view she solicited from him, was optimistic. The ship would arrive in Pernambuco well ahead of schedule, long before the *Crown Pearl,* giving Lisa all the time she'd need to prepare to meet her husband.

"Is there," she asked, "the vaguest possible chance that they'll bypass Pernambuco and go straight down to Cape Horn?"

"That's very unlikely for a steamer," responded Guilfoyle. "From Norfolk to port is well over four thousand miles. That takes a lot of coal. And the run from Recife——"

"From where?"

"The Brazilians call Pernambuco Recife. Only we foreigners still say Pernambuco. But from there down the east coast to Drake Passage and Cape Horn is better than another four thousand. I can't believe they'll pass port when the next coal is way out in the Pacific."

"We ought to have passed them by now, shouldn't we?"

"We probably did, but too far away to see them. Or

even last night when a fog lay over the water like a wall, you remember. It was so thick that even if we passed within three hundred yards we wouldn't have seen her running lights."

They talked on and presently the ship's cook showed his leathery face at the head of the after companionway, ringing the bell for lunch and retreating.

Captain Hughes was the offspring of a Welsh father and a Swedish mother. His father's influence was conspicuous by its nonexistence, not only in the captain's Nordic appearance but in the singsong character of his voice and the manner in which he curled his tongue back toward the center of his mouth and accented the first syllable of most of his words.

Lunch was mock turtle soup, a salad and a *torte*, with freshly-baked bread for those at the table who required more fuel for the afternoon journey to dinner. The soup was tasty. Lisa was unable to resist flashing a look at Miss Osborne. If she liked the soup or disliked it, there was no clue in her expression. For all her complaining, however, she did not look ill. Equally obviously the Reverend Nesmith did not look well, but Clyde Buckshaw consumed his food with the heartiness and dispatch of a starving lumberjack.

"What is our position now, Captain?" inquired Miss Osborne, aiming her pince-nez at Captain Hughes.

"Roughly a thousand miles east of the Grand Bahamas. By this time tomorrow, the Turks and Caicos Islands should be standing off our starboard beam."

"The tail end of the ship, Miss O.," offered Buckshaw. "Bow, beam, starboard, larboard or port."

"Do you travel by ship very often, Mr. Buckshaw?" asked the Reverend Nesmith.

"All over the world, padre. Been across the Pacific a dozen times. International exchange is really international money exchange, except money's a dirty word to some folks. But the international part is just what it implies: the whole bloody world. I love the sea and love to fish. I've caught record-breakers in my time. I once hooked a swordfish thirteen feet, six inches long, weighing three hundred and fifty-two pounds. It's still the record for swordfish off Montauk Point, Long Island— probably the world's record. Had him mounted, naturally. He hangs over my fireplace back home in Baltimore. Takes up practically the whole width of the wall. The missus can't stand the sight of him, but I can't see taking him down and burying him in the cellar just to satisfy her. I mean, a man has few enough outstanding accomplishments in life without burying them out of sight of his friends and admirers."

With a firm hold on his listeners, Mr. Buckshaw tested their attention by shifting subjects with lightning speed. From swordfishing to gardening to tips on selecting diamonds to the financial problems of the city of Baltimore to the Jews. There was little of substance in anything he had to say, but his manner of speaking, his enthusiasm and blatant self-assurance compensated for that deficiency—*at least in Mr. Buckshaw's view*, thought Lisa. Somehow he got onto the subject of marriage and the string of broken hearts he had left in his wake on the way to the altar with the present Mrs. Clyde Buckshaw. Lisa's thoughts went back to Jeremy in the hotel room, his surprisingly generous attitude, his carefree manner disguising his understandable disappointment—the good loser personified. She couldn't help continuing to feel sorry for him and found herself wishing with all her heart that she might do something to help him rid his mind of her. In another two weeks, they would have been man and wife—less, ten days. Lucky for everyone that Middleton's letter had arrived when it did.

She wondered if Jeremy was still taking it well, or if, in the aftermath of her announcement, separated from her, alone and prey to sober second thoughts, he was becoming bitter. Confirmation of that was locked in the future. She and Ross would not be back in Providence before the end of the month at the earliest. In the interim, Jeremy would have plenty of time to get over her. Hopefully he'd meet somebody who could help him. His cousin Emily was bright, perceptive. She'd recognize his need and do everything she could to help him meet somebody new.

The love Lisa had held for Jeremy had fled her heart much faster than it had arrived. News of Ross had pushed it out, almost bodily, the way a barman pushes an unwanted patron out the door. It had never come to a question of choice; there could be none, not even if Middleton's letter had arrived three times three years late. Still, if she and Jeremy had gotten married and in time had had a child, things would have become discouragingly complicated.

He had never discussed the other women in his life with her beyond mentioning, rather resignedly, that his wife had died. A pity she couldn't come back the way Ross had. Jeremy must have loved her dearly, must have taken her loss very much to heart to stay a widower so long.

"Ladies and gentlemen, I have an announcement of some importance," said Captain Hughes. His tone seemed reserved, almost apologetic, as if he were reluctant to open the subject. Everyone at the table perked to attention, except Buckshaw who reacted somewhat miffed at the captain's interruption. The eyes of the others showed gratitude, appreciation for being rescued from Buckshaw's boring recitation of his business successes.

"As you know, we are sailing into waters east of the Indies," began the captain. "The wind is up, the sky clear, the sea quite ordinary for this area. But all morning long the barometer has been falling."

Miss Osborne's fork fell down upon her half-eaten *torte* and she blanched, her eyes seemingly increasing half again in diameter.

"That means we're going to have a storm, doesn't it? It does!"

"Possible dirty weather, yes."

It was a term, Lisa knew, that covered a multitude of degrees of ferocity, everything from a harmless rain squall lasting ten minutes or less to a full-scale hurricane generating waves 60 and 70 feet high.

"We seem to be making excellent time," said Buckshaw. "Can't you get us out of its way?"

The captain smiled tolerantly. "That might not be possible. Of course if it's small, we can slip by it easily. On the other hand, if it's two hundred miles wide——"

"If we have to, can't we put into the nearest port and wait it out?" asked Miss Osborne anxiously.

Hughes shook his lanate head. "We're a good five hundred miles from the nearest island; farther from the mainland." He paused and looked from one to the other around the table. "Believe me, I don't want to upset you. And there's no cause for alarm. All I want is for you to be aware that the glass is dropping and take the necessary precautions, prepare yourselves for a bit of a blow."

"How in the world?" began Miss Osborne. The Reverend Nesmith's hand on her arm stopped her.

Hughes continued. "If and when something starts up, I would like you all to confine yourselves to your quarters. Your meals will be brought to you. Keep your porthole glass closed and fast. Don't open your doors for anything except the man bringing your food. He'll knock and identify himself. And be prepared for heavy seas. The ship will pitch and roll. You'll swear the bow is going straight to the bottom or we're going to tip over, keel to the clouds. But nothing like that will happen. I've been master of this vessel for eleven years. I've seen big storms and bigger ones, but this old girl can stand up to the worst of the lot. We've lost a spar or two in my time, but we've never been in serious danger of going down. I might add, in case you're not aware of it, your fellow passenger Mrs. Dandridge is the wife of the man who built the *Olympia II*. I'm sure she'll vouch for its seaworthiness."

"I will indeed," said Lisa.

XXV

The barometer continued to fall and concern appeared on the faces of the seamen. The ship pushed on, running its southeasterly course, plowing a furrow of whiteness free of the blue water. The wind held steady, corrugating the surface of the water, bearding the waves and laboriously shaping hills and valleys. As the afternoon crept forward, the rich, smoky-sapphire color of the water gave way to pewter—as if the blueness, the sea's blood, were deserting it, settling to the bottom and leaving it as lifeless as a corpse. The sun, as white and lustrous as a Lingah pearl, hung in the West. Its rays retracted, but it continued to emit its oppressive heat, glaring menacingly as it lowered, shrinking into itself, its light increasing in intensity in what appeared to be one final burst of luminescence before dying. Presently it sank in a dark coppery glow.

Watching at the starboard rail in company with Miss Osborne, whom she had persuaded to come out on deck with her, Lisa speculated that it was the last she would ever see of the sun. It was, she thought, expiring for all time, losing itself forever in the sea. Directly above it lay a slender bank of clouds stretching across the distant Caribbean like an immense gray stole. A different shade of gray than that afflicting the sea, infinitely darker, more sullen than sinister-looking. At its distant end, the cloud bank cornered, reaching around the bow of the ship like a bully's arm thrust out to stop his victim in the street. The bow dipped and rose, carving the ocean in two, driving straight for the angled end of the cloud.

Twilight ignited the sky, transforming it into an inverted orange bowl pouring its light down upon the ship. Miss Osborne had little to say beyond repeatedly observing that they were "in for it" and that if Captain Hughes knew what he was doing, he would turn the ship to the left at once and get them out of the path of the oncoming storm.

"I don't think he could get out of its way if he tried," said Lisa resignedly. "That cloud is moving very fast. There must be a heavy gale behind it. It seems to me he's trying to get across its front before it gets to us."

Miss Osborne sniffed impatiently and indicated the arm across their bow. "We're heading directly for it!"

"Yes, but perhaps he feels that end of it won't be as bad as the full brunt."

"We shall see." The older woman consulted her watch depending from a silver chain around her neck. "Twenty past six. I believe I shall take his advice and lock myself in my cabin. You might consider doing likewise. It may be cramped and stifling, but at least it will spare us sight of that evil-looking cloud."

Excusing herself, she walked off talking to herself, upbraiding herself for leaving Baltimore in the first place, for giving up her old job and running off to "of all places, Brazil!"—and subjecting herself to this nerve-racking ordeal in the process.

Lisa stayed at the rail, fascinated by the changes coming over the world, the sea, the sun, the cloud rushing at them. It began to get dark, the hell light overhead yielding to night. On the cloud came, banishing the glow, a swarm of stars adorning its menacing blackness. However they neither shimmered nor sparkled, but glowed dully, like stars cut out of tin and stuck to a scenery flat in a stage play. A stillness at once curious and ominous captured the air, a transparent curtain wrapping the ship in its folds. She trembled slightly, giving it up on the spot, telling herself with macabre humor that she simply wasn't up to witnessing the end of the world. She had started down the deck toward her cabin. Mr. Guilfoyle coming the other way hailed her.

"I'm going," she said with a smile, anticipating his advice.

"It looks like we're in for it," he said soberly. "Just lock yourself in, grab hold of something and hang on."

"Will it be that bad?"

"It's showing all the signs of a hurricane."

"That's bad," she said bluntly.

Locking herself in, she checked both portholes, secured their latches and parted the diminutive drapes, enabling her to watch the arrival of the storm. Presently the sea came to life, the monster in it roused, going into its labors, pushing up mountainous waves. The stars slid up the glass, the sea—gone from pewter to black—followed, filling the roundness of the porthole, the cabin tilting sharply.

Failing to anticipate the floor dropping from under her feet, Lisa was thrown against the door, reeling back from it seconds later and thrust bodily to the opposite wall. Hanging onto the lowboy, she watched the stars return, then the sea displace them as before, up and down, up and down, until a queasy feeling found the pit of her stomach. Hesitating, waiting for the stars to reappear, she then raced five steps up the angled floor to the porthole, seized the latch to keep from falling back with the roll of the ship and closed the drapes with her free hand. Making her way back to the lowboy, she sat on the edge of the bed, hung on for dear life and watched Causling's *History of Sail* slide back and forth across the floor in her stead.

The ship creaked and groaned in its travail. The roar of the waves flinging themselves over the decks became deafening. The rain arrived, an almost instantaneous deluge, combining with the wind-loosened spray to thrash and drench the helpless vessel. The monster in the sea responded to the challenge of the storm, thrusting its black peaks against the now starless firmament and gouging the troughs deeper and deeper yet.

It was as if the ship were a seed afloat in an inch of water in the middle of an enormous bowl that was suddenly subjected to inundation from all sides, an inrush of water hammering down upon it, concentrating its fury upon it, determined to submerge it. This was ostensibly punishment for the ship's audacity in insinuating its presence upon the vast circle of the sea. A tiny man-fashioned alien thing with no more right nor necessity for being there than a gnat on the back of one's hand.

Fear clenched her heart as the pounding increased, ringing in her ears. And over the pounding screamed the voices of the suffering ship, like strings and reeds shrilling above the tympanies in some great cosmic symphony. And the frailty of human judgment, the uselessness of experience, came home to her as she recalled Captain Hughes's words of assurance hours earlier, his well-intentioned claim that they had nothing to fear from "dirty weather."

Closing her eyes, she envisioned the destruction of the ship. Under the brutal assault of wind and water, those sails not yet furled would be first to go, shred to ribbons. Lines would part, down would come yards and spars, and the masts would crack and collapse, smashing against the deck.

The waves would punish the hull with cataclysmic fury, sledging it until the weakest timber yielded. Others around it would quickly give, cracking, shattering, creating a hole gaping at the sea, a mouth to engorge the next wave as the bow dipped, the sprit spearing the water. In would rush the sea, bringing tons of dead weight, pulling the ship lower and lower until the water leveled the decks or until the bow was pulled under by the monster, taking everything and everyone to the bottom.

She thought of Ross and the *Crown Pearl* steaming

along the identical route. Was a metal ship any less vulnerable in such a storm? No canvas to rip, no masts to fall, no timbers to shiver and collapse. But iron could buckle and give, and rivets could pop, opening yawning holes. And yet at only eight knots an hour, the *Crown Pearl* must still be well north of the hurricane's front, not yet nearing its leading edge. Of course the storm could conceivably shift direction and head up the Atlantic seaboard. Hurricanes, she knew, rarely held to projected courses.

Dear darling Ross; she prayed that he was all right and would continue so until she found him. In Pernambuco? Arrival there seemed less and less likely with every passing minute. The savagery of the attack had yet to define its limits, the storm growing more furious, more powerful by the minute. It had become a struggle between the storm's controlling monster and the monster of the depths. The hurricane exploded around the ship with a concussion that wrenched it about, pivoting it on its keel, spinning it like a maple seed pod, dropping it, lifting its stern, holding it aloft for a breath before plunging it down into the sea. The wind was a force flung up from hell bent on destroying the *Olympia* piece by piece, life by life. It roiled the sea, assaulting it, ripping sheets of water from it, hurling them about the arena of its influence. And in its center, ever in its center, anchored there by the elements, the battered ship clung precariously to life, its officers, crew and passengers waiting for deliverance—or for the end, whichever Almighty God had planned for them. The madness of the wind, its calculated rage, its monomaniacal determination to destroy the ship imbued it with something akin to mortal intelligence. A human being gone berserk, annihilating the object of its wrath.

The *Olympia* was doomed, Lisa decided, gradually being pushed beyond its capacity to endure, on the verge of surrendering to its attacker and retreating beneath the waves. There was no defense, no escape, no path of flight beckoning. Suddenly the cabin was a tomb, a vault imprisoning her for all eternity. Down would go the ship and down would go all those who had locked themselves in. And yet outside on the deck, she could be swept away in seconds. If only she could get to a life-boat and with someone's help free it from its davits!

Then what? Go down with *it* instead of the ship? Where was the choice there? Which would it be then, stay in the cabin or go outside? There was no time to argue the merits of one over the other. She made her decision, out she would go. Hurriedly strapping on her life jacket, she reached for the door.

She paused with both hands on the latches. On the other side lay certain death; inside it was just as certain. Was there any difference? If there were, it lay in the element of confrontation: in electing to fight for one's life, to go down fighting, however futile the effort might prove. If, she assured herself, there were to be two survivors, she would be one!

Pulling down both latches, she swung the door wide and started out. A wave careened against the ship below the railing, a sheet of spume tearing free of it and drenching her completely. Salt water filled her ears, nose and mouth. Its force staggered her, sending her bumping down the side of the cabin, her progress finally arrested by the ladder to the wheelhouse. Masses of water swirled and swept across the deck; fragments of the sea loosened by the wind whipped up heaps of foam. A sound like thunder exploded only yards away, battering her eardrums and triggering momentary pain. A wave had struck the bow full force, lifting it clear. The sea rushed in under it, creating a rise where there had been none, forcing the ship to climb it, clear it and drop sharply down the other side.

The eyeless phantom of night hovered overhead cloaking the spectacle, concealing it from divine view. Through the sheets of water flailing the deck, Lisa made out two men forward, one struggling with the other, trying his utmost to pull him back to the cover of the companionway. The man resisting seemed to have lost all control, jerking about and waving his arms crazily. As she watched the two, she could see blood flowering at the side of his head, streaming down his neck. As if discovering their presence, a wave fully 60 feet high, foam dancing along its crest, poised briefly over the two of them. In the next instant, it hurtled forward and crashed down upon the foredeck, carrying across it and rejoining the sea on the other side. It took both men with it, without outcry, without either one even aware of its approach.

She gasped and turned away. Had she been stupid to leave her cabin? Had her courage been fool's courage? The way the waves were sweeping over the ship, one would need eyes in the back of his head to see and dodge one, then a second one building and piling down behind him all but simultaneously. One glance at the mountains bearing down upon the vessel from all sides and she resolved to make her way back to the cabin. Once more she would lock herself in and pray to God that the ship might somehow, by some miracle, survive.

Letting go of the ladder railing, she started back, glancing apprehensively over her shoulder, hoping she could reach the door before another wave struck midships and engulfed her. But like help, luck when most needed is luck that is late arriving or never comes at all. A wave broke over the bow, sending a flood rushing down the decks, knocking her legs out from under her. Down she went, her body buffeted across the deck, her limbs flung out like a rag doll's, her head striking the railing post. The water closed over her, filling her nose and mouth and cutting off her breath, encasing her in the inky chrysalis of unconsciousness broken only by a crimson flare pulsing through her brain.

XXVI

She awoke to a horrendous splintering sound. She was lying in her bed, the copper lamp overhead swinging all the way to the left, banging against the ceiling and seemingly sticking there as the ship rolled. Buckshaw was sitting on the edge of the bed leaning over her, his eyes anxious, a sodden handkerchief in his hand. He patted her forehead with it and trembled nervously.

"Are you all right?"

Again the loud splintering sound.

"What's that?"

"It's under us. I'm afraid it's the hull. The ship is going down. We've got to get out of here!"

He shot to his feet and she saw that his life jacket and white cotton suit were wringing wet. His shirt was drenched, his pink, hairless chest clearly visible through the weave. She raised herself on one elbow, then the other. But the effort made her dizzy, the cabin whirled and she sank back down onto her pillow.

"I can't seem to."

"Let me help. I examined your head. It's just a bump. I don't think there's any fracture."

The instant that the last word was out of his mouth they heard a crackling sound overhead, like firecrackers exploding in brief series, so loudly that her hands flew to her ears. A mast came crashing down upon the line of cabins, buckling the corner of the ceiling and the walls supporting it. Instinctively Buckshaw threw his body over hers protectively. Then slowly lifted himself from her. Taking her hands in his, he pressed them encouragingly though his eyes were wide with dread.

"Missed by a mile."

"We really must get out of here!" she exclaimed.

"Let's go."

He helped her to her feet and together they made for the door. But the impact of the falling mast had crushed the top of it, the weight locking it securely in place. His right foot against the jamb, Buckshaw tugged at the door, but it was useless.

"We need something to pry it!" he rasped, looking about. "A crowbar, a pipe, anything."

She flew to the lowboy and jerked open one drawer after another, searching them hurriedly.

"Anything!" he repeated, continuing to strain at the upper latch.

She found nothing. Rising from a crouch, she turned toward him gesturing helplessly.

"Damn! Come help me. Grab the lower one."

She strained with all her might, but the door refused to budge. Outside the waves continued their relentless onslaught and the ominous sound of cracking timbers could be heard. Then luck, tardy and wholly unexpected, arrived. A wave swept over the port side and carried away the broken mast. Relieved of the weight, the door sprang open.

They rushed outside, Buckshaw flattening himself against the side of the cabin and holding her in the same position with his forearm.

The sea spread waveless before them under the pressure of a violent gale. Then it raised itself, coming straight at them, overwhelming the ship, lathering it white from prow to taffrail. Having started forward, they slipped behind the wheelhouse ladder, permitting it to break the full force of the wave, and managed to keep their feet. They gazed in wonderment as the foam whipped up by the roiling water began receding, revealing battened companions, the tops of covered winches, the bases of broken masts with their clutches of splinters thrusting skyward, hatch tops and the drumhead and sockets of the anchor capstan.

Downship three crewmen and the Reverend Nesmith, Miss Osborne and Mr. Guilfoyle were crowded about a lifeboat. The first mate and one of the men labored feverishly over the two belaying pins holding fast the davit lines. As Lisa and Buckshaw looked on, the ship shuddered and a great rumbling sound was heard. It was the water flooding the hull, surging forward, bringing the bow down under and holding it there.

"We're going down! We're going down!" shouted Buckshaw.

They started toward the lifeboat but stopped suddenly as a wave came careening over the rail, sweeping across the ship, deluging the six people, setting them scrambling for their lives.

The water receded, revealing the five men regaining their feet. Miss Osborne lay crumpled in a heap against the near davit. Lisa squinted through a shower of spray and made out Guilfoyle down on one knee beside the woman, lifting her, cradling her upper body in his arms. Her head lolled at an unnatural angle and, aghast, Lisa turned from the grisly sight.

"Broken neck!" shouted Buckshaw over the noise of the raging storm. Lisa glanced quickly around the doomed vessel. The bow had leveled off, but any moment now, she knew, the hull would refill and pull her back down. Perhaps this time never to rise again. All four masts were down and swept away, taking yards, booms and gaffs with them. From sprit to stern, the storm monster had plundered the helpless ship. Captain Hughes and the rest of the crew were nowhere to be seen and the chilling conviction that all had been trapped below deck sent a tremor across her shoulders.

"We've got to get down there!" roared Buckshaw. "It's our only chance. Are you game?"

She nodded, fighting off her dizziness, watching

Guilfoyle let go of Miss Osborne and cross himself. Gripping Lisa's hand, Buckshaw grinned.

"Here goes nothing!"

They ran for the boat, sloshing through water up to their knees, the leavings of the last wave that had collected along the deck by the cabins in a trough created by the angle of the ship. Now, as the ship rolled back the other way, the water flooded across into the scuppers.

They were only halfway to the lifeboat when another wave hit, coming down upon Lisa and Buckshaw like a dam breaking above their heads. They clung to the railing, Lisa wrapping one arm about it and ducking her head, balling her body tightly. The driving force of the wave nearly wrenched both of her arms from their sockets, and by the time the water fell away and she could catch her breath, she felt more drowned than alive—and she was certain beyond doubt that she hadn't enough strength left to take another such battering. Pulling herself to her feet, she glanced about. Buckshaw, too, had survived—barely. A piece of a boom nearly eight feet long had come tumbling down from the ship's superstructure and had landed across his legs.

"My ankles. I think they're broken." His teeth were clenched so tightly that the muscles of his jaw were all but bursting from the flesh. She scrambled to him, lifting the length of boom free. Down the deck, they spied Guilfoyle releasing one of the davit lines and the stern of the lifeboat dropping sharply.

He was alone. Apparently the wave had swept the Reverend Nesmith and the three crewmen overboard. Lisa gasped, sucked her lungs full of air, steeled herself and ran to help him. Buckshaw crawled after her, pulling himself down the deck.

"Good girl!" shouted Guilfoyle. "Loosen the tarp if you can and get in! Get in!"

"We've got to help Buckshaw. His legs."

"I'm all right!" snapped the older man behind them. "I can make it. Just get it down!"

They were in luck. While Guilfoyle eased the bow-line down, Lisa untied the tarpaulin, flung it back and clambered into the boat. The lowering level of the ship shortened the distance down and prevented the stern of the lifeboat from going under. She helped Buckshaw aboard. The man's homely face was ashen; his flaccid mouth was contorted with pain. And his hands were bloodied.

Down came the bow and Guilfoyle jumped, plunging into the water alongside, surfacing, whipping the water from his face with a jerk of his head and climbing into the boat.

"We've got to get clear of the side!" he shouted. "She's going down, and she'll suck us with her if we don't get away!"

Snatching up an oar, he shoved it at Buckshaw, who was sitting in the bottom of the boat gingerly massaging his injured ankles. All three of them jammed the tips of their oar blades against the side of the ship and pushed away, then hurriedly locked their oars and began rowing. Guilfoyle held the tiller back with one foot, steering them away from the ship.

By the beneficence of Providence, they escaped another wave until they were some 30 feet clear of the hull. Then suddenly the sea drove straight upward under their boat, lifting it well above the floundering ship and slinging it across the deck in a welter of foam far beyond the starboard side. It came to rest, rocking crazily, threatening to fill and go down. Water sloshed in, building to the gunwales, but gradually the boat came to rest. Lisa and Guilfoyle snatched buckets out from under the stern seat and bailed frantically. Buckshaw had lapsed into unconsciousness. He lay in the bottom of the boat, water swirling about him, his face barely clearing it, his eyes tightly closed.

"Is he dead, do you think?" she asked in a tremulous voice.

"No, but he's badly hurt. Let him be for now. Keep bailing."

Their unexpected flight over the ship, as terrifying as it may have been, proved to be their salvation. Within seconds, the *Olympia II* threw her stern skyward into the teeth of the storm in a final gesture of defiance, then slipped bow first beneath the waves, actuating a violent whirlpool and a snowy froth that gradually flattened and blended with the rolling black surface of the sea.

And their lifeboat started down an apparently endless valley between two waves peaking so high that their crests were lost in the darkness, the mammoth walls on either side threatening to close and fold them between.

XXVII

Lavinia's mind was awake, clear and at work before her eyes opened. Sunrise was moments away as she stretched, stifled a yawn and arose from the bed, leaving Enrico snoring serenely against his pillow. Quietly and speedily she made her toilet, and as the sun came up, setting the dew glistening across the grass at the front of the house, she took a last look at Enrico, satisfied herself that a barrage of mortars couldn't awaken him and went upstairs to Philomena's room.

She would discuss the situation with the traitorous bitch one more time, appeal to her sense of loyalty, overcome her with kindness, feign penitence, trot out all her gifts of persuasion.

To her surprise, Philomena appeared at the door fully dressed, a straw hat perched at an absurd angle on her head, tied under her chin with a green ribbon. But for the hat, anyone passing by at that moment might well have wondered who was mistress and who servant, so supercilious was Philomena's bearing upon seeing who was at her door. Lavinia looked past her to the unmade bed, upon it a large, maltreated-looking portmanteau packed and standing beside a suitcase bound with two ropes.

"You're not leaving!" exclaimed Lavinia, affecting disappointment.

"I was just coming down," interrupted Philomena, "to tell you."

"But you can't leave. You wouldn't!"

Philomena's slender jaw jutted forward belligerently and her eyes narrowed. "There is no point in discussing it. We both made our true feelings known yesterday. For me to stay in this house is impossible."

Lavinia acted crestfallen. "Can't we at least talk?" she asked in a subdued tone.

Philomena shrugged. "If you feel you must." She stood aside and gestured her into the room. "But my mind is made up."

Lavinia gazed at her with a look of pained sorrow, the sort a child bestows upon a broken favorite toy.

"I know how you must feel, Philomena. And I can't blame you. I'm not going to try to talk you into or out of anything. I only want to apologize."

"There's no need."

"There is. I must. It's all my fault." She smiled wistfully in an appeal for sufferance. "I said things yesterday that were spiteful and cruel. I was frightened, you see, unnerved—frantic actually." She stared at the floor. "What I did was unforgivable, but my husband, that dear good soul——"

"I am really not interested, *Signora*. Your and the *signor*'s marital problems are no concern of mine."

A barb, but Lavinia let it pass.

"I feel so awful about it. Is it possible you can find it in your heart to forgive me? My insults, my shrewish behavior?"

"I forgive." It was said with little conviction, more like mere acknowledgment voiced in the hope of putting a quick end to the matter.

"Can't we erase yesterday? Can't we pretend we never spoke? I want to so very much, Philomena."

"You know that's impossible."

"Is there nothing I can say to change your mind? My dear, we've been together four long years. Happy, wonderful years."

"Five next month. But that's all in the past, *Signora*. I have to look to the future. After yesterday, how can things ever be right again between us?" Having retrieved her crucifix, she fingered it at her breastbone. "I could never feel—comfortable. Could you?"

"Perhaps not, but that doesn't mean we shouldn't at least try."

"*Signora*, if the *signor* chooses to—how shall I say?—overlook your indiscretion, he will feel as uneasy with me around as you would. Nor would I want to be the cause of any friction between him and his mother."

"But she'll be angry with you for leaving."

"She will understand. That woman is a saint. She has treated me like her own daughter." Again her fingers went to the crucifix, demanding attention for it.

"*Signora* Aldoni is one in a thousand, so sweet, so considerate," said Lavinia. "Still, my dear, she is not your employer. She has no say over the goings on in this house."

"Whether she does or not. . . ." Philomena hesitated as if, Lavinia surmised, debating her decision, re-examining it. When she resumed, her tone had become almost conciliatory. "I am sorry for my part in what happened in this room between us. But who's right and who's wrong doesn't matter now. I must go. I have to."

Lavinia's shoulders sagged. There was a long moment of silence. "If that's what you want. But not right away, please. You must wait a moment."

"For what?"

"I have something I want to give you."

"There's no need."

"Please, a favor for me. For old time's sake."

Philomena stared, her eyes glistening in triumph. Lavinia held up one hand in a silent plea for her to remain and went out and back down to her bedroom. Enrico was still snoring, clutching his pillow, his body tangled in the bedclothes. Ignoring him, she puttered stealthily about the room, paused, ruminated, came to a decision and going to her armoire swung open both doors. Examining her gowns and dresses, quick-handing her way down the line, she selected a lovely creation of

Chinese painted silk with a gold-gauze collar and midriff and a *robe à la française* of yellow flowered silk.

A dress over each arm, she went back upstairs.

At sight of them, Philomena gasped. "Your most beautiful dresses!" Her eyes sparkled as she looked from one to the other.

"Your favorites!" exclaimed Lavinia.

"Signora."

"I want you to have them both."

Philomena caught her breath, one hand going to her face to clasp her jaw in disbelief.

"I couldn't!"

"I insist."

"You are too generous. For me to take them——"

Lavinia cut her short. "You're not taking them, I'm giving them to you. It's the least I can do."

Philomena hesitated, torn, her face aglow with admiration and appetency for the dresses. Laying them down, Lavinia opened the portmanteau and, folding first one then the other neatly, put them into it, closed the latch and turned back to Philomena. There were tears in Philomena's eyes and her face had softened considerably.

"You are too kind, *Signora.*" Impulsively she took Lavinia's hands and bussed her on the cheek. Lavinia threw her arms around her, hugging her.

"Good-bye, dearest Philomena. I shall miss you dreadfully."

"I will miss you."

"Please remember, the door is always open, if ever you change your mind."

Philomena nodded. "Thank you."

"Let me call the *carrozza* boy for you."

"I would appreciate it."

"And before you go, you must have a bite of break-fast."

"I'm not hungry."

"Not even coffee?"

"No, thank you." Her tone had become chastened and her eyes still glittered with tears.

"Whatever you say." Lavinia snapped her fingers, remembering. "There's something else you must have before you go. A letter of reference. I'll go down to the study and write one immediately. Just a few lines to persuade your next employer that she'll be getting an absolute gem, the most marvelous maid on Capri. You *will* be staying on the isle, won't you?"

"I'm afraid not."

"But we may never see each other again. Why must you leave Capri?"

"I have relatives in Naples. My cousin Beatrice on Riviera di Chiaia near Staz Mergellina. I will stay with her until I find a job."

"You mustn't be in a rush to get back to work. Take a week or so, relax. I'll have Enrico send your wages to your cousin's. With an extra month's salary."

"Oh, *Signora*, that's too much! A whole month."

"We owe you so much more than money. What is your cousin's married name?"

"Pelosi. Carlo Pelosi. Number forty-two."

"I'll see your money is sent there." She caught her breath sharply. "Oh, my dear, I so hate good-byes!"

"I, too, *Signora*."

A tear started down Philomena's cheek and she wiped away its trail self-consciously. The conversation was becoming tedious and embarrassing to her, noted Lavinia. Taking her hands and kissing her, she left to summon the donkey boy and to dash off a note of reference.

To whom it may concern,

> *The bearer, Philomena DiCostanzo, has served Villa Aldoni faithfully, conscientiously and graciously for nearly five years. Signor Aldoni, our daughter and I consider her irreplaceable. Her*

presence in our household has enriched our lives.

Her decision to seek employment elsewhere is a personal one and were it within my power to dissuade her, I would not hesitate to do so.

Those with whom she finds a place should consider themselves most fortunate. Their gain is our loss.

Sincerely,
Lavinia Aldoni

XXVIII

Two days later, Lavinia with Deirdre by her side sat in a rickety, shield-back chair across an equally insecure table from a sergeant of police in the police station in the town of Capri. It was one of those uncomfortably hot days that rush the summer season, particularly disagreeable for being preceded by days whose weather befitted their position on the calendar. Flies buzzed about the nondescript little office, the air hung heavy and stifling, and the afternoon sun assaulted with cruel ferocity the high narrow windows that looked out upon the stables.

The windows might have been flung wide to introduce what little fresh air was frequenting the area, but the stench of mule and donkey dung offered by the stables rendered such an effort unthinkable. Lavinia patted her face and neck with her hanky and suffered in silence. The sergeant, a young, painfully homely man in a uniform a size too small, licked the end of his pencil and continued writing in a slow and deliberate hand.

"One figured bracelet in two-colored gold. Design: small circles with box borders. Value?"

"That's hard to say, sergeant," said Lavinia in a discouraged tone.

"Approximately?"

"Two thousand."

"Three thousand," said Deirdre.

The officer looked from one to the other, Lavinia nodded and he wrote.

"Three thousand lira." A fly landed on the paper, strutted about brazenly as if to satisfy its curiosity as to what the man was writing and flew off. A drop of sweat fell from the sergeant's chin striking the report. With the heel of his hand, he wiped it away.

"One diamond-crescent brooch, two inches in width. Value?"

"Six thousand."

"Tsk, tsk tsk, six thousand lira."

"Custom-designed for me in Rome just last year. An anniversary gift from my husband."

"My sympathies, *Signora*."

A lieutenant came in the door, wiping his brow with his forearm.

"What a day; you can't breathe," he complained to Deirdre. He loosened his collar. The sergeant's chair scraped the floor as he half rose to salute his superior. The newcomer towered over him, listening raptly to his explanation of the business at hand. A disturbed look clouded his plain dark features.

"You say these pieces were taken out of your bedroom?" he asked Lavinia. She nodded. "So when did you discover that they were missing?"

"About two hours ago. My daughter here and I searched. There was no sign of them."

"You keep your jewelry casket locked?"

"There's only a latch."

"Were the door and the windows locked?"

"No."

"Then there were no signs of breaking in."

"Inside job," ventured the sergeant. "One of the servants, obviously."

"How many servants do you employ, *Signora*?" asked the lieutenant.

"Four inside the house: the cook, a serving girl and two maids. One maid. One recently left."

"Left or you fired her?"

The sergeant had begun nodding, his head bobbing as if fastened to his neck by a spring.

"She left of her own accord," said Lavinia, going on

to explain Philomena's departure. "The day before yesterday." She drew in her breath sharply. "See here, you don't for a minute suspect——"

"In a crime of this sort, everybody is under suspicion," said the lieutenant. The sergeant continued nodding.

"That's insane!" exclaimed Lavinia. "Philomena was my personal maid for nearly five years. I would trust her with my life!"

"What was her excuse for leaving?"

"She——" Lavinia hesitated, as if reluctant to betray a confidence. "She wants very much to find a man and get married. She feels the selection is somewhat limited here on the isle."

"So she went to the mainland."

"Yes."

"Where specifically?"

"She didn't say."

"Where do you think?"

"I have no idea," said Lavinia quietly. "Anywhere."

"She has a cousin in Naples," said Deirdre. "She was always talking about her cousin Beatrice. Isn't that so, Vinnie?"

Lavinia thought a moment. "Beatrice. Yes, Mrs. Carlo Pelosi."

The sergeant went back to his writing, still nodding.

"What's the address?" asked the lieutenant.

"I don't know. I'm sorry."

"Describe this Philomena."

Lavinia did so. "But this is ridiculous. Outrageous, really! She couldn't possibly have done such a thing. We were like sisters. I gave her two of my best dresses."

"Perhaps she didn't do it," said the lieutenant. "I'm not accusing her. Still we have to question everybody."

At once Lavinia was very nervous, troubled by this turn.

"But to question her makes it look as if I suspect her."

"You should," piped the sergeant. The lieutenant flashed him a look that said 'I'll do the talking,' and the sergeant lowered his eyes to his pencil holding down the paper.

"Is there anything else you can think of?"

Lavinia shook her head. The lieutenant looked at Deirdre.

"No."

He tapped the report. "These pieces are insured?"

"Yes, fully. But it's not their value; they happen to be among my favorites."

"Sentimental value. I understand."

She frowned. "This is getting worse and worse. Perhaps if I went to her and questioned her myself. Discreetly. In a way so that she'd never suspect. You don't know Philomena like I do. She's extremely sensitive. If she had any idea she was under suspicion, she'd be hurt to the quick. I'd hate for that to happen."

"Please, we will do the questioning. Not just her, everybody—inside the house and out."

"She can't possibly have done it," said Lavinia, "not if her life depended on it."

"If that's all, I suggest you ladies go home and wait for word. We'll be in touch."

They got up. Lavinia shook hands with the lieutenant and thanked both men. Outside the building she stopped halfway down the steps, catching Deirdre by the arm.

"What have I done?" she exclaimed. "I never should have told them she left. It makes it look terrible for her!"

"You had to tell them, except that business about her looking for a husband. What made you say such a thing?"

"She told me so in so many words. You don't know her like I do. She has an absolutely morbid fear of dying an old maid. She has good reason to feel so."

"That's unkind."

"Yes, it is. I'm sorry. The poor thing. She'll never forgive me for sending the police."

"You didn't. It's their duty to talk to her. If she's innocent, she needn't worry."

"If? Really, child."

"Please don't call me a child!"

"She's as innocent as you or I!"

"Vinnie, somebody took those pieces. The fact that she didn't tell you where she was going does look suspicious, doesn't it?"

"Let's stop talking about it. We never should have come here in the first place."

"That's ridiculous. You're talking about nine thousand lira's worth of jewelry."

"I'm hungry. Let's have lunch."

They sat at a little table for two under a red-and-white umbrella so close to an olive tree bordering the sidewalk that it it practically joined them. Both ordered avocado salad and iced tea. The place was jammed with the lunch-hour crowd, and the clinking of silverware threaded through the rumble of a score of indistinguishable conversations. Lavinia fanned herself with her sodden hanky and glanced about. Nearby two tourists, ostensibly Americans, both pale as china and suffering from the heat, stared at their menus with bewildered expressions. Byond them, seated alone at a table, a strikingly handsome man in a linen suit without a tie finished his lemon ice. Getting up, he tossed money on the table and started toward them.

He was beautiful, thought Lavinia, unable to take her eyes off him. Perhaps 30, strong-looking, powerfully muscled, his face and neck deeply tanned, his hair so blond it was almost white. And his eyes as blue as the sea. He passed their table without looking down and Deirdre caught a glimpse of his profile as he strode off down the street in the direction of the Anacapri road.

The waiter had come up to their table, dusting the edge of it aimlessly with his napkin.

"Good-looking young fellow, eh?"

"He's handsome," said Deirdre. "Did you see him, Vinnie?"

Lavinia's attention was drawn to the remains of her avocado. She brought her head up sharply. "Did you say something, dear?"

"That man who just left. You saw him."

"Yes, yes, nice-looking."

"*Inglese,*" said the waiter. "*Scultore.* He studies with *Signore* Passimante in Anacapri. He comes every Monday noon for the mussels. He is mad for mussels. All the English are crazy for our seafood."

"May I have the *tortoni* for dessert?" asked Lavinia.

"*Si.*" He scribbled on his pad and turned to Deirdre. "The same."

Away he waddled. Lavinia steeled herself to keep from turning around and looking after the retreating Englishman. God, she could eat him up, he was so delicious-looking! The face and body of an Adonis! Studying sculpture with old Passimante, was he? That was interesting.

XXIX

"I mean to get a man up here to install a safe first thing tomorrow morning!" snapped Enrico. "Though it's obviously a case of locking the barn door too late."

"I knew you'd be upset, darling."

"Why shouldn't I be? Nine thousand doesn't grow on trees! Thank God we're insured."

A timid knock sounded at their bedroom door.

"Come in," said Lavinia. It was the maid, a dumpy little ox-eyed *napoletano*, her hair a disaster as usual. "What is it, Terese?"

"The police come, *Signora*, two. They ask to see you."

Lavinia threw a quick look at Enrico. He seemed disturbed by the news. Amusing, she thought, one would have guessed they'd come to question him about Fernando.

"All right, all right," he said testily. Teresa withdrew. "I don't like this, Lavinia. I don't like the police in my house. It's undignified."

"It also appears necessary."

"You talk to them. It's your business."

"Very well."

"I'm going to the garden for a breath of air. Where's Dee-dee?"

"In her room probably. Spring vacation ends this week. She's no doubt boning up on something or other. You know how conscientious she is."

"Talk to them and get rid of them as fast as you can, understand?"

She nodded. They went downstairs together, Enrico walking by the waiting lieutenant and sergeant, nodding and going out into the garden. Lavinia ushered them into the study and closed the doors.

"Would you like me to bring the servants in?"

"That won't be necessary," said the lieutenant smiling. *Mischievously*, she thought. *The cat that had swallowed the cream*. He produced a small cloth sack and, after loosening the drawstrings, emptied its contents out onto the desk.

"You found them! How marvelous! Where? How?"

"In her portmanteau, wrapped in a handkerchief, shoved down into the corner," said the lieutenant.

"Philomena!"

The sergeant clapped his hands together and shook them. "We caught her red-handed. She's insane, that woman, a lunatic! I've never heard anybody carry on so in my life."

"She was like a wild woman," said the lieutenant. "We had to tie and gag her to get her to jail and into a cell. She wanted to scratch our eyes out."

Lavinia sank into a chair. "I can't believe it. I never dreamed."

"Of course she denies it," said the sergeant. "She insists that you——"

The lieutenant interrupted. "We made arrangements to keep her in Naples. When the case comes up, she'll be tried there anyway. It saves going back and forth."

"What will they do with her?"

"That's up to the court. But you, *Signora*, will have to sign a formal complaint before charges can be brought."

"Must I? It seems so cruel."

"It is the law."

"May I discuss it with my husband?"

"If you like. I will see that the necessary forms are prepared." He picked up the brooch and bracelet, dropped them into the sack, tightened the strings and put it into his inside breast pocket. "These I must keep for a time. Evidence. Regulations. I will give you a receipt."

"That's all right."

"I must. That's the law."

She was given her receipt and the two went away. Enrico came in as soon as they were out the garden door. He stood by the desk tapping the fingers of one hand aimlessly on the bust of Verdi serving as a paperweight. Lavinia repeated the substance of her conversation with the lieutenant.

"I don't believe it," he said solemnly.

"Nor I."

"I don't believe Philomena would do such a thing."

"I'm afraid I was very nasty to her, very bitter."

"No."

"Oh, but I was."

He was not listening. "You know what I think?"

"About what?"

"You planted those jewels in her portmanteau!"

Lavinia began chewing her lower lip with her teeth in an effort to keep from responding to this at once. Getting up, she walked to the study doors, closing and securing them.

"That, Enrico, is the cruelest thing you have ever said to me. The most unfair and the most absurd. I will pretend you never said it."

"Very magnanimous of you, my dear, but I did. The idea's absurd. Philomena wouldn't steal a common pin. There isn't a more trustworthy servant on the entire isle."

She studied him in disbelief, shaking her head as if affecting pity for him. "Why in heaven's name would I put my jewels in her bag? And how?"

"How? I can't say; some way clever and sneaky. Why? To get her out of the way, naturally. If she's behind bars, she can't very well gossip about us, can she? Who would listen, the rats?"

"She wouldn't gossip about us. Even if she wanted to hurt me, she wouldn't say anything about it. She has no ill feelings toward you. Why should she deliberately harm your reputation?"

He laughed, but there was no humor in his eyes. Quite the contrary. "I doubt if you even thought of me when you cooked up this little soufflé."

"I was talking about her."

"I heard. I'm talking about you. What a marvelously devious bitch you are, my beloved. How extraordinarily crafty. And totally amoral. Look me in the eye and tell me you didn't plant those jewels in her things. Say you didn't, Lavinia."

"I most certainly did not! What do you take me for, a monster? If you think I'm lying, that's your privilege. A liar as well as dissolute, is that it? Why do you put up with me?"

"You've got to drag that into it by the hind legs, don't you!"

"You're doing the accusing!"

"You're doing the word twisting, as usual. Shrug it off, my dear."

"I beg your pardon."

"The mantle of martyrdom. It doesn't suit. It doesn't fit you. You will bring no charges against Philomena, is that clear? You will forgive her her 'crime.' If you can benefit from others' charity, you can reciprocate in kind."

"You're not thinking, Enrico. She will crucify us! She'll begin blabbing and keep on blabbing until the day she dies!"

"And what do you think she'd do in court, shed bitter tears and hide behind her beads? You're a fool, Lavinia, a stupid, vicious, heartless fool! And you've put yourself on dangerous ground. She can sue you for a million —for framing her, falsely accusing her."

"I did no such thing!"

Like a too-taut E-string of a double bass, something snapped. In a rage, she began screaming at him, cursing, inundating him with vile language. Enrico blanched, his cheeks sagging. Shaken by the suddenness and bitterness of her assault, he backed away, sidled toward the door, turned in silence, unlatched it and left, closing the door behind. And closing his ears to her shrill voice that was only slightly muffled by the closed door.

XXX

Like a beast after battle exhausted from exertion, the bellows of its belly pumping, the sea panted, its surface surging restlessly, its fury abated, its power contained. The winds that had goaded and infuriated it had fled, supplanted by an indolent breeze. Lisa could see clearly in every direction. Nothing. A world empty, abandoned by every living thing save herself and her companions.

Guilfoyle had hoisted their sail and the breeze filled it, sending them easing smoothly over the water. From nowhere to nowhere, she fancied. Clyde Buckshaw lay in the bow, his shoulders supported by the narrowing gunwales joining at the back of his neck, his legs propped up by a seat, his eyes closed, his normally pink skin infused with a grayish-green hue, the color of silt. Overnight his broken ankles had swelled into large purple globes connecting his feet to his shins. He breathed deeply, his exhalations fluttering the loosened ends of his tie, but, though his eyelids flickered now and then, he made no noticeable effort to desert his semi-conscious state.

It was just as well, Guilfoyle, seated at the tiller, had remarked. Should the injured man move even slightly it would only aggravate his pain. The first mate, though unhurt in any way, appeared exhausted to Lisa. His normally well-tanned face was drawn and pale and his eyes drooped like a well-run hound's. Seated between the two men, she herself was conscious of having all but reached the end of her energy. She would not, however, lie down for fear that once she closed her eyes she might never open them again.

They had come within an eyelash of foundering no fewer than seven times after the wave rising beneath them had sent the boat careening over the ship's foredeck. While Buckshaw lay helpless, voicing encouragement, she and the mate had bailed furiously, dipping and emptying their buckets mechanically as fast as they could. Seven such engagements with the enemy 20 minutes or more each time had turned her arms, shoulders and back into solid masses of pain. From her fingertips to her neck on either side and down her back to her waist it felt as if each muscle had submitted to its own individual vise clamping it tightly.

To merely move her fingers sent pain coursing clear up to her shoulder. Had a wave appeared sweeping over the boat, inundating them, forcing them to resume bailing, she would not have been able to reach down and take hold of the bucket at her feet. Guilfoyle assured her that the vises would "go away in two or three days." But his admission that he was in no better shape, although intended as consolation, had little positive effect upon her spirits.

How they had managed to survive the final fury of the hurricane was a mystery she would be unable to unravel if she lived another 50 years. Although they came perilously close to going down many times, they had somehow managed to bail fast enough to remain afloat —aided by strength born of utter desperation, she had decided at the time.

Now, approximately four hours after sunup according to Guilfoyle's reckoning—six since the departure of the hurricane—they sat in their boat in the sea, in the center of a vastness that seemed to stretch to infinity. And considered their plight.

The boat had proved itself eminently seaworthy. *If,* she mused, *the people who had built it had seen it in performance the previous night, they would have burst their breasts with pride.* In the stern box, Guilfoyle had found dried biscuit, salt beef and a three-gallon keg of fresh water. Fresh was what he had termed it, but when Lisa sampled it, it tasted as if it had been kegged sometime back before the war. Biting into the biscuit was like attempting to chew stone. They were obliged to soak each one in water to be able to get their teeth through it.

The salt beef tasted more of salt than of meat. This worried Guilfoyle. They would need the meat for energy, but consuming it would force them to consume more water than they would have needed to had the meat been fresh. Or half as salty.

Buckshaw did not eat nor did either of them try to feed him. Lisa contended that letting him sleep was best for him, at least until the evening meal. She had no intention of cheating him out of his share of rations, but his condition was poor and gave no promise of improving, so, at least for the time being, it was decided that he be spared the pain and discomfort awakening him would surely cause.

Her hands were cramped from hanging onto the side of the boat; they hurt so, she was forced to clench her teeth as hard as she could to keep from crying out. She began gently massaging her aching fingers, working blood into them, easing the soreness.

"Thirty-seven dead and three survived," observed Guilfoyle morosely. "It makes you wonder, doesn't it? Why us? Why three? Could there be some process of selection?"

"It isn't that *we* survived that amazes me so much," she said, "it's that the *Olympia* went down and this little batch of boards was able to stay up."

"Do you think it's God's intention to let us survive? I mean not just the storm but all the way?"

"I don't know as you can connect one with the other. I would think they're two separate tests."

Guilfoyle's eyes went to the sleeping Buckshaw at the bow. "I don't think he'll make it. He needs a doctor badly. His ankles should be set in casts."

"The bone has broken through the skin on the left one. I'm worried it'll become gangrenous. I don't like the way he's breathing, either. This past hour he seems to be fighting for breath."

"He's swallowed a lot of water. Maybe we should try to roll him over and pump it out of him."

She shook her head. "Maybe later, not now. If he gets some sleep, gets some strength back, maybe it won't be so painful."

"He looks terrible, poor man."

Shading her eyes against the pale-yellow sun lifted clear of the sea off the port beam, she swiveled full circle to examine the horizon.

"Do you have any idea where we are?" she asked.

"I can make a rough guess: about eight hundred miles northeast of Puerto Rico."

"That's the nearest land?"

"I'm afraid so. That's where we're heading."

"Eight hundred miles."

"Maybe a thousand."

"Let's be optimistic," she said brightly. "It could be six hundred. How fast can we go? Fifteen, sixteen knots an hour?"

"Eight or ten maybe, with a breeze like this. Just barely a breeze is what it is. And who can say how long it'll last? Then, too, eight hundred's only an estimate. More a guess based on our original course. The storm could have thrown us fifty or sixty miles off."

"Let's cross our fingers that we don't run into any more bad weather, even a sun shower. Do we have enough food and water?"

"If we can stretch it two or three weeks."

Lisa relaxed in relief, smiling cheerfully. "So if we

make only ten knots an hour, we could get there in less than four days."

"It won't be that easy. We could wander off course at night, we could hit bad weather, the wind could take away the sail."

"My, but you're optimistic!"

"I'm trying to be realistic. I'm saying, don't get your hopes up too high."

"Can't we steer by the stars at night?"

"Only roughly. You know, stay to larboard of the North Star. Cross our fingers, like you say, and hope for the best. We have no charts, no sextant, not even a compass."

"We can relieve each other at the tiller every four hours."

"That's not going to change our luck any."

His attitude worried her. He was by nature such an optimistic sort, always finding the bright side, never conceding there was anything but. Now, suddenly, he was sounding more pessimistic than poor Miss Osborne on her worst day.

The breeze died entirely and the little sail went slack. It remained dead calm for the ensuing four hours, past noon, while the sun climbed to its zenith. Gradually it became hotter and hotter still, pouring its fire like molten metal down upon them. Lisa tore wide strips from the hem of her cambric underskirt, soaked them in seawater, gave one to Guilfoyle and tied the others around Buckshaw's head and her own. It cooled while it lasted, but the cloth quickly dried and had to be taken off and resoaked repeatedly. This routine continued until sundown.

They had decided on two meals and two rations of water daily, and at sunset when Buckshaw stirred and opened his eyes, Lisa went to him, comforted him and tried to feed him some small pieces of softened biscuit. He had a difficult time swallowing, but finally succeeded. Then, to her disappointment, vomited it over the gunwale. It brought a young tiger shark, flashing its brilliant colors adorned with brown spots, its treacherous jaws snapping at the undigested biscuit, its flat head thumping against the side of the boat. Then, flipping its tail, it glided off.

Lisa groaned aloud in relief.

Guilfoyle pointed, swinging his upraised hand around the bow. "He's circling. Now that he's found us, he'll probably hang around all night. Whatever you do, don't trail your hand in the water to cool it."

"Help—me—up," said Buckshaw weakly.

"Don't try to move," cautioned Lisa. "Your legs."

"My stomach, my stomach!"

Rejecting the biscuit had roiled his stomach, actuating the seawater he'd swallowed earlier. It came dribbling out of the corner of his mouth. Getting hold of his left arm, she struggled to lift him, but he was dead weight and too heavy for her. Guilfoyle let go of the tiller, coming forward. Together they raised him to a sitting position, so that by supporting himself with both hands on the gunwale, he could lean over. He spewed up a great quantity of water.

"Please excuse the disgusting display," he said forcing a grin.

"Feel better?" she asked.

He smiled and nodded. "Can I have some more biscuit?"

"Of course."

He ate and this time kept it on his stomach. Then he began examining his ankles.

"They look beautiful, don't they?"

She tore off two more pieces of her underskirt, dipped them in the sea and wrapped them carefully around the injured areas.

"This may bring the swelling down a bit."

"You're very kind, nurse."

She could see from the way he narrowed his eyes that the mere touch of the cool cloth on his ankles triggered pain. But he did not complain. Her thoughts went back to their first meeting the afternoon she had boarded ship. Her initial impression, subsequently affirmed, was that Clyde Buckshaw of Baltimore, Maryland, and the International Exchange was a crude, loudmouthed drummer with the table manners of a jungle savage and the grace and charm of a dockside sot. Everything he said, every action, every reaction, everything about the man rubbed the nap wrong from the outset. To know Buckshaw was to dislike him with an intensity bordering on hatred.

He knew everything. Nobody else had the right to know anything. Interruptions he rarely countenanced, except for the time Captain Hughes had cut into his intolerant diatribe against the Jews. On the other hand, he himself interrupted others continually, with abandon. He was a bore; he was irritating; he was bigoted, opinionated, chauvinistic, malicious and obnoxious. Clearly lacking a sense of humor, he persisted in telling poor jokes as badly as she'd ever heard a funny story told. In short, the man was practically everything anyone blessed with sensitivity despised in a fellow human.

As far as she was concerned, the ship could have been three times as large as it was, it still wouldn't have been large enough to hold the two of them. Whenever she spied him coming toward her, she took flight. His presence at the captain's table all but made the meal, whatever it happened to be, unpalatable. Mr. Clyde Buckshaw of Baltimore, Maryland, and the International Exchange was what Cyrus would have called "a royal pain in the arse sixty-one ways from breakfast."

There was only one thing missing in the entire repugnant portrait: The man had saved her life. And in doing so had exhibited a coolness and disdain for danger that generally distinguished only rash lunatics and heroes.

From the time she had awakened in her cabin with him leaning over her to this very moment, he had conducted himself in the most manly fashion imaginable, with scant consideration for his own safety and with unselfish dedication to hers.

Slumping back against the prow, his eyes searching the growing darkness, his jaw set tightly, clenching away the pain, he spoke.

"You two saved my bacon. Don't imagine that I don't appreciate it. But, lying here with my eyes closed sort of half-sleeping, I've been thinking. I'm just excess baggage."

"Nonsense!" snapped Lisa.

"It's a fact, nurse. I'm not going to make it."

"You'll be fine now that you've got that water out of you."

"Nope. Even if I did manage to pull through, I'll sure enough never walk again. I'll be in a wheelchair the rest of my days. They'll probably have to lop off both of my feet to keep me alive. I wouldn't want that—the rest of my life in a wheelchair!"

"You're going to be fit as ever, mister," Guilfoyle assured him. "We'll be raising Puerto Rico in four or five days. We'll get you to the best doctor they got. He'll shape you up good as new."

"Excess baggage, that's me. Dead weight. I'm not only eating your food and guzzling your water but I'm slowing down this damned boat. Hell, I weigh as much as the two of you put together."

"You'd better try to get some more sleep," said Lisa. "It's the best thing for you." She had seen a piece of repair canvas in the stern box. Now she got it out, folded it into a square and slipped it in back of Buckshaw's head.

"Thank you kindly, nurse."

"You're welcome, patient. Now stop spouting so much pessimism and get some more sleep."

Darkness came stealing over the water. The breeze had come up and died again. There was no motion of the boat whatsoever, not even the gentle surging of the sea to which they had awakened that morning. *As idle as a painted ship upon a painted ocean*, she thought.

And no way to get to Puerto Rico. For all his pessimism, Guilfoyle was proving right. Without wind, the sail was useless, hanging from its mast, the colors of the battle for survival struck, at least for the present.

Night's coming wrapped her tightly in a feeling of awesome loneliness. The smallness of the boat, the inch-and-a-quarter planking that separated them from the depths and all the dangers within, the vagaries of weather and wind, the distance between them and land combined to invest her with a stifling sense of hopelessness—a gloom that brought her close to despair. And the weight of it all was increased almost beyond endurance by the need to concede that once more she had lost Ross.

There would be no reunion in Pernambuco. If she managed to survive this ordeal, wherever they landed, she would have to resume the pursuit from that point. She would head straight for Singapore. And pray that she would arrive before the *Crown Pearl*, or shortly after—before Ross and Regan were swallowed up by the city, by the Orient.

She yearned for him so. To race all the way to Williamsburg only to miss him by a few hours. To escape that animal in the warehouse only to reach the dock in time to see his ship rounding the bend, heading out to sea. To no doubt actually pass the *Crown Pearl* east of the Caribbean. And to speed toward Brazil buoyed by the conviction that she could not help but reach there before he did.

So near, so far, so lost—if not irretrievably, at least as close to it as seemed possible.

Far from reaching Puerto Rico or any other land,

they could conceivably sit where they were for all the time it took to run out of biscuit and meat and drinkable water.

It was time for prayer. Thanks to Almighty God for deliverance past; plea for deliverance future.

XXXI

She dozed and awoke, jerked upright by the sound of loud thrashing close by. The boat was rocking, swinging first one edge, then the opposite almost down to the waterline. Guilfoyle was pounding forward, yelling loudly. She turned to the bow. Her heart leaped in her chest at the sight. In his sleep, Buckshaw had slumped to his right side, his forearm slipping over the gunwale. By the light of the moon, the water was boiling furiously. And Buckshaw was screaming, his heavy body twitching convulsively as if the reticulation of his nerves had caught fire within him. Guilfoyle reached him, continuing to yell and pulled his arm out of the water. Up came a bloody stump where the older man's right hand had been. Holding it up, Guilfoyle pressed the wrist with both hands cutting off the arteries, the crimson fountain subsiding, dying.

"Good God in heaven!" burst Lisa.

Pulling off her headband, she flipped it around Buckshaw's forearm, knotted the ends in a tourniquet, slipped the tholepin of an oarlock into it and turned it until she could turn no further.

"Hold it!"

Guilfoyle obliged. Snatching his headband, she folded it into a pad, which she set flush against the wrist stump. Then she took over the tourniquet with her free hand.

"Rip his headband in two and tie this pad in place," she said.

Guilfoyle did so without a word. Buckshaw, meanwhile, had fainted, his head rolling back over the bow, his face contorted in agony.

"The poor bastard," said Guilfoyle hollowly, turning his eyes from the sight. "That goddamned shark! We should have tied his wrists. Damn it! Damn it! Damn it! Goddamn rotten luck!"

"He's lost a lot of blood," she said resignedly.

"Too much. Look at his face. He's white as a sheet." Guilfoyle groaned tiredly and sat down. "Well, we've done all we can for him. I tell you, if he pulls through this on top of his ankles, he's got to be superhuman."

"That's the thing that worries me."

"What?"

"You heard him talking. He doesn't want to live."

Guilfoyle dismissed this with a disdainful glare. "Talk, that's all that——" He froze in midsentence, his mouth dropping open as if pulled down, his eyes bulging froglike. "Good God!"

She turned. The pole mast had snapped off at its base and fallen over the side, taking the sail with it. Guilfoyle hurled his body halfway across the gunwale, his arm shooting out after the sheet* slipping down into the water, sinking into the moon-silvered water.

He missed it by inches. Cursing loudly and scrambling about, he got hold of an oar and shoved it as far out as he could after the sail and mast. But he was unable to reach them.

"I'm going in after it!"

He started over the gunwale, but she caught his shirt in her fist, stopping him.

"No you don't! That shark's in there somewhere."

"Lady, we got to get that sail! That's our ticket to Puerto Rico! Without it we're dead. Dead!"

"It's gone. Forget it!" she shouted.

The logic of her words sank in. Slowly he eased back into the boat, sitting down beside her.

---

*The rope fastened to the corner of a sail used to control its trim.

"What a clumsy bastard! How could I do such a thing?"

"It was an accident."

"I brushed it with my shoulder when I ran by. But not hard."

"It was probably rotten."

"I didn't even hear it crack. Did you?"

She shook her head. "We couldn't hear a thing with him screaming."

"I should have made the damned sheet fast instead of holding it in my free hand."

"You're supposed to hold it."

"We're really finished now. We could sit here 'til doomsday! Jesus Christ!" He continued to lament their situation.

"I'm going to try to get some sleep," she said, interrupting. "You ought to, you need it."

Together they tied Buckshaw's arms loosely, so that in turning in his sleep he wouldn't accidentally do again what he'd already accidentally done. Then she gave Guilfoyle what remained of her underskirt and he fastened it to an oar blade, placing the handle into the mast hole.

"For all the good this is going to do us," he said in a defeated tone.

"Cheer up. We're alive; we've food and water. We're in the line of traffic to and from Europe."

"No, we're not. We're too far south." He pointed. "That's not Europe, it's the Canaries and beyond 'em Africa."

"So ships come and go from there. Somebody's sure to sight us and pick us up."

"Nothing's sure when you really need it, don't you know that?"

He was becoming irritable, his frustration blending with exhaustion and his mounting despair. She patted his hand consolingly.

"We'll make it, we will."

"I wish to God we were a thousand miles north."

"We're not. And there's nothing we can do about it. So why worry? Why get discouraged?"

He flared up. "Lady, are you stupid? Are you blind? *We—are—dead.* Can't you see that? Look at your friend there: He's the lucky one, not us! He can sleep his way to death! You and me got to sit here like two bumps on a log waiting for it! How? Starvation? Dying of thirst? Our brains broiled by the sun? Washed over and drowned in the next blow? Take your pick!"

"That's enough! Get a grip on yourself. And count your blessings. Thirty-seven people are dead and he's dying. You and I are the lucky two alive right at the moment. We'll be picked up. I know we will. We just have to be patient. All the complaining in the world isn't going to help or hurt, so why don't you save your breath?"

He stared at her, a look of mild shock evident in his eyes. Then slowly a smile took shape.

"I'm sorry. No more moaning and groaning. Cross my heart, hope to——"

"Tut, tut, tut." They laughed. "Good night, Mr. Guilfoyle. Happy dreams."

He went back to the stern and with no further need to steer, fell asleep in minutes. She curled up on the seat and did the same.

XXXII

She was awakened by the warmth of the sun caressing her cheek. Seconds later Guilfoyle was on his feet, standing over her, shaking her by the shoulder.

"Buckshaw's gone!"

She blinked and looked forward to the bow. The image cleared. The bow was deserted; a few bloody stains were the only evidence that a person had been lying there.

"He must have fallen over," said the mate.

"He didn't fall. He put himself over."

"Suicide?" He scratched his jaw. "You're probably right. He couldn't take the pain."

"And something else."

"What?"

"He made a choice. He decided that if he went overboard, it would better our chances. Two of us sharing the rations instead of three."

"I don't think so. He wasn't thinking about us, he wasn't that sort. You know how he carried on, a real pain in the neck. Bigmouth know-it-all."

"The storm changed him. Or brought something to the surface that had been buried inside him. He was a courageous man, maybe the most courageous either of us has ever seen."

"You make him sound like a saint."

"He was the stuff saints are made of. Rare and unusual clay."

"The poor bastard." Guilfoyle crossed himself, murmuring something, his lips moving slightly.

The second day became the third, the third the fourth.

Seven days and nights came and went. Guilfoyle's beard sprouted and grew. Lisa's hair became tangled and stiff with salt, her skin caked with it. And sunburned. Despite thorough soaking, the biscuits got harder, the meat saltier; the water developed a metallic taste. On the afternoon of the eighth day, they sighted a brigantine cruising the horizon at least 30 miles distant off the starboard beam. It inched across the sun, full canvas spread, pennants flying, sharply silhouetted by the bright-orange light on the far side of it. By nightfall, it had shrunk to a tiny dot.

Early the next morning Guilfoyle spied jetsam 100 yards back of their stern. Using the oars, he put about and approached it. It turned out to be a number of fruit crates.

"Do you think the ship went down?"

He cast about. "There's no flotsam. These were probably empties thrown overboard by a cook. Boy, what I wouldn't give for an orange. Nice, cool, fresh orange juice."

"Talk pessimistically if you have to, but please don't mention food and drink. Do your biscuits sit on your stomach like lead?"

"Please don't mention food or drink."

They were four days into their second week, each having detailed practically his entire lifetime to the other when she caught sight of a ship coming from the east, bearing down upon them. Closer and closer she came, a paddle-wheeling steam freighter in the class of the *Crown Pearl*. She was painted as black as pitch from her waterline to stacks to masts, which were topped by large golden balls. Smoke poured from her stacks in great black streams and her paddles churned powerfully, rolling up Catherine wheels of foam.

Guilfoyle grabbed the oar with her underskirt tied atop it and waved frantically, shouting. She joined him, screaming and waving her arms. Almost immediately, they were seen. The wheels of the vessel slowed and stopped, water cascading down from them in torrents. Setting oars, Guilfoyle began pulling for the ship and within ten minutes their gunwale was bumping against a waterline plate.

XXXIII

The ship was the *Vampata, Burst of Flame*, flying the green, white and red of Italy. She was out of New Orleans, homeward bound for Naples by way of Tenerife, her holds crammed with sugar and cotton. Captain Marsala was an Italian, as was most of his crew, with the exception of a few Lascars, three or four Portuguese and an Irish engineer.

Marsala welcomed them in his quarters. His cabin was lavishly furnished with expensive teak and mahogany pieces, Persian rugs and elaborately worked gold-and-navy drapes "custom-made for me in Antwerp." He was a big man in, she guessed, his late 40s, getting heavy about the waist, jowls developing, but discernible only when he offered his profile, because his chin and neck were hidden under a full beard. He was going bald—*ergo the beard*, she thought—and conceit, or something like it, encouraged him to lay his few surviving strands across his pate in the manner of Dr. Howard Middleton. Locking the sides of his head together, as it were.

"Just as I, for one, was seriously considering giving up hope," she said.

"We owe you a debt of gratitude beyond our means to pay," added Guilfoyle.

Lisa shook her head. "Not quite. Captain, I wish to purchase your boat."

"You what?"

"Set your price and I shall meet it. I want you to turn about and head for Pernambuco!"

Up came his hands defensively. "Please, please, not so fast. Did you say Pernambuco?"

"Brazil. It is absolutely vital that I reach there as quickly as possible. A man's life is at stake. How much?"

He smirked. "You talk so fast, dear lady, I can hardly keep up with you. English is my second language." He stared at her, his eyes deserting her face and running down her body, lingering at her breasts on the way, holding at her hips. "Besides, you have no money."

"I can get all I need like that!" She snapped her fingers.

"How fortunate for you. I wish I could say the same, don't you, Mr. Guilfoyle?"

"I'm serious, captain."

"So am I. Unfortunately it is not within my authority to sell you the *Vampata*. Or, for that matter, to alter course." He turned to a calendar hanging between the portholes. "We are scheduled to arrive in Tenerife in four days. We must be there, not in Pernambuco."

"Name your price!"

"You're asking the impossible. I am the master, not the owner. If you wish to purchase this ship you'll have to consult with them. Messrs. Carlone and Dinaldo in Naples."

It was patently useless. As he admitted, he had no authority to sell his ship, for any price. And yet it struck her that having good and sufficient reason for turning down her demand was proving a source of considerable satisfaction. Something in his eyes betrayed it. On the spot, she decided that she did not like this Captain Marsala. She was not quite certain why this was so, but the certainty of it arrived and fixed itself securely in mind with the tenacity of rivets fixing plates to the framework of a ship.

As they responded to his questions and he voiced his reactions, she began to isolate the reason for her negative impression of him. He was, she decided, a creature of excesses. When he laughed, he laughed too loudly and too long. He was either unable or unwilling to make distinctions between that which called for a chuckle and that prompting uproarious reaction. His wandering eyes disturbed her. His smile stretched so broadly, bursting upon his face, she suspected that he was inwardly laughing at her. He talked too loudly; he talked too much. He was, she concluded, a nautical version of Clyde Buckshaw prior to the hurricane. Adding one deficiency Buckshaw had never manifested. The captain smelled—of garlic, rum and body odor commingling in the stuffy atmosphere of the cabin and actuating unpleasant awareness of the last leaden biscuit lying undigested in her stomach.

They were fed, sumptuously—fresh meat and vegetables from the ship's ice hold, Madeira and sweets for dessert, the captain insisting that the sugar would serve to replenish their energy.

After dinner, they were shown to their quarters. She bathed in a copper tub brought to her by the cabin boy and was given a plain cotton dress a size too small for her with the explanation that it had been left behind by a ladyfriend of one of the hands.

Marsala appeared, hanging about making conversation and inviting her back to his cabin for tea. His manner was humble, the wording of his request gracious. But though she accepted, she was not altogether certain it was the wisest course. His odors and his excesses notwithstanding, however, he had saved their lives. In conscience, she could hardly turn him down.

Once inside his cabin, though, she quickly changed her mind.

"Is there any reason to lock the door?" she asked.

"I wish to speak with you in private, without interruptions. Please, have a chair." He set a bulky but surprisingly comfortable chair resembling a section of a church pew in front of his desk for her. The desktop was littered with charts and books and writing materials. A carafe of rum on a tray with three glasses occupied one corner. He saw her looking at it as she sat down.

"Some rum, perhaps?"

"No, thank you."

"It's delicious. It will bring a glow to your cheeks. And beautiful cheeks they are."

"I thought we were going to have tea. Why don't I unlock the door? When the boy comes he'll have his hands full of tray, won't he?"

He laughed. "What boy? What tray?" He reached for the rum, pouring half a tumblerful. His dark face assumed an unpleasant look, a look all too familiar to her: one she had last seen on the face of the animal in the warehouse room in Norfolk. Sight of it sent a tremor racing through her.

"You are a beautiful woman—your hair, your eyes, your figure."

She half rose from the chair, but he was around the desk and looming above her, one hand on her shoulder staying her, the tumbler in his other hand.

"Please, captain."

"Let me look at you. You are a feast for the eyes, dear lady." Licking his fat lips he filled his eyes with her breasts, tearing her clothes off in his mind.

"Take your hand away! I want to go back to my cabin."

"*My* cabin, dear lady. *My* ship, remember? I am the master here, the law. I say you stay. You will stay. Why are you so nervous, so jumpy? Drink this, it will settle you down."

"I said I didn't want any!"

"Drink!" Seizing her by the hair, tightening his grip, sending a stabbing pain shooting through her head, he forced the rum down her. It tasted strangely bitter and almost at once she became lightheaded, all the colors of the room washing away leaving various shades of gray. All that she could see became liquified, undulating, as if it had suddenly been plunged into water.

And she felt strangely languid, sapped of her will to resist him. Indifferent to his menacing presence. When he spoke, his voice sounded oddly hollow.

"Drink some more."

She did so without protest, swallowing it easily. Gradually the taste became pleasing. And still the grayed room swam. He was breathing heavily now, his massive chest rising and falling, his tongue traveling his upper lip obscenely, sweat pouring from his brow, running down his cheeks to his beard. His hands came shooting up, clasping her head, holding it firmly as he bent down bringing his wet, evil-smelling mouth into contact with hers. She wanted to struggle, to twist free, but she lacked the will to do so. Her brain silently shouted warning, but she could not resist yielding. Now he held her mouth against his with one hand, the other going to her breasts, encompassing one and squeezing it roughly.

Then he was carrying her into the bedroom, throwing her down bodily and pulling off her dress. She wanted desperately to resist, to fight him off, to kick and scream and rip his eyes with her nails, but an all-pervading listlessness held her in its thrall. Her mind was alert, keyed to action, to defense. But her body ignored its commands. In seconds, he was down upon her, crushing her with his weight, the sudden excruciating pain between her thighs sending a shrill scream from her throat, the voice of anguish trailing off pitifully, losing itself in the thunder of the engines under the floor.

He made her his prisoner, assaulting her, forcing her into indecent acts, abasing her completely. And taking care always to force the strange-tasting rum down her throat before he began. In time, a feeling took possession of her that neither the hurricane nor its harrowing aftermath in the lifeboat had been able to instill: a conscious yearning to die and have done with this mindless torture.

He derived maniacal delight in hurting her, in mistreating her in scores of ways. He would force his mouth against hers, holding it there until she nearly suffocated, the room whirling, her heart pounding like stone on stone. He would not allow her to dress, not a stitch, keeping her naked, degrading her, cursing and reviling her, ordering her to her knees when she addressed him, demanding she call him master, slapping her stingingly across the face when she displeased him. The cabin became her living hell, an unending nightmare of torment, of suffering and humiliation. He rarely left her, but when he did, he locked her in the closet where she would sit for hours in total darkness shrouded in soreness and discomfort from his abuse. He drank constantly and the drunker he got the more bestial he became.

Again and again he assaulted her, each time more brutally, more viciously than the one preceding, desecrating her beauty and her body with insidious zealousness.

On the morning of the fourth day, he came back into the cabin and, unlocking the closet door, greeted her mockingly:

"Good morning, your highness."

"Why must you lock me up when you go? Isn't the cabin door enough? I can't possibly get out. No one can hear me screaming above the noise of the engines."

"I lock you in not for safekeeping, dear lady, but to teach you humility. To remind you that you are my prisoner. I bring news. We've sighted Hierro. We will be in Tenerife by nightfall. Into the bed with you. I desire you, dear lady."

She glared, seething.

"Ah," he continued, "I forgot. You need your tot of rum to put you in the proper mood. To sharpen your craving for me." Going into the cabin, he poured the rum and brought it back, proffering the glass.

"You'll hang for this, and I'll stand by cheering! So help me!"

"What's this? My love slave voicing threats?" His hand flashed out, slapping her hard across the face.

"Bastard! Filthy pig!"

Setting the rum down, he pushed her down onto the bed and crouched beside her, his eyes slits, his face dark with fury.

"You little minx, do you take me for a complete fool? Do you think for one instant you and your friend will ever get off this ship alive? I must have broken something in your beautiful head! We are thirteen days from home port. We will enjoy each other's company for thirteen more days. And on the way to the last hour, after we pass Sardinia, you, dear lady, can begin saying your prayers!"

"You'd dare murder us in cold blood?"

"Cold, warm, what choice do I have? Would you rather I let you walk down the gangplank and into the nearest police station? And begin spouting pernicious lies about me?"

"Captain——"

"It's obvious. You would lie and tell them I abused you. When the fact is I haven't laid a hand on you. Look at your body. Your cheek is a trifle red, but that will go away. A few black-and-blue marks here and there—inside your right thigh there—but that will be gone by the time we pass Gibraltar."

"If you think the police will take your word over mine, why bother killing me? Why add murder to your crimes?"

"Why take a chance when I don't have to? A man has to protect himself in this world. I must consider my reputation, my wife and family."

"*You* have a wife and family?"

"You look surprised. Why shouldn't I?" He reached inside his jacket and brought out his wallet with a tintype showing himself standing alongside a pretty, dark-haired woman with a small boy and girl standing in front of them. "My wife, Maria. And Mario and

Angelica. This was taken outside church after Easter Mass just last year. Isn't my wife lovely? Her father is one of the wealthiest businessmen in all Campania."

"How do you intend to keep murder a secret from your crew?"

"Murder, you keep saying that word. There's not going to be any murder. It will all be accidental. That's so much more refined."

"*Two* fatal accidents?"

"It's simpler than you imagine. Here you are a man and a woman picked up at sea. You're not passengers from New Orleans. You're not in the log. You have no clothes, no effects, no baggage. Dear lady, you don't exist!"

"Every man saw us come aboard."

"Every man is deaf, dumb and blind." His hand went to the back of her head gripping her hair, the other hand bringing up the rum to force it upon her.

"Drink. You like it now. You know you do. You can't get enough of it."

Her mind and body screamed resentment, but he was right. She liked it, the taste, the drowsy, soft and comfortable feeling that came over her once she'd swallowed it and it took effect.

The feeling that made what he did to her, *whatever* he did, not worth the effort to resist.

BOOK THREE
CONFRONTATION IN CAPRI

XXXIV

Lavinia lay in bed staring at the angels frolicking around the periphery of the darkened ceiling and considering the present state of things. There was no longer room in her thoughts for Fernando. Mourning the dead was a waste of sympathy. She had banished him, giving his place to Adonis. But even the pleasure of imagining him making passionate love to her, her body arching to encompass and engorge his member, their naked flesh gleaming, all such imagery had to be relegated to a position at the back of reality. The reality was Enrico. He was extremely upset with her. She had affronted his sense of honor along with what he kept insisting was "human decency." Twice within the space of a few hours. With the result that she suddenly found herself gingerly picking her way down the edge of the blade. One more slip and——

Her only protection, the single obstacle to an irreparable breach between *signora* and *signore* remained Deirdre. The fact that she would most certainly take his beloved "Dee-dee" with her should he order her out was the only thing that gave him pause.

Be that as it was, Lavinia needed no outside consul to remind her that in her eagerness for revenge against Philomena, she had succeeded in creating a catastrophic mess. The young bitch would never forgive her. Once out of the law's clutches, she would go running to the old bitch. Mama Aldoni would hear her out and come charging back to Capri. She would castigate her Rico, order him to firm his backbone, stand up on his hind

legs like a man and do what his two favorite noble
attributes, honor and decency, demanded:

"Throw the *prostituta* out!"

So the fire was far from extinguished. It could flare
up again at any time. Deirdre or no, she, Lavinia, could
find herself a passenger on Giorgio's boat for the last
time. Heading for the mainland never to return.

Future possibilities disconcerted her so that she was
unable to sleep. Why was it, she asked herself, nothing
ever seemed to disturb Enrico's sleep? Financial set-
backs, grand plans collapsing, loss of an account to his
most detested competitor—none of them had ever so
much as broken the rhythm of his snoring.

He lay beside her emitting his customary night
sounds, a satisfied smile on his face, as blissful as he'd
ever worn. Arising, she donned her robe and going to
the window looked out at the moon floating above the
pool, cloaking the Triton's face and chest in its bluish-
white light. Studying him, she looked back at Enrico
and sighed. Then she noticed that his smile had vanished. His face was solemn now; he worked his lips one
against the other, his brow furrowed deeply between his
eyes and his breath hissed out of his nostrils.

"Dee-dee, Dee-dee," he said aloud.

Lavinia went to him, standing over the bed.

"*Bellisimo, bellisimo.* Your breasts, your beautiful
body. My darling Dee-dee. Come to me. Come to me!"

Lavinia gasped. The filthy degenerate! Disgusting
animal! She shook him vigorously.

"Wake up! Enrico, wake up!"

He rubbed his eyes, staring about in confusion, raising himself on one elbow. Lighting the lamp on the bedside stand, she glared down at him.

"What's the matter?"

"What did you do to her, Enrico?" she asked icily.

"To whom? What are you talking about?"

"Deirdre!"

His face sagged and he swallowed. "Ahhhh . . . !"

She mimicked his voice. " 'Dee-dee, Dee-dee, your breasts, your beautiful body. My darling Dee-dee.' " She leaned over, her eyes burning into his. " 'Come to me. Come to me!' "

"What nonsense. What are you stirring up now?"

"So you finally went off the deep end. Tell me about it, my devoted husband, Mr. Honor-and-decency. Tell me what you did to your fifteen-year-old daughter!"

"Nothing! I swear by the Holy Mother, I never——"

"So don't tell me." She turned from the bed. "I'll get the whole grisly story from her."

"No, leave her alone!"

"Let's hear it! What did you do, attack her in the woods, smother her with kisses, fondle her, finger her, rape her? What did you do?"

"I didn't hurt her, I swear it. I would never. I—touched—her breasts. I—kissed—them. O Jesus, O God."

"You kissed your daughter's breasts! Slobbered all over her like the pig that you are!"

He struggled to explain, telling her how he'd run off to confession.

"Oh, why didn't you say so in the first place? That makes everything all right, doesn't it? Your voice in the priest's ear and your sins are washed away!"

Getting out of bed, he walked to the armoire and turned to face her. "Don't mock me, Lavinia. Don't do it. I'm trying to explain——"

"What's to explain? You attacked her, ran away, confessed and everything's wine and roses again. But what I don't understand is that she's never said a word."

"She wanted to protect you."

"Me? *I* need protection?"

"You know what I'm saying. She didn't want you to be hurt."

"Who's hurt? Shocked, disgusted, the sight of you makes me want to throw up, maybe, but hurt? Not at all. I have a thought. Why don't we wake her up, get her in here and thrash out the whole lovely business?"

"No!"

"Why not? Are you afraid she'll tell me something you may have overlooked?"

"I've told you everything. Word for word exactly as it happened. I—lost my head."

"Not at all. You simply reverted to type."

"She has forgiven me, why can't you? She's the offended party."

"And she's told you she's forgiven you?"

"She—hasn't—said—anything," he confessed in a rueful tone.

"But in your heart you know you're forgiven."

"She *has* to know I meant no harm!"

"Of course you didn't." Her sarcastic tone thickened each syllable.

"It was impulse, something came over me."

"You just couldn't resist putting your hands and your mouth on her." She sat down on the edge of the bed shaking her head slowly back and forth. "How could you do such a thing? Whatever possessed you? Still, I suppose part of the blame has to be mine."

Bewilderment flooded his features. "What did you say?"

"I'm to blame for everything else that's happened these past few days, why not this?"

"You're not making sense."

"Oh, yes, I am. If I were a good and faithful wife. . . ." Her voice trailed off. "The problem is I've grown too old for you, my darling."

"Nonsense!"

"It's true. You're still young at heart. Younger women appeal to you. You're not the first middle-aged man to have his head turned. Now if I were younger."

"Lavinia, Lavinia." He came to her quickly, grasping her elbows, lifting her. "You are the youngest woman I know. You are my life, my darling."

"Oh, Enrico, you can't imagine how much I wish

that that were true. You can't conceive!"

"It is! It is! I adore you. And I'll not let you shoulder any part of the blame for this. It's not your fault or hers, nobody's but mine. If only she could find it in her heart to forgive me. Could—you—talk to her?"

"I'm afraid it's too late. The wound is healing. It wouldn't do to reopen it, would it? Besides, now that I think about it, I'm inclined to believe you're right. She's forgiven you. She'll forget." She kissed him on the cheek, pushing her body hard against his. "So it seems we both break the rules."

He nodded. "Imperfect human beings. Flawed. We're tempted; we're weak."

She stopped his mouth with her fingertips and kissed him. His arms tightly encompassing her, he returned it. Then, nestling her head against his chest, she was unable to hold back a smile. Part relief, she thought, part triumph.

XXXV

Enrico arose early the following morning and went to Naples where he advised the *commandante di polizia* that neither he nor *Signora* Aldoni intended to press charges against Philomena. She was promptly released, but before she left the station, he had a long talk with her. He succeeded in cooling her anger and gaining her assurance that she had no brief whatsoever against him, though she pointedly refused to include the *signora* in this munificence. Nevertheless, he came away confident that out of sympathy for him she would neither air her grievance nor betray what she knew about her former employers. His check for 10,000 lire in no way harmed his cause. He brought back both pieces of jewelry, returning them to Lavinia.

"The matter is closed, my dear."

"Ten thousand lire!"

"I would have cheerfully given her ten times ten thousand."

"But how can you be sure she'll keep her part of the bargain?"

"I can't be, not a hundred percent. But I got the impression that she's serious. And also that she's not going to be around here much longer. I think she's heading for Rome."

"Don't be surprised if she runs straight to your mother's."

"She won't. I was very specific on that point. Besides it was she who suggested Rome."

"Why Rome, I wonder?"

"To find a husband?"

"Could be. She's always complained how lean the pickings were around here. For a witch like that, they're lean anywhere." She laughed. "See Rome and die, Philomena!"

"Tsk, tsk, tsk." He examined the brooch, polishing it against his sleeve then holding it at eye level to catch the sunlight. "Think what you please of her, she's not stupid. That's why I don't worry about her."

"I do."

"Don't bother. She knows that malicious gossip involving people in our position is a risky business. Take my word for it, she won't stir up any trouble." He pinned the brooch in place on her dress. "There we are. Now then, a question: What are you doing today?"

"Why do you ask?"

"I thought I might take a day off for a change."

"I think I'm losing my hearing!"

"I'm serious. We can spend the whole day together." She frowned. "Can't we?"

"Not the whole day. Why don't I meet you at Di-Caldo's in Naples at twelve sharp? We can have lunch and spend the afternoon together."

"What are you planning for this morning?"

"I have to go somewhere."

"Where?"

"It's a secret."

"I'll go with you."

"Then it won't be a secret anymore."

"I thought there weren't going to be any more secrets. Why can't I go?"

"Enrico, stop looking so suspicious. If you must know I'm—going to see an artist."

"For what?"

"What do you think? What do artists do?" She sighed in exasperation. "Very well, I've decided to have my portrait painted. It's going to be a birthday gift for my husband. But don't you tell him. It's a secret."

He broke into a broad grin, pressing her hands

tightly. Then his eyes grew serious. "You're not——"
He gestured, both hands sweeping down his chest.

"No, silly. No nudes. What makes you think I'd want
a frame around this wretched old body?"

"It's not wretched and it's not old!"

"Then perhaps," she began slyly.

"A big beautiful picture of your face will be perfect."

"My guilty secret revealed."

"Forgive me for being nosy."

"Happy birthday—six weeks from today." Bending
over her vanity bench, she put her hat on, driving the
pin through the back. Then she turned for his approval.
"Like it?"

"The brim is too wide."

"The latest style in Paris." She patted one cheek and
kissed him on the other. "See you at DiCaldo's."

"Noon sharp. We'll eat and we'll spend the day shopping together."

"*You* shopping?"

"All afternoon, all night, to your heart's content."

"*Ciao.*"

And she was gone.

Passimante's atelier was in the Piazza San Nicola
across from San Michele, an impressive octagonal
church famed for its majolica pavement depicting the
story of Eden, designed by Solimena and executed by
Chiaiese. The atelier occupied the ground floor of a
small building washed dazzlingly white and carelessly
laced about its windows with shining green ivy. A girl
in kerchief and crisp apron was sweeping the steps, and
through the open door, Lavinia could see the garden at
the rear: Gardenias, lagerstroemias and hibiscus
paraded their colors, with agave, ferns and other native
greens providing a charming setting for them.

"*Mi scusi,*" began Lavinia. "*Dov'è Signor Passimante?*"

Leaning on her broom the girl pointed at the church
across the way.

"San Michele."

"*A chiesa?*"

"*Sto lavorando!*" snapped the girl impatiently.

"*Grazie.*"

Passimante was a stubby barrel of a man with well-rounded powerful shoulders and wedged between them a miniature version of his trunk serving as his head. He wore a second skin of grayish-white dust, his face caked with it, his eyelids resembling crescents cut from mother-of-pearl. The steady clink-clink-clink of iron hammer against point chisel echoed through the otherwise empty church and the sunlight that filtered through the stained glass window depicting Christ on the cross behind the altar outlined Passimante sharply as his arm rose and fell.

Behind him, stripped to the waist, his hands gloved with dust, his body glistening with golden beads of perspiration, stood Adonis. At sight of him, she caught her breath. He was even more beautiful than she had remembered him.

Neither man noticed her standing on the next to the top step looking in through the open doors.

"See the shadow under the brow?" inquired Passimante, pausing and indicating with his chisel. "It can mislead you. It can make you set the inner corner of the eye too deep."

"Leaving no room for the width of the nose."

"Right. Very good. There's another trap you can fall into. You can make the whole edge of the profile as high as the center of the head." He indicated. "But because it's closer to you, it's got to be higher."

"I understand."

"There are lots of little traps. *Haut-relief* and *bas-relief* are as different from busts as fish from fowl." Passimante handed him the tools. "Start on the eye."

"I beg your pardon."

Both turned and Passimante, who had been kneeling, rose to his feet.

"Good morning. Can I help you?"

She came in slowly, studying the work. It was a *bas-relief* of the Madonna and child in a sylvan setting and was nearly two thirds completed. She introduced herself. Hearing the name Aldoni, Passimante's initial reaction —a trace of disappointment in his eyes at being interrupted—speedily fled.

"*Signora*, may I introduce my associate, Derek Childs."

She shook hands with Adonis. "He flatters me, *signora*. I'm no associate, only his pupil," Childs said.

"He is too modest. He is very gifted. Strong hands. I am the eye on this job, he is the hands when my hands get weary."

"Please forgive me for interrupting your work. It's beautiful, magnificent."

"Thank you."

"If I can steal one minute, then I'll leave you alone."

"Steal five," said Passimante good-naturedly.

"I have a commission for you. I wish to have a bust done of *Signor* Aldoni. Preferably in marble."

Passimante pursed his lips, glancing at the younger man, then at her. "I am sorry, *signora*, it's impossible." He indicated the wall. "As you see."

"When do you think this job will be finished?"

"Not until September at the earliest." He flung out one hand sweeping down the wall. "There will be six scenes in all. This is the first. I haven't even begun sketches on the others."

"I see. But if you could do it—I'm speaking hypothetically—may I ask what you would charge?"

"It would depend," said Passimante.

"A marble bust perhaps twice life size. Just a rough estimate?"

"Two thousand, give or take a hundred."

"I will pay ten thousand."

Their reaction was all she could have hoped for. The older man's eyes began blinking rapidly, dust freeing itself from his eyelashes. With his left hand, he scratched his neck under the opposite ear, his mind racing.

"I am sorry, I——"

"Then neither of you," she began looking at Childs.

Passimante leaped to the bait. "You could do it, Derek."

"But the *bas*——"

"Half and half, my boy. You work with me in the afternoons. In the mornings, you work for the *signora*. Or one day on, one day off. He's very good, *signora*. The best I've seen."

Childs actually blushed, his eyes downcast, shifting his feet self-consciously. *He is more than beautiful,* she thought. *Fernando had been beautiful. This one, this Adonis, this gift to me from Queen Victoria, is enchanting!*

"What is your schedule, *signora*?" he asked in a subdued tone.

"Six weeks."

"Plenty of time!" Passimante was suddenly all enthusiasm for the idea, the *bas-relief* abandoned completely for the moment. "Take the lady back over and show her your work, my boy. The muses and your archer. Show her your Saint Francis. Yes, yes, by all means Saint Francis! And don't forget the head of Lorenzo de' Medici! Wait till you see! He's another Pisanello!"

She walked with Childs across the piazza. He had put his shirt back on without buttoning it, the breeze rippling it revealing his bare upper body. She could scarcely tear her eyes from the sight.

"Would half the money down and the rest on completion suit?" she asked quietly.

"Whatever arrangement you like. When can I see your husband? When can he come in?"

"Oh, he won't be coming in."

He stopped short staring perplexedly.

"But——"

"I have pictures here." She patted her bag. "Seven photographs. All excellent. Even a couple profiles."

"*Signora*, it's impossible! Unless I can see him in the flesh, take his measurements, work closely——"

"He can't possibly come in. It's to be a surprise, you see. I will be here every day. As long as you need me, whenever you need me. I'll work with you. You'll start with a clay model, won't you?"

"Yes, but——"

"Good. We'll work and work and work on it until it's absolutely perfect. You'll see. Once that's done, the stone should be simple, shouldn't it?"

"I've never worked this way. It's very unusual."

Good, she thought, *he's the sort who can be talked into anything. Mild-mannered, shy, easily buffaloed.* Which in a sense made the whole situation slightly hilarious. If Enrico was to be putty in dear Derek's hands, Derek would be putty in hers!

XXXVI

What a perfectly delightful six weeks in paradise it would be! she had promised herself. But here she was in the midst of her third visit to the atelier with disappointment and doubt gnawing at her conviction.

She sat on a high stool a few feet from him as he worked over the clay likeness of Enrico, applying the final touches, moving the turn top of his stand one way then the other, busily deepening a hollow with his wire loop, brushing over one cheek. The sun poured through the high wide north window, falling upon the clay features of Campania's most illustrious wine merchant. The faucet in the corner dripped loudly in imitation of lead pellets dropping in steady rhythm into an iron bucket. And Lavinia ringed her lips to hold back a yawn, glancing about. As usual the floor had been swept; other than that, the place was a mess, with work completed and half completed and virgin wood, plaster and stone scattered about. Tools and clay and clothes were strewn around as if someone had stood in the center of the room and flung them in every direction. That beauty could emerge from this slovenliness and disorder was inconceivable!

It annoyed her more than it should have for a very good reason. She was bored. Watching him she could almost hear the afternoon drone toward evening. And she could hardly believe that this was happening to her. The first day she had worn a tight-fitted shirt-waisted jacket and walking dress hitched up provocatively, showing her red petticoat. The second, a white chemisette with Gabrielle sleeves and lemon-yellow skirt with a silk sash hanging from her waist. And today, her black silk "Rome" dress with pagoda sleeves and *engageantes*, so formfitting at the bodice as to leave nothing to anyone's imagination.

But if there was the slightest glimmer of interest on his part, nothing he said or did betrayed it. It struck her that if she were to stand up and rip every stitch off and pose naked in front of him, he wouldn't have blinked an eye. The clay alone commanded his attention. One would have thought from the depth of his concentration that he was a doctor bringing a child into the world. He wasn't playing games; he wasn't teasing her; he wasn't even consciously ignoring her. He was simply captivated by his work and all the turning and touching, picking and poking, pushing and probing required to bring it to perfection. She was tempted to rush forward hands high and topple it, send Enrico tumbling to the floor flattening his forehead or his face or his pate!

She had never met a man like this indifferent, this thoroughly detached Britisher. Was he a homosexual? There were none of the telltale indications. Was he madly in love with and sworn to be faithful to some dark-eyed peasant bitch two years older than Deirdre? Was he artfully concealing his fear of the great man's great lady? What, in all that was holy, ailed him? What was under all that heart-rousing perfection? That divine flesh? What thoughts intermeshed under those tight golden curls? What was going on behind those sinfully blue eyes?

He wasn't going to get away with this; that she wouldn't allow! No man born could treat her so, whatever his reason! Worse than disappointing, it was humiliating. She could almost hear her pride moaning in resentment.

"Is that better?" he asked.

"I'm sorry. What did you say?"

"The left cheek." He picked up a photograph of

Enrico, holding it at arm's length, angling his head this way and that as he compared it with the bust.

"It's perfect."

"All right, I'm going to turn it slowly. If you see anything at all that doesn't strike you as perfect, stop me."

"Why don't I walk around it?"

"No, no. It's got to pass through the full light of the sun." He began inching the turn top to the left.

"The nose at the left." She indicated the interstice at the wing of the nose. "It's not deep enough."

He deepened the indentation. "How's that?"

"Fine."

"I wish I could get him in here for half an hour. Or perhaps you could invite me to tea day after tomorrow. It wouldn't be as good as bringing him in, but——"

"No, no. There's no need. It's excellent. It really is."

He continued turning. At her direction, the fold of flesh at the back of the neck was reduced in size, one earlobe refashioned and the clay stage declared finished.

"Day after tomorrow we will go to plaster," said Derek, moving to the sink and scrubbing his hands. She stood at the stand aimlessly turning the bust. Suddenly she gasped. Her hand went to her forehead, she cried out and sank to the floor. He hastened to her, going down on one knee, lifting her to a half-sitting position.

"What is it? What happened?"

"I——" She rolled her eyes, pretending uncontrollability, drawing her breath in sharply, the cold chilling the underside of her tongue. "I feel—weak—I——"

"I'll get you some water."

"Is there someplace I could—lie—down?"

Gathering her in his arms, he carried her upstairs to the living quarters, laying her down upon a narrow metal bed, her head against a pillow so hard it felt as if it were stuffed with grain.

"I'm so sorry," she said weakly.

"It's my fault. I should have opened a window. It gets stuffy as a tomb down there. And this heat."

"May I have that water now?"

"Of course."

He left the room. She stared about her. What a lovely place to make love, so small, so intimate. If only he lived here alone. He came back with a cup of cold water, supporting her head with one hand, feeding it to her. She took two swallows and waved away the cup.

"I don't understand, I never faint. I. . . ." She struggled to breathe.

"I'll open the window." He did so, returning, sitting back down on the edge of the bed, hovering over her, staring at her anxiously. She relaxed her lower lip languidly and with calculated effort brought the back of her left hand to her forehead letting it settle there like a wounded dove. The tip of her tongue moistened her lower lip and she moved her right hand to undo the buttons at her throat. But her fingers had no strength.

"Would you, please—I. . . ."

He unbuttoned her and her outspread hand came to rest between her breasts. "That's better, now I can breathe."

He stared. "You're beautiful," he said quietly.

A wounded fawn, she thought, that's what he was seeing, wide-eyed, innocently sensuous, helpless. He leaned down to kiss her, his hand finding hers, easing it aside and going to her breast. And the music of love began in silent performance. The perfect joy of submission, of yielding mind and body to his advances infused her with a sense of triumph that all but inspired a squeal of delight. She trembled all over as he undressed her, running her hands down his naked chest, undoing his belt.

A cloud surrounded them, obscuring any view of the world. He lay beside her, his tawny flesh fused to hers, the paleness of it in contrast cloudlike, overcast with the soft pinkness of life, the smouldering fire beneath. Their eyes met and she slipped into the blue depths of his, feeling herself borne away. His fingertips touching, caressing, thrilled her so that she all but fainted as the cloud surrounding closed about them.

XXXVII

Two visits later, while Passimante labored at his *bas-relief* in the church across the way, Derek completed his initial drawings on the Seravezza block, making his rough outlines on all five surfaces and began the cutting.

He had started his workday an hour later than was his custom that morning, the first hour after Lavinia's arrival being devoted to *divertissement*. In embrace, their bodies intertwined, undulating in the dance of carnal expression. They shaped Eros, breathing life into his being with kisses, caresses and whispered words of love. With Derek the act was so entrancing, so incredibly fulfilling. She silently prayed that it might never end. And to think there were five glorious weeks still to come!

Conquering his heart had to be the most supremely satisfying triumph in memory. He was so intensely desirable, so possessable she wanted to steal him from his stone and his chisels, run with him to the end of the earth, lie with him for all eternity, love him until they crumbled to dust in each other's arms.

She had never felt this way about any man before. When he swept her back to reality with the quiet announcement that it was time to get up, go downstairs and get to work, she wanted to leap up, lock them in and toss the key out the window. And when the shadows of afternoon had lengthened, the sun began losing itself behind Monte Solaro and it was time to stop working, it was all she could do to resist seizing him and begging him to carry her back upstairs.

Back at the villa she spent the days between visits,

when he was busy with Passimante on their Biblical scenes, wandering from room to room whispering his name as if half expecting him to reveal himself in a doorway or a corner. Or she would lie in bed losing herself in fantasy, conquering him over and over again in imagination.

Late in the second week, with Enrico again away on business, she decided to take Deirdre along to show her the work in progress. It was Friday, the birthday of Santa Stefano and a school holiday.

"But," she emphasized, as the two of them started down the road to Caprile and beyond it Anacapri, "I must swear you to absolute secrecy. You're not to even hint to Enrico what I'm up to. He thinks I'm having my portrait painted for his birthday."

"I won't say a word. But how can he do it?"

"Who do what?"

"How can this man carve Enrico without seeing him?"

Lavinia explained, adding: "It isn't perfect—not as good as if he were sitting there day in day out—but there's no mistaking the head and face. Besides, your father will be so flattered I doubt if he'll look for imperfections. After all, it's the thought that counts, child."

"Please."

"I'm sorry, Deirdre."

They walked along, Deirdre picking a daisy, spinning it, plucking its petals one by one. "You are insane, you know that, Vinnie? Doing a bust of somebody from photographs. I'll bet you commissioned him just so you could go every day and watch him work."

"What a horribly suspicious mind you have!" Lavinia giggled. "Still, I must confess it's not exactly distasteful being with him. But it's all work," she hastened to add. "Strictly business."

There was a slight chill in the air despite the ministrations of the sun. From Punta del Monaco to Cala del

Rio, it spread its light, the isle becoming an enormous chunk of gold-speckled gray-green ore set in the sapphire of the Tyrrhenian Sea.

Derek was working over the pointing machine, adjusting the point and legs to their proper settings. Then he penciled a dot on the plaster at the point of contact, adding to the myriad collection of pockmarks already in evidence. This accomplished, he lifted the machine off the plaster, lowering it onto the marble, gently pressing the needle onto the surface.

"Derek, this is Deirdre. Derek Childs, my dear, all the way from——"

"Avenmouth. It's near Bristol on the Welsh side of the island," said Derek, smiling and shaking hands. "I'm delighted to meet you, Deirdre."

Deirdre stared, practically openmouthed, drinking in the sight of him, responding mechanically. "How do you do."

"And this," said Lavinia, pointing, "is your father. Twice the size, but that's in keeping with his ego, wouldn't you say?"

"It's marvelous," said Deirdre in an awed tone. "The plaster looks just like him."

"*That's* marvelous," said Derek, "precisely what I wanted, a second opinion. Your mother's prejudiced, you see. Much too unfinicky. And she's hiding your father in a closet somewhere."

"I never realized sculptors used something like that to copy," said Deirdre pointing at the machine.

"It's life's biggest boon. It measures at hundreds of different points. See all the dots? All about a quarter of an inch apart. So even a clumsy pounder like me can't go very far wrong between points." He patted the machine. "We owe it all to an Italian, Antonio Carona, the marquis of Ischia. Without this clever brainchild of his, I shudder to think how stone would come out."

"What do you do if you knock off a larger piece than you intend to?" asked Deirdre.

"I try not to. When you rough out, you allow an extra half inch outside the actual form. Stone, like wood, has a definite cleavage; it always works better in one direction than another. Once you establish your cleavage, you try and follow it. Even if it means altering an angle, a turn of head or thrust of knee, like Michelangelo did.

"Still, if you knock off a good-sized piece, it's irreplaceable. Then," he shrugged, "you persuade your patron that it was entirely the fault of the stone, wangle additional monies out of him and start over."

"What a tragedy!"

"Indeed it is." He winked and grinned. "For whomever is paying."

They watched him work until the sun climbed directly overhead. All at once a loud shouting was heard outside the door in the piazza. Lavinia went to look. Two women were fighting over a live chicken, its legs bound, wings flapping, feathers flying. One woman was struggling to wrench it from the other. A fat, cherry-cheeked man in disreputable clothes topped by a brimless straw hat was attempting to mediate. A crowd assembled rapidly. The women screamed at each other, the chicken flapped back and forth between them, the man separated them, then was pushed out from between as they rejoined the battle. Louder and louder it became, and funnier and funnier. One of the women was at least a foot taller than the other, but her opponent was wider and quicker and the match appeared even. In no time the arena was littered with feathers. And more continued to escape the beleaguered bird as it was jerked back and forth between them, cackling its resentment at the top of its voice.

Lavinia laughed until her sides hurt, calling to Deirdre and Derek to come and watch. Suddenly the fray took an unexpected turn as both women whirled on the self-appointed mediator. The one holding the chicken let it drop and both went for the man.

"Deirdre!" Lavinia turned. There was no one in the

studio. On the far side through the open door leading into the garden at the rear of the building she saw them standing, talking animatedly, Deirdre holding a beautiful white daffodil. She turned and came at Lavinia's summons, Derek following. They said their good-byes and, circling the feathery residue of the squabble, which had concluded as abruptly as it began with the taller combatant in possession of the chicken, walked off in the direction of Capri.

They had lunch at the same restaurant, at the same table given them on the day Lavinia had reported her jewels missing. The day they had first discovered Derek Childs.

"He's beautiful," said Deirdre solemnly, stabbing her *quiche* with a fork. "He's like a statue come to life: his head, his face, his shoulders. He's absolutely dreamy!"

"Tsk-tsk, such talk. I didn't bring you up there to salivate over him. I wanted you to see the bust."

"The bust, yes. How can anyone that handsome be that talented? It seems downright unfair!"

"With your permission is it possible we can stop talking about Mr. Childs?"

"Just beautiful."

"Deirdre!"

XXXVIII

Her next appearance in Passimante's studio resulted in a mild shock, which lost its mildness after the first few moments.

"Why don't we skip it today, Lavinia," said Derek in what she took to be an apologetic tone. "I'm just not up to it."

"Not up to it? I love your choice of words, darling." She stroked his cheek. Taking hold of her wrist, he kissed the palm of her hand. Throwing her arms around his neck, she pushed hard against him, kissing him passionately.

"There, does that help get you 'up to it'?"

"I'm serious, darling. The problem is time. I seem to be spending more in bed and less working. You seem to forget I've a deadline to meet."

"But you're almost done."

"Not exactly. Besides, from now on, I've got to give more time to Julio. After all, his work is my reason for being here. I should be working with him every day, not every other."

"So our lovemaking is interfering with your work? How discouraging."

"Let's not be bitter."

"Do I sound bitter? Disappointed perhaps, but never bitter." She brightened. "I have a thought: I'll go and come back tonight after dinner. We can spend the whole night together. Darkness is so much more romantic."

"I don't think that would be good. We have to consider Julio."

"You don't sleep in the same room."

"No, but it's his house. He's very straight-laced, very religious."

"He wouldn't approve."

"He's been very good to me, Lavinia. I shouldn't want to——"

"To what, upset him? Really, Derek, you're a grown man. Your private life is your own—at least it ought to be. I'm the one who should be sensitive about his being on the other side of the wall. But who cares!"

Derek pondered. "He's going to Rome to visit his sister some time soon."

"Wonderful!"

"We'll be able to see each other then. But as to staying over tonight——"

"Forget I mentioned it. It's much too risky."

"He has been very decent toward me. I'd hate to offend him."

"Say nothing more. I understand."

"Now I should get to work."

"And I'll go."

"You needn't."

"I'd rather. I wouldn't want to distract you. Darling, you're looking at the new me, all concern and consideration for others. Doesn't love work the most magical changes in people?" She kissed him again, holding him tightly.

She came away from the studio, crossing the piazza, half hearing the muffled clinking of Passimante's hammer coming from inside the church. Starting down the Caprile road, she turned the incident over in her mind. He was like a different person, she thought. Having classified him as a conquest, it was totally unexpected. He seemed disinterested, looking past her as he spoke, giving the conversation little thought or friendliness. Artistic temperament surfacing, perhaps?

She'd see him again day after tomorrow. She'd wear something more daring, more deliberately seductive.

Deirdre was hours late getting home from school. The sun set and the afterglow had come stealing up the mountain invading the trees and spreading across the front of the house and the pool when Lavinia sighted her approaching the front door. Her book bag was slung from her left shoulder and her face wore a bemused smile.

Waiting impatiently, Lavinia had been pacing her own bedroom. Now, through the partially opened door she heard Deirdre come up the stairs and go down the corridor to her room. Lavinia followed, knocking, opening the door.

"Well, well. How thoughtful of you to come home at last."

"I'm sorry I'm so late." Deirdre slumped into the peacock chair, her eyes on her hands, an oddly serious expression capturing her features.

"May I ask where you've been?"

"School."

"School lets out at two o'clock. It's going on six-thirty." Lavinia came into the room closing the door. "Once again I'll ask you: Where have you been?"

"Nowhere. Please, Vinnie, I'm exhausted. Can we discuss it after dinner?"

"We'll discuss it now. Nowhere is no answer. Suppose I guess. Could it possibly be Anacapri—again?" Deirdre brought her head up sharply, her eyes anxious. "Yes, again, the second time this week."

"So I went to Anacapri. I didn't sneak out of school, if that's what's worrying you."

"You know damned well that's not what's worrying me! We can cut this very short," she said icily. "You, my dear, are to stay away from Derek Childs. Is that clear?"

"Why? He asked me to come."

"Did he really?"

"Didn't I just say so? We don't do anything, if that's what you think."

"What should I think?"

"We talk, that's all. It so happens he's the most interesting man I have ever met."

"I would say he's the first man you've ever met, so who do you measure him against to make him 'the most interesting'?"

"What in the world are you so upset about?"

"The man is a cradle robber, Deirdre. That's the only way to describe him!"

"Vinnie!"

"He's over thirty. What could he possibly find to talk about with a fifteen-year-old? What's so fascinating?"

"You're fifty-six. What's so fascinating about a thirty-year-old?"

Like a snake striking, Lavinia's hand flew out slapping her loudly across the cheek. Deirdre gaped at her in shock and amazement, but though her cheek reddened perceptibly, she did not touch it.

"How dare you say such a thing!"

"It's true!"

"You insolent little bitch!"

"Thank you, Mother dear!"

Suddenly Lavinia was livid, her eyes furious. She started to say something then stopped abruptly, catching herself, forcing herself to calm down. Biting her lip, she leaned against the closed door.

"I'm sorry I said that. I'm sorry I hit you. I apologize."

"It's all right." It wasn't. The hurt in Deirdre's tone, the look on her face clearly said it wasn't.

"I've never struck you before. I don't know what came over me. Deirdre?"

"Yes, Mother?"

"Why mother all of a sudden? I like you to call me Vinnie. I like it very much. Darling, please promise me you won't ever go over there to see him again. Never, unless we go together."

"If you insist."

"Deirdre, I do wish you wouldn't take that tone. I'm trying very hard to be understanding, to be fair. It's you I'm thinking of. It's for your own good, darling. Derek is much too old for you. I know you're not a child, but you live a cloistered life. A circumstance that's more or less unavoidable living here as we do. In some ways, you're still immature. In the ways of the world. I don't say that to offend you or to hurt you, but because it's true. Men like Derek Childs, good-looking experienced men, can be loads of fun to be with, for a time. Then they tire of you and end up breaking your heart, making you miserable. The Bible says 'Enter not into temptation: The spirit indeed *is* willing, but the flesh *is* weak.'"

Deirdre lifted her eyes searching Lavinia's. "You are a damnable hypocrite, do you know that, Vinnie? A total fraud!"

Setting her jaw, her eyes blazing, Lavinia strode to her, readying her hand to bring it down with all the force she could muster.

But Deirdre's eyes stopped her. Slowly she lowered her hand. Whirling about, she stalked out of the room, slamming the door behind her, rattling the figured bowl sitting on the windowsill.

XXXIX

Cape Carbonara at the southeastern tip of Sardinia had long since vanished into a thick gray mist off the stern of the *Vampata* as Lisa awoke, sitting up in the bed. For the first time since her capture by Captain Marsala, husband, father and sadistic brute, he had become too stultified with undrugged rum to remember to lock her in the closet after he was done with her.

She had no idea how far they had yet to travel across the Tyrrhenian Sea to Naples, located mid-shin of the leg in the boot of Italy. But whatever the distance, the more miles slipping from under the stern the closer she and Guilfoyle came to their "accidental" deaths. If she was to act, it would have to be soon. Preferably the next time her captor returned.

Acting, however, overpowering him, knocking him out with a candlestick, his sextant, the rum carafe was easier imagined than done. If he followed his customary pattern, he would come in fairly to roaring drunk, pour an ounce or so of the evil yellow powder he carried in an envelope in his back pocket into rum in a glass and force her to drink it.

Force her? Force was no longer necessary. She drank it willingly, unable to resist drinking it, her willpower deserting her, her addiction to it worsening daily. And once under its influence, he had his way with her.

Still, her course was clear, if difficult, perhaps impossible to follow. Somehow, to save her life and Guilfoyle's, she must resurrect her enfeebled will, imbue it with the vigor of purpose, the sinew of self-preservation, and deal with her captor. She had to withstand the impulse to swallow the rum, fight back and get the best of him. The key lay in taking advantage of his intoxication. Render him powerless and lock him in the closet.

Wrapping herself in the blanket, she rose from the bed and went into the other room. As always, the carafe stood on the tray at the corner of the desk. It was half full. She could empty it out a porthole, but what would that gain her other than additional abuse? If only he kept his insidious yellow powder in the cabin instead of on his person, she might find it and dispose of it. And in doing so arouse his anger so that he might very well beat her to death!

Twilight came and night, darkness stealing through the portholes in both rooms, seeking the corners and filling their narrow limits. In that time, she had searched every inch of the cabin and bedroom hoping to find a gun or knife, anything sharp yet small enough to conceal behind her wrist with its hilt in her fist. There was nothing. It was hopeless. Despairing, she sat on the edge of the bed, the blanket pulled about her nakedness, waiting for him—the rattle of his key in the lock, his hulking body filling the doorway, the foul stench of stale rum about him as he lurched into the room slamming the heavy door. Preparing her rum, the taste of it slipping down her throat, the terrifying effect upon her vision, her will, her body. And the nightmare resumed. Only this time for the last time.

She must not drink, not a drop. She must steel herself as she had never before. Let him thrash her, force the tumbler to her lips, let him do his worst. She would not drink! After a time, he would give it up, throw her down on the bed and begin. Then, or after it was over —if she had any strength left at all—when he lapsed into his drunken stupor, she would cave in his skull with whatever heavy object was at hand. She would pound and pound until she could no longer lift her arms. He had to be killed, it was the only way.

It seemed all so simple, so easy of execution in the mind, one logical phase linking up with the next, creating a series that would culminate with him lying at her feet, the floor drenched with his blood, his head crushed like a melon.

It would be anything but simple. A dozen things could go wrong, a score. And were she to try and fail, he would kill her in ten seconds. Wrap her in this very blanket, weigh her down with a length of pipe and drop her over the fantail.

His key sounded in the lock, an ominous clicking, turning, the lock releasing, the door opening. He came staggering in singing loudly, ignoring her standing in the bedroom doorway. Straight to the desk he went, fumbling in his pocket, finding his powder, adding it to a glass of rum. Continuing his song, he lit the kerosene lamp then he held the glass up before him, examining the rum in the wan yellow light.

"Your tonic, dear lady, see it glow in the glass. The fire that binds the will." Lowering the glass he stared at her. "You have no idea how lucky you are. I could dose you so full your brain would crack into little pieces. You wouldn't eat, you wouldn't drink, you wouldn't want to. All you would want is more powder, more and more and more to shrivel you up inside like a dried prune, to consume you. You should be grateful I'm the considerate sort. I'm very careful to give you just enough to relax you, to soften the world so that it wraps itself around you. And you feel, I know, like you're quilted in a cloud that seeps inside you, through you. Until you and it are one. So drop the blanket and come and drink."

"No!"

"No? My, my, my. Are you trying to say you don't want it? That's absurd; you know you do. Look at your eyes. They're snapping like tiny whips. You can almost taste it."

"I refuse to drink it. Why do you force it on me, because you have to have me helpless? That's the reason, isn't it? Because you cannot get up the courage to rape me unless you're sure I'm too weak to resist."

"Get up the courage to rape you? Don't be stupid. I can do what I like with you. I can break every bone in your body and rape you dead! I once raped a corpse, if you could call it rape. Interesting."

"You rape me only after I drink. Why is that?"

"Because I want you to enjoy our play as much as I, dear lady. Not resist me, scratch and kick and scream and carry on like an animal. Think of it as a sedative. Come, drink."

"If I enjoyed making love with you, I wouldn't need it, would I? I mean, think how much more enjoyable it would be if I gave myself willingly, with passion, with desire."

His eyes gleamed in the amber light. He was thinking. Then he shook his head. "You drink. Now!"

She resisted, pushing him away, but he was much too powerful for her, opening her mouth with one hand, pouring the rum down her with the other. She choked and spewed, beating her little fists against his chest until the glass was empty and further renitency was useless. She collapsed in his arms, the blanket slipping from her body. He carried her into the bedroom and dropped her on the bed. Then he fetched the rum and the lamp and brought them in, closing the door with his foot. He placed the lamp on the table beside the bed and drank from the carafe, the crimson liquid running down the sides of his chin in twin rivulets. Then he set the carafe on the floor, divested himself of his trousers and lay down on top of her.

And all the while she fought, arousing her will, goading it to action, inciting it to throw off its supineness and resist. Resist! His rigid member slipped between her thighs and she gritted her teeth against the pain to

come, turning her head to avoid sight of his leer, his vile
breath. He had pushed her diagonally across the bed
and her right hand dropped over the side, her knuckles
touching the cold floor. Wandering forward, her hand
came in contact with the carafe. Hope seized her. His
body pinning her to the bed, he brought both hands up,
clamping her head between them and smothering her
with kisses, thrusting his tongue into her mouth.

Fighting back the effects of the rum, the all-possess-
ing constraint of it, she roused her strength, gripped the
carafe and with a supreme effort of will brought it up,
smashing him full in the head with it, the rum spilling
down upon her.

For a moment he lay still, then lifting himself upward
on his stiffened arms, he glared, his eyes protruding
grotesquely. With all her remaining strength, she
pushed his chest. He dropped sideways, losing the
balance of his arms, flailing wildly for something to
hang onto, his left hand striking the lamp. It teetered
and, as he fell to the floor, toppled over shattering on
his face, spilling its fire over his beard, igniting it
swiftly, turning his face into a torch!

He screamed horribly, his hands flying to his face,
beating it, quashing the flames. She neither saw nor
heard his agony. Relieved of his weight, she was up out
of the bed, snatching up the empty carafe, dropping to
her knees and bringing it down upon his burning face
again and again and again and again!

Faint from exhaustion, she dropped the carafe and
staggered to her feet. Rushing to a porthole and opening it, she sucked in the cold sea air. It cleared her head
and restored her strength. She looked down at his pros-
trate figure. The moonlight slipping through the porthole fell upon his battered face. He appeared more
dead than alive. But he was not dead; the breath hissed
from his shattered bloody nose.

The key to the closet door in the other room protruded invitingly from the lock. Swinging the door wide, she held it back with a chair and dragged and pushed him out of the bedroom and into the closet, then locked the door and placed the chair back under the knob at a tilt.

XL

Finding matches, she lit another lamp, washed, dressed and straightened her hair. Locating an unopened bottle of rum, she availed herself of half a tumblerful to steady her nerves and silence her heart.

One problem still remained: the crew. If she appeared on deck, they might seize her and lock her in another cabin. Or would their loyalty extend to voluntary complicity in their captain's crimes? Crimes which, now that she thought about it with a clear head, would have to be proved before a judge. Perhaps it would be wiser to stay put, not show her face outside the door until Naples.

But the ship could be hours from port, and when Marsala failed to appear on deck, somebody—probably the first officer—would go looking for him. Head straight for his cabin. He'd search, he'd find him.

As she leaned against the desk weighing the future possibilities, the engines ground to a stop and the sound of loud voices topside was heard. Opening the door a crack, she heard whistles blowing and steps directly overhead, people running back and forth. A light flashed at the top of the companionway and a loud voice began barking orders in Italian. Her curiosity aroused, she slowly ventured up the steps, emerging onto the deck. The crew was lined up along the starboard gunwale and a number of uniformed men were striding about. Two boats, both flying the Italian colors, were drawn up alongside the ship and an officer in a light-blue uniform and white cap came over the railing by way of a Jacob's ladder. Guilfoyle came running up to her all smiles.

"Mrs. Dandridge! I've been worried sick about you!"

"What is all this? What's going on?"

"It's the customs people and the police. They're taking command. Where's the captain?"

"Below. What's going on?"

"They're smugglers, caught in the act. Somebody in Naples tipped off the authorities." He pointed toward the bow, where the lights of the city were visible, orange and white jewels strewn across black velvet.

"What are they smuggling?"

"The manifest says their cargo is sugar and cotton, but there's bullion aboard."

"Gold?"

"And counterfeit American money and God knows what else!"

A swarthy little man resembling a chicken, with his sharply pointed features and narrow chest, interrupted. He wore the bar of a police lieutenant. "*Mi scusi*. The lady is with you, *signore?*"

"Yes, lieutenant."

"You were picked up when he was, is that correct, *signora?*"

She explained. The officer touched the brim of his cap in salute. "We will be pleased to bring you both to port. This ship is impounded. The officers and crew will not be permitted to disembark for at least two hours. But you can go."

"What will happen to them?" asked Lisa.

"To the crew, probably nothing, unless there is provable complicity. The captain is another matter. I understand this is not his first offense. He can be sent to prison for a long time."

"He's in his cabin, in the closet."

The officer stared. In as delicate terms as possible,

she explained what had transpired. Guilfoyle's face filled with admiration, and when she had finished, he shook his head in disbelief.

"Mrs. Dandridge," he said quietly, "you never cease to amaze me."

XLI

The villa came into view as a great orange blur with needles of light surrounding it through the tears in Deirdre's eyes. She wiped them away with her well-dampened hanky, touching her nose and sniffling before restoring it to her pocket. But the blur came back within moments as more tears accumulated. She circled the house and came in the garden door, heading up the stairs for her room. The door to the master bedroom was ajar and she could hear Lavinia and Enrico talking as she arrived at the top of the stairs.

Lavinia sat at her vanity brushing her hair, sighting a gray intruder and plucking it savagely.

"I practically begged her to come straight home from school. She promised me faithfully she would. Now she's disobeyed again. I don't know what we're going to do with her!"

"Perhaps I should have a word with her," said Enrico, standing behind Lavinia, studying her in the mirror. "You flare up too easily."

"Don't be ridiculous! I'm her mother; I can hardly treat her like a sister. I'll nip this in the bud."

"Perhaps somebody at the school knows what she's up to, a teacher or one of her classmates."

"No, no, no! Besides, 'what she's up to' isn't that important. What upsets me is her disobedience. I won't stand for it!"

"You're too hard on her."

"And you're too soft! Somebody around this place has to discipline her."

"You fly off the handle. Darling, I'm not criticizing

269

for the sake of it. You react much too strongly to what she says, what she does. I've seen you."

"You don't know what you're talking about!"

"Yes, I do. Every time she mentions her mother and father, you get all nerved up. And let her even hint that she wants to go back to Rhode Island and see the house and talk to friends of theirs and you turn six colors and come apart at the seams. Don't you think she's bright enough to notice? She must be curious as the Devil. Even I get curious."

"About what, may I ask?"

"The whole business: the fire, her mother and father burning to death. And you just happening to be there."

Lavinia got up and closed the door, sitting back down on the bench. "What's so strange about my being there? I was one of the family. Why shouldn't I have been there?"

"Why should you? You claim they treated you shabbily. You hated the sight of the two of them. You should be the last person to be there. And how is it Deirdre escaped the fire, but neither her mother nor father was able to? She was a babe in arms. One of them had to have carried her out."

"The nurse did."

"So you say. What caused the fire, anyway?"

"How should I know? Lower your voice, the servants aren't deaf!"

"It's all so hazy. I find it difficult to believe both father and mother were the only two casualties."

"Don't bother 'finding it difficult to believe,' Enrico. It's none of your business."

"If I have doubts, what makes you think she doesn't?"

Lavinia stopped brushing her hair in mid-stroke, bringing the brush down loudly against the marble counter of the vanity.

"If you dare discuss it with her. If you so much as hint you're curious——"

"See, there you are, overreacting again. If you're telling her the truth, what are you worried about? But it's not true, is it? Somebody's still alive."

She turned on her bench, her eyes suffused with contempt. "You fool."

"Ahh."

"You actually think I'd kidnap her?"

"I wouldn't put it past you. I wouldn't put anything past you. I know you too well."

"You don't know me at all! You may know wine, but you don't know two pins about women."

"Her parents *are* alive, aren't they?" She laughed, but it was brittle and tinged with ice. "I knew it. And so does she, she's got to."

"So what if they are?"

"If they are, you'd better talk with a priest. You're in bigger trouble than you know."

"They're dead, my darling, dead, buried, turned to dust!"

"How strange."

"What now?"

"When you lie, your cheeks don't redden like most people's. But the lie is on your face, spread all over it."

"I thought we were talking about Deirdre. It's curious, darling. Aren't you concerned? Aren't you the least bit worried about her?" She stood up. "I am. I'm going out to look for her!"

"Don't be silly. She could be anywhere on the isle. Besides, it's only four o'clock."

"She should have been home an hour and a half ago."

"So give her another half hour."

"No!"

"Do you want me to tag along?"

"No I don't!" She pinned on her hat and drew a figured woolen shawl over her shoulders. "I need a respite from you and your nasty suspicions!"

XLII

Lavinia confronted the maid Terese at the front door. "I'm going out to look for Miss Deirdre."

"Oh, she came home, *signora*."

Lavinia paused in putting on her gloves. "When?"

"I don't know when; I did not see her come in. I saw her go out. She was carrying her bag."

"Schoolbag?"

"No, the *valigia*."

"Damn!"

She half ran all the way to Anacapri, nearly half a mile. Arriving breathless, she looked about the piazza. There was no sound of hammering coming from the church and the door to the studio was closed and locked. She beat upon it loudly with her fists.

"Derek! Derek!"

He came to the door in his trousers, shirtless and barefoot. "Lavinia, what is it? What do you want?"

"Where is she?" Brushing past him, she spun about angrily. "Where?"

"Where is who? What are you talking about?"

"Don't start games with me, you cradle-robbing bastard! Get her down here this instant! You hear me!"

"Deirdre?" He stared in confusion. Ignoring him, she ran across the room and up the stairs. "Hey, come back here!" He was after her quickly, passing her before she got to the top, stopping her at the closed door to the bedroom.

"Open it! Let me by!"

"Now just calm down."

"Deirdre! Come out of there, do you hear me!"

272

"I'm telling you she's not here!"

"You're a liar! I could brain you for this, you ungrateful son of a bitch!"

He stood with his feet spread before the door, his arms outstretched and angled downward in the classic thou-shalt-not-pass pose. The lock clicked and the door opened slowly. A pretty dark-haired girl, the sheet drawn snugly about her, stared at Lavinia with a puzzled expression. Derek grabbed the knob and pulled the door shut.

"Now do you believe me?" he asked in a hostile tone.

It was as if a huge stone had been dropped on her. For a moment, she could not believe her eyes. Then fury and loathing swept over her, she brought her nails down across his bare chest, raising bloody lines, and cursed him at the top of her voice. He winced but made no move to retaliate.

"Get out of here!" he snapped, cutting into her diatribe. "Now! And don't come back!"

Down the stairs she stomped, striding across the studio, passing the half-finished bust of Enrico on its stand, pausing, looking about, finding nothing to suit her purpose. Seizing the bust, oblivious of its great weight, she pushed it high over her head, then sent it crashing to the floor. It broke into three large pieces.

Outside she heard a voice above her and looked upward. It was the dark-haired girl leaning out the window, smirking down at her.

"Hey, Grandma Moneybags, what are you so mad about?" she asked mockingly.

"Bitch!"

"Hey, if you're looking for your little girl, she was here before, but we sent her packing. Hey, hey."

The girl was jerked back bodily, the window slammed shut.

The bastard, the stinking rotten pig! The beautiful son of a bitch!

XLIII

"No!" Enrico brought his fist down sharply against his thigh.

"But she's gone to Naples!"

"Calm down. It's getting dark. You can't go prowling about the docks looking for her. You'd get raped and your throat slit. The first thing in the morning we'll go together. With a couple of policemen."

"Tomorrow will be too late! If she isn't assaulted and murdered tonight, she'll be on the first ship out!"

"No ships will be leaving after dark."

"And what's to stop them?"

"She'll have to book passage. She'll have to make arrangements. All that takes time."

"And where do you suppose she'll stay tonight?" He shrugged. "You don't know, of course you don't!"

"With a friend; in a hotel. She won't be curling up in an alley. She has plenty of money."

"If we doled out two or three lire a week to her instead of spoiling her with tons of money, she wouldn't be able to buy passage!"

"Of course, blame me!"

"Whatever possessed her to do such a thing?"

"Isn't it obvious? You say she came back and then went out. She must have overheard us."

"She did! She did!" Lavinia stopped abruptly, her hand flat against her forehead. "What could she have heard?"

"What difference does it make? The milk is spilled."

"We've got to go to Naples at once. Straight to the

police. Get them to blanket the entire harbor with men."

"No."

"You are the stubbornest bastard alive!"

"Don't take it out on me; I'm not the reason she packed up and got out."

"Don't be too sure. She may have gotten sick and tired of living on the edge of uncertainty, wondering when her dear father would attack her again!"

"There's no need for that. There's nothing more to say. You are not to leave this house tonight and that's final! If I have to tie you up and lock you in this room, I'll be happy to. Now shut your big mouth and give my ears a rest!"

XLIV

Mr. Alfred P. Winslow, American vice-consul in Naples, was a diminutive tightly wound spring of energy with a head as bald as a bone, a wedge-shaped chin and small-boy features neatly assembled between. He sat before an enormous American flag practically concealing the entire wall. And talked to her over his desk, over the tips of his fingers forming an inverted V.

"You have all the clothes you need?"

Lisa nodded. "Yes, thank you."

"And money?"

"Plenty."

"Mr. Brubaker, our consul, tells me you'll be taking a ship to Boston day after tomorrow."

"That's right."

"You'll forgive me for saying so, but you seem——"

"Disappointed? I am." She smoothed her lap, the tips of her fingers lingering on the pale blue brocade, and explained.

"But you'd have to wait a month for passage to Pernambuco from here," he said. "It's not a major port, like Naples, or Boston, or New York, merely a convenient fueling stop on the way to Cape Horn."

"So I understand. The irony of it is that before the storm we had actually passed his ship."

The double doors behind her opened and a secretary wearing spectacles much too large for her face cleared her throat, excusing the interruption.

"There is a gentleman outside asking for Mrs. Dandridge, sir."

"Thank you," said Lisa rising and offering her hand

to the vice-consul. "You've been most helpful, Mr. Winslow. I can't thank you and Mr. Brubaker enough."

"That's what we're here for—mostly. I trust you'll have a comfortable trip home."

"More comfortable than coming over, hopefully."

The gentleman asking for Mrs. Dandridge was the first mate of the *Olympia II*.

"Listen to this," Guilfoyle began as the two of them started down the steps into Piazza Principe di Napoli. "I'm pulling out."

"Where to?"

"I reported to the company's Naples office and I've been reassigned to Rotterdam. I'm sailing with the tide, about half an hour."

"What ship?"

"The *Sea Devil*."

"I've heard of it."

"Your husband probably built her. She's an old clipper with a history of mystery that would fill a bookshelf: stolen by pirates, hauling slaves, you name it."

Lisa searched his eyes. "Haven't you had enough excitement for the time being?"

"There's never enough. I came to say good-bye."

"Don't be in such a rush. I'll come down and see you off."

"You really shouldn't, not these docks. Not in that outfit."

She swung about. "Like it? A gift from the American consul. I'm going to see you off and there'll be no argument."

They headed in the direction of the Piazza Municipio. It was a warm and lovely day, a cloudless blue sky canopying the dockside, the sea birds wheeling and darting, ships and boats trafficking into and out of the harbor. The clock in the steeple of nearby San Ferdinando struck nine as they walked by Castle Nuovo, built in the late 13th Century for Robert I of Anjou and diligently restored by doting and appreciative Neapolitans down the ensuing centuries. Guilfoyle stopped to light a cigarette, cupping his hands against the breeze. She waited for him. It took three matches and all of 30 seconds. Thirty seconds in which just around the corner they were to turn a young girl carrying a small valise, her lovely red hair loosened to the breeze, was marching determinedly up the gangplank of a nondescript-looking sailing ship. Reaching the deck, she was shown down a companionway by a bearded officer.

Guilfoyle's ship to Rotterdam was the *Sea Devil*, a four-masted paddle-wheeler similar in appearance to the *Vampata*, sufficiently like it to stir memories.

"What do you suppose is happening to the *Vampata*?" she asked.

"She's still impounded, as far as I know. Your friend Marsala is in the hospital." He laughed. "Recovering from a recent encounter with a certain lady passenger."

"If I had time I'd really fix him."

"Neapolitan justice will do it for you. He'll get a good ten years."

"What a blessing for his family!"

The *Sea Devil*'s whistle sounded, scattering a flock of terns.

"That's me," he said soberly, lowering his newly acquired seabag from his shoulder and offering his hand. "Good-bye, Mrs. Dandridge."

"Lisa, please. For the first time and I'm afraid the last. And you're John?"

"Jack. The very best of luck to you. I hope you catch up with him."

"I will, probably in Singapore. But somewhere, someday," she added wistfully.

"It sounds stupid, I know, but, well, it's been a pleasure, a great pleasure. Not what we went through but meeting you, knowing you. Your husband is a lucky man."

She tightened her grip on his hand. "I'll miss you,

Jack. Take care of yourself. And if ever you get to Providence."

"Blackwood. I'll remember. Good-bye again, Lisa."

"Good-bye, Jack. Godspeed."

He restored his bag to his shoulder, hefting it into a comfortable position, walked off, climbed the gangplank, turned at the top, waved and vanished.

She waited, and moments later he reappeared on deck. The bow and stern lines were loosened, the ship hooted farewell and, with the assistance of a stubby little barnacle-studded tug, it started out into the bay. He stood at the rail waving and minutes later the *Sea Devil* turned and headed in the direction of Sardinia.

She started back the way they had come. The docks were even busier than Norfolk, cargo being laded and unladed, stevedores sweating and swearing under the broiling sun. But there was an order, a neatness to the activity here conspicuously lacking in Norfolk. There were few loafers, practically everyone within view was busy doing something. And the police were all about, strolling around in pairs with their pompous-looking Bonaparte hats, brown uniforms and short swords dangling from their hips.

She would register at a hotel in the vicinity for the two nights before her ship departed for Boston. Once arrived, she'd go straight home, check on things and make immediate preparations for the long trek west. Cross country this time to San Francisco, and from there by clipper ship to the Orient. Depending upon how long it took her to reach the West Coast. . . .

Stopping, as if blocked by an invisible wall, she blinked in astonishment. Her hand flew to her breast; she was convinced her heart was about to jump out of it! Not 50 feet away a tall, dark-haired woman in a floppy white hat and orange-silk dress, a fringed cashmere shawl about her shoulders, stood haranguing a policeman, loudly demanding that he take her aboard the ship anchored nearby. She pointed at it and gesticulated angrily, then threw up her hands and stalked off.

Lisa followed, so completely astonished by the sight that she was tempted to pinch herself.

But there was no mistaking that face, that voice. Fourteen years, or 40 years, she would have recognized her instantly! All morning long and into the afternoon she followed her about the docks.

XLV

To Lavinia's surprise, Enrico was sitting in his study working when she got home, slamming in through the garden door, storming into the drawing room and pacing up and down loudly upbraiding the Greeks and Trojans peopling the murals, the closest and most convenient targets for her calumny. Enrico came in.

"No luck?"

"What do you think! Why bother to ask?"

"Calm down. It's possible she didn't even go to Naples."

"Of course she went to Naples, stupid!" Slumping into a chair, she buried her face in her hands. "Gone, she's gone! I'll never see her again! It's so unfair, so wrong! What have I done to deserve this?"

He comforted her. "Don't get all upset. The police are looking for her."

"The police! Those idiots couldn't find a stray dog! Stupid popinjays strutting about in their silly uniforms!"

The garden-door bell jangled and Terese padded by the drawing-room door to answer it.

Lisa pulled the cord a second time impatiently. The door eased open. The maid beamed.

"Miss Deirdre, your mother. . . ." Her voice trailed off, a nonplussed look replacing her smile. It was and yet it *wasn't* Deirdre!

"Good afternoon. My name is Dandridge. Mrs. Ross Dandridge. May I please speak with your mistress? We're old friends."

"Who is it, Terese?" called Lavinia from within.

Terese opened the door, standing aside. Lavinia appeared gaping in amazement, blood draining from her cheeks.

"You!"

"Good afternoon, Lavinia. Well, you've led me a merry chase. It's been a long time. May I come in?"

"Come in, come in," burst Enrico, coming up behind Lavinia.

"What a beautiful home," said Lisa pleasantly, entering the foyer, glancing about. "So cool. It's so hot outside." She extended her hand to Enrico. "How do you do. I'm Lisa Dandridge."

"A pleasure, madam. I am Enrico Aldoni. My wife, Lavinia." He angled his head studying Lisa. "Remarkable, the resemblance. Oh," he looked from one to the other, "you two know one another, don't you?"

"Mrs. Dandridge and I will talk privately, dear, if you don't mind," said Lavinia.

"Of course," said Enrico. He nodded to Terese. She walked off and he went into his study and closed the door.

"The drawing room," said Lavinia. She followed Lisa in, closed the doors and indicated a chair. They sat across from each other.

"You followed me from Naples."

Lisa did not hear her. Her attention was on Lavinia's face, her mind racing, peeling away the years. "Lavinia, Lavinia. Of all people. Of all places. You're looking remarkably well——"

"Preserved? You certainly haven't changed. Not a whit. As lovely as ever, although a little thin."

"Mrs. Enrico Aldoni? How did that happen?"

"Does it matter? Are you really interested?"

"Not as interested as about other things, namely Deirdre's whereabouts."

"Your daughter?"

"My daughter."

"What on earth would she be doing here?"

"I wouldn't know. She certainly didn't come all the

way from Providence of her own accord. Where is she?"

"Why ask me?"

"Lavinia, when your maid answered the door, she mistook me for Deirdre. Just for a second, long enough to blurt out the name Deirdre. My daughter. Or *our* daughter so it seems. It's all rushing through my mind so fast it's making me dizzy. I've lived these years with so many unanswered questions and now suddenly they're all answered. The fire, us getting out alive, the knock on the head, Deirdre missing, no trace, not a clue. We assumed something evil had taken her. We'd expected it. And how in the world would we get her back?"

"Is it possible we might skip over all this?"

"It never occurred to either of us that you'd come sneaking back."

"You've figured it all out, haven't you? All except the ending, my dear."

"Lavinia, don't make things difficult. I can walk out of this house and come back in three hours with one hundred policemen. There's no place you can hide her."

"My, my, such tenacity. Such confidence. And to think I always took you for a lacy little girl." Lavinia got up and, walking to the wall, ran her hand over the chest of a Greek warrior poised to drive his spear through a fallen Trojan. "This is so ironic it's almost frightening."

"What are you talking about?"

"Would you care for some tea? Coffee, perhaps?"

"Nothing. Get to the point; then get Deirdre!"

"Deirdre. She's been with me almost fourteen years. Beautiful years, Lisa, beautiful for both of us. Now you show up and I have to tell you she's gone."

"You're a liar!"

"Unfortunately it's the truth. You missed her by a day. You saw me down at the docks. I was looking for her, searching frantically," Lavinia explained, covering all that was necessary to clarify the situation.

"You think she's on her way to America?"

"I couldn't begin to guess where she's going. She could be heading for the North Pole."

"In other words, you'd rather not tell me."

"Don't you think I'd tell you if I knew?" Lavinia laughed thinly. "Poor Lisa, poor long-suffering dear. Mistress Misfortune. When I think of all you've gone through."

"You mean, all you've put us through."

"You could throttle me, couldn't you! Scratch my eyes out for all the satisfaction it would give you. Unfortunately that won't bring Deirdre back, will it? I've lost her, you've missed her. Now she belongs to the world." She stared at Lisa, her eyes dark with loathing. "Pity about Ross. I read about it in the New York newspaper. We get it weeks late, but I follow the news from abroad very closely." She laughed. "Can you imagine me being homesick?"

"Let's stick to the subject, shall we?"

"Deirdre, yes. Even if you do locate her, you'll find she's no longer a child. All the fun of seeing her grow up is gone. So what was it that brought you to Naples?"

"It's a long story."

"Boring?"

"I'm afraid so. Why don't I spare you?"

"If it's any consolation, Lisa, Deirdre's had an excellent home here with us. She's been deliriously happy. And she's wanted for nothing."

"Except her parents. But then we were dead. Killed in the fire."

"One doesn't miss what one has dismissed, does one?"

"If she was so deliriously happy, why did she leave?"

"She's confused, poor child."

"She's not confused." Having opened the doors without either of them being aware of it, Enrico stood staring at Lavinia. "She's the furthest thing from it."

"If you don't mind, dear——" began Lavinia.

"I mind you deliberately misleading her mother about her. Mrs. Dandridge, Deirdre left here to go home to Rhode Island because she overheard a conversation. I suggested that you and your husband might not be quite as dead as my wife insists. It's comforting to see that my suspicions were well-founded."

"You fool!" shrilled Lavinia. "Will you ever learn to keep your nose out of other people's business?"

"Lavinia, do you know what this world needs more than anything I can think of at the moment? It needs you put into a sack and stored away in a vault somewhere. No lock, no key, just six solid sides. To protect all the decent people from your conniving and your mischief."

"Get out, leave us alone!"

"Mrs. Dandridge, I can't find the words to express how deeply I regret this sorry business and my part in it. I believed her story about the fire. I didn't suspect anything until recently. Perhaps its because loving Deirdre as I do, I didn't want you to be alive. We had a golden wall around our little world here. Very fragile protection it seems, when truth intrudes." He shook his head resignedly. "It's really very distressing. Mrs. Dandridge?"

"Yes?"

"If you wish to speak with me tonight or tomorrow, if there is anything I can do to help, please feel free to call on me. I have an office in Capri down below and in Naples." Handing her his business card, he withdrew.

"What a fine man," said Lisa quietly. "You're a lucky woman, Lavinia."

"Yes, exceptionally. In many ways. These years with Deirdre have been the happiest of my life."

"You could be sent to prison for what's left of it. How lucky for you you're nearing sixty. I understand judges and juries are usually lenient toward older criminals."

"Don't be ridiculous. If you tried to bring charges, it

would be your word against mine. I could say I thought the two of you were dead. I'd even whip up something that could pass for proof, showing that by taking her, I was only doing my Christian duty."

"Oh, I don't underestimate you, Lavinia. I'm sure you'd put on a rare good show in a courtroom. Lucky for you I'm not the vengeful sort. All I care about at the moment is finding her." She started for the door, then stopped and turned. "Just one other thing."

"Yes?"

"If you value your skin, take my advice: Don't ever show your face in Providence."

Lisa left. Lavinia closed the doors and dropped into a chair, staring fixedly at the end wall and turning the events of the past 24 hours over in her mind. Her thoughts were interrupted by a knock.

"Yes?"

It was Terese carrying a large rectangular box bound with cord.

"This was delivered earlier, *signora*."

She set it on the regency table and withdrew. Lavinia undid the knot and opened it. Inside were 100-odd fragments of marble. Folded neatly and lying among them was a piece of paper:

"FOR SERVICES RENDERED
PRICE: 10,000 lire
BALANCE DUE: 5000 lire"

Slowly and deliberately she tore the bill into tiny pieces, dropped them onto the fragments in the box, restored the cover and dropped it with a thump into the wastebasket.

XLVI

Deirdre's voyage to Providence was to prove un-
eventful but so pervaded with anticipation that every
hour seemed to drag by as slowly as the blocks of the
Great Pyramid dragged by Cheops's workers. The
fourth day out, nearing the mouth of the Mediterranean
and within sight of Gibraltar, she took to standing at the
prow of the ship and staring down at the white furrow
separating the surface of the water, consciously urging
the vessel to increased speed, even pushing her shoulders forward to help it along.

The ship, the *Agatha Mayer*, a barkentine of American registry, was originally out of Charleston, South
Carolina, and was now homeward bound with stops at
Providence and New York. She was well-tended and
run, skillfully canvased to catch the cooperative
easterly. Day after day, the weather held uniformly
good. Indeed the only drawbacks throughout the entire
journey were the ship's naggingly tedious progress
westward and the food, which Deirdre shared with the
captain, officers and three other passengers, a New
Yorker and his two maiden sisters. Boiled beef and
potatoes and a gooey pudding, which boasted the consistency of library paste and a taste not altogether unlike it, dominated the bill of fare. The gentleman and
his two sisters were in their 60s and were determinedly
private individuals, with discouragingly little in the way
of interesting conversation to offer; so it was not surprising that most of every day found Deirdre on deck
mutely urging the ship forward—and going over in her

mind the events that had culminated in her departure from Capri.

After what seemed the better part of an eternity, the *Agatha Mayer* reached Providence. Debarking, Deirdre engaged a carriage and asked to be taken to Blackwood. She sat nervously fumbling with the handle of the bag on her lap as the horse trotted through the outskirts of town. They reached the woodland, the narrow road becoming a slender rutted dividing line and beginning to rise. Looking out the window, Deirdre could see the house rising like a shadow liberated by the nether world, the thick stand of maples enclosing it protectingly. Closer and closer they drew, the house pushing above the treetops, its slate-topped granite eminence resembling a fortress, seat of safekeeping for the area surrounding. She could almost picture cannon spewing noise and smoke, driving back an army sent up the hill to subdue the place.

Somewhere behind the windows her mother and father would be busy: she sewing, or in the kitchen with the cook, or supervising the hanging of new portieres; he cleaning his guns, or discussing finances with whomever was in charge of the servants, or perhaps sitting alone in his study sipping brandy and reading his newspaper. Bursting in on them like this, their seeing her returned from the grave so to speak, thrust at them out of the past, might shock them so their hearts would be unable to stand the strain.

No, hardly that. The door would open, there would be that brief brittle moment of reaction and recognition and then joy and tears and embracing, shouting, laughter. Her homecoming: out of the world of the isle into their world, this world of 10,000 black maples, this awesomely imposing house, this Dandridge world. The carriage deserted the trees for the approach circle and the driver pulled up at the front door. A bent old man came running up as speedily as he was able, opening her door. His face flared recognition at sight of her.

"Mrs. Dandridge——"

Something suddenly wrong.

"Deirdre Dandridge," she said, concealing her amusement at his look of confusion.

He held his hand out a foot off the ground. "The baby—the baby."

She nodded. "You're?"

"Enos Pryne, stableman. Forty-two years on the job. Worked for your great-grandfather, your grandfather, your father." He helped her down, collecting her valise.

"Is Daddy home?"

"No, miss. He's gone."

"Where?"

"Clear to the other side o' the world they say— Thursby says. Of course, Thursby'll say most anything."

"My mother?"

"Gone too, looking for him."

Her heart sank. Enos paid the driver and she watched him leave, completing the approach circle and heading back down the way they'd come. A spare man, old, but not nearly Enos Pryne's equal in years opened the door to Enos's lazy knock. The second man's watery-blue eyes saucered at the sight of her.

"It's Miss Deirdre, Thursby, come back home. Your mouth's open, man." Enos chuckled.

Deirdre smiled cordially. Thursby rapidly got himself together.

"Miss Deirdre! This—is—a surprise!" He took her bag from Enos, who shuffled off with "Welcome home, welcome home" floating back over his shoulder.

Thursby summoned a maid for tea for the two of them, and after introducing her to the household staff, they sat in the library. In his painfully boring mono-tone, he detailed the entire situation for her adding:

"She and your father should be back from Brazil any day now."

"That's good news."

"We're all on tenterhooks waiting. But see here, you

must tell me all about yourself. Where have you been all these years?"

She covered everything of importance. Mention of Lavinia sent one eyebrow hooking up Thursby's forehead, bringing a scowl of disapproval to his face. When she had finished telling her story, halfway through their fourth cup of tea, he set his cup down and rose from his chair.

"With your permission, I have something to show you." He led her into the drawing room, walking her slowly along the line of portraits. "This is your grandfather, Mr. Gray Dandridge. A fine man, the salt of the earth. Accidentally killed. And this is your grandmother, Madam Justine. Also, I regret to say, killed. A riding accident here on the grounds."

"She's beautiful. She looks exactly like Lavinia."

"They were identical twins."

"She never said, never mentioned it."

"Forgive my bluntness, miss, but your Aunt Lavinia is not a very nice person."

"So I've discovered."

They moved to a portrait of her father, her mother and herself.

"You, miss, less than six months before the fire. You see, you and your mother could pass for twins as easily as your aunt and grandmother. She was in her early twenties when this was painted. As you see, your father resembles both his parents." He talked on, caught up in the spirit of the moment. She only partially listened, engrossed as she was in studying her mother and father's faces. Her feelings thrashed about in turmoil.

It was all so marvelous and scary and incredible. The past 14 years lost all reality, magically transformed into a dream—happy, perhaps, but as chimerical and unsubstantial as her wildest fantasy, becoming little more than an abyss in her life separating the night of the fire and now.

Vinnie must have been completely mad! How her

mother and father must have suffered, the heartache, the emptiness, the hopelessness! Thought of it filled her with sadness and sympathy for them. But the bright side dazzled! Any day now they would be back and the three of them reunited.

And what of Vinnie and Enrico, Villa Aldoni, Derek and Anacapri, Capri, Naples? All had suddenly vanished, the entire tapestry ripped from the wall and crumbled into dust. It was all so wrenching that it exhausted her completely. She stopped a yawn with her fingertips. Thursby barely paused for breath as he ushered her through the two sets of open doors to the living room. Then he caught himself. "See here, miss, you've come such a distance. You must be worn out."

"I'm all right, thank you."

"Still perhaps we might continue all this later. Would you like something to eat?"

"First a bath."

"Of course." Standing back, he cast a critical eye over her dress. "You'll want that thrown away, I'm sure," he said.

"This and a blouse and skirt in my bag are all I brought. I came away from Capri in such a rush."

"Your mother has rafts of clothes. Everything should fit you beautifully." He pulled the bell rope. "The maid will show you to your room. Ask to see your mother's room and her things. You can pick something out while Molly's filling your tub. And tell her what you'd like for dinner. She'll see that the cook prepares it.

"And may I say again, Miss Deirdre, welcome home. This is the most exciting, the most joyful day we've had around here in ages!"

XLVII

Three days later, Lisa returned home to Blackwood, having been met in Boston by Muybridge Senior, whom she brought along with her to the house. Thursby greeted them at the door and while Lisa was removing her hat and gloves, Deirdre appeared at the top of the stairs and started down. Lisa lifted her eyes and saw her daughter. She caught her breath and her hand went to her heart.

"Mother!"

"Deirdre, darling!"

Deirdre ran down the remaining stairs into her arms, tears bursting from their eyes, each one hardly able to speak. They held one another closely, tightly, as if neither dared let go for fear the other would disappear.

"Deirdre, Deirdre, Deirdre."

"Oh, Mother." Tears ran down Deirdre's cheeks, her emotions overflowing, her elation uncontrollable.

Her arm around her daughter's waist, Lisa walked her into the drawing room, leaving both men staring after them misty-eyed.

"I can't stop crying," said Deirdre beaming through her tears. "And I'm not even a crier."

"Nor I. They just seem to come and come, don't they? Oh, my darling Deirdre." Lisa clasped her shoulders, kissing her forehead, her eyes, her cheeks, holding her possessively, reveling in her nearness, the warmth of her presence.

They talked all afternoon, through dinner into the night, sitting in the master bedroom until the rest of the house was asleep. Lisa explained in detail about Ross, his misfortune, his flight from Norfolk.

"At this moment, his ship is probably making its way around Cape Horn to start north then west across the Pacific."

"To Singapore." Lisa nodded. "I'm going with you. Say I can, please!"

"No you may not! It's too long a trip and far too dangerous."

"So we'll bring guns. We can protect ourselves."

Lisa smiled tolerantly. "Which reminds me, you did a very very foolish thing running away like that. Being around that dock area unescorted——"

"I had to leave. How could I stay? Oh, Mother, you can't know how much I hate her. She's despicable!"

"Did she treat you badly?"

"No, but——"

"She was good to you, wasn't she? Both of them were. You had nothing in common with Oliver Twist."

"I don't believe you! How can you forgive so easily? How can you wipe out fourteen years?"

"I'm not forgiving her, and I'm not wiping out anything. The subject is you and how you were brought up."

Deirdre seethed. "How I wish we could make her pay for it, make her suffer the way you and Daddy did!"

Lisa brushed the hair back from Deirdre's forehead. "And would that make you happy?"

"She'd be getting what she deserves!"

"Don't you think she's suffering right now? She loved you. She must have to have been so good to you. To suddenly lose you, to walk into your room and see it empty, see your photograph on the dresser and know she'll never see the real you again, don't you think that's painful? Deirdre, stealing you and marrying Mr. Aldoni represent the only two triumphs of her entire life. She tried to get rid of me, she failed. She tried to steal your father from me and failed again. She almost married your grandfather. But she never did, after waiting half a lifetime for the chance. She's a murderess. She can never come back here, the police would be onto her before she unpacked.

"She was over forty in a life as barren of happiness, of love and contentment, satisfaction, before she got her hands on you."

"And Enrico."

"I got the impression talking to them that she's exhausted his patience. He's a perceptive sort. He said something to her while I was standing there."

"What?"

"About how the world needed protection from her. If your father ever said such a thing to me——"

"Enrico can't divorce her though; he's very Catholic. Even though he never goes to church. You can't get a divorce over there."

"I pity him. He knows what she is, what she's done, all the bad about her."

"Still he loves her passionately."

"I was going to say dearly."

Deirdre placed her hand over Lisa's. "You look tired, Mother."

"I can hardly keep my eyes open."

"But we can't go to bed, we've so much to talk about. We must stay up all night and watch the sunrise!"

"No, thank you, miss. It's your bedtime! Come, I'll walk you down the hall. You get ready for bed and Mommy will tuck you in."

"Mother, I'm fifteen. I'll be sixteen in two months!"

She took her hands and gazed into her eyes. "Deirdre, for tonight, just for tonight can we pretend you're a very little girl? Say four or five? My little girl?"

"I wore pigtails. O God, when I wake up tomorrow, you're not going to put my hair in pigtails. You wouldn't!"

"I'd love to."

"They stick out on both sides! They make me look like an old-fashioned doll! They bump against things."

"Very well, no pigtails tomorrow, brushing out tonight. Come."

Arms around one another, they walked down the hall to the last bedroom at the right. Just beyond by the end window a cast-iron spiral staircase wound its way up to the third floor and the captain's walk above. Lisa paused at the bedroom door.

"Is this the room Molly gave you?"

"Yes, why? It's very pretty. I love the view of the rose garden, even though it's so scrawny-looking this time of year."

"She didn't know—Molly, I mean. She's been with us only two years. Are you superstitious?"

"Not a bit."

"Darling, this room was Lavinia's."

"Oh, no! Get me out of here!"

"I thought you weren't superstitious?"

"I'm nauseated. Just the thought of sleeping in her bed. And I did, last night and the night before!"

"We'll find you another room."

XLVIII

All things considered, theirs was a splendid reunion, as successful as Lisa could have hoped for. There was so much to talk about that it kept them close to each other morning and night. But when the recollections had run their course, when each had come to know the other's earlier years and only boring repetition could extend such conversation, the first phase gave way to the second, in which, for want of common interests and experiences, they retreated into the roles of strangers. The period of getting-to-know-you began, an interval replete with false assumptions, misunderstandings, second thoughts and more thorough, more candid and less idealistic evaluations on the part of each. By the fifth day, it had become ominously apparent to Lisa that Deirdre's life with Lavinia had been as cloistered as that of a postulant in a nunnery. How she had managed to get from Naples to Providence without encountering disaster in one form or another amazed her mother. Deirdre was a little girl in a grown woman's body: sweet, warm, kindhearted, considerate, but also petty, prone to vexation and infantile pouting over silly little things that went wrong or that she disagreed with. And she was surprisingly naïve. It was plain to Lisa that Lavinia had kept her locked up in the tight little world of Capri, treating her more like a priceless toy than a human being, thus making her uncertain and difficult way through adolescence even more difficult.

It was disappointing to Lisa, but not surprising. Lavinia being Lavinia, self-indulgent in the extreme, pampered and coddled, she could hardly expect her to bring Deirdre up any other way.

Somehow over breakfast, the subject got onto men and boys, and Deirdre confessed that she had fallen madly in love with Derek Childs only to discover that he was sleeping with "a local," a term Lavinia reserved for her social inferiors on the isle—approximately 99 percent of the populace.

Lisa's knife invaded the jam then spread it over a triangle of toast. "What did she say when she found out?"

"She was furious. Jealous as could be. She wanted him for herself, of course. She was always sneaking off with younger men. She thought she was very clever about it, that nobody suspected, but the more she did it, the more careless she got. Enrico was always away, so she got away with murder. Now it's catching up with her."

"How?"

"Word gets around. Capri is very small. Then, too, she's getting on."

"That shouldn't stop her. The older she looks to herself in her mirror, the faster she'll run."

"But she's not blind. When she wakes up one day and sees an old lady."

Lisa laughed. "That she'll never let happen. She'll forbid it!"

Deirdre considered this and nodded slowly. "You're right, she will. She'll be eighty and out prowling around with a twenty-five-year-old. But let's not talk about her. She ruins my appetite. Tell me about Daddy."

"I've told you everything."

"I know he's handsome; his picture's beautiful. He's warm, too, and enormously sincere, isn't he? And funny."

"He's also bullheaded and temperamental. But he's got one thing I've never seen in any other man. Do you know he'd never done an honest day's work in his life, not really, up to the time he brought me back from Europe? When Tom Overstreet, the foreman at the yards, told him your grandfather had been killed, he stepped into the breach and worked like a demon. He put Dandridge Shipbuilding back on its feet. All through the Fifties he never let up. And when the war came, he worked even harder."

"If he was doing war work, why did he give it up and enlist? I would think he would have been more valuable staying on the job."

"I thought the same thing, but the bug had bitten him and nothing I said could change his mind. And when I got that letter——"

"You must have died."

"I felt like I had. Still, it wasn't a complete surprise. When your husband, or your brother, or son, goes off to war, the first thing you think is that you'll never see him again. That he'll be killed or taken prisoner and die. Of course I prayed and prayed he'd come back, with all his limbs, all in one piece. Every day I'd read about the war in the newspaper. They published the casualty list and I'd take a deep breath, hold it and run my eyes down it to the Ds and see he wasn't there and sigh relief. For twenty-four hours. Until the next list."

"It's worse than the actual fighting!"

"In a way it is. But never say that to a man wearing medals."

"Do you think he'll have changed?"

"Three years is a long time—and after all he's been through—yes, I'm sure he's changed. Perhaps we'll have to get to know each other all over again," she added pensively.

"Perhaps not. You'll probably hit it off stupendously. You and I are doing all right." Deirdre's hand covered hers on the table. "Aren't we?"

"We're doing marvelously, although I don't know what the regulations are for mothers who meet sixteen-year-old daughters who burped and burbled and cooed in their arms the last time they saw them. It's a bit tricky. I guess what I really want is to be your best friend, even big sister. You're so grown it's frightening."

"Am I heaps different from what you expected me to be?"

"I didn't expect anything. I never dreamed I'd see you again. After that first year, I guess we both gave up hope."

"What don't you like about me?"

"That's a foolish question. Nothing."

"That's not so; it can't be. There have to be some things. Do I prattle too much? Am I immature? Am I demanding? What?"

"You're you, silly. How can you ask such things? For that matter, what about me? Am I too overmothering? Is there such a word?"

"You think I'm horribly spoiled, don't you?"

"No more so than you would have been had you lived here."

"Ha! Tons more! You have no idea. If I as much as looked a second time at a dress, or a piece of jewelry, or shoes in a shop window, Lavinia would insist on buying it for me. And she'd push everything under the sun on me. She'd sneak into my room when I was downstairs or out of the house and stick scads of money in my drawer or under my pillow. And there were always presents. Practically every other day."

"Did she talk to you, mother-daughter talk?"

"She talked about me constantly, but almost never about herself. Or about the past. Of course she'd much rather forget that."

"Did you discuss your problems with her?"

"When I was little. But not this past year. Now that I think about it, she seemed to be losing interest. Playing mother was getting to be more duty than fun."

"You're very refreshing, Deirdre."

"How?"

"You're very discerning. In some ways, you're surprisingly mature."

"In others, I'm not?"

"Of course. It's your age; it's normal."

"What ways?" Lisa made a face, wordlessly pleading ignorance. Deirdre threw down her napkin. "Oh, you're too much!"

"That way, for one. You take hold of little things with your teeth. And chew till they make you ill. Don't you imagine everybody is a mix of mature and immature, however old people are? Do you fancy yourself the exception?"

"You think being temperamental is immature?"

"Certainly."

"And yet you say Daddy is temperamental."

"So am I. Who isn't in this house? Which only proves my point."

"What else don't you like about me?"

"I didn't say I didn't like it. I love it; it's the Dandridge in you."

"And the Allworth in you?"

"I shouldn't wonder. Oh, your father and I used to have some priceless squabbles."

"You're sneaking out on my question."

"Which one?"

"What don't you like about me?"

"Please, don't ask me to pick your personality to pieces. Number one, I don't know you well enough yet. Secondly, I wouldn't do such a thing if I did. I'm much too grateful to the gods for having you back." She patted her hand across the table. "You're filling a great emptiness in my life, my darling. To be able to touch you, feel your warmth, see you smile, hear your voice. To know you're home at last. I can't tell you how much it means."

"I can't either." Deirdre glanced about. "I used to lie awake nights thinking about this house. Pretending the

villa was Blackwood and my bed was in my room upstairs. And you and Daddy were sleeping down the hall.
That the fire and all of it had never happened. I wanted
that so very much."

"Why don't we make a pact?"

"What sort of pact?"

"Let's promise each other we'll never talk about it
again. About her, Capri, any of it."

"Make believe it never was."

Lisa nodded. "We're together, we've always been.
We'll never be separated. And soon, hopefully sooner
then we dare to expect, it'll be the three of us again."

"We'll be the happiest family in the world!"

"We will." Lisa stared across the table at her
lovingly.

"I love you, Mother."

"I love you, dear." They continued eating in silence.
Then Lisa touched her mouth with the corner of her
napkin. "I almost forgot."

"What?"

"Very important. School. We've got to take you into
town and get you enrolled before the school year ends
in June."

"Why bother? It can't be more than a month. Besides, we'll be leaving soon."

"*I'll* be. I'm afraid you can't go with me, Deirdre. It's
just not possible."

"You promised!"

"Did I really? I don't remember saying so."

"Not in so many words maybe."

"It's a long long journey. It could be extremely
dangerous."

"All the more reason I should go. I can't let you go
alone; I won't."

"I appreciate your loyalty."

"Now you're poking fun!"

"No I'm not."

"Mother, I'm almost sixteen!"

"Be realistic, darling. I'd no more consider your going along than if you were half that."

"Well if I can't go, you can't!"

"I don't have any option."

"You could send somebody, a private detective. Somebody trained in that sort of thing."

"He'd never find your father. For somebody like that, it would be just another paid assignment. If he came up against what looked like an insurmountable obstacle, he'd give up and come home. Something I'd never do."

"But to go alone . . ."

"Mr. Muybridge Junior is considering coming with me. Let's not discuss it any further now. We've yet to have our first squabble, and today's much too nice."

The doorbell. Sitting in silence, they heard Thursby answer it.

"That'll be Mr. Muybridge Senior," said Lisa softly. "Come."

Thursby appeared at the dining-room doors, the sunlight captured by the crystal chandelier focusing on his bloodless features causing him to blink.

"Pardon me, madam. Mr. Jeremy Slater is here to see you."

XLIX

"I can't get over it," gasped Jeremy. "I'm seeing double!"

They had secluded themselves in the library with coffee and the melodious performance of a brazen catbird perched on a branch framed by the window. Lisa had just finished recounting everything that she had been involved in since Baltimore.

"And what have you been doing? Deirdre, Jeremy is an excellent painter."

"Amateur," said Jeremy.

"He's fibbing. He's another Rembrandt Peale. Are you still at the Slaters'? Have you been to Philadelphia lately?"

"Matter of fact, I just came back," he said stirring his coffee methodically. "Beating the bushes looking for something in the law business nearer my liking."

"You're giving up painting?" asked Lisa.

He nodded. "I've decided it's best I keep it strictly a hobby. So it's back to the bar. Though it appears I'll have to wait till something in the way of a job opens up in September."

"Being a lawyer must be fascinating," said Deirdre spiritedly. "Defending murderers. And proving them guilty!" She couldn't take her eyes off Jeremy, noted Lisa. He smiled.

"Actually I'm looking into corporation law. It's dull to most people, but I've always wanted into it. It'll be a long summer waiting. But what are your plans, Lisa? When will you be leaving?"

"Tomorrow or the day after. When Fred Muybridge

finishes paving the way. There's a possibility his son may go along."

"How about me? Lisa, I have to tell you I walked away from that hotel in Baltimore feeling very dissatisfied with myself for letting you talk me out of going to Pernambuco with you. That was a big mistake."

"Not so big. As things turned out, you might have drowned."

"Well I have no intention of making the same mistake twice. You're talking about Singapore this time, ten thousand miles from here."

She smiled ruefully. "Not exactly Seekonk Beach."

"Do me one small favor. Don't try to talk me out of it this time. I'm your friend. It's times like these when you need a friend."

She shook her head. "It's too much of an imposition."

"You're not imposing; I'm offering my services. I've got nothing to do till September. We'll be back before then."

"It's too much to ask."

"I'll pay my own expenses."

"Don't be silly."

"I can help you in a dozen ways. You'll be coming up against red tape and officialdom that can block a lone female completely. It's a man's world, Lisa."

"Not so you'd notice it. No man's telling me what to do. If I can't talk my way past people, I'll pay. Thanks to Fred Muybridge, when I get to Singapore, I'll be in a position to practically buy the city outright, turn it upside down and shake Ross out of it—if it comes to that. I won't have to wander about like a lost soul begging information. Believe me, I'll make the Dandridge power and influence felt."

"Ten thousand miles from home?"

"Anywhere in the world."

"All the same I want to go along. I demand to. Whether we travel together or not."

"Very well, if you insist. I must admit I don't think Muybridge Junior is too keen over the idea of going. I believe his father is trying to talk him into it."

"I'll be much better company."

"Yes, you would be."

"Where does all this leave me?" asked Deirdre. "Mother, give me one good reason why you won't let me go!"

"I'll give you three. You're too young. You're too precious, and I refuse to expose you to danger when there's no need to!"

Deirdre turned to Jeremy. "Do you believe this? I came all the way from Naples by myself."

"Naples is not Singapore."

"Mother, how can there be any risk? I'll be with the two of you all the way to San Francisco, all the way to Singapore. When we get there, you can lock me up in the police station or the American Embassy, any safe place. You can go find Daddy, come back for me and the four of us will head home. What could be simpler?"

"It couldn't possibly be that simple," said Lisa tersely.

"Jeremy, will you please talk to her? A daughter's place is with her parents."

Jeremy held up both hands. "Can I be neutral?"

"No, you can't!" exclaimed Deirdre. "That's the coward's way out!"

"That's me."

"We'll discuss it another time," said Lisa.

"There isn't time for another time. You two'll be gone and I'll be left standing at the window. It's not fair!" Jumping up, her empty cup and saucer rattling to rest on the coffee tray, she threw up her hands, muttered something with a nasty edge to it and stalked out of the room. Turning in the doorway, she scowled at her mother.

"You!"

And she was gone.

"Are you finding motherhood a trifle difficult?" asked Jeremy.

"Not funny."

"Sorry." Getting up he moved to the globe in the corner, turning it aimlessly in its stand. "Look." She joined him. "It's a wide country. How does Muybridge propose to get you across it?"

"The railroad runs to Council Bluffs, Iowa. From there, we'll take a coach." She traced a line with her finger. "Omaha, across Nebraska, Denver, Salt Lake City, Carson City, San Francisco."

"How far is that? How far would you guess? I'll tell you, the better part of sixteen hundred miles and over the Rocky Mountains, the most treacherous going in North America."

"Do you know a better way?"

"There's got to be. Besides, cross country is nearly three months. There's got to be a faster way. See here, what if we went to St. Louis by rail, down the Mississippi to New Orleans, by ship to Veracruz, less than four hundred miles overland to the West Coast—perhaps the ruggedest part of the trip but nothing compared with the Rockies—then by coastal sloop up to San Francisco? With any luck at all, we could save a whole month."

"We could use it. I've added up the miles and the days. At its very slowest, the *Crown Pearl* has to be rounding Cape Horn and starting up the west coast of South America. Even if we make the best possible connections all the way."

"St. Louis, New Orleans, Veracruz, San Francisco. You'll need every single day you can save."

"Exactly."

"Do you have a pencil and paper and piece of string?"

She found the pencil and paper and a ruler in the reading table drawer. He made rough calculations.

"Giving the *Crown Pearl* two hundred miles a day just to be on the safe side, by the time we get to the West Coast, it'll be well out in the Pacific."

"It's really disheartening. On the way to Pernambuco, we actually passed it. Before we hit the hurricane."

"Figuring very very roughly, we could beat them to port by two or three days, or. . . ."

"Or what?"

"They could beat us."

"We've got to get there first. If they dock, and Ross and Regan get into the city or, God forbid, out of Malaya, we could be ten years catching up with them."

"Then let's get started. Tomorrow, not the day after. Get your things and we'll go down and see Muybridge. I'll light a fire under him."

"Lead the way."

At Lisa's direction, Thursby hurried down to the stables to alert Enos Pryne, and minutes later, the old man was perched on the cabriolet at the door. They drove away, leaving Deirdre standing in an upstairs window, a look of fury on her face.

L

Lavinia stared at her mirror. And considered the barren years before Deirdre had come into her life. The lady in waiting she had called herself for that hundred years. How cruelly appropriate. Waiting for love. After Justine's death, waiting for Gray to turn to her. Waiting for him to propose marriage. Waiting for their wedding day that was never to come. Waiting for Ross in his father's stead. Waiting for love, claiming it at last not in a husband but in the child. Deirdre had loved her as Enrico did. But of course Enrico didn't count. True love was two-directional. She didn't love him back; she couldn't. It was Deirdre, only Deirdre.

Now Deirdre hated her. Now the love of 14 years had run out like the grains of sand in an hourglass, leaving a vacuum that too quickly filled itself with hurt and loneliness. What a woefully wanting life. So much had gone wrong, so little right. Her hands went to her face, her fingertips touched her cheeks, moved down them, coming together at her chin.

Her face was a mask. Slip her fingers under the top of it and peel it slowly down. It would be painless and underneath, under the years, was the face of a young girl.

Lavinia Cartwright. Happy birthday, Lavinia. Happy birthday, Justine. The Cartwright twins are 15. Such pretty girls: jet-black hair, creamy-white skin, lovely eyes and smiles. We'll invite all the girls from school to your party. Miss Talbot's School for Young Ladies. Latin, Greek, grammar, American history, mathematics, music, art, gymnastics, dancing, riding. Justine is superb on horseback, so steady, so confident. And look at Lavinia waltz with the Frazier boy. His sleeves are too short, he's pimply and clumsy. But she's beautiful, moving like a flower bending in the breeze. Aren't her hands lovely, the fingers so slender and perfectly proportioned. As if carved of white marble.

The party, the party! Two cakes, one for Justine, one for Lavinia. Blow out the candles, birthday girls! First make a wish. One, two, three! There we are. What was your wish, Lavinia? If I tell it won't come true.

It won't. It never does. Justine's going to be married. Hear the church bells! See the carriage! Hurrah, hurrah. She's marrying Gray Dandridge. Isn't he handsome! And he's rich! The Dandridges are wickedly wealthy. Cyrus Dandridge owns half the state. Isn't Justine lucky? When will Lavinia get married? Poor Lavinia, her sister's marrying Gray and she's to be maid of honor. There she is, standing by holding a bouquet while Justine says I do! I do! Here comes the bride! And here comes Lavinia trailing after. Strange, isn't it? She's just as pretty. Why isn't she married? Justine's married, and all her friends, why not Lavinia? Who will marry Lavinia? Will some nice young man come dashing up on a white horse? Who will he be? Who?

I love you, Lavinia. Will you do me the honor of becoming my wife? I accept, Enrico.

Dear lumbering Enrico, the good-hearted bear with popping eyes and fat lips. Buying her everything. Buy this, buy that, buy it all. Whatever your heart desires, my love. Snoring. Sweating. And his breath. Apologizing, fawning, boring her beyond belief!

But life was different, so much better married. Livable—all thanks to Deirdre. My little girl, my darling child. Throw the ball to Mommy. Bring your kitten and we shall have tea and cookies in the garden. Don't eat the sugar off and leave the rest. There's a good girl. I love you, Deirdre. I love you, Vinnie. Love, love, love, love, love!

Arising from the bench, Lavinia selected her black pannier dress with the large side puffs to the overskirt. The Vandyke hem. No crinoline. Fancy buttons set with classic heads in relief. For jewelry, the dog-collar necklace, inch-wide velvet with beads sewed on. The silver-plate earrings. The silver double-chain bracelet. Polished boots, high, tasseled, with colored heels. Tall-crowned hat with pale-blue feather. Black-kid six-button gloves and her new pagoda-shaped parasol of brocaded silk.

One last glance at her mirror: beautiful, never lovelier. A hastily scribbled note to Enrico. Leave it folded and on his desk in the study.

Twirling her parasol aimlessly over one shoulder, she walked down the mountain road to within sight of Villa San Michele and the ruins of the castle of Castiglioni perched on the summit of San Michele itself. To the right was the Castello di Barbarossa. A frolicsome breeze bent the clover and wild daisies along the road and the sun was as yellow as a daisy's eye in the cloud-cluttered heavens. Bow, daisies, it is *Signora* Aldoni. Heads down in proper obeisance as she passes.

Eight hundred steps up to the castle gate. Her heels clicked against the sunbaked stones. Up, up, up, the isle shrinking beneath her, drawing into itself. She paused to rest, leaning against the railing, shielding her eyes from the sun with her parasol. So clear and clean was the air that it tasted like fresh water. What a rare and perfect day! So cool up here despite the sun cutting away the blueness above. Resume the climb, 400 steps now, halfway. She was beginning to pant with the effort despite the slowness of her pace, breathing rapidly, her breasts rising. Such beautiful breasts. No woman alive her age possessed such magnificent breasts. Beautiful breasts, beautiful woman. Soon to be 40. Happy birthday, my dear? Forty? She wished.

She paused for two minutes' rest every 50 steps and surveyed the isle in every direction. Reaching the 800th and last step, she walked through the shadows of the towers, through the open lichen-laden gate into the outer ward. Overhead the wind whined welcome as it impudently assaulted the towers and battlements. She climbed the stairs into the light, pausing at the top to take in the sight of the ramparts. Then she crossed the inner ward to the battlements and, bracing herself, looked down upon the sea.

It was claimed that during the past two years alone no fewer than 11 people had leaped from these heights to their deaths, burying their bodies in the blue water below. Leaving scarves or boots or lovers behind to apprise the world of their departures. At that, there seemed little point in electing suicide if one didn't tell somebody. To move on to the next world without letting anyone know how or where seemed wretchedly inconsiderate.

But the number disturbed her. So many people, too many leaping from here made emulation gauche. The site and the privilege had been abused. Of course once one was gone, one could hardly be embarrassed.

Undoing the scarf from her hat, she looped it about the telescope mounted on the merlon. Then she knotted it securely. The bullying wind teased the silk, rippling it, snapping the loose ends noisily.

She looked about. Castello di Barbarossa. To think all these stones had to be carried all the way up here. For what? To lift the Turkish plunderer of Capri closer to Allah to facilitate heavenly recognition of his depredations? How infantile, how useless and absurd! One might just as well build a city on the moon!

Steeling herself a second time, hanging tightly to the stones on either side, she looked down. The sea's surface was roughened by the breeze, as coarse as gravel and flecked with slender white plumes. How high up was she, she wondered. It seemed miles.

Suddenly the wind caught her parasol, tugging it from her grasp, sending it sailing outward and down, the weight of its short thick bone handle holding it upright. Following it down with her eyes, she discovered a fisherman seated in his dinghy, picking at his net. He was hatless and bare to the waist, and at this height, his sun-browned body appeared almost black. Moving to the telescope, she adjusted it, finding and fixing him in the glass. He was young, his shoulders extraordinarily broad, heavier, more muscular than Fernando's had been. At that moment, a gull detached itself from its flock, swooping down upon his boat. Up came his arm, as if he had imagined it had come closer than it actually had. His body angled and she caught a glimpse of his profile, the strong firm lines of his cheek and jaw. He wore a mustache; she adored a mustache on young men. She had once argued with Fernando for half a day trying to induce him to grow one.

He stood up, stretching his arms, casting his net. How like a dancer, so effortless, so fluid. Younger men were so delectable, so firm and hard and—capable. The clearness in their eyes, the supple movements of their bodies, their freshness, their animal energy. As she looked on, he reached under the stern seat, brought out a wide-brimmed straw hat and put it on, shading his shoulders and upper body from view.

He was fishing close to the shore, within 100 yards. Fifty yards farther out a ketch was passing, its sails fore and aft stout with wind, cutting through the water at right angles to the isle. Unaided by the glass she could make out four people on board, two men, two women. Focusing on the boat, she followed its progress. Both women were honey blondes, young, shapely, one insufferably active, scurrying about, waving her arms and her hat, carrying on like an undisciplined child. The other girl sat aft, holding tightly to the arm of a man old enough to be her grandfather.

He turned his head. Lavinia gasped. There was no mistaking that hair poking out from under the cap, those glasses, that face.

"Bastard! Deceitful pig! Cheating on me, chasing about with some vulgar little baggage behind my back!"

She let loose a torrent of vulgar language, screaming loudly, heaping vilification upon him.

"Bastard! Bastard! Bastard! Bastard! Baa——"

Having straightened up, slamming the glass aside, turning from it, she stopped suddenly, her jaw dropping. Two nuns stood gaping at her, the obstreperous wind ruffling their skirts, teetering them slightly where they stood. Between them, neatly lined up according to height, were eight to ten pairs of schoolgirls attired in crisp, spotless, black-and-white uniforms bearing the emblem of the Santa Monica School in Naples.

LI

The rain had diminished, finally stopping completely, but the air remained heavy with dampness and Jeremy's clothing under the oilskins provided by the first officer of the *Marigold* felt like a sopping-wet glove covering a hand around his body. Down the small but ruggedly built ship the twin paddle wheels continued digging into the gray water of the gulf, churning up small bergs of foam. Above, the coal smoke trailed back from the single stack and stretched far over the taffrail.

A sailor finished coiling a hawser nearby and joined Jeremy at the bow.

"Some rotten weather, eh, sir?" The man had no teeth, his mouth was a pocket of skin in his dirty face and his two-day-old beard a thousand black needles erupting from his chin and cheeks. Producing a filled corncob pipe from his inside pocket, the sailor rounded his shoulders against the wind, lit up and began puffing.

"How far to Veracruz?"

"Fifty, maybe sixty miles. We'll be there middle o' the afternoon. You and the lady staying there?"

"We're heading overland to the West Coast."

"Whereabouts?"

"San Marcos."

"Horseback?" Out came the pipe and up went his forehead inquiringly.

"Coach."

"Mind the Frenchies."

"I was told they're withdrawing, going home."

"True, but there's many a bunch sore as boils over

that. Ready to take it out on anybody passing through.
Especially Americans. It was Secretary of State Seward
talked old Napoleon into getting out, you know. And his
people come over expecting to fill their pockets with gold."

"I know, I know."

"I'm sure you does. Keeping it in mind and being
careful won't hurt none, though, especially with a
woman along."

"Do you think it's stopped raining for good?"

The man fisted his pipe bowl and scanned the sky.
"Don't see no break. It could start in again anytime
and keep up till hell ices over."

"That's a pleasant prospect."

"You asked; I told. Ain't you 'fraid o' catching cold
out here?"

Jeremy tightened his muffler about his neck and
pulled the oilskins over it more securely.

"I don't catch cold easily."

"Your traveling companion don't hardly show her
face out her cabin door though, do she? Right purty
woman that. I'm shore partial to red hair and that pale
skin goes with it. Well, I'd best stop jawing and get aft
afore I get yelled at." He touched his cap with the tip
of his finger. "See you, sir."

Jeremy took no notice of his departure, concentrating
on the view, gazing out over the bowsprit into the mist
rushing to blanket the vessel. The 1000-mile train ride
from New York to St. Louis had been the most ex-
cruciatingly uncomfortable four days he had ever experienced. His back and backside had recovered
somewhat on the three-day journey by flatboat down
the Mississippi to New Orleans, although the boat trip
had inspired new depths of boredom. Now, well into the
third week of travel with months more ahead, he was
speedily coming to the conclusion that Baltimore to
Providence, with welcome stops between, was the limit
of his ability to travel. Only the optimistic trend of

events seemed capable of salvaging his spirits. And kept the smile that Lisa had fallen in love with spread across his face.

He could not deny it. His luck verged on the incredible. Teddy Vossbacher had obligingly removed himself from the scene. Taking care of Ned Loomis had been a well-timed masterstroke. He could just picture loud-mouthed, nosy, obnoxious Mrs. Harrigan invading the room, discovering the body, screaming, carrying on, summoning the police:

"Charles Fitch. I don't know where he came from. He left, said he was going to Philadelphia on business. Fitch. F-i-t-c-h."

Running back to Providence, but not to his uncle's, thank you. No need to court unnecessary risk. Holing up in a room down by Fox Point. Watching the news-papers, waiting.

"MRS. ROSS DANDRIDGE RETURNS FROM EUROPE"

Jeremy on the spot! Amazing how things always seemed to turn out for the best if one had patience. She'd been absolutely right, of course. Had he insisted on accompanying her to Pernambuco, he might well have drowned. Instead here he was, popping up just when she needed him. Desperately, when he thought about it. Good old loyal Jeremy, always there when help was short. On to Singapore! Heartening news. Any man, especially an outlander like Ross, could catch a knife in the ribs or between his shoulder blades easily in such a barbarous place. British law had to be as loose as a sot's tongue. All but unenforceable, according to Muybridge Senior's research. Muybridge Junior had been so relieved when told that there was no longer need for him to go along that he had practically fallen to his knees and kissed the lady's hand!

Jeremy laughed aloud. Then there was Deirdre; what a pretty little thing, the image of her mother, a wide-eyed, easily astonished, passionately green schoolgirl who gazed at him as if he were a god. Tempting that, but much too young. And damned if he'd jeopardize the perfectly marvelous relationship he was constructing with Lisa, friend and friend. Ever the gentleman, Mr. Slater, sir, eyes and hands off the little miss. His stock, already soaring with mother, would be through the bloody roof by the time they got to where they were going. That he'd see to.

His hand went to his pocket and the pearl-handled derringer filling it. His little secret from the lady. She knew about the Colt .45 in his valise, necessary protection. Although she despised guns, she recognized the need and approved. The derringer, reserved for her dear husband, she mustn't know about.

Patience, luck and courage. All three in concert had brought him a long way, he reflected proudly. This jaunt was the next-to-last lap. Do what had to be done with his customary cleverness, then return. On the way back, he would spend every minute of every hour consoling the grief-stricken widow. Poor creature.

Give the lady six months, perhaps less.

LII

Veracruz emerged from the mist on the horizon, the narrow channel of its harbor slipping behind a line of reefs and small bleak-looking islands. The city itself rose beyond a flat, barren beach barely a few feet above water level.

The *Marigold*'s wheels spun her into the channel and Lisa drew Jeremy's attention to the French tricolor hanging limply against its mast, which rose over the fort.

"Do you think they'll give us any trouble?" she asked in a worried tone.

"I doubt they'll delay us, if that's what you mean. I'll have to get transportation as fast as I can. The quicker we get out of town the better!"

She pulled the collar of her pelisse tightly about her throat against the lingering dampness. "Why don't we ask the captain to send a man ashore to get a coach? He can see it's brought straight to the gangplank."

"Good idea."

"It might be safer."

Like all paddle wheelers, the *Marigold* was not easily docked. To prevent the incoming current from pushing her against the stone quay and smashing her starboard wheel and housing, boat hooks had to be placed over the rail fore and aft and Veracruz held away while double lines were made fast, securing the vessel.

The first man down the gangplank had been given orders to hire a coach for the two Yankees. Their baggage at hand, Lisa and Jeremy waited at the rail while the ship's cargo—timber and cotton—was lifted from

318

its holds. The coach, an overly decorated Mexican version of a four-in-hand American Studebaker, was driven up and the two of them were starting down the gangplank when a familiar voice called out of the crowd below.

"Mother!"

"No! Dear God." Lisa groaned, her hands flying to her cheeks.

Jeremy blinked in disbelief, then burst out laughing.

"You think it's funny?"

Deirdre came running up to the foot of the gangplank waving. "What took you so long? I've been in for hours!"

Lisa's first impulse was to seize her, throw her across her knee and administer a sound spanking in full view of captain, crew, stevedores, dock officials and all other assorted Veracruzans. This urge she managed to stifle, instead calling her daughter down in a voice seething with rage. Culminating with the firm declaration: "You, you mischief, are leaving! Going straight back! To New Orleans, St. Louis, home!"

Jeremy interrupted. "It's none of my business, Lisa," he said quietly, "but I'd think twice about that. New Orleans looked pretty seamy to me. I know she made it once, but let's not press our luck."

"You're not suggesting she come with us?"

He hesitated, studying her face with something like misgiving in his own. Then he responded with a noncommittal shrug.

"I can't possibly go back, Mother."

"You can and you will!"

"I can't!"

"Can!"

"Can't!" Eye to eye, nose to nose, mouth to mouth, both with their fists planted firmly on their hips, they screamed at each other. Jeremy glanced about in embarrassment and sighed relief when Lisa lowered her voice and capitulated.

"Why not?"

"There's no boat, not for a whole week. Isn't that wonderful? I'd have to stay here in Veracruz alone!"

Lisa's shoulders sagged. She glanced about the dock. It was a fair duplication of Norfolk, she thought, only with an unfamiliar accent distinguishing the babble filling the air. The Norfolk dockside types, however, were present in abundance: dozens, scores of Marsalas. She suppressed a shudder, then she turned her eyes on Deirdre standing before her grinning, brimming self-confidence, as fresh and pretty as a bridal bouquet in her Isabeau dress, her lovely face framed by the brim of the spoon bonnet.

"Dear God."

The coach rumbled through town and out into the flat open country over a road that Jeremy insisted was no road at all:

"It's a dried-up streambed. It feels like every rock in Mexico has been tossed into it. Would you believe I think I'm getting seasick?"

LIII

Lavinia had put a great deal of thought against the idea, examining it with the scrupulous care and patience, the fastidious devotion to detail, that a diamond cutter reserves for a valuable stone entrusted to him for the breaking: one blow of the hammer against the cleaver set in its pre-cut notch. Only one try, therefore there should be no stinting in forethought and preparation.

Unfortunately there was more to it than the act alone. There was the morality of the thing. Not that Enrico didn't deserve to die. Well, perhaps not deserve. A husband that cheats is not automatically fit subject for removal. After all, cheating has to be as instinctive as breathing with the male of the species.

To be honest with herself, the real reason she wanted him out of her life was akin to the reason one rids oneself of an incurably sick pet—like an aging dog that habitually throws up on the carpet just before company arrives. Any usefulness he'd ever had he'd outlived. Besides, life would be more comfortable, richer, happier, safer, more relaxed, infinitely more satisfying and fulfilling in the role of wealthy widow. In addition to which she could never again let him touch her with his sticky hands or his fat wet lips, not after what she'd seen through the glass!

In her attempt to eliminate Enrico, she must take pains to conceal her true feelings. Never let him suspect she knew he was keeping company with some slut of a secretary, probably one of his own. Still she couldn't keep him away from her in bed without some excuse.

For a week, perhaps, but for longer than that she'd have to give him a reason. In his defense, as weak as it was, she had to admit that he'd been very good to her all these years, even to forgiving her Fernando. Which had been a crack-brained thing to do, totally spineless on his part. For that, she could never forgive *him!* Any real man would have broken her jaw and sent her crawling off with nothing but the clothes on her back— that ridiculous business involving him and Deirdre or no. But shooting Fernando and forgiving her was unforgivable.

She had little stomach for weak men, men one could walk over. Where was the satisfaction in that? Where the challenge? Now Derek Childs, there was a different breed entirely. His flinging her aside like an old boot had made him even more fascinating, the luscious bastard!

Life in widow's weeds looked outrageously attractive. After the funeral, she'd dismiss the staff, sell the villa and everything in it and run away from Italy. She'd had her fill of it. Too many churches, too much pasta, too many dirty, grubby types clogging up the public thoroughfares, the shops, the restaurants. Too much sun; it was like living in a steam bath. Always having to hide from it, the eyes, the face, one's skin.

She'd go straight to Paris, buy an apartment on the Seine and a shop close by. Jewelry. She adored jewelry —not costume junk, either, good pieces: money-money pieces to attract money-money people. And every 30 days by the calendar she'd take a new lover, none older than 35. No, none over 30!

Ashes to ashes, dust to dust. She'd inherit the business and sell that, too. She'd come out of it with barrels of money, drowning in it!

She stood outside in the garden looking up at the villa. It was homely when one really studied it: a heaping pile of orange pillared in white marble, statues standing about on the railing supports like pioneers defending their fort. Sell them, sell it, every foot of land, every stick of furniture.

Poison was the way. The proper selection, properly used, enjoyed a reputation for success that far outstripped all the other popular devices. This was probably so because nobody ever killed with poison out of anger, the way a gun or a knife was so frequently employed. With poison, one needed to plan, set the stage as simply as possible in order to reduce the chances of a slipup. Administer it in the victim's food or drink or medicine, and there you were, a widow.

Oil of sage. In Enrico's study she had come across a medical book that very morning that asserted that the ingestion of a mere eight ccs. of sage oil caused circulatory failure, difficult breathing, convulsions and death after a few hours. Given it at bedtime, he would be dead before sunup.

And she would put on a performance worthy of Julia Dean's Juliet, collapse and be carried off to Santa Sebastian's Hospital suffering nervous prostration, shock and seven other ominous ailments.

They had dinner that night promptly at eight, beefsteak, vegetables and potatoes "the size of a grown man's thumb," as Enrico put it. He loved them. They graced the table as often as five times a week. As usual, the serving maid came and went soundlessly, like a shadow in the night. When she was present, he took no notice of her, probably, surmised Lavinia, because she was flat-chested and a brunette.

"You're quiet tonight," he said looking up from his plate. "Feeling all right?"

"I feel fine."

"You're not eating."

"I'm not hungry."

"It's been almost six weeks. I would hope for your sake you'd have started getting over her."

"What makes you think I want to?"

"For your own good, Lavinia, your peace of mind."

He ate in silence, stabbing his peas one by one, locking them onto his fork with a potato. "Are you angry with me over something?"

"Should I be?"

"Not that I know of."

"Want a moment to examine your conscience?"

He smiled. "We've sharpened our tongue tonight, haven't we?"

She bored her eyes into his. "I was thinking. Wouldn't it be nice if you and I could get away? Perhaps to Nice for a week."

"It would be nice, but not now I'm afraid. We're getting into our busy season."

"Oh?"

"I'll be traveling more than ever, I'm sorry to say."

"Switzerland?"

He nodded. "And Rome and Milan."

"How lucky for you."

"It's not for enjoyment, Lavinia. It's all business."

"Isn't business enjoyable?"

"Sometimes; sometimes it's deadly."

"What about after hours?" He brought his head up, his eyes, enlarged by his glasses, staring inquiringly. "What do you do to relax?"

"Go for a walk, read a magazine, dine with the people I'm doing business with."

"How dull."

"It is. I generally get to bed by nine."

"Isn't there anything else you can do for diversion? To unwind? How about the theater? Are there ever parties? Couldn't you go to church? Sailing?"

Nothing. Not the slightest suggestion of surprise in his eyes, his face. No muscles tightening, not a hair turned.

"What's for dessert?" he asked.

"I have no idea. We're to be surprised."

The bastard. Mr. Innocence. Not the least bit

ruffled. On the night she picked, she would sit with him in the drawing room, they'd play Russian backgammon and drink anisette. He loved anisette and it always made him thirsty. He'd drink a liter of cold water before retiring.

LIV

"I still say it tastes bitter," remarked Enrico lowering the water glass from his lips.

She accepted it from him. "It's all that anisette."

"It's the well. This time of year lime or something seeps into it." He was sitting up in bed, the lamp on the nightstand casting an eerie glow over the left side of his face. He looked frightening, like a half mask cut out of fire. "I'm getting a headache."

"I'll get you a powder." She held up the empty glass. "And some more ice. You really shouldn't drink so much before bedtime."

"Please."

She went downstairs to the kitchen, returned with ice swimming in the glass and got two headache powders out of the medicine box in the top drawer of the bureau.

"One at a time, and drink it all."

He did as she told him and lay back on his pillow. "That's better. I'm tired. I could go right to sleep."

"I'm tired myself."

"Then you won't need Dr. Inglese's yellow pills. Blow out the lamp and come lie down."

"Not tonight, Enrico."

"Don't worry, I haven't the energy."

She lay down beside him and his hand was upon her, fondling her breast clumsily.

"Enrico."

"Sssssh, go to sleep."

He was off in seconds, snoring loudly on his way into deep sleep. Turning her head away from him, she tried to relax and fall asleep. If she could, she'd like to sleep

326

through his dying. According to the book, it wouldn't be particularly pleasant. Better she let Terese or one of the other servants awaken her with the good news.

Clouds covered the heavens, obscuring the moon and stars. The room was pitch black. She could barely distinguish the molding on the ceiling. His snoring continued sonorously, then it softened and gentled into simple heavy breathing. Releasing her breast, he turned on his right side away from her.

Waiting, she dozed, awoke and drifted off again—this time into a dream of Derek Childs. He was busy at a bust of her, working outside in a meadow. A bright sun hovered overhead; wildflowers and tall green grasses encircled them. She was posing nude from the waist up, her beautiful breasts coming to shape in the stone under his skillful touch. Neither of them spoke, but there were love and desire in his eyes. She made herself blush; she could feel the color rising in her cheeks. It was all he needed. Dropping his tools, he came to her, reaching out, his warm hands caressing her.

She awoke. Enrico had turned over on his stomach, throwing his left forearm across her, his hand back at her breast. He was breathing harder now, irregularly, fighting for air, catching it loudly, exhaling. It was becoming more and more difficult for him, as if his throat muscles were contracting, narrowing his windpipe. All at once his head and shoulders began twitching, then his limbs, until his entire body was convulsing. He thrashed about the bed. She got up, standing over him in the darkness, looking down. A human being in the process of dying. Fascinating! The final battle. Death with its arms outreached to enfold him, the pushing and shoving to keep him away, the gradual weakening of limbs and heart and will.

She closed her eyes to prevent any possibility of being able to see him, however dimly. After a time, the thrashing sounds, the guttural noises, the choking and high-pitched croaking diminished and stopped altogether. Gingerly she felt his pulse, holding his limp wrist for fully two minutes. She listened to his heart.

He was dead.

Wash out the glass, she cautioned herself, *carefully, plenty of soap. Oil could cling to the sides, could show up under strong light as some shade of yellow or light brown. There mustn't be any such careless slipups.*

She washed the glass thoroughly in the bathroom, returning to the room, standing in the middle of the floor, filling her lungs to capacity and screaming loudly.

They came running. She could hear them rushing down the stairs from the third floor, two, possibly three people. She screamed again. They were up to the door now. She collapsed.

She kept her eyes tightly closed, letting her body go limp as they carried her down the corridor to Deirdre's room. The bedcovers were pulled back and she was laid down gently. Two women had carried her; she could tell from their voices and the odor of their powder. After she'd been put to bed, one left, closing the door quietly.

Slowly, with contrived effort, she opened her eyes. Holding a candle with both hands, Terese sat at the bedside, a frightened look distorting her homely features. She set the candle in a holder.

"Terese."

"Shhh, *signora*, it's all right, all right."

"My husband!"

The look of fear gave way to pity. "He is dead." Terese crossed herself, jamming the knuckle of her index finger into her mouth, biting on it.

"God in heaven."

Lavinia groaned and raising herself on one elbow fell back immediately in a dead faint, a weak cry of anguish escaping her throat. *A perfect faint,* she assured herself, *as natural as could be.* Terese reacted with a nervous start. She brought her around with a damp cloth across her forehead and cold water applied to her lips.

"It's not true," whispered Lavinia feebly, "it can't be. It's all a bad dream. Tell me it didn't happen, Terese, say it!"

"His heart, *signora*, I'm so sorry. Mother of Jesus." Again she crossed herself and attacked her knuckle with her teeth. She started up from her chair.

"Don't go. Don't leave me!"

"Just to light the lamp, *signora*."

"Don't bother. Stay with me. Hold my hand, tightly." Again Lavinia raised herself. "No, I must go to him."

"No, no! Antonio has gone to fetch Dr. Inglese. He will see to everything. We will help. You must stay out of that room. Try to sleep."

"Yes. My yellow pills." She cast about helplessly. "They're in the top drawer of the bureau. Get me one and some water, please. Get two."

"Oh, *signora*, should you take so many?"

"Please get them."

Terese went out. *As smooth as silk*, thought Lavinia, stretching, relieving the binding at the nape of her neck. Thinking back on it, it might have been better to poison his precious anisette. Anise would have masked the bitter taste much better than water. She hadn't imagined it would taste bitter in water, so bitter he had commented on it. Careless. Still, if that was her only mistake, she had nothing to worry about.

LV

Two familiar faces, the lieutenant and his sergeant from the police station down below in Capri, appeared in the doorway. Terese led them into the room. The sun filled the room with its warm white morning light firing the shield on the lieutenant's absurd two-cornered hat, which was stuffed under his arm. Lavinia had awakened moments earlier feeling barbarously hungry, but deciding at once that new inductees into widowhood did not give in to such indelicate urges. On the contrary: For the next two weeks at least, she must pine away, enshroud herself in gloom and pretend total absence of appetite.

"These two wish a word with you, *signora*," said Terese in a disapproving tone. "I told them you were sleeping, but he——" She pointed to the lieutenant.

"It's all right. You may leave us."

"Some tea, perhaps, *signora*?"

"No, nothing. I can't possibly eat."

"The doctor has come, *signora*," said the lieutenant in a sympathetic tone that was almost sheepish. "We know what a terrible shock this must be, but if you can bring yourself to answer one or two questions, we would appreciate."

"I feel very weak, completely exhausted."

"I'm sorry. Would you prefer we come back later in the day?"

He exchanged glances with the sergeant, who was sweating as usual. His face was soaked, his tightly fitting uniform darkened with perspiration around the collar and on either side of his midsection.

"What do you want to know?" asked Lavinia.

"Can you tell us the approximate time of your husband's death?" asked the lieutenant.

"I have no idea. It could have been ten o'clock or four in the morning. I was asleep. When I woke up, he was carrying on loudly, thrashing about. It was horrible!"

"You have our sincere sympathies, *signora*," said the sergeant gravely.

"Did your husband have a history of heart trouble?" asked the lieutenant.

"Not that I know of. Still, he was a very private person. The sort who if there was anything wrong. . . ."

"Wouldn't tell you," finished the sergeant. He had gotten out a pad and pencil and was writing laboriously, sucking the tip of the pencil at the end of each line.

"If he thought it would upset me. My husband was the most considerate human being on the face of the earth."

The lieutenant nodded agreement. He started to say something, appeared to think better of it, then changed his mind a second time.

"I realize this is a very awkward time, a very painful time for you, *signora*, but there is something enormously important you can do for us."

"I'll do what I can, of course."

"With your permission, may we bring the body in here so that you may observe it?"

She gasped. "Why? What for?"

"There is something."

"What are you trying to say, Lieutenant?"

"If you could see it, perhaps you could answer one last question."

"What question?"

"With your permission."

"Never mind! Never mind!" *What was this, an impromptu inquisition? And why was he beating about the bush so? How perfectly annoying!* Well, obviously there'd be no getting rid of them until she complied.

"Help me up, please."

"Are you quite sure?" began the lieutenant.

"I'd prefer to go there if you're sure all this is absolutely necessary."

The sergeant moved to action, pocketing his pad and pencil and helping her out of the bed. His superior poked in Deirdre's closet bringing out her robe.

"I won't need that," said Lavinia concealing her annoyance with some difficulty.

They walked on either side of her slowly down the corridor to the master bedroom. Dr. Inglese was standing at the foot of the bed staring down at Enrico's body. A sheet concealed it completely. Inglese sucked his teeth and toyed with the end of his stethoscope, its clamps about the lower part of his neck. He appeared confused and anxious, and when they came into the room and he saw her, his forehead knit discernibly.

"Lavinia." He came to her, taking her hands. "I was just about to come and look in on you."

"I'm all right, thank you. A little weak, but——"

Inglese got a chair for her and she sat down.

"With your permission," said the lieutenant.

"You keep asking my permission, officer! I've given it. Will you please get on with this?"

"Yes, *signora*."

Good, she thought, *his tone was properly chastened.*

"We would like you to look at the face," he said quietly.

She glanced at Inglese and he nodded. The sergeant moved to the head of the bed and pulled down the sheet. She started, gulping audibly. The face was horribly contorted and as blue as cobalt; the lips darker, almost purple. Then the sheet covered it again.

"*Signora*," began the lieutenant, "I want you to be very careful as to what you say. I will ask you questions. Please take all the time you need to answer."

"You don't have to answer anything!" snapped Inglese testily. "Not a word before you talk with your lawyer!"

"Really, Tomaso, what on earth would I need a lawyer for? What do you want to know, Lieutenant?"

He cleared his throat. "As you can see for yourself, *Signore* Aldoni did not die of a heart attack."

"Oh, didn't he? Is this your personal diagnosis?"

"Dr. Inglese, is the face we have just seen the face of a man who died of a heart attack?"

"No——"

"Poison," interrupted the sergeant, drawing a glare from the lieutenant. The pad was back out, the pencil scribbling furiously.

"Poison?" asked Lavinia. "That's preposterous!"

"Lavinia, will you please listen!" burst Inglese. "Lieutenant, I forbid you to question her further. She's in no condition."

"The *signora* volunteered, Doctor."

"You heard me!"

"Very well. But in your professional opinion, sir, when will she be able to answer questions?"

"You'll be the first to know!"

"Excellent. Sergeant?" Clicking his heels, the lieutenant bowed stiffly. "*Signora* Aldoni, if I have upset you in any way, you have my most profound apologies. However, I must ask you not to leave the isle."

"Am I under arrest?"

"No. But until such time as you feel up to answering questions——"

"Your lawyer will be present, Lavinia," said Inglese.

The lieutenant nodded. "By all means. Until such time, we would be obliged if you remain here. Once again, may I express Sergeant Colato's and my own deepest sympathies at your tragic loss. We know our way out, thank you. Good morning."

Clamping her lips tightly together, she suppressed a smile. Then she began tittering. Inglese's hand on her arm to stop her only incited her. She broke into raucous laughter, rocking about in her chair, pointing at the body under the sheet, the tears running down her cheeks, her cupped hands pounding her knees. She laughed and laughed.

"Lavinia."

"His face.".

"Lavinia."

"I never thought, never even dreamed! It wasn't in the book, not a word!"

"Book?" He stared perplexed. Ignoring him, she resumed laughing, lurching about in her chair uncontrollably.

LVI

The *Macedonia* was a packet of 908 tons, a clipper from bowsprit to stern flag with a handsome V-shaped bottom, hollow waterlines and, according to her master, the most complex and ingeniously designed set of spars ever to cover a deck since the *Sea Witch*.

The *Macedonia* was a delight to the eye: Her hull was painted a fiery red up to the bulwarks, which were black, while the deck fittings, the cabins and the inside of the bulwarks wore a skin of shamrock green.

Six years earlier, she had made the run from San Francisco to Canton in 39 days, a record that still stood. Five years before that, she had broken four records in 11 months. She had been the first vessel of any class to round the Horn to California in fewer than 100 days. Her top speed had been clocked 19 times at between 22.5 and 22.8 knots per hour over a 90-mile course.

Middle-aged though she was, her paint was new and she displayed canvas only a year old. Under full sail so smoothly did she run that from a distance it appeared she was actually flying, skimming the sea rather than slicing through it. From braid to apprentice seaman, all hands were lavish in their praise of the ship's dependability, her consistency in performance, her heroic behavior in heavy seas.

A single noteworthy shortcoming clouded the *Macedonia*'s dazzlingly bright reputation. Like all clippers, she plied the seas without mechanical assistance, entirely dependent upon the power of the wind. And here in the middle of the Pacific, within a round 100 miles of the

Marshalls, the wind had died. More than died, observed Lisa petulantly. It had plainly deserted the earth, gathered its various representative selves into one massive draft, contracted itself to a ten-square-mile tempest and blown itself to the outermost edge of the universe. Like the dinosaur and the glacial shelf over New England, the weather force defined as wind was no longer with the world.

Lisa, Jeremy and Deirdre sat in the latter's little cabin sipping ice water, fanning themselves when the urge and the energy were upon them, perspiring freely and discussing their plight. It was all sadistically ironic to Lisa. How Ross and Gray and particularly Cyrus had detested steam—dirty, smelly, cumbersome coal, burning and besmirching God's clear clean air. For years, she'd heard the anti-plaint with slight variations as it was passed down the hierarchal line. Sail was all: the speed, the beauty, the clean clipper lines, the incomparable magnificence of canvas filled to bursting, the creaking and groaning of hard-working masts and spars. How like the soaring eagle was the clipper.

All of which notwithstanding, what would she not give at this moment—her money, years off her life, her soul—for a handful of horsepower and a black plume trailing from a smokestack peppering the deck with soot. Soot in her clothing, her hair, her eyes, her ears.

The sea around them had magically transformed itself into green glass; there was not a ripple, no movement of any sort. It was as if far below Neptune was holding the reins of his oceans in firm check while he slept. Flat calm. A sun as white as new snow monitoring it. The captain had ordered the ship's mainsail and mizzen sheeted hard in and the other sails lowered. He had resolutely assured one and all that their route was nowhere near the doldrums, that a calm such as this was a "freak of nature" that could not possibly last for more than a few hours.

This was the fifth day. The captain's early confidence

gave way to palpable concern, which in turn was supplanted by confusion. Now the man was embarrassed, conscientiously avoiding discussion of the condition at mealtimes. Day and night he had taken to locking himself in his quarters with his first mate and poring over charts and books on winds and weather.

It was getting on Lisa's nerves. It was getting on everybody's nerves.

"Harping on it won't do any good, Mother," observed Deirdre.

Lisa studied her daughter with a look of well-controlled annoyance. "You don't seem to understand, dear. While we sit here, sweating and counting the hours, the *Crown Pearl* is steaming merrily along. She's certain to beat us in. Not by two or three days, but more like a week."

"If that happens, she could easily get in and get back out again with another cargo," said Jeremy morosely.

"Precisely. It's conceivable that we could chase her all over the world and never catch up with her."

"I doubt that, Lisa," said Jeremy.

Deirdre nodded. "Me too."

Lisa sipped her water in silence, putting down the half-emptied glass and patting her face with a handkerchief. "Everything was going so smoothly up till now. Do you realize we got off the train in St. Louis and onboard that flatboat in less than half an hour? Then across the gulf and that spine-cracking jaunt through those mountains to San Marcos."

"Aren't you glad my calculations were a good hundred miles off?" asked Jeremy. "It was less than three hundred overland; I estimated four."

"It felt like four thousand," said Lisa drily. "Up the coast to San Francisco, almost perfect timing." She threw up her hands. "We just happened on the wrong ship."

"Mother, the wind will come back. It has to."

"When? A week? Two? Have either of you ever read about anything like this?"

They shook their heads. Then Deirdre changed the subject. "Mother, are you going to be angry with me the rest of our life together?"

"What you did was unbelievably foolish."

"That depends on one's point of view."

"My point of view is when we get there I shall lock you in a hotel room and keep you there till we've found your father and we're ready to leave."

"Really. Isn't that overdoing it?" Deirdre turned to Jeremy. "Isn't it, Jeremy?"

"No comment. I have a powerful aversion to the middle. I feel very uncomfortable there."

"You're completely ignoring the fact that I can help," insisted Deirdre. "I'm not crippled. I'm not stupid."

"And you're not getting involved!" snapped Lisa. "You——"

A snapping sound directly overhead stopped her.

"Heyyyyy!" yelled Jeremy. Pulling open the door, he ran out and looked upward at the sails. "Wind! Wind!"

"Praise the Lord!" exclaimed Lisa.

The crew came to life, swarming skyward, dropping skysails, topsails, gallants and royals, dressing the *Macedonia* in a great white cloud filling with the arriving westerly that sent her scudding over the suddenly choppy water. Lisa stood gripping the rail against the force of the wind, letting it pummel her face, her heart filled with joy and relief. But at the back of her mind, an annoying awareness of what they were entering upon persisted. It had come home to her while she was climbing the *Macedonia*'s gangplank in San Francisco. A woman, a girl and a man, who to her knowledge had never been south of Baltimore, embarking on a mission that was to take them into the heart of the Orient, into a world of strange cultures, unfamiliar tongues, a place where danger lurked down every alley, around every corner.

The mission was to find Ross and bring him home. The objective eased the doubt and apprehension. For, examining it in a manner as detached as her heart would permit, it was a step that had to be taken. There was no alternative.

Thank the Lord for Jeremy. His mere presence held off pessimism. He was bright, able, gritty, and if it came to trouble, she could rely on him to protect them.

Friend Jeremy; friend, indeed.

BOOK FOUR
AT THE GATES OF HELL

LVII

The rain fell in crystal sheets, dropping like liquid metal, pounding on their umbrellas as they stood waiting at the rail. It had been 53 days since San Francisco, including weather conditions that ran the gamut from a complete lack of wind to blustery squall to the most magnificent sailing conditions an embarking captain could wish for. Here they were in Singapore at last. Lisa's optimism was intact, while Deirdre's was, to some extent, overcome by girlish eagerness for adventure in this area of the globe renown for mystery and intrigue. Jeremy's smile remained fixed in place while he continued conscientiously to ignore his conscience and to concentrate on the task he had come halfway around the world to complete.

The *Macedonia* eased into its berth; the lines were flung, looped and made fast; the gangplank was lowered and secured. Through the downpour, Lisa could see the dim shape of the harbor. The land reaching to it was as flat as her hand and crammed to bursting with attap-thatched shacks, brick shops, warehouses and orange-roofed stone buildings. So closely built were they that it struck her that if the gods saw fit to lower one additional small building from the heavens and thrust it into the midst of the area, the buildings already there would pop from their foundations like fire spears from a Roman candle.

Sampans clustered at the water's edge, their flat tops curving downward to their sides like turtle shells. Groups herded together, seemingly for mutual protection out in the traffic water, and jammed between them

343

—and junks, pinnaces, bunderboats, tongkangs, proas, dinghies and dugouts—were commercial sailboats and steamers of every size and nationality.

The orange roofs contrasted with the blue water and shining green foliage, and she could almost feel the pent-up energy of the city, its vibrant activity temporarily contained by the punishing force of the storm.

Nine of ten men scurrying about the docks, legs and arms bare, their heads protected by coolie hats, were Orientals—Malays, Indians, Burmese, Tais, Japanese. But the majority of the people in the city were Chinese, according to the *Macedonia*'s master. If, he asserted, the British controlled Singapore aboveground, it was the Chinese, through their criminal secret societies, who controlled it underground. And this was the source of his concern over the welfare of his three passengers once they debarked and got beyond reach of his protection. The death rate among Europeans in Singapore was well above the assumable average for their numbers. The number of those dying "by unknown hands, without apparent motivation other than fanatical xenophobia" was alarmingly high. Any Christian captain worth his certificate got his ship into and out of ports such as Hong Kong, Canton, Macao, Yokohama and Singapore as speedily as possible.

According to the captain, in Singapore, as in Canton and Hong Kong, the Chinese secret societies waged continuous warfare with the authorities—quiet warfare that occasionally erupted into overt hostilities. As in 1846 when 100 Chinese were given permission by the magistrates to follow the funeral of the head of one of the secret societies and 6000 people assembled. The result was a bloody street battle in which hundreds were killed or injured; the military was called out to conclude the warfare. Five years later, 500 people were killed and 27 plantations attacked and burned within one week, in the course of sustained aggression against Roman Catholic converts. The secret societies regarded the Catholic Church as a rival society. In 1856 and 1863, two wide-scale bloodbaths underscored the city's reputation as something less than a peace-loving multinational community.

"I didn't pick this place," said Lisa to Jeremy as the three of them started down the gangplank. "Blame it on Wiley Thomas Regan."

Jeremy glanced about warily. "He might have settled for New Orleans. What's next? I vote we head for the best hotel in this lovely metropolis."

"Later," said Lisa, reaching the bottom and helping Deirdre off the gangplank. "First, customs. If anybody knows where the *Crown Pearl* is docked, it'll be the director."

"Lead the way," said Jeremy.

The port customs house was up a muddy stream bottom masquerading as one Chichak Street, designated by a small wooden sign hanging at an angle from one hook. Though it was early in the afternoon, lamps were lit inside to enable the two clerks busy at their tall wooden desks to distinguish their letters and numbers from the specks left by the army of flies in residence. The director was a small, undernourished man with a trace of cockney in his accent; from the depth and evident permanency of the color covering his nose, he was partial to gin.

He was also partial to pessimism.

"The *Crown Pearl*'s in, but she's on the book for the tide tonight," he announced offhandedly.

"What slip? Where exactly?" asked Lisa.

"This is Singapore, madam, not New York. Our slips aren't numbered. Dock space is catch-as-catch-can and push four sampans out of the way to get in. Besides which it stretches nearly forty miles from Changi to the south run of the Johore Strait. Plus fifty-four islands."

"What would be the point of putting in at an island?" asked Deirdre.

"Ships do, child." Obviously he didn't appreciate being questioned by somebody a quarter his age.

One of the clerks interrupted. "The *Crown Pearl* is at Telok Blangah; Captain Stahl commanding; cargo of teak, rice and mother-of-pearl."

"You're in luck," said his superior.

"How far is——" began Jeremy.

"Telok Blangah. Two miles from here." He pointed. "Back down the way you came and turn right. Follow the line of the harbor. You can engage a gharri at the corner."

"Thank you," said Lisa. "Good afternoon."

The rain began letting up by the time Jeremy reined up at a sign identifying Telok Blangah. A welcome sight met Lisa's eyes just beyond: the cumbersome black-under-white snub-nosed bow of the *Crown Pearl*, her name clinging to it, the two words separated by a four-inch hawser. Getting out of the gharri, Lisa lowered her umbrella and handed it to Deirdre.

"You two find a hotel, something decent close by."

"Mother, you're not going onto that thing alone?" exclaimed Deirdre.

"Don't bet your last dime," said Jeremy.

"Jeremy, I want you to come back and pick me up in half an hour."

"Will do." He saluted. "But whatever you do, don't let that scraggy-looking tub haul anchor and leave with you on board. I don't trust this part of the world, this city, that lovely bunch of rivets and plates, or anybody you're likely to find on board."

"Relax. I don't think it's another *Vampata*."

"Let's hope not."

"Half an hour. And when you locate the rooms, get them as close to the front desk as possible. Our little girl here is going to need somebody to keep an eye on her when you and I are out."

"I want to go with you, Mother."

Lisa glared and spoke through clenched teeth. "Don't start; just leave."

Jeremy drove off with Deirdre and Lisa boarded the ship, asking directions to the captain's quarters. The boatswain escorted her to the door and knocked.

"What?"

"Lady to see you, Captain Stahl."

He was very old—too old for the rigors of mastering a hard-working steamer, she decided—and, as she was quick to discover, into that phase of his life where impatience, short temper and shorter shrift are conduct preferred over gentlemanly congeniality. She showed him the picture of Ross and explained her visit.

"I can't tell you what name he's been using, but his real name is Ross Dandridge. He's my husband. He may appear normal, but he's suffering from amnesia."

"Never seen him before." She described Ross in meticulous detail. Stahl shook his head slowly. "I think you got the wrong ship."

"They boarded you in Norfolk. I know that."

"Then you know more than I do."

He had been standing. Now he sat down tiredly, yawning, settling his body into his chair, bringing out a cigar and lighting it.

"May I sit down?" she asked.

He shrugged. "What you got to understand, missus, is every port I put into I lose men, pick up new ones. Some skin out without their pay even. I give up minding faces or names. Just as long as I can get a day's work out of 'em." The door opened and a white-jacketed steward came in carrying a small tray of coffee. He poured for the captain who continued talking, oblivious of his presence. "Nobody really wants to work. They just think they do. Work on board a ship like this is no rose garden. I put in here, half the crew lights out. So I get new hands."

"Captain Stahl, a man's life is at stake. I beg you,

think! The man in this picture and Wiley Thomas Regan, who is six foot, five, completely bald with a scar on his head, a cross heavily welted. A big man, two-hundred-twenty-five pounds. Heavy drinker, hot temper."

"I already said I don't know either of 'em. Never seen 'em in my life. I got work to do. You better go."

She left, descending the gangplank and waiting for Jeremy under a tarpaulin raised to protect a pile of crates marked GUTTA-PERCHA. Jeremy picked her up. She recounted her meeting with Stahl.

"He's lying," she added bitterly.

"Maybe not. Maybe they jumped ship in Pernambuco months ago and he's completely forgotten them."

She gasped. "Lord, I never thought of that! Stahl could have stopped off at other places enroute. They could have left anywhere!"

"I hate to say it," said Jeremy, "but the further we get, the harder it looks."

"I still say Stahl was lying. There was something in his eyes. He was almost afraid to look at Ross's picture. And he was in a great rush to get rid of me, to get his ship out of Singapore. The way he behaved you'd think I was bringing the plague aboard."

"What do you want to do now?"

"Call a council of war and discuss what our next move is to be. What luck. Everything hinged on the *Crown Pearl!* How many times did I say to myself coming over 'If only we get there in time'? We did, and look what good it's done us!"

LVIII

The Equatorial Hotel was in Orchard Road approximately a mile inland. A four-story sand-colored building, it supported a typical orange-tile roof and was surrounded by temple trees and coconut palms. Potted palms littered the lobby, and the furniture, although for the most part new, was obviously inexpensive. Two small boys pulled indolently at punkahs, stirring the stifling air made heavy by the moisture that was left after the rain. The ceiling was hung with Argand lamps and the floor was covered with mats that cracked softly beneath their feet as they made their way past the desk and up the stairs to the second floor.

The three adjoining rooms were comfortable and more tastefully furnished than the lobby, with a partial view of the harbor—the full view being cut off by a newly constructed municipal office building.

They discussed the situation, Lisa continuing to contend that Stahl was lying.

"I know he was. The question is why, for what reason?"

"Perhaps he'd rather not get involved in something that could conceivably delay his sailing," said Jeremy. "Two missing men could bring in the police."

"I wonder if there's any other way to track them down besides the *Crown Pearl*?" mused Deirdre aloud.

Lisa shot to her feet. *"You are right!"*

Deirdre looked bewildered. "All I said was———"

"There *is* another way. If crewmen leave ships and replacements have to be hired, there must be some central place. Some sort of hiring location. There was

a grog house in Norfolk. Everybody coming in and
going out collected there. If I were a captain looking
for hands, it would be the first place I'd go to!"

"That's Norfolk, Lisa. In places like this, they're
much more likely to pick up men hanging about the
docks," said Jeremy.

"Forty miles of docks, the customs man said,"
observed Deirdre glumly.

"You two sound deliriously optimistic, I must say!
Hold on, I've got a better idea." She started putting
her hat back on. "I'm going straight back to the *Crown
Pearl*, stand by the gangplank and stop every man getting back on. I don't know whatever possessed me to
leave. It was bone stupid!"

A knock at the door. A hesitant, timorous tapping
that said the knocker was afraid of waking whoever
was inside. Jeremy opened the door. Lisa recognized
the steward from the *Crown Pearl*, his white jacket
exchanged for a raincoat.

"Come in, come in, Mr.———"

"McNulty, ma'am. I'm the steward."

"Yes, yes. Come in, please."

He was comically bashful, working his cap in a circle
with both hands, his eyes darting about the room,
spying Deirdre, looking away.

"I come about the two fellows."

They leaned forward expectantly. "Yes!" burst Lisa.

"Both o' them was aboard."

Lisa brought out the picture. "This man?"

"Smitty, yes. Him and the big loudmouth, his pal."

"Regan."

"I can't remember his name."

"It doesn't matter," said Lisa. "You're absolutely
certain about this one, though." Again she held up the
photograph of Ross.

He nodded emphatically. "They left ship here in
port. They got into Dutch."

"What happened?"

"They got caught smuggling *chandu*."

"*Chandu?*"

"Cut opium."

"O Lord, no!"

McNulty nodded, his pale, gaunt features fixed with all the conviction they could possibly muster. "The coppers got 'em. I know because Deering was with 'em and he got away. Deering's my pal."

"Then they're in jail here in Singapore?"

Again the nod. He continued to spin his cap nervously. "They're to go up before the justice."

"When were they arrested?" asked Jeremy.

"Three nights back."

"How could they be going to trial so fast?"

"Mr. Justice Sir Reginald Lowell. Any white man caught with opium in Singapore is for it with him." He drew his index finger across his throat. "Fast as he can get at him."

"No wonder Stahl pretended he didn't know them," said Lisa disconsolately.

"The captain washes his hands of them what gets into smuggling trouble, ma'am. They're on their own."

"They're being held at the police station?" asked Jeremy.

Lisa interrupted. "Where, tell me?"

"In South Bridge Road."

"Is that far from here?"

"It's close, only a few blocks. You could get a carriage."

"We will. Mr. McNulty, I don't know how to thank you," she said. She pressed money into his hand. To her surprise, he refused it.

"I couldn't, ma'am."

"I insist. You've earned it, coming here like this on your own."

He was suddenly a different person, stonily obdurate, his jaw set, his hands with his cap behind his back, out of her reach.

"No. I heard you and old Otto talking and I could see that fella in the picture was dear to you. Your brother or——"

"My husband."

"Yes, ma'am. And it ain't right to take money for doing what's right for decent folks. I couldn't; I'm Presbyterian."

"Then may I shake your hand? And thank you from the bottom of my heart?"

They all three shook his hand. His embarrassment returned, his sallow cheeks reddening. "I hope you can get him out of old Lowell's clutches. He's a bloody severe one, so they say."

"We'll do our best, Mr. McNulty," she said. "And thank you again."

Mr. McNulty said "You're welcome," put his cap on, tipped it and withdrew.

"Smuggling opium," said Jeremy quietly.

She bristled. "It's Regan's doing. Ross is just a cat's-paw; he has to be. He's never done a dishonest thing in his life." She glanced at her watch. "It's getting on to five. I'm going over there and find out what this is all about."

Jeremy's hand went to her arm. "Slow it down, Lisa. Let's think this out. First off, do you seriously think he'll be able to tell you anything? He's probably thoroughly confused by it all. And if he still has amnesia, he won't even recognize you."

"I'm not about to let that stop me."

"I'm not implying you should. I——"

"We've found him, Jeremy. That's what we're here for, remember?"

"I know, I know."

"God willing, when he sees me, it might trigger something in his mind. Dr. Middleton said it could happen that way. It's possible." She paused, placing her open hand over his held against her arm. "You'll represent him in court. I'll find out all the facts and you'll——"

"Hold everything."

"What's the matter? You're a lawyer; you can defend him."

"That's just it, there's no way. I'm no criminal lawyer. Even if I were, I'm not licensed to practice here."

"In a case like this, with a man's life at stake, I'm sure the law makes allowances. We're talking about Ross Dandridge!"

"I can talk to the justice, but what possible good that will do I can't begin to guess."

"We'll discuss it later. I'm leaving."

"I'll go with you."

"Let me come," said Deirdre, "please."

"I'd rather the two of you stay here."

"If I'm to help, I ought to talk with him," said Jeremy.

"Yes, yes. Deirdre, we'll be back in an hour or so. Lock the door and keep it locked. I don't care if Queen Victoria asks to come in, you're not to open this door. Is that clear?"

"Mmmmm."

LIX

Singapore's police station in South Bridge Road more closely resembled a cow barn partitioned into rooms. The noxious odor of camphor filled the air and the floor was badly in need of sweeping. Isinglass windows yellow with age successfully obscured view of the outside, and legions of flies buzzed merrily about. A single policeman was on duty, a bulbous-looking Chinese with a face that threatened a minimum of intelligent conversation. His tongue pushed his lower lip down ludicrously and his eyes protruded from the folds of fat encompassing them, creating the blankest expression Lisa had ever seen on human features. He spoke no English and apparently understood very little, if any. His response to every question was the same.

"Debuchi, debuchi."

"From his face, I'd say it means pardon me, some kind of apology. I doubt if he even understands Chinese," said Jeremy.

Lisa persisted, holding Ross's picture in front of the man's eyes. "We—want—to—see—this—man."

"Debuchi."

Using a form of pidgin English devised on the spot by Jeremy and the broadest pantomime imaginable, they struggled to make him understand. They failed completely. Her patience exhausted, Lisa started for the door to the rear half of the building, behind which it was obvious the prisoners were kept. But he was down from his desk stool and blocking her way before she could get to the door.

354

"This is ridiculous!" she snapped. Pulling out money she held it up. "Money, American dollars. For you!"

At that instant, the door in front of them opened and out came a second man, also Chinese, but older and infinitely brighter-looking.

"Good evening, sir, madam. May I help you?"

Lisa explained. He listened intently, with evident understanding. Then he shook his head.

"We are not authorized to admit visitors to the pen after sundown." Again she showed the money. His eyes sparkled and he wet his upper lip with the tip of his tongue. Out darted his hand, snatching away the money. "Five minutes, that's all."

"Only five?"

"If I am found out, I lose my job."

"Very well."

He stepped aside, his attention on the money, counting it. Jeremy opened the door for her and she started in. The policeman's arm shot out blocking Jeremy.

"Just the lady, sir."

"See here—"

"Just the lady."

"It's all right, Jeremy. Stay here; I'll be fine."

The officer closed the door at her back. To her surprise, she found herself in a large room filled with prisoners—no bars, no individual cells, the windows boarded up from the outside and the interior illuminated by a single Argand lamp suspended from a rafter. The reason for the camphor became clear. It acted as a mask for all the human odors emanating from this room. It did its job outside; in here, it shared the air with a variety of stenches.

Her heart leaped as she recognized Ross standing in the middle of the crowd with Regan. Unmistakably Regan. Dr. Middleton's description had been perfect. She stared at Ross, who was looking off to the right, staring into space, listening to Regan. *He looks dis-*

couragingly thin, she thought, *underweight 15 perhaps 20 pounds. And pale, with none of his usual vigor, tired-looking, slumping where he stood.*

Her entrance attracted the attention of the prisoners sitting and standing near the door—Chinese, Malays, Indians and a handful of white men, for the most part vicious-looking men, their eyes narrowing at the sight of her. She could guess what ran through their minds. She pushed forward, her heart beating wildly, her throat suddenly dry as tinder. *Three years, my darling, three years and more now. A lifetime. To see you again in this hellhole. Locked up like an animal with all these animals. Ross, Ross, my darling Ross.*

"Ross!"

Regan heard her first, turning to stare. Nearing them, she could see the scar on his forehead just as Middleton had described it. He was a fierce-looking man with evil in his eyes, the worst sort for Ross to become associated with. A killer. He directed Ross's attention to her. Their eyes met.

Dear God, let him know me. Make him know me!

No. He looked at her and back to Regan questioningly, his eyes mystified.

"Who are you, lady?" asked Regan. "What can we do for you? What are you doing here? This is no place——"

"Please!"

There was no hint of recognition in Ross's eyes, not the vaguest semblance of it. He was staring at her now, looking through her as if it were the first time he had ever seen her. She reached him, taking his arm, holding it tightly.

"Ross, it's me, Lisa. Look at me, Ross. *Look at me!*"

Again he looked at Regan questioningly.

"He's my husband," she explained. She produced the picture and showed it to Regan. "His name is Ross Dandridge."

"His name is John Smith."

"He's my husband, I tell you!"

To her horror, Ross began snickering at her, a broad smile spreading across his face.

"What's so funny, Smitty? You heard her, she says you're her husband. Look at her, you dumb bastard. She's pretty as silk." It was all a big joke to Regan. He was enjoying himself immensely. "This is your picture, look."

Ross studied the likeness. "That's me, yeah."

"Ross, darling." Unable to hold back, she threw her arms around his neck and began kissing him, tears rushing to her eyes. It was like kissing a dead man. There was no response, no yielding to her, no return of affection whatsoever. Instead the mystified look came back.

"He don't seem to know you, lady." The man's tone was almost jubilant. He was finding her mounting frustration amusing. She hated him, his familiarity with Ross, his nearness, his obvious sway over him.

It was horrible, ghastly, much worse than she could ever have anticipated! If only she could get him alone, just the two of them in a room where she might talk to him quietly, gently stir the embers of his memory. Ignite the smallest spark of recognition, fan it with all the words—Cyrus, Gray, Dandridge, Dandridge, Dandridge. Blackwood, Lisa, Lisa. Deirdre, the war, Ericsson, the *Monitor. My darling, the storm, the sinking! Lisa, Lisa, Lisa! I love you, Ross, my dearest darling Ross! Hold me! Kiss me!*

"Who are you?" he asked.

"It's Lisa, Ross, Lisa, Lisa."

"Lisa." He scratched his head and shook it slowly, wrinkling his chin, his eyes dull with confusion.

LX

The bribe taker came in for her, and the three of them stood outside talking, with the other policeman looking on, listening, unable to understand one word.

"The trial will be tomorrow morning," said the policeman. "Mr. Justice Lowell goes to watch the cricket matches on the Esplanade every afternoon, so the whole show stops at noon."

"What time does the court open?" asked Lisa.

"Nine o'clock."

"Too early. We'll go see him tonight, have it out with him. He's got to be made to understand."

Jeremy consciously avoided her eyes. "Lisa, you're not being realistic. This isn't Providence."

"It makes no difference. The man is civilized, he speaks English. When I tell him the whole story——"

The policeman shook his head. "You can't tell him tonight."

"And why not?"

"You won't be able to get to him."

"Where is he?"

"At Fort Canning, *Bukit Larangan*, Government Hill. Playing bridge with Brigadier Washburn. The husbands and the wives play every Wednesday night. They go up early for cocktails."

"How do we get there? Give me directions!"

"Why bother? You can't go up. You can't get by the guards."

"Officer, the man inside is my husband! He's going on trial tomorrow morning. It's all a farce. It's all nonsense, but if he's found guilty, he could hang! Do

358

you understand me? Time is vital; it's absolutely essential that I——"

"You can't get by the guards."

"To hell with your guards! I will see this Justice Lowell tonight!"

"He won't see you." He held up three fingers touching each in turn. "Three things are sacred to him, the law, cricket and bridge. When he is wrapped up in them, the whole world is locked out."

"Very well." She paused and pondered. "Listen to me, I'll pay you five hundred American dollars or the equivalent in British pounds, whichever you prefer, if you will take a message to him."

"Five hundred dollars?"

"Cash. Payable first thing tomorrow morning!"

"Oh, my, I am sorry. I am so sorry."

"You refuse?"

"I would be glad to take a message to him. I would be joyful to, but it can't be done. Not by me, not by anybody. To disturb his bridge game is unthinkable, especially if he is losing. He once sentenced a Tai to hang for shooting a policeman. Just before the execution another man was found to be guilty. But the innocent man was hanged, all because no one could get in to tell the justice."

"I don't believe it. It's monstrous! And ridiculous!"

"It is also true. I give you my word of honor. I swear by Shang-ti. It's no big stumbling block. You can see him tomorrow in his chambers, early, before the trial. He comes fifteen minutes before."

"It might be better," said Jeremy. "Breaking into his precious card game could get his dander up and wreck any chance we have."

"Where will the trial be held?"

"At the High Court Building, at the front of the Padang. It is the biggest building for miles around. You can't miss it."

"This is the most farcical thing I—I've never laid

eyes on him and already I hate him with a passion!"
She turned again to the officer. "What do you know
about this case?"

"They were smuggling *chandu*. Bad business, very
bad."

"If my husband is found guilty, what will they do to
him?"

"Transport him."

"I don't understand."

"To the penal colony."

"Good Lord!"

"I'm afraid it's so."

"Where? Near here?"

"Maybe, maybe not. There is one at Pulau Senang,
but it is very overcrowded. The men are packed in
there like rice in a sack. And all sick with malaria and
dysentery. He will probably order them sent to Tasmania, Port Arthur or Macquarie Harbor. Who can
say? Whatever comes into his head. If he's in a good
mood, if he and Mrs. Lowell beat the Washburns at
bridge——"

"I don't believe this," said Lisa in a hoarse whisper.
"It can't be happening. I'm dreaming it!"

Jeremy put his arm around her shoulder. "Now don't
go jumping to conclusions. He hasn't even gone to trial
yet. Come eight forty-five tomorrow, we'll see Lowell."

"I'll be waiting for him. I want you to arrange a
meeting for us with the governor. We can lay the
groundwork with him tonight."

"The governor?" The policeman sucked in his
breath, a frightened look on his face. "That's no good.
Very bad."

Lisa ignored him. "We've got to get a leash around
Lowell's neck before he goes wild."

"The governor won't help you. Mr. Justice Lowell,
he made Mr. Cuthbertson governor. He brought him
here from New Delhi. Old school chums."

Jeremy looked glum. "This is getting stickier by the minute."

They talked on, the policeman acquainting them with local politics and the unwelcome though unassailable fact that Mr. Justice Sir Reginald Lowell wielded absolute power over the island city-state. And Ross's fate appeared to be entirely in Lowell's judicial hands.

"At a quarter to nine," said Jeremy. "Let's cross our fingers and hope for the best."

"For Mr. Justice Lowell," she said solemnly. "He'd better listen to reason. If he refuses to, if he dares convict him, I promise you both I shall make him wish he never heard of Singapore!"

The policeman smiled weakly and swallowed. He believed every word. Jeremy did also, although he betrayed no reaction. It was all becoming extremely complicated. But he was confident that it couldn't continue stretching out very much longer. He wouldn't put it past her to make the justice "wish he never heard of Singapore," but he doubted she'd get him to reverse whatever verdict for conviction he might come up with. Bearding the lion in his own back yard was no easy chore.

And if and when Ross were sent out to Tasmania, his chances for survival would be next to nil. In which event, he Jeremy would very likely be spared the job of getting rid of him.

As matters stood, good old reliable Jeremy could not lose.

LXI

At the suggestion of the policeman, they left the Equatorial in their rented gharri at eight o'clock the next morning. It was a 15-minute ride to the High Court Building. But the policeman had advised that traffic would be unusually heavy, because it was Thursday, the day when food hawkers invaded the city by the hundreds. With their appearance, practically everyone turned out. Well-intentioned though the officer had been, he greatly underestimated the situation. Within shouting distance of the hotel, they were overswept by a sea of humanity that promptly closed behind them. Six or seven thousand people were locked into place seemingly unable to move in any direction. Gharries and carriages were wedged in by the pedestrians—*Samsui* laboring women, cone-hatted Cantonese women food hawkers, turbaned Sikhs, Punjabis and *chettiars* from Madras, Malayan women in colorful close-fitting jackets and long batik skirts, Malayan men in *bajus*—loose collarless jackets worn over ill-fitting trousers—saffron-robed Tais, pig-tailed Chinese businessmen and patriarchs, their ladies in brightly colored *cheongsams*, straw-hatted coolies, Japanese, Eurasians, British civilians and pith-helmeted soldiers. A seething mass of people frozen in place and wholly indifferent to Lisa's plight.

"Incredible!" she snapped irritably. Abandoning their gharri, they attempted to shoulder their way through the mob, Jeremy leading the way, but no one seemed disposed to let them by. Nobody was annoyed, nobody upset. Everyone smiled and nodded pleasantly. Some even greeted them with *Ni hao** and *nah-mahs* TEH†, but their forward movement was comparable to that of a snail over a flagstone walk on a particularly hot and humid summer's day.

It seemed like hours before they got to the source of the holdup, a multivehicle traffic accident that had attracted hundreds of onlookers and blocked the streets in all four directions. They were delayed one hour by Lisa's watch, finally emerging onto the Padang within sight of the High Court Building, its lofty dome and cupola shadowing the smaller surrounding buildings. They hurried across the parade grounds to the entrance, located under a balcony attached to four Grecian columns and supported by four square pillars of its own.

Two uniformed guards attempted to block their way, but they hurried past them through the open door into the building. The doors to the courtroom were also open and the room was filled to overflowing. People flailed the sultry air with their fans and Mr. Justice Lowell's boring voice vied with the swishing sound.

"In the view of this court, your contention that your fellow seaman Cyril Alfred Deering was wholly responsible for the crime of which you are accused is without merit or foundation. I therefore have no recourse but to find you both guilty as charged of the crime of opium smuggling. I sentence you John Smith and you Wiley Thomas Regan to seven years hard labor at Macquarie Harbor."

Down came his gavel, the hammer of doom.

"Take them away. Next case."

Lisa made no sound other than a barely audible gasp. Both hands went to her mouth and she went limp, leaning back against Jeremy for support. His arms were around her waist holding her securely.

"Easy, easy." he said quietly, clamping his jaw tightly to keep from laughing gleefully.

**Chinese for how are you.*
†*Hindi for hello.*

LXII

A portrait of Sir Thomas Stamford Raffles hung in a polished-teak frame on the wall. Modern Singapore's founder sat cross-legged in a square-backed leather chair, a letter in one hand, his jauntily angled elbow supported by his work table, his free hand drooping carelessly over the arm of the chair. It was a relaxed, bored, almost sleepy-eyed image of the man, manifestly belying his inexhaustible energy and extraordinary capacity for action.

Opposite, hanging between two Chinese watercolor panels, was a portrait three times the size of Sir Thomas's: Mr. Justice Sir Reginald Lowell in judicial cap and robes, holding the gavel of his office. His pale blue eyes, rendered steely by the artist, bored into Raffles's. Even without his portrait, Sir Reginald's influence in the room was evident. Framed photographs depicted him in his undergraduate days at Harrow, at Oxford, at cricket and crew. With a hunting party, rifle cradled over his forearm, his naked knee elevated above the remains of a Bengal tiger. Photographed hand in hand with a plain, dowdy-looking woman, garlands of flowers circling their necks. On the massive mahogany desk was a stone bust of his honor, his chin protruding defiantly well beyond its normal natural thrust exhibited in the courtroom.

Having been shown into the justice's study at ten minutes before five with the assurance that the master would be home on the hour, Lisa had been sitting for nearly one hour and thirty minutes. This delay served to stir the fires of resentment, although glancing about the impressively appointed room and listening to the figured ivory clock atop the glass-doored gun cabinet ticking away the afternoon gave her time to mentally prepare precisely what she would say. Jeremy had insisted on coming along, but she did not want him to.

"If I'm to make any headway with him at all, I'll have to play on his sympathies," she had said, "try to find a human chord and touch it. A lone female coming to him heart in hand might stand a chance. But to march in with my lawyer in tow——"

After hearing Lowell's verdict, they had gone back to the hotel to consider strategy. Even before they got there she was suggesting hiring a ship and men, storming the jail, freeing Ross and rushing him away to Indonesia or Australia, anywhere out of reach of Singapore justice. But once reason and common sense took over, she decided to approach the justice in his den.

"Too bad we weren't able to catch him before the verdict. Getting him to reverse himself may be next to impossible," said Jeremy gloomily.

With this she could hardly disagree, although she refrained from commenting. She was beginning to wonder about Jeremy. He was behaving rather oddly, she thought, loyal, helpful, calm and rational but increasingly pessimistic. It was as if he had privately given up and was now merely going through the motions for her sake and Deirdre's. It wasn't so much what he said but the hollow hopelessness of his tone. And the look of discouragement. In one normally so optimistic, the turnabout was distressingly obvious.

The punkah suspended over the desk hung motionless. Past the vase filled with yellow black-eyed Susans on the windowsill, she saw a white-collared kingfisher land in the rhododendron and perch there, jerking his head absurdly. The image of Lowell sitting on the bench delivering his verdict came back, his head snapping forward punctuating his words.

Through the partially opened door she heard the outside door open and men's voices: those of the ser,ant who had shown her into the study and, unmistakably, Lowell. He came striding in one hour and thirty-four minutes past his usual time—according to the clock on the gun cabinet. She introduced herself. He closed the door, brought her chair up to his desk and sat down behind it. He was in a good mood, chipper and relaxed—or as close, she surmised, as one of his old-school stuffiness could ever get to.

"A cricket match like I haven't seen in years! The Eighth Grenadiers against a bunch of Punjabi chaps. Very very good for duskies, uncommonly fast. By George, they had a bowler faster than Harvey Fellowes in his prime!" He pulled his head back and made a ridiculous face. "Dear me, I do beg your pardon. I'll ring for tea and crumpets."

He rang. She hadn't realized how much she needed tea until she'd downed nearly a full cup. It braced comfortably, steadying her nerves. She told her story putting emphasis on who she was, who the Dandridges were and Ross's contribution to the Union cause in the war. Lowell seemed impressed, but by the time she had brought him up to date, his interest appeared to be flagging. She hurried to the core of the matter.

"My husband is a man with the highest regard for law and order. He would never knowingly break the law."

"Be that as it may, dear lady, I'm afraid he has." Up came both hands, forestalling interruption. "I know, his amnesia, his relationship with the other one, Regan, all the unfortunate ingredients. Word seems to fit, doesn't it? Nevertheless, the law is clear. The smuggling of opium in Singapore, dealing in narcotics in any way, is expressly forbidden. An infraction of this magnitude is punishable by lengthy penal servitude. Statute forty-four B, paragraph seven, the Penal Code."

"My husband is accused, but did he admit to the crime? Did he confess?"

Lowell's smile was infuriatingly patronizing. "My gracious, dear lady, there was no need for a confession. The arresting officer caught the two of them red-handed."

"That was the information given you?"

"Most assuredly. The information upon which I based my verdict."

"The arresting officer's testimony."

"No testimony. His report. The arresting officer is not required to testify."

"He spoke with you?"

"Dear me, no. I couldn't even tell you his name!"

He was leading her by the hand now, feigning surprise at her ignorance of judicial procedure.

"There was a written report?"

Lowell shook his head, freezing the annoying smirk on his face. "No, dear lady, why should there be? The arresting officer's information was given to his superior. And relayed to me."

"So sending two men to a penal colony in Tasmania for seven years was based entirely on one man's version of what happened."

"That's right." She emptied her cup and he hastened to pour her more. "Gunpowder, my favorite. Isn't it delicious? Have a crumpet."

This, she silently shouted, *has to be the most self-centered, implacably self-assured know-it-all in authority in the entire Orient, a sector of the world notorious for colonial-service tyranny.*

"What if the arresting officer was wrong? What if he failed to see what he claimed? What if he misunderstood what he saw? What if he lied?" she asked.

"All possibilities, I grant you. Reasonable and logical, but no concern of mine."

"No concern of yours!"

"Precisely. I don't arrest people. I don't question those who do. I accept their version and render judgment."

"You never question their version?"

"Certainly not. That's not my responsibility. Given the facts, I examine them under the glass of the applicable statute and fix sentence."

"With no proviso whatsoever that the facts might conceivably be distorted or wrong?"

"Didn't I just tell you——"

"Doesn't it occur to you that you might be sending an innocent man into penal servitude or to the gallows? That you could be making a perfectly simple mistake? Which in effect means *you're* committing the crime of punishing somebody who's entirely blameless?"

"Mistake?"

"Yes, mistake!"

Lacing his fingers over his watch chain, he leaned back and searched her eyes. "I never make a mistake."

"You never make a mistake? Not once?"

"Never. Such a thing is impossible. Oh, the police may, but you see—and once again let me make this very clear—I address only the law and the sentence to the facts given me. The punishment fits the crime."

"Even if there is no crime."

"Their mistake, should it happen, not mine. Never mine."

"Have you ever found out after sentencing that you've sent up the wrong man?"

"Definitely. You can't possibly pass judgment on nearly two thousand cases a year without that happening once in a while."

"What do you do then?"

"Not a blessed thing, dear lady."

She was finding it increasingly difficult to believe she was seeing and hearing this. He was not the least bit defensive about it; he wasn't even self-conscious. And the furthest thing from regretful. Nor at the opposite end was he proud. It was all unbelievably matter-of-fact, rather do-you-understand-and-if-you-don't-why-don't-you?

He seemed to sense the timely need for simplistic explanation.

"Think of my job as a house with a thousand doors. Every case completed, every verdict rendered and sentence passed, one door gets closed. Slam, click. But most remain open, waiting for me to get to them. And new ones are always popping up. But I work hard, I work steadily and one by one I close them. Slam, click."

"Never to open them again."

"Never. Oh, I confess injustices occur, mistakes are made. But we can't go back and glue the broken window back together now, can we? To do so would be to take three times the time it took to break it in the first place. Leaving three other doors still open that should be closed." He grinned and winked. "And putting me three doors behind. Can you imagine the chaos that would ensue, if the backlog began growing?" He shuddered childishly. "Perish forbid!"

"You're content to let the minority suffer from injustice as long as justice of sorts is done the majority."

"Of sorts? Dear lady——"

"You sent two men away for seven years today in fourteen minutes. Fourteen minutes."

"Twelve. We started two minutes late this morning. My clerk mislaid my gavel."

"Twelve minutes for seven years."

"I heard the facts. I heard the defendants. I found defense wanting." He laughed. "To say the least. I found both men guilty, I sentenced them. Slam, click. And they're on their way to Tasmania before lunch."

"Twelve minutes."

"A routine case. Not at all complicated. I've had any

number even simpler. Just yesterday I sent a chap to be hanged for stabbing his landlord in three minutes and thirty-two seconds by the clock over the door."

"May I ask you a favor?"

"If it's in my power to grant it."

"Could you call in the arresting officer so that the three of us might discuss this case?"

"To what purpose?"

"To possibly reconsider your verdict. Possibly reopen the case."

"But why bother? I'd never reverse myself. I never have. I never would. The doors, the doors."

She stood up. "Thank you for your time, Sir Reginald. I must be going."

"You haven't finished your tea. Nor even tasted the crumpets."

"I've had enough, thank you. Good afternoon."

"Good afternoon." He pulled the wall bell cord. "I'll get Dharmi in here to show you out, Mrs.——"

"Dandridge."

"Quite right."

"Before I go I must tell you that you, sir, are an amazing man."

"I——"

"I've never met anyone quite like you. Never known anybody who played God with such confidence and comfortableness in the role. I'm curious what the members of the bar back in London will think of your door theory of law when word gets back. I can imagine their shock. Obviously you imagine that distance lends justification to such asinine conduct. You're very wrong. There can be no justification, no possible excuse.

"You may begin counting your days. I have friends in Washington who have friends in London. I have wealth, power and influence. I intend to use this case as the basis for a complete investigation into your activities here. The Prime Minister will be apprised. If necessary I shall request an audience with Her Majesty to inform her of your flagrant distortion of the law, your unconscionable dereliction of duty. This case will be reviewed by your superiors. My husband and his companion will be set free and I will see you brought down in disgrace, stripped of your office and dishonorably dismissed. You will never sit in judgment in a court of law again as long as you live. On that I give you my word. Good day."

"You're quite certain?" She had started toward the door. Stopping she turned. "About the tea? You're more than welcome to a good-bye cup."

He smiled benignly and pointed to her chair.

LXIII

For every self-respecting woman there comes a time when the only recourse, the only balm to heart and soul, the only defense against the slings and arrows, is tears. To let go. To give in. Rising from the springs of misery, they reach the eyes, collect in abundance, blessedly dim sight of the bullying world and fall into that world. A sign of weakness, surrender? Just the opposite. At least in Lisa's case. They signaled release, an unlocking, the lid removed from the well-crammed cask of emotions, the pressure loosed, the mind eased, the heart soothed, the soul wrung out. The last tear, the last sob, the final application of sodden hanky to eyes and nose and she reached inward getting firm hold on herself. Straightening her shoulders, she lifted her chin defiantly, girding and psychologically arraying her resources for the attack.

The feeling inside after a rousing good cry is similar to that outside after a good rain. A clearing, a cleanness to the air, one's surroundings, life. A fresh start.

She returned to the hotel with her plans formulated, examined for flaws, found workable and worth the implementing. Even before recounting her meeting with Lowell, she announced their next move.

"Jeremy, I want to hire a ship, fully manned, every man armed. Destination: Macquarie Harbor. We will attack the colony, overcome the defenders and rescue Ross."

"Just like that."

"Hardly. How to get onto the island without endangering him or any other prisoner will require a

372

scheme that has to be planned down to the tiniest detail, obviously. But we need the ship, the arms and the men right away. Every day we waste sitting here twiddling our thumbs brings him closer to Tasmania and that hellhole. I saw the poor darling. He's in no condition for that sort of life. Regan will be able to take it, but not Ross."

"This is going to cost you a fortune."

"I don't care if it costs a million in gold bullion."

"I'm only saying——"

"We'll start at fifty thousand for ship and crew, plus expenses for supplies and arms and ammunition. I suggest you talk with captains only. You've got to tell them our destination; it has to come out sooner or later anyway. I'd prefer a ship that's combination steam and sail, at least a thousand tons. How far do you think it is to Macquarie Harbor?"

"Tasmania's due south of Melbourne. We'd have to head south down through the Java Sea to the Sunda Strait past Batavia* out into the Indian Ocean, down, down to Cape Leeuwin at the southwest corner of Australia, then east south east to Tasmania."

"Which is?"

"Four, maybe five thousand miles. It could be more."

"That's good."

"What's good about it, Mother?" asked Deirdre.

"Over that long a distance, we might be able to catch up with the prison transport."

"I doubt that," said Jeremy. "To hire a ship, the men, get arms and ammunition all takes time, a week or ten days. They'll have a fifteen-hundred-mile head start."

"Then bother their ship; we'll attack the colony. We'll need at least fifty men, guns, bombs, dynamite."

"First the ship."

Jeremy skipped dinner, going straight to the docks to

*Modern Jakarta.

make inquiries. He came back to the hotel three hours later, walking into the lobby, his face cast with dejection. Lisa and Deirdre were occupying overstuffed chairs on either side of a huge potted palm. He shook his head.

"Not a whisper. I might as well have been asking them to take us to hell."

"Let's not tell the world about it," said Lisa, glancing about the lobby. A dozen people sat about chatting or reading newspapers. "Let's go up to the room."

The change in location had no effect on either his mood or his pessimistic appraisal of their chances. "I talked to nine men. Every one was all for it, right up until I mentioned Macquarie Harbor. It was as if I pulled a gun on them. Practically every one the same reaction: Each one would shrink back, hold up his hands and shake his head."

"You'll just have to keep trying."

"I don't know what good that will do."

"Double the money: a hundred thousand, ship and crew!"

"Lisa, you'd understand if you could have seen their faces. I could have offered them ten million. They weren't the least bit interested."

"There has to be somebody with a little steel in his backbone."

"It isn't courage you want, it's more like old-fashioned lunacy. Somebody who'll jump into a snake pit just for the thrill of it. With fifty men who feel the same way behind him."

She thought a moment. "Tomorrow morning I want you to go back down there, find four or five more and set up appointments for them with me here in the room. Tell them the money; tell them they're going on a long trip. Don't say where."

"But——"

"Send them back here one by one."

"If that's the way you want it."

"One at nine, one at nine-thirty, ten o'clock, and so on. All day long until we get one I can talk into it."

He was up and out at seven-thirty the next morning, and promptly at nine a knock sounded at the door. Deirdre opened it to sight of a man six-and-a-half feet tall, so wide he was obliged to turn sideways to make it through the door. A man so hard-looking his face appeared fully capable of breaking the most powerful fist. All but hidden behind his back was another man, half his size and weight and twice as ugly, bearing scars that wandered about his face as if seeking wrinkles in which to hide.

"Alger Foote, master-owner of the *Wanderer*, little miss. This is my first mate, Mr. Terence O'Hara. Are you the lady?"

Lisa appeared behind Deirdre. "Mrs. Dandridge, Captain. Mr. O'Hara, come in and sit down."

Both men removed their caps and, stuffing them into their pockets, came pounding into the room, the mate bringing with him the powerful stink of bay rum mingled with fried onions. Lisa had set up a table with a chair on either side and Deirdre brought another chair for Mr. O'Hara.

"One hundred thousand dollars, the gentleman said," began Captain Foote. "Now the *Wanderer* is rigged and fueled and ready to go. We was just sitting in port waiting for cargo, but this sounds much more to my liking than rice and lumber. A hundred thousand. And where will we be going?"

"Tasmania."

Disappointment flooded the captain's face and his mind wheels began turning behind his eyes. "Tasmania."

"That's what I said."

"Are you familiar with Tasmania?"

"No."

"It's a convict island."

"That I know."

"Where exactly were you planning to put in, Hobart?" asked Mr. O'Hara.

"No."

"Devonport, then, or Stanley, Wynyard or Ulverstone?"

"Macquarie Harbor."

The captain's generous mouth fell open, exposing a gaping void where his teeth should have been. Mr. O'Hara got his hat out and onto his balding head, starting up from his chair.

"You're not serious, missus!"

"One hundred thousand dollars serious. That's cash, payable in full upon departure from the harbor."

"You want to get somebody out of the colony?"

"Exactly."

"It can't be done."

"It will be done. By you or by somebody, but I assure you it can and will be done."

"You mentioned you're not familiar with Tasmania, missus," said Foote, "I can tell you that it's circled by an ocean full o' the most furious storms in all the seven seas. They collect there before starting out to work their mischief all over the globe. It's the west winds of the roaring forties that stir 'em up. So even landing on Tasmania is touch and go. Many a good ship's piled up."

"It's even worse what you're talking about," interposed Mr. O'Hara. "The Gates of Hell."

"The what?"

"The entrance to Macquarie Harbor, missus," continued Foote. "Would you like me to picture it for you? Not that I claim to have been in there, only passed by at a distance. A safe distance."

"Go on."

"Every man who sails this part o' the world knows of the Gates of Hell. They lie in the hardest to reach part of the west coast of the island. The entrance to the harbor is scarcely wider than this room, with tide rips

fit to pull the plates off and shifting sands that can suck
you in tight as a trivet. It rains every day, some days not
all day, but every day. Southwest and westerly gales
come sweeping in from the Antarctic Ocean, bringing
hail squalls that hit like a fusillade o' bullets. It's icy
cold. Coming in from Hobart, say, you'd have to stand
on against that westerly wind along a lee shore that's
the most dangerous on the island. So you could sit for
two months in a sheltered spot, at Recherché Bay or
Port Davey, waiting in the rain and the cold until a
slant in the gale lets you stand in. The reason it's so
hard to get in is the reason it makes such a perfectly fine
penal colony. It's just as hard to get out.

"I wouldn't accept a commission to bring supplies in,
let alone stand to and wait for a rescue party to debark,
pick up a convict and come back."

"It has to be done."

"It can't be. Nobody ever escaped from Macquarie,
not in fifty years!"

"Dietrich did," said O'Hara.

Lisa sat up very straight, her eyes wide with interest. "Dietrich?"

Captain Foote dismissed this with a gesture. "So one
man, with the luck o' the devil."

"How did he get away?"

"Swam," said O'Hara. "He could swim like a por-
poise and he made it to a wreck four miles oot. Then
he got picked oop! A broth of a boy."

"Where is he now?"

"Swallowed up by the world," said the captain, "a
few thousand miles away from Macquarie, you can
wager." He got to his feet, towering over the table, his
palms firmly braced against it. "The money is very
attractive, missus, but I could lose ship and crew in
those waters as easy as pulling a cork. It's not worth
the gamble, I'm sorry to say."

"What if I were to double the money?"

He shook his head. "There's no amount you can pay

for men's lives. And I don't know a soul, including Mr.
O'Hara here and myself, willing to risk their hides over
there. The place is bloody notorious." He glanced at his
mate for confirmation. O'Hara nodded.

"Notorious, that's the word. The Gates o' Hell."

"Mind you, missus, we've no qualms about rescuing
a poor soul from that pesthole of a colony. Many o'
them that get theirselves transported are either innocent
or guilty o' something as criminal as picking flowers out
of the governor's garden."

"It's the seas and the weather," said Lisa.

"The risk. I'm sorry."

"There's no need to apologize, Captain. I appreciate
your frankness. I had no idea it was so dangerous." She
glanced from one to the other. "I expect you don't
think anyone will take us there."

"Nobody in his right mind," said O'Hara. "Wit' no
intention o' bein' roode, missus."

"No white man," said the captain.

"But somebody whose skin is a different color?"

Foote lowered his voice as if in fear of being overheard. "Are you familiar with the name Wo Sin?" She
shook her head. "A Chinee, a big man in Singapore.
Number-one headman of the number-one secret society."

"The captain of the ship that brought us over mentioned the Chinese secret societies. Criminals, aren't
they?"

Both nodded. "Bad as they come," said the captain.
"Real ruffians. Knife you as easy as look at you. Wo Sin
is Captain China of the Sing Yops. Very big in opium,
prostitution." His eyes strayed to Deirdre. "I apologize,
missus, it slipped out. Wo Sin is big and powerful in all
the bad enterprises, you might say. With the biggest
collection of *boo how doys*, fighting men."

"And professional murderers," said O'Hara, spacing
out the word melodramatically with his brogue.

"But," went on the captain, "coming right down to

the peg, for all his unsavory reputation, Wo Sin is one sharp businessman. And scrupulously honorable in a decidedly dishonorable operation. And he's always getting his fingers into wild money-making schemes."

"You think he might accept my offer?"

"It's possible. You see, he can order a Chinee captain and crew to do the job with no skin off his nose if the ship goes down. All in the line o' duty, you might say."

"Wit' us, it's different," said O'Hara.

"Gentlemen," said Lisa, smiling, "if the ship that goes out goes down, I'll be one of those going down with it."

"Why would you have to go?" asked Captain Foote.

"To identify my husband, of course."

"Husband?" She nodded. "Gracious me. Well, for a hundred thousand dollars, I should have guessed."

"Where can I find this man?"

"You can't," said O'Hara. "Wo Sin don't operate like that."

"What you do is get word through a Chinee to one of his men, and if he's curious, he'll send somebody to meet you to bring you to him, blindfolded," said the captain. "He's underground, remember."

"Any particular Chinese? I've only met two and they're both policemen."

The captain shrugged. "Either one'll do."

"You're not serious."

"Missus, the police in Singapore are eighty percent Chinee and they see nothing wrong with buttering their bread on both sides. Chinee here are all for one and one for all. Even though the different societies are always at each other's throats. You see each one represents one particular dialect group from some province in China. They're like a family, always quarreling among themselves, but if an outsider threatens, they pull together like a tortoise."

"The outsider being the British?"

"And the Malays, the Indians, the Japs—anybody who's not Chinee."

"Captain, Mr. O'Hara, I thank you both again. You've been very helpful."

"We wish you the best o' luck," said the captain, moving with O'Hara to the door.

"Wo Sin and the Sing Yops."

"Remember, I can't promise he'll do it," said the captain, "I'm only suggesting he might. It's a lot of money and he likes money. The only thing I can say with certainty is that none of us'll take it. But if he turns you down, I wouldn't bother going to any o' the other headmen."

"I shouldn't trust them?"

"Not for the time it takes to turn your head."

She closed the door after them. "Wo Sin, the Sing Yops."

"They even sound menacing," said Deirdre, with a shudder.

"I've got to make contact right away."

"What about the other captains Jeremy's sending up?"

"We'll see the next few, but if Captain Foote is right, and I have a feeling he is, we'll just be wasting our time with them. This Wo Sin is the one we want."

LXIV

"No, it's too wild, too dangerous, too——"

Lisa cut him off, slicing away his objections with both hands. "It's our only chance, Jeremy. We're taking it!"

"Then get him up here to the hotel."

"Impossible."

It was early in the afternoon. She had interviewed four other master-owners. All had turned her down flatly, despite her intimation that half a million dollars for the job was within her means to pay. Not one of the four was as friendly nor as helpful as Captain Foote and Mr. O'Hara had been. The last one, arriving with Jeremy, had accused both of them of "putting up a practical joke that in my opinion is in outrageously bad taste, thank you!"

"One of you has to go to Wo Sin, Jeremy," said Deirdre.

"I will go," said Lisa. "If it works out, I'll be doing business with him eventually. I might just as well start it off."

"You'd actually put on your hat, your parasol over your shoulder and go marching off to some stinking opium den six cellars under a brothel to sit and pow-wow with a Chinese hatchet man?"

She couldn't recall Jeremy being quite so upset and she found this sudden obstreperous arousal of his protective instincts touching as well as flattering. But her mind was made up. She could not, however, bring herself to confront the policeman who had let her in to see Ross and ask him to put her in contact with the

Sing Yops' headman. So she went to the trishaw driver on the nearest corner and handed him money and a sealed note for Wo Sin, explaining her proposition. At four that afternoon, a slender young Chinese, his queue wound around his head under a broad-brimmed low-crowned black slouch hat pulled down to his eyes, came shuffling into the Equatorial lobby and asked to see:

"Missy Dandlidge."

Jeremy and Deirdre stood with her as she prepared to leave with him.

"I still don't like this," said Jeremy tightly. "I don't like his looks."

"He's right, Mother. This is crazy."

"Let him wait," said Jeremy. "I'll go upstairs, get the gun and go along with you."

"Missy come alone."

"I go with missy!" snapped Jeremy impatiently.

The man shrugged and turning, started off. Lisa caught him by the sleeve. "It's all right, I'll come alone. Jeremy, Captain Foote assured me. He knows; he wouldn't have spoken of him if he didn't."

"And what do you know about Foote?"

"What does one know about anyone except the impressions you get? My impression of Foote was that he was honest and sincerely trying to help." Jeremy turned to Deirdre. She nodded and shrugged. "I'll go talk to Wo Sin and come straight back. It shouldn't even take an hour."

They left, turning right outside and heading toward the heart of the city. Within twenty minutes, walking at a rapid pace, they reached Chinatown, an island of single-story shop-houses built originally with one room open to the street for business and another in the rear where workers and their families lived. Each was now divided and subdivided into cubicles, enabling scores of people to crowd together in a single house. The fronts of practically all the buildings were decorated with garish patterns of acanthus leaves on mock Corinthian pillars and color-washed in brilliant pinks, greens and blues.

At the head of an alley, her escort stopped her and, blindfolding her securely, led her down it to what sounded like the door to a shed, rattling as it was opened, the hinges creaking, the smell of stale incense coming from inside striking her nostrils.

"Slowly," he hissed.

He led her expertly, as if he had had sufficient practice in the art, and presently she found herself walking down corridors, around corners and up and down stairs unhesitatingly. He opened a door, the odor changed to perfume—lilac she thought—the soft sound of a drape being raised was audible and, as she moved into the room, she was stopped and her blindfold removed. The dark room was filled with lighted candles, their flames sputtering, throwing eerie shadows over the walls and ceiling. Fear seized her and she shrank back from the sight of the dozen or more half-naked coolies lying about on worn pallets spread upon the rough-hewn plank floor. Grabbed from behind, she was thrown down. She screamed and struggled, her heart hammering her ribs. Sheer terror tightened its grip on her as a leering face, scarred and disfigured, rose up before her. The glow of the candles fired the man's pupils and a loathsome sound issued from his throat.

LXV

One after another they ravished her, chattering loudly, gleefully. It was a horror come upon her so quickly, so unexpectedly that the full shock was scarcely arrived before the pain between her thighs, the odor of their bodies and their breaths, the cruel torment of their hands tearing away her clothing, pinching and twisting and punching her combined to inspire a giddiness that sent her off into the blessed realm of unconsciousness. The last sensation she felt was the pain; the last sounds she heard their laughter and loud voices commingling in an unintelligible jabber that became progressively fainter as it retreated from her hearing.

She awoke aching all over, discovering herself in a small, low-ceilinged room with a single window looking out upon a deserted alley. Fresh lotus blossoms occupied a shallow glass bowl on a low table at the foot of the narrow bed upon which she lay. A cotton-white kitten squatted beside the bowl eyeing her resentfully. A pretty Chinese girl in a gold and crimson *cheongsam*, her hair piled high upon her forehead in characteristic fashion, bent over Lisa, daubing her face with a damp cloth.

She tried to rise, but the girl kept her from doing so with the gentle pressure of her hand against one shoulder. Not until then did Lisa notice that she herself had been dressed in a *cheongsam*, the high collar touching under her chin, one side slit to her thigh. The girl smiled and began feeding her a delicious hot soup that soothed her mouth and throat and almost immediately began restoring her strength.

384

"Feel better?"

"Yes, thank you. Where am I?"

"In the house of Wo Sin."

"What time is it?"

"Early in the morning. Just past sunrise. You have slept all night. Very good for you."

A beaded curtain at the far end of the room parted with a soft jangling sound revealing a tall middle-aged Chinese in a white-cotton business suit. He held a black briefcase under one arm, in his hand a cigarette in a long ivory holder. He came into the room, a somewhat timid smile on his face, as if he were reluctant to show friendliness. The girl got up from the stool and backed to the other side of the room. He came and sat.

"Mrs. Dandridge, I am Wo Sin. Are you feeling better?"

"Yes, thank you."

"What befell you here last night was not of my doing. The men responsible have confessed and will be punished severely. The man who brought you here has had both eyes removed for his trouble." She gasped. "Do not be shocked. He deserves no less than that for his despicable action. It appears he intercepted your note intended for me. Alas, I never received it. But before he contributed his eyesight, in the cause of retribution he admitted everything. He and the others have dishonored my house and my name. I am desolate with shame. I would like nothing better than to make amends. Alas, how can I atone for the desecration of a lady's honor?"

"I came to you with a business proposition."

"What sort of proposition?"

She explained. He listened attentively, politely, but with little evident interest. No glint in the eyes, no nodding, no hint whatsoever that the undertaking was inspiring approval.

"This is most embarrassing," he said quietly when she had finished.

"I will pay one million dollars."

"I believe you. I believe you'd pay twice that."

"If necessary."

"Unfortunately what you ask can't be done."

"You're afraid it's too difficult, too dangerous, the seas too rough for your men?"

"Not at all. My people have taken worse risks, for far less important reasons. Not nearly so humanitarian. It is hard to explain." He snuffed out the remainder of his cigarette and lighting a fresh one, inserted it in the holder. "It is a question of politics."

"Sir Reginald Lowell?"

He nodded. "He's part of it, yes. It is the British and us. We have had difficult times in Singapore, sharing the area, the commerce and industry here, the authority. One thing that we have learned is never to tread upon the other chap's flower bed. If your husband were one of us, we would no doubt consider taking action. But he is, I presume, a white man." He smiled. "Transported by the white man, under his law. I'll put it another way. If one of us took it into his head to put his knife into a letter writer in Tiba Street, the British would not lift a finger. They would expect us to deal with the murderer ourselves, in our own way. Hands off the other chap's problem, do you see? The unwritten law. It makes for peace between us, however uneasy that peace may sometimes be. For if the same chap with the knife decided to put it into the governor's brother-in-law——"

"It would complicate the unwritten law."

"To say the least."

"So my husband and I are to be bound and helpless in your red tape."

"Not mine, Mrs. Dandridge, not even Lowell's. Singapore's. I know, it's heartless, it's cruel, but are my reasons clear to you?"

"I suppose."

She got up, sitting on the edge of the bed.

"You're not leaving?"

"I must. My daughter will be very worried about me."

He gestured helplessly. "This is very bad. You come here. You are mistreated wretchedly! You ask my assistance and I turn you down. You must think me a dog."

"Not at all."

"There must be something I can do for you."

"Perhaps I'll think of something."

"If ever another need should arise, do not hesitate to call on me. Alas, in this one instance——"

"Impossible, I know."

"I am very sorry."

"Everyone seems to be, lately."

"Before you go wouldn't you like a physician to come and see you? I can get the finest man in the city up here in ten minutes."

"It's not necessary, I'm all right. I'll just finish my soup, if I may. It's delicious."

"By all means."

She ate slowly, savoring the soup. He sat with her chatting amiably.

"A thought occurs to me, Mrs. Dandridge. Perhaps Singapore is not the best place from which to launch your attack on the Gates of Hell."

"You know a better place?"

"Hundreds. Melbourne, for instance. It's less than four hundred miles from Macquarie. And in Melbourne you would likely find many English-speaking seamen with a grudge against the colony. If you follow my meaning."

"Is Melbourne as picturesque as Singapore?"

He smiled. "All ports in this part of the world are picturesque. But Melbourne has fewer foreigners. Then, too, word of your preparations and your mission would not get back to your friend, Sir Reginald. As they must eventually here in Singapore."

"Melbourne. I'll think about it. Thank you."

"There are vessels leaving here for all Australian ports almost every day. It is less than a month by clipper ship to Melbourne."

She finished her soup, her heart lifted, her hopes reassembled and readied for the inevitable next step.

LXVI

She had returned to the hotel and gone immediately to bed—after telling Deirdre what had happened, taking care to delete the more grisly aspects of the episode.

"Jeremy was right; I was a fool to go there alone. I could have gotten my throat slit."

"You had to go. It was our only chance—our last chance," added Deirdre sadly. "What rotten luck!"

"Maybe we still have a chance, dear. Where's Jeremy?"

"Out looking for you. I imagine he's got every policeman in town knocking on doors."

"When he comes back, if I'm asleep wake me."

"But you need rest."

"Please do as I ask. I want him to go and book us passage to Melbourne. To leave tonight, if possible."

"Melbourne?"

"Australia. He and I will be leaving from there for Tasmania."

"And what about me?"

"I intend to lock you in a room in the American consulate until we get back."

"But you can't come back here with Daddy."

Lisa paused. "You're right. I never thought of that. Well, we'll work something out. You'd better start packing. Everything, even Jeremy's things."

Deirdre muttered something calculated to display the strongest possible disapproval and left the room. Through the door left ajar Lisa could hear her opening and closing doors and drawers, and slamming luggage about. She lay with her eyes closed in a half sleep, visions of Ross moving slowly across the screen of her imagination. In her dreams, since he'd been away, he had always looked so handsome, so strong and vigorous. Now, since she had seen him in the jail, he appeared drawn and tired, with a pallor of one who hadn't seen the sun in ages. At that, what sun could there be in his life, what living? He was only going through the motions, without memory, without a mind of his own, without aim or purpose. And now, consigned to hell, to be starved and beaten and worked to death. There had to be an end to it! She must make an end! She must find and rescue him from that dreadful place. And bring him home to Blackwood.

Blackwood. Ten thousand miles away. It seemed a million miles at the moment, not on the other side of the world, but out of it, situated on some distant planet. The house, the maples, the beauty of spring, the warm and comfortable summers, the wild colors of autumn, the laughter, the love, all a dream, locked in the past, denied forever the blessing of new reality. No! She must not let herself even think such thoughts. Slender the thread of hope may be, but there it was for the grasping. To hold tightly and never let go.

"Mother, are you asleep?" Deirdre was standing in the doorway holding a small oilskin packet. "What's this?"

"Bring it here."

She loosened the cord and opened it, revealing a number of letters, the Blackwood address scribbled on each envelope.

"Daddy's letters. You saved them."

"Every one."

"Oh, Mother." Deirdre began to cry, tears falling into her lap where she sat, her pretty mouth clamped tightly closed, holding back the pain of the moment.

"There, there, you mustn't cry. We'll find him, we'll bring him home."

"Promise?"

"Cross my heart."

Deirdre threw her arms around her and kissed her. "I love you so. I hate to see you suffer."

Lisa retied the packet and handed it back. "Put this in a safe place. Your father will want to read them."

Somebody was at the door.

"It's Jeremy!" exclaimed Deirdre jumping up. "Will he be glad to see you!"

"Poor dear."

"Why do you say that?"

"I've dragged him all the way out here, and ever since we arrived, he's been running about like a messenger boy doing all the dirty work, taking orders."

"He doesn't mind. He likes being able to help. He likes you, Mother. He loves you."

"What makes you think so?"

"Don't be coy. You know he does. He adores you. I see the loving looks he gives you."

"And what, pray tell, do you know about loving looks?"

"I know them when I see them."

"Very good. In the meantime, he's waiting patiently for somebody to answer the door."

"O Lord, yes!"

It was not Jeremy but a stranger, an elderly man in the uniform of a ship's captain. He wore a beard joining the mass of snow-white hair piled on his head, and at first glance, he resembled Santa Claus gone to sea.

"*Verouw* Dandridge?" His accent was thick, the words rolling out with exaggerated emphasis.

"She's sleeping," said Deirdre.

"Oh, I'm sorry to intrude. I will come back later."

"May I tell her who called?"

"Captain Jacobus Franeker."

Lisa could hear them talking and got up and pulled on her robe. Deirdre was preparing to close the door when she stuck her head out.

"Captain?"

He came in, limping tiredly, as if having dragged himself through so many years that making it to the end of his life was proving far more physically wearing than it ought to have been. But his eyes were bright and his smile friendly and infectious. Deirdre brought him a chair. He sat, placed his cap on his knee, cleared his throat ceremoniously, excused himself and began.

"There is word going around the docks that you are looking for a ship to take you to Macquarie Harbor in order to rescue a convict from the penal colony there. Is this so?"

"It is. Exactly as you've put it."

"Then I offer you my ship and my crew. I was for six years on the run from Adelaide to Hobart. I know Van Diemen's Land very well."

"I beg your pardon?"

"Forgive me, it must be ten years since they began calling it Tasmania, but we Dutch have always known it as Van Diemen's Land. The seas are ferocious, the weather extremely harsh, brutal, but everything considered, my men and I feel it can be done."

"Mother!" burst Deirdre.

They talked, examining all aspects of the venture. The captain suggested that rather than a full-scale assault on the Gates of Hell a small boat with a handful of armed men be put over the side, rowed to shore and Ross seized from the work gang to which he would undoubtedly be assigned.

"The convicts work at felling timber, you see," said the captain. "Huon pine. It is sent to Hobart. Very good for shipbuilding."

"Then the men work outside the stockade," said Lisa.

He nodded. "When they cut trees, they are in crews of ten or twelve scattered all over the island."

"All over Tasmania?"

"No, Sarah Island. The penal colony is on Sarah Island."

Lisa brought up Dietrich, the convict who had succeeded in escaping from the colony. Franeker nodded his head rapidly.

"He must come with us. He knows the island, the work shifts, all the little helpful things that only a man who's actually lived there could know."

"The trick is to find him."

Franeker held up one finger and winked. "That may not be too hard. I have heard he is in Batavia, Java, down south. Batavia is my home port. Dietrich can live there openly, you see."

"As long as it's not British territory, I take it."

"Batavia is Dutch."

"I'm curious, Captain."

"What about?"

"About you. I have had five captains sit in that very chair and tell me that they wouldn't take this job for all the money in the world. That it's too dangerous and that there's no hope of succeeding."

"You wonder why I'm willing to stick my head in the tiger's mouth? Because there are times in life when, if you don't gamble, you can lose everything—in this instance, our plantation. I will explain. Outside Batavia, at a place halfway to Bakasi, my sons and I have a large plantation. It's devoted to raising rambong, Assam rubber trees. The *Ficus elastica*. I have six sons; five of them live and work on the plantation overseeing the native help. My eldest son, Hendrik, is in Leyden. He is a chemist. Some years ago, at Hendrik's urging, we pooled our resources to buy the land. Hendrik believes that one day rubber will be very important commercially, much more important than it is at the present time, much more valuable. One day, he says, it will replace gutta-percha. But it takes seven years for trees to grow large enough to tap for the latex. We will not begin tapping until next year. In the meantime, however, we need capital to pay the workers and to finish paying the bank loan. We need, with the interest compounded, 63,000 *rijksdaalder*. A *rijksdaalder* is equal to two and a half gulden or one American dollar, almost exactly."

"I will pay you one hundred thousand American dollars. Plus expenses."

He shook his head. "Sixty-three thousand, exactly. Expenses are another matter, of course, but the only reason I take the job is to save the work of nearly six years. To lose our plantation now, after all the work my boys have put in, would be a disaster."

"I can imagine how you feel. But what about your crew? Would they be willing to risk their lives to save your property?"

"They would follow me down into the pit. For one reason, because they know I would lead them back out. And Macquarie Harbor is not so different; the entrance is called the Gates of Hell."

"So I've heard."

"If you agree that I am your man, I will make the necessary preparations."

"I agree, Captain. I will pay you with a check drawn upon your bank in Batavia upon our return."

"Is such a thing possible?"

"It is. I have with me letters of credit good for any sum payable by any bank in any major city in the world."

He sat up very straight, his eyes rounded, his lips pursed and emitted a low whistle. "That is something, *Verouw* Dandridge."

"Whether we succeed or fail, you will be paid."

"No. Only if we bring him out. We will not fail. You'll see."

She shook hands. "I believe you. Is your ship ready? I'd like to see it. Is it steam or sail?"

"Both."

"How large?"

"Four hundred thirty-eight tons. One hundred thirty feet long. Gross capacity——"

"That's not very large."

"Large enough for this, I assure you. The tide rips outside the harbor and the reefs are not easy to handle. The larger the vessel, the harder they get. You'll see."

"What about arms and ammunition?"

"Those we pick up when we pick up Dietrich in Batavia."

"When can you leave?"

"Whenever you say. I brought a cargo of silk and spices in from Ceylon for transshipment to San Francisco, but my holds are empty now."

"Would tonight be satisfactory?"

"Tonight it shall be. From now on, you give the orders. I and my men follow them."

"There is one other detail that must be attended to." Lisa put one arm around Deirdre's waist and drew her close. "My daughter will be staying here."

"In Singapore?"

"Yes, although frankly I've had my fill of this place."

"If I may say so, *Verouw* Dandridge, Singapore is no place for a little girl without her parents."

"I'm not a little girl!" said Deirdre.

Lisa nodded. "I was thinking of the consulate."

"She would be welcome to stay at my home in Batavia. With my wife and her sister and all their cats. It's a beautiful spot, with gardens and fruit trees. All sorts of things to do. You'll have the time of your life."

"It would be an imposition," said Lisa.

"Nonsense! There's plenty of room. My sons bring their families to visit, boys and girls your daughter's age some of them. So many I can't keep their names straight. And we'll be back with your husband before you know it. You'll see!"

LXVII

The *Sea Urchin* was appropriately named, in Lisa's opinion, undisclosed to the others. It was an old ship, an ancient ship, frighteningly small for the open seas, she thought, almost tiny. But it was easy to see that it was well cared for, clean, in excellent repair and as smooth-running as Jeremy's Geneva watch. Captain Franeker's crew numbered only 19 men, but unlike most captains of commercial ships that plied the coastal waters of the Orient, he had little turnover in manpower, no fewer than 12 of the 19 having been with him for more than ten years. And what his crew lacked in numbers, he was eager to point out, they more than made up for in hard work and dedication to the *Urchin*.

Jeremy, as had become his habit of late, entertained doubts about the whole expedition. Lisa and Deirdre shared the only cabin on board and he was obliged to bunk with the crew. All three sat in the cabin discussing the immediate future as the ship puffed and paddled its way through the choppy gray waters of the Riouw Strait on the first leg of the 600-mile trip down to the Java Sea and Batavia perched at the headwaters of the Sunda Strait "like a sparrow near a horse's ear," as Franeker phrased it.

"I wonder if this tub will make it to Batavia, let alone Macquarie Harbor?" asked Jeremy gloomily, eyeing the metal plates bolted together to form the walls and ceiling of the room. "And back to Batavia—what, nearly ten thousand miles? It's like heading back to San Francisco, practically the same distance."

"We've been all over that a number of times," said

Lisa. "If you can think of a way to shorten the distance, I'm all for it."

"It's not only the distance, the danger, the seventeen other lovely prospects, it's you."

"Me?"

"You shouldn't be going along. You know you shouldn't. This is man's work."

She smoothed her lap, braced her elbows on the table, rested her chin on her palms and stared at him balefully. "That phrase has always fascinated me. What does it mean exactly, heavy work? Dirty work? Dangerous work? I've done my share of all three in this life. The only difference I can see is this particular 'man's work' has to do with rescuing him. Who can pick him out of a crowd of men on a dark night better than I? Who can comfort him, care for him, hopefully tear away the curtain over his mind? You? Captain Franeker? I belong there, Jeremy, where he is. It's the only place on God's earth I want to be. And all your logic, your well-intentioned concern, your declarations that this is 'man's work' aren't going to keep me away!"

"You are the stubbornest female I have ever known, Mrs. Dandridge!"

"Oh, good, let's you two have a fight!" exclaimed Deirdre, clapping her hands and grinning impishly.

"Let's you go to bed," said Lisa. "It's nearly midnight."

"I can't. Too many people in my bedroom."

Jeremy covered a yawn, excusing himself. "You say midnight and suddenly I could fall asleep sitting here."

"It's the sea air. When the four of us get back to Rhode Island, please remember to remind me that here and now I took an oath to stay off ships and oceans for the next fifty years."

"Amen. Good night, ladies."

Batavia rose from the Java Sea, a mass of two- and three-story buildings, the streets and squares fringed with trees, the whole divided by the Djakarta River.

Occupying a swampy plain at the head of a capacious bay, it boasted nearly 70,000 inhabitants, according to Captain Franeker.

The heat was savage, the sun firing the heavens as white as spume as they stood with him at the rail, the larboard paddle churning the clear-blue water to their left below, all eyes watching the *Sea Urchin* berthed and made fast by four members of the crew.

"You must come to my home, enjoy lunch, relax and get back your land legs," said the captain jovially. "The boys will bring your things up on deck and we will summon a carriage."

"I'd like to start looking for Dietrich as soon as possible," said Lisa.

"No need. A couple of the boys will dig him up and bring him to the house." The captain paused, filled his lungs, his red cheeks popping out above his beard like Christmas-tree balls. "Taste that air, clean and sweet off the Indian Ocean and up the strait. None of the fishy stink of Singapore, you notice. This is God's country!"

LXVIII

Klaus Dietrich was one of the strongest-looking men she had ever seen, but topping his muscular body was an oddly emaciated face, his cheeks unnaturally shrunken, the bones protruding above them grotesquely. His hazel eyes sat in their hollows staring like those of a predatory beast, a creature lurking in a cave peering out of the darkness waiting for its prey.

Under any other circumstances, she wouldn't have trusted him to help her over a mud puddle in the street. He was too clearly a man who had lived his life outside the law, beyond the bounds of decency and on the run. A man who felt everybody's eyes upon him; a friendless, unloved man shunned by the world he had spent his life cheating and betraying, a world that had little use for his sort and less tolerance for his sins. He was the kind of man she would ordinarily have crossed the street to avoid, but she needed him, ironically, for what he was: a clever, unscrupulous, opportunistic scoundrel. A man filled to overflowing with hatred for the penal colony from which he had escaped and lust for vengeance against those in authority there.

"I'd help the Devil himself escape that hellhole," he announced loudly. Lisa, Jeremy and Captain Franeker sat at a table with him in a bar on the Leidseplein, a dimly lit, disreputable oasis in the seedy section of town. She was the only woman present and the regulars in attendance appeared somewhat shocked by sight of her. She and her companions ignored them, none of the four having either the time or the patience to worry about the social conventions of Batavia's public places.

"You know why they picked Macquarie Harbor for a penal colony in the first place?" continued Dietrich too loudly. "I'll tell you why. It has three great things going for it. With all the pine there to cut and pile and load, it keeps the poor slobs busy in such a way so they can feel their punishment. Second, nobody but yours truly ever got out of there and lived to tell of it. Thirdly, breaking the prisoners' backs working 'em fourteen hours a day helps repay the cost of keeping up the dear place."

He held up his empty glass and the captain half-filled it with rum. Dietrich gestured with the glass and Franeker added more.

"How many men are kept on Sarah Island?" asked Jeremy.

"Two hundred."

The questions came from all three at a rapid pace, and just as rapidly Dietrich downed glass after glass of rum, his deep-set eyes becoming glassier, his body loosening perceptibly and his words running against each other in growing confusion before departing his mouth. By the beginning of the second bottle, he was as drunk . . .

"As a Tipperary stoker," whispered the captain sourly to Lisa.

But the thirsty one continued to insist his glass be refilled. His condition notwithstanding, he was a trove of information on their destination and what they might expect to encounter there. The more he told them, the clearer it became to Lisa that getting Ross off the island and the *Sea Urchin* safely out to sea would take as much luck as ingenuity, resourcefulness and courage.

Dietrich seemed to derive sadistic delight in dwelling at length on the more grisly realities of life on Sarah Island. The working and living conditions were, in his words, "pure hell." Punishment was flogging "strip after strip peeling off your back, falling to the ground, the ants feasting on 'em." The food "ain't fit for a stray dog," and the work dangerous as well as backbreaking. He was also full of tales of cannibalism among those so foolhardy as to attempt to flee. Men would run off into the jungle to be eventually reduced to "eating each other raw, or starving to death—if the dogs don't find 'em. Men commit murder in order to be hanged and set free of the place!"

It reached a point where he appeared on the verge of passing out, so, taking the initiative, Lisa asked him the question uppermost in her mind.

"How much do you want to go with us and help us?"

"A lot."

"Give me a figure, please."

"Fifty thousand American dollars."

"You're out of your head!" snapped Jeremy. Captain Franeker resisted the impulse to comment, rolling his eyes to the ceiling and holding them there. Lisa caught Jeremy's forearm, holding it tightly as if afraid he would leap out of his chair and grab the man by the throat.

"I will give you five thousand, payment in full when my husband boards the *Sea Urchin*."

Dietrich pretended shock. "You don't hear too good, lady. I said fifty. Five-O thousand. You're looking at a first-rate businessman. I know the value of my services. I'm the only man on the face o' the earth can help you! You could putt-putt up to the harbor entrance and stand off and search the shore with a glass and see men working and the stockade, the whole of it. So what good is that? What then? How do you get onto the God-forsaken place? And if you did, where would you go to keep hid? How would you reconnoiter? And how would you pick out the fella you're looking for? Questions, questions, questions." He tapped his head and leered. "And all the answers locked in here. Fifty thousand, that's my price. Cheap enough for a man's life."

He reached for the bottle, but her hand shot forward snatching it from him.

"No more. Our business meeting is over, Mr. Dietrich. You want to drink, you pay."

He stared unbelievingly, a look that slowly evolved into confusion. "You said——"

"I said five thousand dollars."

"That's crazy! You're asking me to risk my skin for a paltry five thousand?"

"Would you mind lowering your voice?"

"There's nothing paltry about five thousand dollars, mister," Jeremy said icily.

"It's very simple," said Lisa, "take it or leave it."

"I'll leave it, and you be damned!" He staggered to his feet, but instead of lurching away as they expected, he leaned over the table glaring at her.

"You're making a big mistake, lady."

"One of us is. Good day, Mr. Dietrich. It's been a pleasure."

He flung out one hand dismissing her, the three of them, the whole proposition. Then he turned and started toward the street door.

"Now let's discuss the armament we'll need," she said in a commanding tone. "Any ideas on the subject, Captain?"

"You don't know how to do business, that's your trouble!" bellowed Dietrich loudly. Having reached the door, he had turned and was leaning against the jamb for support. "You got no head for it. You're supposed to know value of services rendered. Hell, without me, you're finished before you start!"

They ignored him. Their heads lowered conspiratorially and they talked in subdued voices. He swore, spun about, started out the door, changed his mind, turned back, swore again and came reeling toward them.

"All right, all right, all right, all right. Goddamn me

for a spineless bastard! I'll take it! Five thousand, cash!"

"Cash," said Lisa quietly.

"Be at dock number four at six A.M. day after tomorrow," said Franeker stiffly. "Bring your seabag with anything you like except guns or knives. No weapons. We supply the arms."

"Six o'clock. Day after tomorrow."

"Wednesday, mister," said Jeremy.

Dietrich paid no attention to him. His eyes were riveted on Lisa. "You're getting the damned bargain of a lifetime, you know that, lady? Biggest bargain you ever saw. Without me, you're finished before you start, you know that?"

"Good day, Mr. Dietrich," she said softly. "It's been a pleasure meeting you. And I know it will be an even bigger pleasure working with you."

"You're a bloodsucker. You're all bloodsuckers!"

He left, lurching back across the floor and out the door as if the bar were a keelboat running through heavy seas.

"You wouldn't have let him walk out, would you?" asked Jeremy.

Lisa sighed and let out a long breath. She shook her head. "I don't know what came over me."

"He made you mad," said the captain, "that's what."

"He made me furious. I was actually seeing red! It was very stupid. We could have lost him."

"Not a chance," said the captain.

Jeremy nodded. "He's right. If you'd knocked him down to two thousand, he would have cursed a little louder and a little longer, but he would have taken it."

"Such a fine man," said Lisa. "What a colorful traveling companion he's going to be."

LXIX

Captain Franeker's home was a modest two-story stone house painted yellow with white trim, with a mansard roof and colorful window boxes filled with orchids. Morning glories, inglorious in the evening, climbed a large trellis at one side of the house, and palm trees and shrubs were tastefully positioned about the lawn. The citrine sun had long since darkened to carnelian red and slipped into the Indian Ocean to the west, the dinner dishes had been cleared from the table, Jeremy had gone down to the docks to supervise lading of the arms and ammunition purchased that afternoon and Lisa and the captain had retired to the veranda to sit and listen to the owls hooting and the booming call of the goatsucker over the chorus of insects.

Franeker adjusted his spectacles on his nose, angling them and going over his copy of the list of acquisitions.

"Dynamite—two cases. Fire bombs—three cases. A thirty-millimeter mortar and, most important of all, thirty Spencer rifles."

"Are the rifles effective?" she asked.

"My friend Cornelius Maater claims they're the most modern rifles available. They'll soon make the muzzle-loaders obsolete. Very rugged. Seven-shot lever action with the magazine fixed in the stock itself. Good protection against rough handling. Remember what Dietrich told us?"

"About what?"

"The guards at the penal colony. They are armed with Austrian muzzle-loaders. No match for Spencers at all."

"Let's hope it doesn't come to a battle. If he ever got hurt, God forbid killed, by gunfire I'd——" A loud screeching above their heads caused her to start. He patted her forearm and chuckled.

"A goatsucker. We call them night jarrers. They do jar the night. But for them isn't it peaceful here?"

"It is. So unlike Singapore."

"Every time I come home, I find it harder to leave. Soon now I'll be packing it in for good, retiring to the plantation. Ah, Batavia." He sighed contentedly, pausing to let his thoughts wander, then surrendering to the business at hand. "As to the arsenal, we'll need it for protection, not to attack."

"Why the mortar?"

"That's your friend Dietrich's idea. For lobbing fire bombs, if needed. Just the thing to create panic."

"What do you think of Dietrich, Jacobus?"

"What can I think of his sort? He needs us for his money as we need him for his help. Rescue missions make strange bedfellows, eh? Still, I wouldn't worry about him, if that's what you're getting at."

"He and I got off badly. He seems a very basic sort, the kind of man who'd hold a grudge against me, against the three of us."

"I don't know as I agree with that. With the life he's led, he's gotten a gutter shrewdness about him. If we can keep him sober, he should be useful. Are you afraid he'll let us down at the critical time?"

She nodded somewhat dejectedly. "Call it intuition."

"I must say I doubt if you'll get him to go onto the island."

"He didn't mention that. He more or less steered the conversation around it."

"That's what I mean by shrewd. They'd shoot him on sight if they recognized him. I imagine you'll get your money's worth of information out of him—what we should and shouldn't do—but I wouldn't count on him to be one of the rescue party."

"I'm not. Jeremy's the one I'm relying on."

"Is he related to you or your husband?"

"No. Why do you ask?"

He shrugged, folding the paper and putting away his glasses. "It seems strange."

"What?"

"That a man would come all the way from Rhode Island to help a beautiful woman find her husband. Friendship is one thing, but that's more than friendship. What would you call it?"

"I didn't ask him to come. He insisted. We were going to be married when word came that my husband was alive."

"So you tell him you can't marry him and he turns around and offers to help find your husband. Unusual."

Deirdre appeared at the door. "Mrs. Franeker and I baked an orange nut cake. Come, you two."

Elspeth Franeker was Mrs. Santa Claus, a plump motherly woman with steel-gray hair and an omnipresent smile. She had fallen in love with Deirdre on sight, and the affection had become mutual. In four days, the captain's wife had taught her more about cooking, baking and the Dutch language than Lisa could have believed possible. Mrs. Franeker's sister was a spinster who bore no resemblance whatsoever to Elspeth. Kristina Pieters taught school in the Molenvliet sector of town. She was tall, ungainly, discouragingly plain-looking, but "very smart upstairs, a very good teacher," according to her brother-in-law.

"The expedition is launched tomorrow," announced the captain, as all five sat down at the table. "We must toast our success. I have a bottle of wine that's been sitting in the cabinet for two years." He rose from the table. "Just long enough to make it perfect."

Locating the bottle, he set it in the middle of the table with comical ostentatious ceremony and *Verouw* Franeker brought out five exquisite cut-crystal glasses on a teak tray.

"Zagarese. Sweet as honey, a very delicate bouquet," said the captain.

"Mother, look!" exclaimed Deirdre, interrupting him as he was preparing to raise his toast. She pointed at the label on the bottle. "E. Aldoni Ltd.—Naples! Enrico! Enrico!"

The captain and the two ladies looked bewildered. Deirdre explained.

"Mr. Aldoni's wine is excellent," commented the captain. "I'm particularly fond of his Rosato del Salanto."

"Too fond," said his wife winking. His sheepish reaction brought a laugh from the others.

The cake was consumed to the last crumb and the bottle emptied and an hour later Lisa sat at Deirdre's bedside saying good night. She gazed about the room. It was a bedroom for a girl half Deirdre's age, too frilly—pillow case and bedspread and curtains. There were a number of framed photographs of self-conscious-looking little boys and shy, pretty little blonde girls done up in their Sunday best, the Franekers' small army of grandchildren.

"We'll be off before you wake up, dear, so this is good-bye," said Lisa with a trace of wistfulness in her tone.

Deirdre threw her arms around her mother's neck and kissed her. "Please be careful, I mean really careful. I'm afraid for you, Lisa."

"Lisa? That's the first time you've called me that."

"May I?"

"Of course. Although you know what it means."

"What?"

"We're getting used to each other."

"We've seen and done an awful lot in these few weeks. Aren't you glad I came?"

Lisa nodded, squeezing her nose playfully. "Though I could have spanked you screaming in Veracruz, you mischief!" She became serious. "Don't be afraid for me, Deirdre. Think of all the protection I'll have: twenty-two men and all those guns and bombs and things."

"What do you think the chances are of getting him out? Without his getting hurt?"

"I think they've gotten a great deal better since Jacobus walked into our lives. Getting better all the time."

"But it's so dangerous: the sea, the weather, that awful place. It'll be like trying to pluck a pearl out of a pile of nettles."

"That's very descriptive. Where did you hear it?"

"I read it. Still it's true, isn't it? And the worst part is having to sit here waiting for months and months."

"It won't be months and months. Jacobus figured it out. A little more than ten thousand miles round trip. From here to Fremantle on the west coast of Australia to Macquarie Harbor."

"Ten thousand! It might as well be ten million!"

"At the very slowest, the *Sea Urchin* will make close to two-hundred-and-fifty miles every twenty-four hours. That's about forty days, even stopping at Fremantle to take on coal."

"Jeremy says you could get down there close to the harbor and not be able to get in because of the weather, the hailstorms, the winds. You may have to sit in a cove and wait for ages!"

"Jeremy said that?" Deirdre nodded. "Pay no attention, he's being pessimistic again. Jacobus says we shouldn't have any trouble getting in. If there is a delay, it'll be only hours, a day or two at most."

"I'll hold my breath till you and Daddy are back here safe, all three of us together at last."

"You do that," Lisa said, laughing.

"Seriously, I won't sleep a wink I'll worry so."

"You'll sleep and have the time of your life. This is a vacation for you, Deirdre. Shopping in town, boat rides, horseback riding, picnics, sightseeing and the plantation. I understand it's a fascinating place."

"What can be fascinating about a bunch of dumb old trees standing around?" She sighed. "I'm sorry. I'm just on edge, I guess. I wish I could go along. I'd give anything——"

"I'd give anything if you'd close your eyes and go to sleep."

"I wouldn't be any trouble."

"Deirdre, drop it and go to sleep or I'll—put your hair in pigtails!"

"No!"

She began picking at the fringe of the coverlet, her mouth drooping dejectedly.

"What's the matter now?" asked Lisa.

"Nothing. It's just that when I was fifteen, I couldn't wait to be sixteen. I was dying to get there. Fifteen, you're a child, a baby. Sixteen, you're grown up. Except that now I am sixteen, it's no different than before."

"Why not give it five more years?"

"Five! God, I'll be twenty-one, an old lady!"

Lisa groaned, then laughed, and Deirdre laughed with her until she caught herself abruptly, her eyes misting. Again her arms went around her mother, pulling her close, stroking her hair affectionately.

"I love you. I'll miss you, be careful. Please. And please come home safely, both of you. Promise?"

"Promise."

LXX

Through the Sunda Strait south-southeasterly past Christmas Island, a welcome wind bellied the *Sea Urchin's* sails, idling the 20-horsepower Maudslay engine. And saving precious coal. A propitious sign indicating a lucky voyage, according to Captain Franeker.

"If this wind holds and we're able to keep the engine shut down until Fremantle, we can bypass her and fill our bunkers on the return run," he observed, standing at the rail with Lisa looking over the idle port paddle wheel.

The wind was ideal, a cut under blustery, the sky the color of ashes, the weak white sun occasionally sneaking through the clouds as if peering down out of curiosity to check on the vessel's progress. Spirits were high; confidence reigned. Even Jeremy's optimism was aroused and audible. The only disconcerting element was Klaus Dietrich. As instructed, he had fetched his seabag aboard with everything he wanted to bring. He appeared to have brought all the hard liquor he could find in Batavia. The man drank with the relish a starving dog displays for fresh meat. He treated his body as if it were a sack that by kingly decree had to be kept filled with spirits. Oddly, although consuming enough for three men, he got only so drunk and no drunker. He became loud, obnoxious, even physical on one or two occasions, but he did not have the decency to carry his condition one step further and obligingly pass out.

To worsen matters, he sang, loudly and badly, sea chanteys mostly, well off-key, the words garbled but sufficiently comprehensible to permit his unwilling listeners to recognize the foulest among them. He was forever excusing his bad behavior to Lisa, but by the fifth day out, the situation had reached such a pass as to be more comical than annoying. And she calmed an irate Jeremy with the assurance that Dietrich's language didn't offend her nearly as much as the man's breath.

"He's pathetic. Besides, I have no intention of getting on the wrong side of him."

During Dietrich's infrequent sober periods, he would sit on a capstan on the afterdeck holding his thumping head between his fists and moaning, lamenting his rashness, begging sympathy of anyone within earshot. Once his head stopped hammering and before he resumed filling his skin, he was fair quarry for lucid conversation. Lisa kept a close watch on him, and when such rare interludes cropped up, she lost no time in taking advantage of them. Escorting him to the captain's cabin, she would sit him down and pump him with a vengeance.

"What do they feed the prisoners?"

"When no food comes in from Hobart, they get half-a-pint o' skilly in the mornings before they start work."

"Skilly?"

"Flour and water with a pinch o' salt."

"My God!"

"If supplies do get through, they get their one real meal at night."

"What?"

"Whatever the ship brings. Rotten meat, salt fatback fit to bust your teeth, biscuits like rocks. It's the Palace Hotel Restaurant in Melbourne."

"They have horses and mules to help them with the work——"

"Not a chance. They harness men to plows and whip 'em like horses. Fourteen hours a day, day after day. Or you work in icy water up to your neck all day long, battling logs. Or cut and saw till your arms feel like they're pulling loose."

"Don't they try to escape?"

"Logging in the water, they just lower their heads and

drown. That's the only real escape. Oh, they try, poor devils. And some get away, only to die of exposure or starvation, if a guard don't shoot 'em before they get fifty feet clear. Men get into the bush and die there. Eight got away once and when they found 'em only one was left. They'd eaten each other, you see."

"Let's talk about something else."

"You asked me. You want to know about escaping? Attempting, you mean, not escaping. You'd be amazed. They build log rafts and coracles on the sly and hide 'em in the bush. Coracles, just green wattle branches covered with shirts and rotten canvas stolen from supplies. Hoping, praying, begging God that the damned things'll float. Ha, they never do. Corpses wash up on the beach every day. And the prisoners get to bury 'em.

"But the worst of it isn't the work or the flogging or the chains, even the food. It's the rain. It whips you day after day after day after day, beating you down, breaking your spirit, rotting everything you touch, you wear, rotting your soul inside you, shriveling it up like a piece o' beef jerky. Funny, you can never see whether a man is crying or not 'cause there's most always rain dripping down his face. You can't even show the other fella how miserable you are!"

"What happens if the supply ship from Hobart is delayed? What do you eat?"

"Anything you can swallow. Greenhorns eat leaves and grass and throw 'em right up again. You eat bark, paper, rotten leather. You chew it, get the juice out of it."

"The men are chained?"

"You bet. In long lines in the fields. Not logging, though, you got to be free to move and swim in the deep water. Shackles off in the morning, back on at night. I'm thirsty. I got to have a drink."

Which always put an end to the brief question-and-answer period. And invariably she would come away from it wondering why she'd bothered to initiate it in the first place. What he told her only depressed her. Still she felt she had to know everything she could about the place. Like rice in a broth, there were helpful bits scattered throughout his responses. Just knowing the loggers worked without shackles, that the bush offered temporary safety, that it came all the way down to the shore at certain points.

Ten days out, they passed a point 100 miles west of Perth and Fremantle, the sister towns lying through and beyond the gray mist of morning settled over the placid sea. Within two days, well ahead of Captain Franeker's schedule, they would round Cape Leeuwin at the southwest corner of the continent and proceed easterly along the outer edge of the Great Australian Bight—into heavy seas and unpredictable weather, rain squalls, hailstorms and tempestuous winds, an early sampling of what lay ahead. The plan was to strike the *Urchin*'s canvas and start up her engine, reraising the sails only when the weather cleared.

The captain's warning of bad weather came on schedule, as if rounding the cape was like rounding the corner on a city street and coming up against an arrogant bully whose mission of the moment was to insinuate his unwelcome presence on the first person he met. Lisa remained in her cabin listening to the muffled howling of the wind, the waves thundering against the plates, watching the oil lamp swing dizzily until nausea found its way to her stomach. To stave off the consequence of the condition, she lay down and closed her eyes. This, she told herself, was one of the disadvantages of a small ship, the ease with which the elements mishandled it. If the weather was as uncooperative at Macquarie Harbor, things would be considerably more difficult than Captain Franeker planned for.

Her course set east-south-east, the *Sea Urchin* battled the rain, a hailstorm that rattled the deck noisily, smashing a lamp in the process, and even sleet as she carved a path through the waves heading toward her destination. *To think that the convict ships followed this same route,*

Lisa mused, *carrying their cargoes of human misery through such foul conditions of wind and weather to the Gates of Hell and the Devil's Paradise, as Dietrich termed it.* There would be 2200 miles of mostly poor to horrendous travel, the ship slowed to five knots an hour and less, often forced to concentrate on staying afloat with no thought whatsoever of forward motion.

From the Antarctic Circle and the 60th parallel, nurtured by the cold of the polar ice floes, encouraged by the obstructionless expanse of thousands of miles of open sea, lashing hail and snow squalls ahead of it, the wind roared northward, reaching Tasmania and circling it like a dog after its tail, accelerating, building its relentless fury and pinwheeling outward to thrash any vessel coming within its reach. And heading toward it along the edge of the Bight, the *Urchin* drove, its paddle wheels smashing the surging seas, throwing back twin trails of foam. The engine gave its all hour after hour, devouring coal in a steady stream fed into its furnace by the sweating stokers laboring round the clock in six-hour shifts.

Clear skies came upon them with the suddenness of the storms, the seas settling as if exhausted, the wind dying, supplanted by a playful breeze, the wind's child yet to mature into a blustery, belligerent blast of the sort that had preceded it. All the weathers in all extremes called upon the *Urchin* as she pushed the miles out from under her rudder. And then one middling calm night the call came down from the lookout that land was in sight lying off the port bow, mountains rising, thickly entangled vegetation dressing down their heights, collecting about their bases, greening up to the forbidding rock-cluttered shoreline.

Macquarie Harbor.

LXXI

The *Sea Urchin* slowed, stopped and drifted to within 50 yards of the Gates of Hell. The wind was up, the seas became menacingly heavy and, as if to greet the little ship's arrival, the sullen skies opened, releasing a storm of hail—stones the size of a man's thumb rattled down upon the deck of the vessel, bouncing high off the paddle-wheel housings, an ear-splitting volley that kept Lisa in the protection of the companionway looking out upon the harbor. Her heart sank at the sight of it. No lights were visible through the thick foliage, and only a break between the trees wherein the ill-defined outline of the stockade presented itself betrayed the penal colony's existence.

It was still seven hours until dawn and Captain Franeker's plan was to pull farther back from the Gates, stand off a mile or two to the north and, with the coming of day, pass the site on a parallel course in order to familiarize themselves with its physical layout. And hopefully catch a glimpse of the work gangs.

"I suggest you get some sleep, *Verouw* Dandridge," he said, coming up the companionway behind her, raising his voice above the din.

"We'll have to wait all tomorrow until dawn the next day, won't we?"

"It's all right. We can use the time to plan." Together they backed down the companionway, the better to hear each other.

"Something we ought to have done a month ago," she said regretfully.

"How could we? Dietrich has been away from that

415

place some seven years. Things change. Until he sees how things are arranged, the men coming and going to work, the number of guards on each gang——"

"I'm sorry, I'm impatient I know."

"Of course, I understand."

"I suppose he's snoring away in his usual drunken stupor."

"Everybody's asleep, except the watch and you and I."

She nodded toward the island. "He's asleep, shackled, probably cold and starving. I wonder if he's given up hope?"

"That's the last thing a man gives up."

"Before the ghost, you mean."

He patted her shoulder. "It won't be long now."

"The one thing that worries me more than anything else is his condition. He looked dreadful when I saw him in the jail in Singapore. Regan looked healthy as a horse, wouldn't you know. If it comes to swimming for it, Ross'll have a hard time, poor darling."

"You mustn't turn over rocks looking for problems. He may not have to swim a stroke. We can send a boat into two feet of water, even less."

"And have it blown to smithereens?"

"Please, we can stand here chilling ourselves to the bone theorizing all night. Better we both get some sleep."

She nodded assent. "Good night, Jacobus. Say a prayer."

He smiled. "I will."

She was roused from a troubled sleep by a rap on the door shortly before dawn. It was Jeremy.

"Franeker wants us in his cabin as quickly as possible." He stifled a yawn and rubbed his eyes. It had stopped hailing and the sea was down, but a steady rain was falling, splattering the vessel, ringing against the deck plates overhead as they hurried down the narrow corridor. Dietrich was waiting with the captain, his eyes crimson from drink, his face furrowed with pain caused, Lisa surmised, by his customary morning hangover. But ache or no, he was able to think clearly.

"I agree with the captain here. We stand off a good mile or so from the Gates and run across so I can get a look through the glass."

"What can you possibly see in this weather?" asked Jeremy.

"I won't be able to see the teeth in a man's mouth, Mr. Slater, but what I can see will help!" snapped Dietrich. His hand went to his shirt pocket and he brought out a piece of paper, unfolding it on the table.

"Look at this." It was a crudely drawn map. They gathered on his side of the table as he explained it. "If whoever goes ashore lands here near this split rock and moves straight inland through the underbrush about twenty yards, then bears left about fifteen more, he'll come upon a small cave where many a damned fool has tried to hide. It's the first place the guards look when the gang count is made and anybody's missing."

"So what good is it?" asked Franeker.

"It's the only spot close to the stockade that can be used to reconnoiter. A man can burrow down inside it and look out and see on three sides. Gangs work all around there—at least they used to."

"What if a convict runs off and tries to hide there and finds our man already occupying it?" asked Jeremy.

Dietrich shrugged. "I suppose that could happen. Look, nobody said this was going to be easy as picking cherries."

"How many men can fit in there?" asked Lisa.

"Maybe three, in a tight squeeze."

"And that's the only possible hiding place near the work area?"

Dietrich nodded. "Unless you want to climb trees. But that's really risky. The guards are always checking overhead. Force o' habit."

"Then the cave it is. I suggest we start at once," said Lisa firmly.

"Who?" asked Jeremy. "Not you."

"Of course me. Who else is able to identify Ross? I have to go."

Franeker shook his head vigorously. "Oh, I don't like that. I don't like that at all."

"Nor I," said Jeremy. "You've got his picture, Dietrich and I will study it——"

"Hold your horses!" snapped Dietrich. "Count this boy out."

"See here," began Jeremy.

"Not a chance, mister."

"He's right, Jeremy," said Lisa. "That's asking too much. You and I will go, that is if you're willing."

"I'm willing. It's what I'm here for. But you——"

"Jeremy, I don't want to argue about it. I have to go. Don't worry. I won't be a burden. I have no intention of panicking, or turning my ankle or doing anything else foolish. The way I see it, a boat takes us within wading distance, we get to the cave, conceal ourselves, wait for sunup and when the work gangs come out, we look for him."

"That's another thing," said Dietrich. "You may not spot him."

"I have a pair of binoculars," said the captain.

"I mean he may not be assigned to logging. Only half the convicts are on any given day. There's field work and work inside the stockade."

"Great," muttered Jeremy, "what you're saying is we could run in there every day for the next week and look for him. And never find him."

"You could."

"You said half of the convicts," interposed Lisa. "That's a fifty-fifty chance."

"I'd say so," said Dietrich.

"But if we see him today, will he be there tomorrow?" she asked. "Is there a chance he might be shifted to another crew?"

"That can happen. He might even be left at the stockade, if he's hurt or sick or in the hole."

"What hole?"

"In the ground by the main gate. There are eight holes with trapdoors. After a man's flogged, he's thrown into the hole for twenty-four hours. He can't stand, he can't lie down. If he sits, he has to keep his head bowed, because it's so cramped and shallow. Pitch darkness, nothing to eat. He can hardly breathe, except in number four. There's a hole in the trapdoor near one 'o the hinges big as the palm of your hand and plenty of air gets in there. Whenever they give you the hole, you pray for number four."

Captain Franeker cut in. "Forget about the holes. Let's say he's assigned to a logging gang and is found. What's the next move?"

"I say the fire bombs," Dietrich said, slapping the table loudly.

"Lob them into the stockade to create a diversion?" asked Jeremy.

Dietrich nodded. "To upset the guards outside with the gangs. They'll either run back to the stockade or down to the shoreline to fire on the ship. Then you can jump out, grab him and run him down to here." He indicated a spot on the map. "The water is shallow among the rocks until you get about seventy-five feet out. The bottom's sandy, though, and it shifts, so you never know from one day to the next how deep it is. But here there's a channel, a good twenty feet deep or more, which means the two o' you can swim underwater. It's freezing cold, but it can be done. And anyway, you're going to have to go underwater when the guards spot you and start shooting. The boat can pick you up on the side near the ship."

"What about the men waiting in the boat?" asked Lisa. "They'll be exposed to firing from the shore."

"They'll have to flatten out. Men on deck here can cover 'em with the Spencers."

"It sounds like a feasible plan," said Franeker. "But I still bridle at the thought of you going ashore, *Verouw* Dandridge. If there's a slipup, you could find yourself in serious trouble."

"Can you handle a rifle?" asked Jeremy.

She nodded. "And shoot to kill if I have to."

"So the way it looks, there'll be at least two trips to shore, the first to reconnoiter, the second to help him get away," said the captain.

"I'll go in alone the second time," said Jeremy.

"Oh, no, you won't," she said. "You'll need me to——"

"I won't need you for anything! You point him out to me the first time, and between that and his picture, I'll know which one he is." He snapped his fingers. "Damn it!"

"What?" asked Franeker.

"If that Chinese cop in Singapore had let me in to see him at the jail, you wouldn't have to go ashore at all!"

"Little did we know at the time."

"It all depends upon timing," said Dietrich. "And luck, lots of it."

"I still say we should be going in right now, before sunrise," said Lisa.

Dietrich laughed. "What sun is that?"

"We've got to look over the situation first," said Franeker.

"He's right." Dietrich folded his map, stuffing it back into his pocket.

"Can I have that?" asked Jeremy.

Dietrich gave it to him and he began studying it, obviously committing it to memory.

Dietrich continued: "We'll get a look at what's going on first. Who knows whether they're still even sending out gangs? Seven years is a long time." He shuddered visibly and smiled at Jeremy. "You, mister, you must be crazy. You think I'd get into a boat and go over there? Not for all the money in the world!"

Jeremy nodded. How could he blame him? Actually he was grateful. Once over with her and the second time over alone. It was perfect. Risky, perhaps, no question risky, but the ideal opportunity. With all the shooting that was sure to be going on, anything could happen.

LXXII

The rain continued falling, the sky hung low over the sea, buttressed by an impenetrable blanket of dismal gray clouds. Venturing as close to the harbor entrance as seemed safe, the captain posted Dietrich at the starboard paddle wheel. Resting a telescope on the housing, Dietrich scanned the island for signs of activity. He maintained that his eyesight was excellent, and having sustained his sobriety thus far in spite of the rain, he was able to make out a dozen or so gangs setting out in single files for their work sites. At such a distance, under the prevailing conditions, however, identifying Ross was out of the question. Indeed, all Dietrich could make out were the lamps and dirty white uniforms against the dark-green background, small spots threading their way into the bush.

The remainder of the day was spent in restless anticipation, waiting as the hours dragged by, going over the plans a dozen times and consciously avoiding discussion of possible failure.

The following morning at daybreak a boat was lowered and Jeremy, Lisa and a volunteer from the crew clambered down into it, all three attired in boots and black sou'westers, their hats tightly secured under their chins. Jeremy and the other man rowed through the choppy water entering the Gates of Hell well to the left, using the concealment of a collection of boulders coming out of the bush into the shore waters. Pulling up behind the largest, Jeremy shipped his oars and helped the other man get the anchor over the side into the shallow water.

"Figure one hour at least," advised Jeremy. "Five

minutes to get there, five back and fifty looking around."

"Is it necessary to stay so long?" asked Lisa.

The crewman, a young, strong-looking Irish stoker nodded. "If they come out to work the same time as yesterday, it'll be about fifteen minutes from now."

"That's right, Jeremy. Fifty minutes to look around is much too long. Ten or fifteen should do."

"All right, fifteen," he said. "That's twenty-five in all. Estimate the time and sneak a look around the rock. We'll be coming back the same way we go in." Pulling out Dietrich's map, he squinted at it, double-checking their location. Then he repocketed it and, gripping his rifle, nodded to her. "Let's go. Keep your rifle over your head."

The water was frigid, coming up above their waists as they surged forward, picking their way through the rocks, reaching the beach, the rain-sodden sand squishing noisily underfoot. Slipping into the bush with Jeremy in the lead, she began counting paces out loud. The foliage was dense, leaves slapped her in the face, vines as thick as her arm looped down in front of them, the ground underfoot was root-bound, rugged and slippery. Turning left, they came at once to the edge of the bush. Jeremy stopped her with one arm. The remaining distance separating them from the cave was open country, with only stumps and low-lying shrubs to offer concealment. The logging sites began on the far side stretching in what appeared to be a semicircle following the curve of the coastline.

"Keep going," she hissed. "We've got to find the cave and get inside before they come out the gate."

"You all right?"

"I'm fine."

"Here goes!"

Crouching low, they half-ran half-stumbled across the area to the cave, all but diving into it, righting themselves and turning about.

"What is he talking about, cave?" said Jeremy. "This is no more than a hole in the ground on a slant!"

"Let's not worry about details. Ssssh."

Scrambling to the entrance, they lay on their stomachs side by side, the muzzles of their weapons poking forward. Through the continuing sound of the rain they could hear footsteps, faintly at first, then getting louder, pounding the ground, shaking it around them. They shrank back down, well out of sight.

"You know something?" he said. "We're lucky there's still a hole here. In seven years, they could have filled it in."

"Why? Why deprive the guards of their favorite shooting gallery?"

"I suppose."

The work gangs were passing through the area at a rapid pace, urged on by the guards. Presently the last of them had gone by and the sound of their pounding feet was replaced by chopping and sawing and sledgehammers striking wedges in slow, laborious rhythm. Lisa took out the captain's binoculars strapped about her neck.

"I'll take a look."

"Keep down, way down."

She nodded and turning over on her back, slid upward out of the cave. Still on her back, she pushed herself to one side to be able to see by the cave mouth and scanned the scene from left to right. The men worked like automatons, slowly, mechanically, their pale faces glazed with hopelessness, and something like total indifference to their surroundings, to one another, to their efforts.

And then she saw him—Ross, bending over a two-man saw, pushing and pulling it with his partner. She groaned. He looked much more wan and wasted than when last she'd seen him—on the point of collapse.

"The second gang from the right, on the far side of the biggest log, sawing. Look."

Jeremy fixed on him, studying him. "Just like his picture."

"Nothing like his picture! Thank God we got here when we did. Another week and he'd be dead."

"Let's get out of here." Turning, he surveyed the stretch of ground over which they would have to run to reach the bush. "We have a choice, Lisa."

"What do you mean?"

"If we run, we'll get there faster, but they may spot us and start shooting. If we crouch——"

"We'll squirm it on our stomachs," she said flatly.

"Can you?"

"Can *you?*" She started out, wriggling through the mud, dragging the rifle behind her.

"Watch it," he rasped. "Don't let the muzzle hit the mud. It'll close it up like a cork."

It was slow going, her feet slipping time and again as she strove to push herself forward. He came up beside her and passed her, making it to the bush ahead of her, reaching back and pulling her in by the shoulders. She was gasping for breath as she sat up and the front of her sou'wester was caked with mud.

"I hope Dietrich's idea for a diversion works," she said gloomily, "because if it doesn't, with this open ground, there's sure to be shooting. And at close range. That's the last thing we want."

"Yes," he said, "the last thing we want."

LXXIII

The next morning the weather conditions were identical to those of the previous day—for which Lisa thanked God. A clear sky, a bright sun would have spelled disaster. Moments before the boat was to be lowered, she spoke with Jeremy.

"I suppose all I can do is wish you luck and wish I were a man for one hour."

"You wouldn't look very good as a man. You're much too beautiful a woman."

"Be very careful. He's important, but you are, too." She paused looking away from him. "I have to ask you."

"What?"

"Why are you doing this, risking your life?"

"My but we're dramatic this morning."

"But you are, all for my sake. Our sake."

"What's the answer to that? Things might have been different for us, but they're not. What's left for me but to do the least I can do?"

"*Least?* Good Lord."

"Any man who knows you would."

"I doubt it." She kissed him on the forehead and tapped his rifle. "Don't use that unless it's absolutely necessary. If somebody starts shooting——"

"Lisa, they'll have to once you people out here start lobbing your fire bombs into the stockade."

"I mean no shooting at the work site. How will you get to him?"

"Once all the racket starts and hopefully the guards rush away, I'll walk up, introduce myself——"

"Jeremy."

"Sorry. At times like these I get nervous-silly."

"Are you afraid?"

"Don't ask me that. You wanted to know about getting Ross. The thing is I've got to get his attention right off. Try and get him to run toward me."

"What if they all run?"

"Let them. We'll bring back as many as we can."

"Again, be careful."

"Careful's the word."

Grinning, saluting, he was over the side into the boat and moments later he and the stoker had drawn clear of the *Urchin*, pulling steadily toward the boulders. They rowed without talking, giving Jeremy opportunity to go over his plans—although there was nothing overly complicated about what he had in mind: Reach the edge of the bush, conceal himself behind a tree or shrub and await the beginning of the barrage. Once it started, he would fix Mr. Dandridge in his sights, squeeze off one shot, a second to make sure, back off into the bush and return to the waiting boat.

"I don't know how it happened, Lisa. One minute he was working, the next he was lying on the ground." No good, she'd ask how he could be sure Ross was dead. *"It was crazy, Lisa, when the bombing started he lost his head. He went after the guard, tried to grab his rifle. The guard hit him in the head with the stock, then shot him in cold blood! It hit me like a brick. I got furious, I killed the bastard with one shot!"* That would do it. A bit grisly, but neat, impossible for her to poke holes in. *"I stood there helpless. You can't imagine how I feel. To almost pull it off, to come that close. Whatever made Ross do it? He panicked!"*

He'd follow with a singularly impressive display of guilt. She would comfort him, assure him that it wasn't his fault, only bad luck. He'd sink into the doldrums for a few days. She would do likewise, then gradually——

"Heads up, sir," said the stoker, "coming up on the boulders."

The anchor went over and Jeremy followed, sloshing through the shallow water heading for the bush, feeling the sand under his heels, the wet foliage confronting him, pushing through it, following the direction of the previous day. He turned left and in seconds found himself at the edge of the clearing. He spotted Ross and was preparing to kneel and take aim when a loud explosion lit up the sky beyond the trees in the direction of the stockade.

Instantly the guard began herding his prisoners together, yelling loudly, brandishing his rifle. One after another, fire bombs landed inside the stockade, but the guard never even turned his head, instead concentrating on the men, ordering them to drop their tools and herding them into a tight group.

Jeremy swore out loud, dropped to one knee and fired at the guard. He missed. Spinning about, the guard hit the ground, at the same time bringing his rifle up into position. He fired. Crabbing backward into the bushes, Jeremy wiped the rain from his eyes, levered the Spencer and fired again hastily, wildly, cursing his luck and the early arrival of the fire bombs. *Damned Dietrich, damned stupid drunk!* Given five more lousy seconds and Jeremy would have picked off Ross and the guard, and would be heading back—before the other guards could even react. *Stupid imbecile!* While he fumed, the guard quickly rammed and reloaded his ancient rifle. A shot whined by Jeremy's ear and he pushed farther back. But not too far for fear of losing sight of his target. The convicts were bunched too closely for a shot at Ross. For the moment, Jeremy would have to concentrate on knocking the guard out of it. But sight of the man defending himself and ignoring them charged the convicts with courage. They broke and began running, fanning out in a crescent, heading for the bush and the sea beyond.

Again Jeremy cleared his eyes. He levered another round into the chamber, aimed and fired, catching the guard in the face, snapping his head back, killing him instantly. Jeremy looked to his left and spotted Ross vanishing behind a shrub; he emerged, only a few strides from the cover of more bushes. Levering again and fixing Ross in his sights, Jeremy fired. The shot grazed Ross's shoulder, twisting his upper body. His hand went to the wound, gripping it, but he continued moving forward without breaking stride, reaching the bush, diving into it. Again Jeremy fired.

Had he hit him in the back? He couldn't tell. Jumping to his feet, Jeremy began thrashing through the dense undergrowth toward the spot, cursing the thickness of it, as it slowed his progress. The vines, the mass of shining green, blocked both his path and his view. Reaching the bush Ross dove into, Jeremy looked about for Ross's body.

"Missed, Goddamn it!" Whirling, he headed toward the sea, breaking clear of the bush to the sight of a dozen convicts splashing amongst the boulders. The fire bombs continued raining down upon the stockade, and directly in front of it on the open beach, a handful of guards were down on their bellies firing at the *Sea Urchin*. Answering fire came pouring at them from both sides of the paddle-wheel housing and the afterdeck. A man was running up and down the deck waving his arms exhorting the attackers. *Dietrich*, thought Jeremy, *so ravenously hungry for vengeance he'd gone wild.*

With their backs to him and their clothing identical, Jeremy was unable to distinguish one convict from another.

"Ross!" he yelled, "Ross Dandridge! Smitty! Smitty!"

No one turned. He couldn't tell if he'd been heard and ignored or if Ross had failed to recognize either name. A thought struck him. Raising the rifle he fired into the air. Every man fleeing turned to look back. He spotted Ross, aimed and pulled the trigger. It clicked harmlessly. Hurling the weapon aside, he tore off his hat and oilskins, kicked off his boots and ran into the water after Ross, rapidly narrowing the distance between them. Now some of the guards on the beach had sighted the fleeing men.

They began firing at them. The convicts rushed forward into the freezing sea, dodging behind boulders. First one, then another fell dead. The rain continued falling steadily, splattering the boulders, pocking the surface of the water.

Reaching Ross, Jeremy threw himself upon him, his hands tightening about his throat, squeezing and pushing him downward. But Ross reacted with surprising swiftness, jerking his arms up between Jeremy's wrists and breaking his hold. Smashing his attacker alongside the head, Ross sent him tumbling into the waist-deep icy water. Quickly, Jeremy was up, cursing viciously, rushing at Ross, pounding him with both fists. He could see in Ross's eyes that he wanted no part of a prolonged fight, that he was bleeding from the shoulder and rapidly losing what little strength he had left after the long run from the work site. He was breathing hard, his narrow chest visible through his open shirt, rising and falling, his eyes suffused with fear like those of a cornered animal.

On board the ship, the mortar had stopped lobbing fire bombs shoreward and the gunfire from the afterdeck and around the paddle wheel was becoming sporadic. *They are running out of ammunition,* reasoned Jeremy. *Either that or Dietrich, continuing to run back and forth at the rail, has ordered a slowdown in the firing.*

But allowing his attention to wander to the ship was a mistake. A mistake Ross was quick to take advantage of. Bringing his right fist straight upward, he struck Jeremy flush on the jaw, felling him in a daze. By now other guards had rushed past those returning the fire from the ship, splashing in amongst the rocks, seeking out the helpless convicts, clubbing them senseless and dragging them one by one back into the shallows.

Another convict joined the bleeding Ross and sighting the ship they raced for deeper water, diving, swimming for it. Rapidly revived by the icy water, Jeremy cleared his head and struck out after them, breasting the water easily with powerful strokes. Ten yards ahead of him Ross's companion suddenly stopped swimming and began fighting the frigid water, splashing about frantically, struggling to stay afloat. Ross tried to aid him, throwing his arm under the man's armpit, tugging, straining to keep his head above water. But the effort proved too much for him and he, too, began going down. Then the man slipped from his grasp, vanishing. Relieved of his burden Ross struggled to stay up, sweeping his arms from side to side.

Crying out exultantly, Jeremy started for him. Seeing him, Ross resumed swimming. Just as Jeremy reached the spot where the other man had gone down, he pulled up short, recoiling in astonishment and horror. An enormous black shadow was bearing down on him from the side, undulating through the rain-swept water, gliding easily like some hideous specter out of a nightmare. Before he could twist out of its path, it was upon him, its great weight driving him under, its barbed tail ripping across the back of his neck, the two venomous spines piercing the soft flesh, poison shooting from their conduits into his neck, flooding his upper body.

Raising his head, Jeremy shrieked, then sank, his mouth filling, burbling water loudly. Its tail locked to his neck, the creature dove, circling beneath him, wrapping him in its massive folds, enshrouding him and continuing to turn, revolving slowly. Then it flattened out and released him.

Ross looked on in fascination and dread as Jeremy's head surfaced, his eyes rolling upward. Then his body turned over face downward. Ross began swimming, finding strength born of terror and the instinct for survival, speedily doubling the distance between himself and the site of the grisly attack. The guards shooting from the beach and the shallow water strewn with boulders sighted him; bullets sang about his head, slapping the water on all sides. He dove, swimming underwater, then resurfaced and pushed forward, his arms and legs becoming heavier with each stroke. Rolling over, he tried to float, but water splashed over his face, into his nose and mouth. He spewed it out and was preparing to turn back over and attempt to begin swimming again when his pounding heart leaped in his chest. To his left behind him was a boat, its bow splitting the sea and sending lacy foam arcing up to its gunwales. The man seated in it was pulling for the ship, his arms pumping furiously, the shafts of his oars bending.

"Help! Help me!"

LXXIV

He slept. She sat beside the bunk staring down at him, occasionally mopping the perspiration from his forehead. A knock and the door opened. Captain Franeker.

"Come in," she said softly.

"How is he?"

"Still asleep. He's swallowed water. It dribbles out of his mouth every so often."

Franeker eased his bulk down onto the edge of the anchored table, folded his arms and studied Ross. "He can't have swallowed too much. He's breathing steadily and his color isn't bad. How's that wound in his shoulder?"

"It's nothing, the bullet just grazed it. What worries me is how thin he is; he must have lost at least thirty pounds." She paused. "How's Dietrich?"

"That's what I came to tell you. He's dead."

"Oh, no."

"He was like a maniac, running up and down the deck, exposing himself to their fire. I wonder."

"What?"

"All that hatred spewing out of him, the way he screamed and carried on. Do you suppose having gotten out of the place alive he had some sort of delusion that he was—immortal?"

"I don't know. We'll never know now. I've heard it said that men do strange and unpredictable things in battle. I take it there was no sign of Jeremy."

Franeker shook his head. "We sent both boats out

433

searching. My guess is the guards either killed or captured him."

"He's dead," said Ross, opening his eyes.

"Ross!"

"The one with the rifle that didn't need loading every shot?" He nodded. "Poisoned and drowned."

"Poisoned you say?" Franeker's rosy features assumed a puzzled expression.

"A gigantic stingaree got him. I saw the whole thing."

"The biggest in the world are in these waters, some fourteen feet long; six, seven feet across," said Franeker.

Again Ross nodded. "It was easily that. You sent him to rescue me?"

"We did," responded Lisa. "Poor Jeremy, the poor dear."

Ross shook his head and laughed weakly. "He tried to kill me."

"Impossible. He couldn't have."

"He did. It was he who shot at me in the clearing. He was wearing black oilskins. He shot the guard, then went for me. And in the water, he tried to strangle me, push me under. He wanted me dead, sure enough. If it hadn't been for that stingaree——"

Lisa gasped. Franeker stared at her, as if he were letting Ross's words sink in before saying anything.

"Why would he try to kill him?" he asked Lisa. "Because he was in love with you?"

She was thinking about it. It came clear to her, the truth flowering suddenly, rising above her jumbled thoughts. "In love with me, or maybe in love with the Dandridge millions. You said it was strange, his coming all this way to help. Poor man."

"You feel sorry for him?" asked Franeker.

"I don't know what I feel."

The captain stood up. "Why don't I give you some privacy?"

"It's all right, I'm not going to try to stir his memory

now," she said. "He's exhausted and it can wait. It's a long time till Fremantle."

"Ten days, if the weather doesn't get any dirtier."

"Ross, would you like something to eat, some broth?" She stopped. He had fallen asleep again.

"Cook's got a pot of soup on the stove," said the captain. "He'll keep it simmering."

"I won't wake him, but when he does wake up, I'll start feeding him, building him up."

Over the next few days, Ross ate, sparingly at first; then when his appetite improved, more and more frequently. His color deepened and the dullness deserted his eyes. He became noticeably livelier and more spirited.

Lisa awoke one morning and decided that this was to be the day to try. She talked with him at great length about Blackwood and the past, bringing him unhurriedly through the early years up to his enlistment. He tried to cooperate, sitting on the edge of the lower bunk, his head between his fists, pushing his brain to grasp and hold what she was saying. Turning it over and over in an effort to identify himself with any part of it. Hour after hour she patiently tried to break through the wall, to kindle a tiny glint of recognition in his eyes, the first glimmer of recall.

To no avail. Just before noon on the eighth day after their departure from Macquarie Harbor, they were standing at the rail watching the paddle wheel lifting and dashing the sea, the white-bellied terns high above them weaving the low leaden sky when Franeker appeared at the companionway, motioning to her.

"I'll be right back, Ross."

She stood above the captain looking down the steps. "Any luck?" he asked.

"No. I need a doctor, someone like Middleton to work with him. Only better, somebody brilliant. I don't know what else I can do. I can't even seem to dent the surface."

"Be patient. Nature takes her time."

"I had a chilling thought last night. What if it's been too long? It's going on three-and-a-half years now. Perhaps he's too far removed from it ever to snap back. When a man's own wife holds him, kisses him and he——"

"What is it?"

She brightened. "I just thought of something. Maybe I'm going about it all the wrong way."

"How the wrong way?"

"I keep trying to get through talking about all the things he's familiar with, the house, the firm, his father and grandfather, me. Maybe that's the wrong tack."

"What then?"

"He himself, don't you see?"

"I'm afraid I don't."

"Go to him, stay with him at the rail. I've got to go down to the cabin." She descended the steps, brushing past Franeker. "Bring him down in five minutes."

Inside the cabin she pulled out her suitcase, unbuckling it, rooting about inside and finding the oilskin envelope containing the packet of letters. His letters to her. Her fingers trembled as she leafed through them, selecting the one with the latest date. Taking the letter out, she browsed through it. Footsteps sounded outside the open door. Ross and the captain appeared.

"I promised Ross a surprise," began Franeker awkwardly.

"Sit down, Ross," she said. "I want to read you something. Please listen very carefully. 'My darling Lisa. Tomorrow we're taking the old girl out again. Rumor has it down to Beaufort, South Carolina. If that's a military secret, bad luck, it's been making the rounds for days. There'll be no action, so don't worry. I thank you for the muffler you sent me. There's no snow down here, but the wind off the water gets fierce, especially after sundown, so it comes in handy.'"

She stopped reading, staring at him hopefully.

"Yes?" he asked.

"You wrote this, Ross. These are your words, your letter sent to me. Four days after Christmas, December 29th, 1862. The very next night the *Monitor* went down off Cape Hatteras."

He started to speak, hesitated, his brow knitting, his eyes bewildered. Slowly he shook his head.

"I'm sorry. I'm trying, but I can't seem to remember. It's all a blank."

LXXV

She awoke the next morning, the sun flooding through the porthole striping the blanket and the table in the center of the floor. Stretching, she rolled over on her left side and pondered the situation. Alex Craven must know somebody with the proper credentials, somebody like Middleton who specialized in the mind, in amnesia. If she had to, she'd get the two of them back on a ship and head for Europe. There must be somebody in London, Paris, Berlin or Vienna who could help.

"Lisa, are you awake?"

Turning the other way, she looked down at him in the bunk below. "Good morning."

"Brace yourself. I think. . . . Please don't say a word, just listen." He cleared his throat. "Did the rest of the letter say something like this: 'I—thank you for the muffler you sent me. There's no snow down here, but the wind gets fierce, especially after sundown, so it comes in handy. You can't imagine what they gave us for dinner last night, Yorkshire pudding, the foulest swill I've ever tasted.' "

She gasped, then squealed with joy as he talked on. Jumping down, she rushed to the suitcase, located the letter and read along with him.

"Cameron has gotten a dog, a mutt, all ears and legs."

He was sitting up now grinning broadly, tears rolling down his cheeks. Wiping away her own, she flew to his arms, gripping him tightly, kissing him, his eyes, his cheeks, kissing, kissing, sobbing.

"My darling, my darling, my darling, my darling."

438

LXXVI

His arms surrounded her, encompassing the world. Their world of love revived, of passion's golden embers leaping to flame. To be locked in his embrace once more after so many centuries, to feel his love, her flesh absorbing it with a conscious tingling sensation. And returning it in abundance, to see love clearly in his eyes. This was all her heart could hope for. His face above hers as they lay entwined, the lingering soulful kisses, the welcome throbbing at her thighs, the yearned-for acceptance of his manhood and the beautiful act, the floodgates of desire flung wide, the sensuous surging.

"I love you, my darling, I love you."

"Lisa, Lisa."

A shrill voice outside on deck somewhere forward: "Land ho! Off the starboard bow!"

Fremantle.

She stirred. Releasing her, he sat up.

"Let's go ashore, Ross," she said suddenly inspired. "To a restaurant. We'll order everything on the menu, heaps of food. We'll fill the whole table!"

He laughed. "You sound famished."

"Captain Franeker is a dear, but his cook is no Reyníere. I'm positively drooling for roast beef, lobster, veal cutlets. Wouldn't it be marvelous if we could find veal?"

"You're getting me all worked up. Let's go."

Fremantle was situated at the mouth of the Swain River 12 miles southwest of Perth on the rocky western coast of the continent. The bar at the entrance to the harbor was littered with rocks and Captain Franeker was hard put to pick passage through them, maneuvering the *Sea Urchin* carefully, at length bringing her up to the coal dock, the quay overloaded by a towering black mountain of fuel. The dock area was distressingly dirty, a mixture of soot and salt blanketing everything. After the five-minute walk into the town, however, the streets, small shops and houses interspersed among the one- and two-story commercial buildings appeared clean and tidily kept. They found a restaurant at the corner of Market and Wallaby streets, *Tumbledown Dick's*. Going in, they were shown to a corner table. The dining-room ceiling was obtrusively low and festooned with fishing equipment, nets and floats and the like. The man at the next table was eating squid, attacking steaming chunks of it with his fork and cramming them into his face, his eyes glued to his newspaper.

They ordered roast beef and it came piled high on their plates surrounded with garden-fresh lima beans and potatoes mashed with butter.

As he had since his memory had come back, Ross talked of Deirdre, asking the same questions over and over. She suspected that he only wanted to hear the bits and pieces of good news about her to nourish his fatherly pride. Pride that had had little time and opportunity to assert itself in the early years.

"The three of us together at last," he said in an awed tone. "It doesn't seem possible. To find her in Capri, of all places. That's like finding a needle in a mile-high haystack."

"With all our bad luck, darling, a sudden burst of good was long overdue."

"Describe her again."

"What's to describe? She looks like me, poor dear."

"Then she's unconscionably beautiful!" Lowering his knife and fork, Ross leaned over and kissed her, causing the reader at the next table to frown in puritanical disapproval of such public exhibitionism.

Patiently Lisa told him everything she could think of about Deirdre. He listened raptly, eating mechanically, not even tasting his food.

"I wonder what she'll think of her father?" he asked. "A total stranger bursting into her life."

"You're talking about the man I love, you dolt!" She laughed, patting his cheek affectionately. "She's dying to see you. Counting the hours. I wish there were some way we could let her know we're on our way."

"How long will it take us from here to Batavia, I wonder?"

"Ten, eleven days. We're on a straight line, north northwest. About twenty-two-hundred miles, I think Jacobus said."

"And from there, home. A long trip," he said soberly. Then he brightened. "Lots of time for us to get to know one another."

"Do you and I know each other yet?"

He stroked her hair and looked at her with the eyes of love, the look she adored seeing. "What a question," he said gently. "What I feel for you has been pent up inside me so long, ever since that terrible night. All my love shunted to a cranny at the back of memory. But it must have been building up, darling, because now that I'm back, I feel like I'm drowning in it, liquid sunlight closing over my head!"

"Don't drown, dearest, swim to my arms." They kissed, prompting another disapproving frown from the man at the next table. Paying his bill he got up and without looking at them again strode purposefully to the door and out, leaving his newspaper folded on the table. Ross picked it up, opening it to the headlines. He drew in his breath sharply.

"Good God!"

"What?"

"Lisa." He showed her the headline.

INSURRECTION IN BATAVIA!
Martial Law Declared. Scores Dead. Hundreds Injured as Dipå Negôrå's Followers Attempt Seizure of Power.

Governor Declares Situation Stable.

LXXVII

The journey from Fremantle to Batavia was absolute torture, the suspense taking visible toll on everyone's nerves. Captain Franeker limped up and down the deck in fair weather and foul muttering to himself, alternately heaping vituperation on the fanatical *hajis*, who, according to the article in the West Australian newspaper picked up by Ross, had fomented the uprising, and pleading with Almighty God to spare his wife, his sister-in-law, his sons, their children and Deirdre.

Lisa was stunned, shaken to the anchors of her heart. "God's country," she said over and over. "He kept telling me it was God's country." Ross tried his best to raise her spirits, inundating her with optimism, summoning forth the gods of logic and reason to support his claims.

"She's with Mrs. Franeker and the other one, Lisa, outside the city proper. You told me so yourself. They must have had all the time in the world to get away. How far are the barracks?"

"Jacobus said Welte-*something. In town."

"There you are. The soldiers probably turned out at once."

"Not according to the newspaper. It says the barracks was the first place the rebels stormed. You read it." She brought the newspaper out of her suitcase, unfolded it and smoothed it. "It's more than what it says here anyway, it's—a feeling."

"Feminine intuition?"

---

*Weltevreden—well-content—a sector integrated into the city early in the 19th Century.

"A feeling of dread inside me, weighing down my heart." She tapped her chest. "As if it were filled with stones, with one more added every hour. I want to be optimistic. I'd like nothing better than to feel she's safe, but I can't."

He stood looking out the porthole at the open sea dazzlingly bright under the late afternoon sun.

"I have no such feeling," he said firmly. "I say she's safe. I know she is!"

"Ross, look!" She had aimlessly turned the page, her eyes falling on a column under the headline INTERNATIONAL NEWS. " 'Wife of noted wine dealer indicted in his death. *Signora* Lavinia Aldoni pleaded not guilty today to a charge of murder in the first degree. Proceedings to go before a *juge d'instruction* in Naples early next week.' "

"Lavinia." He stared at the paper in disbelief. "Aldoni?"

"I told you, she married an Italian, a wine dealer. Enrico Aldoni. I met him. She married him; now she's killed him."

"She's pleading not guilty?"

"Knowing Aunt Vinnie, would you expect her to do otherwise?"

"I wonder which of the black arts she'll use to get out of this one."

"Speaking of murdering and murderers, what became of your favorite shipmate, Mr. Regan? When I went over to reconnoiter, I didn't notice him in your work gang. Where was he, back in the stockade?"

"No, old Wiley never made it to Macquarie. He got into an argument with a guard on the ship coming over. He got himself shot in the throat. They threw him over with the morning garbage, poor bastard."

"Oh, my."

"Believe it or not he wasn't a bad sort. We got to be friends back at Eastern Virginia; he enjoyed playing big brother to me."

"And got you seven years in a penal colony."

"Not him. We didn't smuggle anything. It was another guy in the *Crown Pearl* crew, a man named Deering."

"Cyril Alfred Deering," she said thoughtfully.

"Right. How did you know?"

"I've heard the name."

"We tried to tell the judge, but he wouldn't listen. He had his two birds in the hand. Deering engineered the whole scheme. We poor stupid jackasses didn't even know what he was up to. Until he stuck us with the evidence."

There was the sound of footsteps running by the porthole. Suddenly activity on deck.

"Land ho!" shouted the lookout. "Home port!"

"Here we are, Mrs. Dandridge."

"At last," she said. "Although I'm afraid to go ashore. Afraid of what we'll find."

"She's all right, I tell you! She's got to be."

The undersides of the clouds assembled above the harbor were roasted red by the sun, and they spilled the color back down into the sea where it spread like ruby wine overrunning a glass table. Franeker met them at the rail, his usual pleasant smile absent. He scratched his beard nervously, his eyes darting about.

"We'll get a carriage as fast as we can. Leave your bag, Lisa, everything. Let's just go and see what's what."

The docks were a shambles as far as they could see. Hurrying down the gangplank, Franeker hailed the first carriage driver he saw and they climbed aboard. He gave the address and they rattled off. The driver was a young man, bearded, his slender body wrapped in a dirty black-linen duster. Hunching over his reins, he shouted his horse up Canal Street and across to the main thoroughfare. Lisa's heart began hammering at sight of the city. Stretches of rubble abounded on all sides, the streets and sidewalks filled with abandoned furniture, broken building stones and shattered glass.

Franeker sat with his fists in his lap, stirring and flinching nervously, breathing unnaturally, short quick breaths betraying his inner turmoil. The carriage rounded a corner on two wheels and there was his house, razed to the ground, blackened beams scattered about like burned matches in an ashtray, broken sections of the roof atop them. Other homes nearby had also been demolished. It was as though a huge flaming scythe had passed through the area, slowly cutting them down, leaving total chaos in its wake. Lisa swayed in her seat, her hand going to her forehead. Ross gripped her shoulders.

"Pull up! Pull up!" yelled the captain frantically.

A Chinese was walking by, an elderly man with a cane and a straw hat, the brim flapping ridiculously in the breeze. He turned at the arrival of the carriage.

"Ling Chow!" called Franeker, beckoning him over to them. "My wife and the others, where are they? What's happened?"

"At the cemetery, the funeral." Holding his hat, he lifted his cane and pointed down the street.

"The red-haired girl, Deirdre!" burst Lisa loudly. "She's with her?"

The man shrugged. "I don't know."

"Whose funeral?" demanded Franeker.

"Your sister-in-law's. She was hurt getting away from them. She died yesterday morning. Mrs. Franeker is——"

The captain cut him off, yelling at the driver, pushing him in the back. "Hurry, man, hurry!"

They reached the cemetery in less than a minute, clattering in through the opened iron gates and up a small rise to within sight of the funeral in progress. The minister stood at the head of the grave, his hands folded, his head bowed, his face in shadow, the breeze flapping the white tabs of his collar against his chest. *Verouw*

Franeker saw them and came rushing down, throwing herself into her husband's arms, sobbing hysterically.

"Kristina! She's dead, dead!"

"Where's Deirdre?" screamed Lisa running up to her, Ross following.

The woman stared at her, her eyes wide with fear. Then she turned her face into her husband's shoulder hiding it, speaking rapidly in Dutch.

"Gone," said the captain quietly.

"No!"

"She says the rebels took her. Deirdre was at the plantation, staying overnight. They overran the place, burning, looting. They took her and two of the older girls. They took dozens of girls."

"Where?" roared Ross. "Where, tell us!"

"No one knows," said *Verouw* Franeker. Her face was wet with tears, her eyes crimson-rimmed. She looked from one to the other helplessly. "They say they took them to the Chinese. But no one knows for certain."

"What Chinese?" asked Lisa. "Where?"

"A ship." She pointed toward the docks. "Sold them to a Captain China. They say, they say. It's all gone. We've lost everything. The house, the plantation. Kristina's dead, Jacobus. Deirdre's gone, Hendrickja, Anna——"

She was rambling now. Lisa began dying slowly, feeling her whole body disintegrating, silently crumbling into small pieces. Her hands trembled and her eyes drifted past the woman, becoming misty and settling on the minister standing at the grave, his hands clasped together, lips moving.

She imagined him at the point in the oration just before the call to prayer. The words of Job:

"The Lord gave, and the Lord hath taken away; blessed be the name of the Lord."

* * *

"*In* journeyings often, *in* perils of water, *in* perils of robbers, *in* perils of *mine own countrymen, in* perils by the heathen, *in* perils in the city, *in* perils in the wilderness, *in* perils in the sea, *in* perils among false brethren;

In weariness and painfulness, in watchings often, in hunger and thirst, in fastings often, in cold and nakedness."

II CORINTHIANS: 11, 26-27

Aurelia did not usually spend an inordinate amount of time admiring herself in the glass, but now, while she toweled herself vigorously, her eyes wandered appraisingly over her naked form. Slim and boyish it was, she thought, but she wasn't altogether displeased with it. Her breasts, while small for current fashion, were high and firm and looked rather marvelous in a low-cut gown. Her hips, however, were much too full to be called boyish, and her thighs and calves curved nicely above and below the dimpled knees.

She shook her head to rid it of such vanity, pulled on a dry shift and bodice, fitted two unadorned petticoats in place and topped them with a simple gown of a stiff green material, denying herself the cumbersome, fashionable hoops.

Her fine blonde hair had curled tighter with the dampness, but she smoothed it with a few brush strokes and, after tying it back with a pink ribbon, was ready to go down and face de Vries again. Then, on an impulse, she paused and picked up the tiny bottle of perfume her cousin had brought back from his visit to Venice last year. Quickly, before she could change her mind, she touched the glass stopper to the pulse beating in her white throat and to the inner side of each wrist. Then, with her emotions hovering somewhere between anticipation and dread, she descended the stairs to confront her insistent suitor.

"Ah, there you are," de Vries said as she entered the

1

room. "For a woman, you dress remarkably fast, but it seemed like an age to me."

"Really, René, you could turn a girl's head with your flattery," she said with a smile.

"Your head, my dear, is remarkably hard to turn," he said, taking her hands and leaning forward to kiss the soft palms, the perfumed wrists and up to the bend of her elbows.

"René, really, you are much too impetuous," she protested as his arms came around her and his lips burned against the pulse in her throat, then up the firm line of her neck before claiming her lips in another passionate kiss.

It was a long, demanding embrace, and when he released her, she was breathing fast and had difficulty getting the words out. "Please, René, don't kiss me that way, I——"

"It excites you, doesn't it, my love?" he whispered huskily, his eyes bright with excitement and his full-lipped mouth loose with desire. "It excites you almost as much as it does me."

"No. No, I——"

"Yes, you love me and want me as I love and want you," he said, sliding his hands up and down her back to press her body tight against his.

"René, please, no——"

"Aurelia, I've never wanted a woman the way I want you. Like every man of my station, I have had mistresses, no more but no less than any other man of fashion, but I have never in my thirty-two years desired a woman as I do you. Never before have I wanted a permanent arrangement, wanted to give my name to a woman. I've always known I must marry someday and produce heirs for the de Vries name, but until now, I've been content to take what comes easy, what some women give lightly. But with you it is different—I want you body and soul, and I will have you!"

"But, René, I don't feel that way about you."

2

"Ha! Don't you? Then why do you take fire when I kiss you?" he asked. "Why does a virgin like you become as excited as any light-of-love at the touch of my hands, the feel of my body against yours?"

"I don't . . . know," she faltered. "I don't really know. Oh, *mon Dieu,* I am so confused!"

He pressed her closer. "Perhaps I can unconfuse you. A little more intimacy is what you need. A slight taste of what our marriage bed will be like and you'll be begging me to set the date."

Aurelia felt a thrill of fear. She knew he must have sensed the way his touch affected her. He was so assertive in his masculinity, so sure of his ability to arouse her that it was inevitable that sooner or later he would give up pleading and attempt to storm her emotions to gain his way.

"Just relax in my arms, sweet little one, and let me teach you the pleasures of love," he whispered hotly as his mouth covered hers again.

Aurelia knew she should do something, pull the bell cord to summon the servants, call to her father, anything but stand there with her knees going weak, the pounding of her heart so loud in her ears that it drowned out common sense.

Her shock and helplessness spread as she felt his lips force hers apart and his tongue thrust into her mouth. No one had ever done that before, and it was wildly disturbing to feel that hot prong slither around inside her mouth, flicking across her teeth and twisting and turning lustfully as it collided with her tongue and engaged it in slippery combat. Other sensations assaulted her from the contact of their bodies. He was holding her tightly, crushing her tender breasts with their sensitive tips against his chest and pressing his lower body hard into her softness. Even through two petticoats and the heavy stiffness of the skirt, Aurelia could feel the heat of his thighs and belly, the bruising bulge of—oh, no, it couldn't be!

3

She began to struggle, but that only seemed to excite him more and he pushed her down onto the settee and forced her back against the cushions.

"My darling," René whispered hoarsely, releasing her lips and moving his mouth down the curve of her cheek and neck to find again the perfumed hollow where her pulse beat so strongly. "My sweet little wild bird."

In all of her eighteen years Aurelia had never experienced the feelings that were surging through her now. She had been kissed before but more in daring than in passion. There had been the young officer from the garrison at Nantes, and her cousin Raymond, but those kisses had been exchanged flirtatiously and with good humor, not in this intense, demanding way.

She was pressed flat against the pillows, with René half sprawled on top of her, his lips avidly exploring the décolletage of her modest dress, the creamy little crevice between her breasts. Surely he wouldn't—but he was. His hand had come up to cup her breast from the underside, crushing it until it tingled with pain that blended into excitement, and kissing the top, his tongue dipping into the valley between.

Was it the perfume that had aroused him to this pitch? Why had she been so foolish and so vain?

No, it wasn't the fault of the scent. She had known what René wanted right from the beginning, had realized that his overpowering lust would break loose someday. She should have avoided any situation in which she was likely to be alone with him. And now that he was trying to force himself on her, she should be able to resist him, to insist that he stop what he was doing instantly.

She tried to move and found the effort just too much. In her strange lethargy, her arms felt like lead; it was impossible to raise them to push him away. And then her thighs fell apart limply, and he got a leg between them while his lips continued to caress her breasts with burning kisses.

"René . . . please, René . . ." she managed to gasp.

"Yes, my darling, I will. I will. I am going to show you what being loved by a man is like."

In his arrogance, he assumed that she was urging him on instead of pleading with him to stop. His fingers went to the hooks of her dress, pulling at them impatiently and tugging the bodice down off her shoulders. She saw then how wild and glittering his black eyes were and knew that unless she pulled herself together and overrode the strange languor that had taken possession of her, he was going to do exactly what he said.

His breath was like the sirocco that blew in from the North African deserts, and his lips moving over her shoulder and down the side of the breast he had managed to partially expose was setting her flesh on fire. Sensations rippled through her from nerve endings she had never guessed could be so stimulated.

"I've wanted you so much for so long," he said huskily, thrusting his fingers under the top of her shift to fondle the other breast. "I've wanted you as much as you've wanted me."

That cut through the fog that enveloped her. How dare he say she wanted him! The smug conceit of the words angered her and anger lent strength to her voice. "Stop it, René! Stop it right now!"

He gave no indication that he had heard, and his fingers continued to crawl downward, searching for the tiny nipple.

"René, you assume too much! I never gave you leave to——" She sucked in her breath abruptly as the fingers found what they were seeking and stroked back and forth, sending little shocks of ecstasy radiating out from her breast to her whole body. It seemed to have no connection to anything else he was doing. That nipple seemed to have a life all its own, and she could feel it swelling and standing upright under the knowing touch.

This was too much. Why should she have feelings she didn't want to have? Feelings that came not from her

5

mind, and certainly not from her heart, but only from the way his fingers manipulated her flesh.

"René, listen to me! I don't want you to——"

"Be silent, girl!" His voice was a snarl now, filled with arrogance and lust.

"Stop it, I tell you, stop it!" She was struggling with all her strength now. "You have no right to do things to me I do not want done. I am not your property! Neither am I some court lady who amuses herself with games of love."

He paused in his assault on her vulnerable flesh to stare at her in surprise for a moment, then threw back his head and laughed.

"Naturally you must protest, my dear. Do so. Struggle also; it makes the game more enchanting for us both. The doe flees the hunter, and when the chase is done, the hunter takes more pleasure in the winning."

Aurelia resented the comparison. She was no doe; she was a woman—her own woman. Her father's philosophers had taught her that, just as they had taught her that it was the natural right of men to be free. No, she was no doe, and this was her own sitting room, not a deer park such as they had once had at Versailles where young, innocent girls were taken to be hunted down and ravaged by bored and decadent courtiers.

"Let go of me, René!" she demanded, trying to push him away, to break the band of steel his arms formed around her.

He ignored her words and her attempts to free herself. He had worked her shift down so far, her breasts were almost totally exposed, and his lips and fingers continued their assault on her senses, sending shivers of carnal excitement through her which were obviously intended to weaken her resistance.

But anger and the pride she had always taken in her essential integrity, her belief that she belonged to herself, resisted the returning languor, fought the impulse to relax and let him do with her as he would.

6

She took a deep breath and said calmly, "René, if you don't let me go, I am going to scream. I have a strong voice and this is not a large house. I shall scream very loudly and everyone, including my father, will hear me."

She wasn't in the least sure that the part about her father was true—if deeply enough into one of his books, he was unlikely to hear anything—but she was sure the servants would hear. Not that there was much they could do to a man of de Vries' position—to raise their hands to him could mean death—but at least he wouldn't dare go on with what he intended in front of them.

René raised his head and stared at her. "Screaming is not part of the game, my dear."

"I am not playing your game," she said. "I'm quite serious."

"Oh, well." He shrugged, and for a moment she thought that she had won, that he was going to give up. Instead he took a handkerchief out of the sleeve of his coat, crumpled it in his hand and stuffed it into her mouth before she had time to realize what he was up to. With her arms pinned to her sides by the way her dress was pulled down, she couldn't get rid of the gag, and when she tried to sit up, he pushed her back roughly and rucked her skirt up along with the petticoats, exposing her slim white thighs.

For a few seconds Aurelia was sure she was going to faint, but that would have made his conquest too easy and her determination to resist was stronger now that he had openly shown his ruthlessness. She rolled and kicked and tried to throw herself onto the floor, but he was too strong and heavy for her. Slowly he overcame her thrashings and forced her to lie still with legs spread under the weight of his body.

Through the haze of weakness and terror that filled her, she thought she heard the sound of a galloping horse and shouts from outside, but she wasn't sure. It didn't matter anyway, she thought despairingly; nothing could save her now.

7

"And now, my dear," de Vries said, fumbling with his own clothes, "you are going to get what you've been asking for. You know you want it, and later you will thank me for it."

Aurelia thrashed her head from side to side and tried to scream around the gag. She pushed at him futilely with her pinioned hands and kicked her feet furiously without striking him. He laughed and pushed her skirts higher. In a moment it was going to happen and there was nothing she could do to prevent it.

OTHER SELECTIONS
FROM
PLAYBOY PRESS

HISTORICAL ROMANCE

THIS RAVAGED HEART $1.95
  BARBARA RIEFE

Lisa Allworth Dandridge comes to America as mistress
to a vast shipping fortune. Another, jealous woman has
plans of her own and attempts to separate the desperate-
ly-in-love pair. It is a searing romance that moves across
continents and across time—from the 19th Century world
of aristocratic Providence to plague-ridden London.

ROSELYNDE $1.95
  ROBERTA GELLIS

The first book in an epic saga that will span three gener-
ations of turbulent medieval English life. Book I intro-
duces readers to young and beautiful Lady Alinor Devaux,
mistress of Roselynde, whose lands and wealth have made
her one of the most desirable women in the realm. Strong,
self-willed, clever and compassionate, Alinor is truly mistress of her own estate—and of her own heart as well.
Until she meets Sir Simon Lemagne, a man with the
strength of character, passion and wit to match her own.
Their struggle to be united against all obstacles sweeps
them from the peaceful lands of Roselynde to the pomp
and pageantry of King Richard's royal court, culminating
in a daring Crusade through exotic Byzantium and into
the heart of the Holy Land itself.

IN LOVE'S OWN TIME $1.95
JANICE YOUNG BROOKS

Blanche, the illegitimate half sister to the Queen of England, is suspended between two worlds. As a bastard, she cannot marry into nobility, yet as the Queen's half sister, it is not fitting for her to marry a commoner. Life in a convent seems the only path until the Queen asks her to be her lady-in-waiting, and she meets Sir Charles Seintleger and begins a passionate love affair that will endure separation, political intrigue, and bloody battles for thirty tumultuous years during the War of the Roses.

ROXANA $1.95
HELENE MOREAU

Across ancient Persia and India, into the exotic palaces of Persepolis and Babylon, beautiful and brilliant Roxana —daughter, courtesan, wife and mother to the most powerful men of her time—bewitches those around her as her whims and passions alter the course of history.

FLOWERS OF FIRE $1.95
STEPHANIE BLAKE

The best-selling novel of stunningly beautiful Ravena Wilding, the strong-willed woman, who is torn between the passions of twin brothers. It is a tempestuous love story that sweeps from the Irish revolution to the American Civil War, from the slave plantations of the South Seas to the Wild West.

DAUGHTER OF DESTINY $1.95
STEPHANIE BLAKE

In this stupendous sequel to *Flowers of Fire*, Ravena's daughter, Sabrina, scandalizes the lives of all who love her. But her heart belongs to a hot-blooded Irish rebel, and together they carry the torch of their passion from Ireland to India to the twilight of World War One.

THE DRAGON AND THE ROSE $1.95
ROBERTA GELLIS

A rich novel of the intrigue, war and struggle that preceded Henry VII's ascent to the English throne and his romance with the young, betrothed Elizabeth.

THE SWORD AND THE SWAN $1.95
ROBERTA GELLIS

Bold warrior Rannulf meets gentle, radiant Catherine and an urgent sense of desire touches him, a sensation far different from his usual impersonal need for a woman. Their marriage is one of political convenience, but from the strange alliance grows a love so powerful it challenges the will of kings.

PROUD PASSION $1.95

BARBARA BONHAM

The love story of beautiful and brave Odette Morel, who flees the brutal excesses of the French Revolution, endures the hardships of an ocean voyage to America and faces unthinkable dangers in the frontier wilderness.

PASSION'S PRICE $1.95

BARBARA BONHAM

In a heart-rending story set against the harshness and isolation of the vast prairies of 19th Century America, a lovely young widow and a lusty family man are thrown together by fate. Victims of their overwhelming passions, they become outcasts in the community and nearly destroy each other before learning the price of true love and understanding.

ROMANTIC SUSPENSE
BY AMANDA McALLISTER

DEATH COMES TO THE PARTY $1.50

A beautiful woman of wealth and social standing learns her fiance's secretary has been murdered. She attempts to learn how and why the girl died, but someone tries to stop her.

LOOK OVER YOUR SHOULDER $1.50

A young woman's husband is committed to a mental hospital for several brutal murders. Devastated, she moves to Vermont to establish a new identity. New men fall for her, but someone out of her past is spying on her and again she faces panic and terror.

NO NEED FOR FEAR $1.50

The hired assassin who kills a woman's husband is stalking her. An agent is protecting her and a college professor has swept her off her feet. So there are three men in her life—or is it only two?

PRETTY ENOUGH TO KILL $1.50

Three girls enter a campus beauty contest for different reasons and are unaware that a psychopathic killer is after them.

TRUST NO ONE AT ALL $1.50

A young woman receives a letter from her beau asking her to smuggle his father's papers out of Russia. She gives up everything to take the bold and perilous journey.

WAITING FOR CAROLINE $1.50

When her cousin doesn't return to pick up her child, Andrea begins to realize something is terribly wrong. And when a murder is committed in her own back yard, she realizes her own life is in danger.

TERROR IN THE SUNLIGHT $1.50

One year after the murders of three Chilton residents, Gwen Potter, the young English teacher in that town, is jolted by a tiny detail of the crime, which now threatens her very life.

ORDER DIRECTLY FROM:

PLAYBOY PRESS
P. O. BOX 3585
CHICAGO, ILLINOIS 60654

No. of copies		Title	Price
_____	E16450	Wild Is the Heart	$1.95
_____	E16406	Roselynde	1.95
_____	E16427	In Love's Own Time	1.95
_____	E16396	This Ravaged Heart	1.95
_____	E16418	Roxana	1.95
_____	E16377	Flowers of Fire	1.95
_____	E16425	Daughter of Destiny	1.95
_____	E16364	The Dragon and the Rose	1.95
_____	E16389	The Sword and the Swan	1.95
_____	E16345	Proud Passion	1.95
_____	E16399	Passion's Price	1.95
_____	C16387	Death Comes to the Party	1.50
_____	C16360	Look Over Your Shoulder	1.50
_____	C16329	No Need for Fear	1.50
_____	C16327	Pretty Enough to Kill	1.50
_____	C16352	Trust No One at All	1.50
_____	C16328	Waiting for Caroline	1.50
_____	C16410	Terror in the Sunlight	1.50

PLEASE ENCLOSE 50¢ FOR POSTAGE AND HANDLING.

TOTAL AMOUNT ENCLOSED: $_____

Name _____

Address _____

City _____ State _____ Zip _____